SOON I WILL BE INVINCIBLE

SOON I

INVIN

PANTHEON BOOKS, NEW YORK

WILL BE

CIBLE

AUSTIN GROSSMAN

Library of Congress Cataloging-in-Publication Data

Grossman, Austin, [date]
Soon I will be invincible / Austin Grossman.
p. cm.
ISBN-13: 978-0-375-42486-1 (alk. paper)
1. Heroes—Fiction. 2. Good and evil—Fiction. I. Title.

PS3607.R666S66 2007   813'.6—dc22   2006033296

www.pantheonbooks.com

Printed in the United States of America

First Edition

2 4 6 8 9 7 5 3 1

TO MY PARENTS,
ALLEN AND JUDITH GROSSMAN

CONTENTS

CONTENTS

PART THREE

PART
ONE

FOILED AGAIN

This morning on planet Earth, there are one thousand, six hundred, and eighty-six enhanced, gifted, or otherwise-superpowered persons. Of these, one hundred and twenty-six are civilians leading normal lives. Thirty-eight are kept in research facilities funded by the Department of Defense, or foreign equivalents. Two hundred and twenty-six are aquatic, confined to the oceans. Twenty-nine are strictly localized—powerful trees and genii loci, the Great Sphinx, and the Pyramid of Giza. Twenty-five are microscopic (including the Infinitesimal Seven). Three are dogs; four are cats; one is a bird. Six are made of gas. One is a mobile electrical effect, more of a weather pattern than a person. Seventy-seven are alien visitors. Thirty-eight are missing. Forty-one are off-continuity, permanent émigrés to Earth's alternate realities and branching timestreams.

Six hundred and seventy-eight use their powers to fight crime, while four hundred and forty-one use their powers to commit them. Forty-four are currently confined in Special Containment Facilities for enhanced criminals. Of these last, it is interesting to note that an unusually high proportion have IQs of 300 or more—eighteen to be exact. Including me.

I don't know why it makes you evil. It's just what you find at the extreme right edge of the bell curve, the one you'd get if six billion minds took an intelligence test and you looked at the dozen highest scores. Picture yourself on that graph, sliding rightward and downslope toward the very brightest, down that gradually gentler hill, out over the top million, the top ten thousand—all far smarter than anyone most people ever meet—out to the top thousand—and now things are getting sparser—the last hundred, and it's not a slope at all now, just a dot every once in a while. Go out to the last few grains of sand, the smartest of the smartest of the smartest, times a thousand. It makes sense that people would be a little odd out here. But you really have to wonder why we all end up in jail.

Wake-up for me is at 6:30 a.m., half an hour earlier than the rest of the inmates. There's no furniture in my cell—I'm stretched out on the painted green rectangle where I'm allowed to sleep. The way my skin is, I hardly feel it anyway. The facility is rated for enhanced offenders, but I'm the only one currently in residence. I am their showpiece, the pride of the system, and a regular feature on the governor's tours for visiting dignitaries. They come and watch the performance, to see the tiger in his cage, and I don't disappoint.

The guard raps on the plexiglas wall with his nightstick, so I get up slowly and move to the red painted circle, where they run a scan, X ray, radiation, and the rest. Then they let me put on clothes. I get eight minutes while they check the route. You can do a lot of thinking in eight minutes. I think about what I'll do when I get out of here. I think about the past.

If I had writing materials, I might write a guidebook, a source of advice and inspiration for the next generation of masked criminals, bent prodigies, and lonely geniuses, the ones who've been taught to feel different, or the ones who knew it from the start. The ones who are smart enough to do something about it. There are things they should hear. Somebody has to tell them.

I'm not a criminal. I didn't steal a car. I didn't sell heroin, or steal an old lady's purse. I built a quantum fusion reactor in 1978, and an orbital plasma gun in 1979, and a giant laser-eyed robot in 1984. I tried to conquer the world and almost succeeded, twelve times and counting.

When they take me away, it goes to the World Court—technically I'm a sovereign power. You've seen these trials—the Elemental, Rocking Horse, Dr. Stonehenge. They put you in a glass and steel box. I'm still dangerous, you know, even without my devices. People stare at you; they can't believe what you look like. They read out the long list of charges, like a tribute. There isn't really a trial—it's not like you're innocent. But if you're polite, then at the end they'll let you say a few words.

They'll ask questions. They'll want to know why. "Why did you . . . hypnotize the president?" "Why did you . . . take over Chemical Bank?"

I'm the smartest man in the world. Once I wore a cape in public, and fought battles against men who could fly, who had metal skin, who could kill you with their eyes. I fought CoreFire to a standstill, and the Super Squadron, and the Champions. Now I have to shuffle through a cafeteria line with men who tried to pass bad checks. Now I have to wonder if there will be chocolate milk in the dispenser. And whether the smartest man in the world has done the smartest thing he could with his life.

I stand by the door in a ring of armed men while my cell is checked by three specialists with a caseful of instruments. From the tiers come yells, shouts of encouragement, or catcalls. They want to see a show. Then I march, past their eyes, followed by two men in partial armor with bulky high-tech side arms. They have to wait until I pass before their morning lineup.

There's a lot of prison talk about my powers. Inmates believe my eyes can emit laser beams, that my touch is electrical or poisonous, that I come and go as I please through the walls, that I hear everything. People blame things on me—stolen silverware and doors left unlocked. There is even, I note with pride, a gang named after me now: the Impossibles. Mostly white-collar criminals.

I'm allowed to mingle with the general population at mealtimes and in the recreation yard, but I always have a table to myself. I've fooled them too many times by speed or misdirection. By now they know to serve my food in paper dishes, and when I turn in my tray they count the plastic utensils, twice. One guard watches my hands as I eat; another checks under the table. After I sit down, they make me roll up my sleeves and show my hands, both sides, like a magician.

Look at my hands. The skin's a little cool—about 96.1 degrees, if you're curious—and a little rigid: a shirt with extra starch. That skin can stop a bullet; it stopped five of them in my latest arrest as I ran up Seventh Avenue in my cape and helmet, sweating through the heavy cloth. The bruises are still there, not quite faded.

I have a few other tricks. I'm strong, much stronger than should be possible for a mammal my size. Given time and inclination, I could overturn a semi, or rip an ATM out of a wall. I'm not a city-wrecker, not on my own. When Lily and I worked together, she handled that part of it. I'm mostly about the science. That's my main claim to life in the Special Containment Wing, where everything down to the showerheads is either titanium or set two inches deep in reinforced concrete. I'm also faster than I should be—something in the nerve pathways changed in the accident.

Every once in a while a new prisoner comes after me, hoping to make his reputation by breaking a prison-made knife against my ribs, a stolen pencil, or a metal spoon folded over and sharpened. It happens at mealtimes, or in the exercise yard. There is a premonitory hush as soon as he steps into the magic circle, the empty space that moves with me. The guards never step in—maybe it's policy, to alienate me from the prison population, or maybe they just enjoy seeing me pull the trick, proof again that they're guarding the fourth-most-infamous man alive. I straighten a little in the metal chair, set my single plastic spoon down on the folding table.

After the whip crack of the punch, there is silence, ringout, the sigh-ing collapse. The heap of laundry is carried away and I'll be left alone again until the next tattooed hopeful makes his play. Inside, I want to keep going, keep fighting until the bullets knock me down, but I never do. I'm smarter than that. There are stupid criminals and there are smart criminals, and then there is me.

This is so you know. I haven't lost any of what I am, my intrinsic menace, just because they took away my devices, my tricks, and my utility belt. I'm still the brilliant, the appalling, the diabolical Doctor Impossible, damn it. And yes, I am invincible.

All superheroes have an origin. They make a big deal of it, the story of how they got their powers and their mission. Bitten by a radioactive bug, they fight crime; visited by wandering cosmic gods, they search for the lost tablets of so-and-so, and avenge their dead families. And vil-lains? We come on the scene, costumed and leering, colorfully working out our inexplicable grudge against the world with an oversized zap gun or cosmic wormhole. But why do we rob banks rather than guard them? Why did I freeze the Supreme Court, impersonate the Pope, hold the Moon hostage?

I happen to know they've got practically nothing in my file. A few old aliases, newspaper clippings, testimony from a couple of old ene-mies. The original accident report, maybe. The flash was visible for miles. That's what people talk about when they talk about who I am, a nerd with an attitude and subpar lab skills. But there was another acci-dent, one that nobody saw, a slow disaster that started the morning I arrived there. Nowadays it has a name, Malign Hypercognition Dis-order. They're trying to learn about it from me, trying to figure out whose eyes are going to be looking out at them from behind a mask in thirty years.

I have a therapist here, "Steve," a sad-eyed Rogerian I'm taken to see twice a week in a disused classroom. "Do you feel angry?" "What did you *really* want to steal?" The things I could tell him—secrets of the universe! But he wants to know about my childhood. I try to relax and remind myself of my situation—if I kill him, they'll just send another.

It could be worse—there are stories villains tell one another about the secret facilities out in the Nevada desert, the maximum-intensity enhanced containment facilities, for the ones they catch but are truly afraid of, the ones they can't kill and can only barely control. Fifty-meter shafts filled with concrete, frozen cells held to near absolute zero. Being here means playing a delicate game—I'm in the lion's jaws. I mustn't scare them too badly. But Steve has his questions. "Who was the first one to hit you?" "When did you leave home?" "Why did you want to *control* the world? Do you feel out of control?" The past creeps in, perils of an eidetic memory.

It's a danger in my line of work to tell too much; I know that now. And last time I told them everything, giving it all away like a fool, how I was going to do it, how escape was impossible. And they just listened, smirking. And it would have worked, too. The calculations were correct.

By the time the bus came that morning it was raining pretty hard, and the world was a grayed-out sketch of itself, the bus a dim hulk as it approached, the only thing moving. Inside the bus shelter, the rain drummed hollowly on the plastic ceiling, and my glasses were fogging up. It was 6:20 a.m., and my parents and I were standing, stunned and half-awake, in the parking lot of a Howard Johnson's in Iowa.

I knew that it was a special morning and that I should be feeling something, that this was one of the Big Events in a person's life, like marriage or a bar mitzvah, but I had never had a Big Event and I didn't know what it was supposed to be like. An hour earlier, my alarm had gone off; my mother stuffed me into a scratchy sweater that was starting to itch in the late September warmth. We trooped out to the car and drove through the gray, silent town, the deserted city center, and turned into the lot by the mighty I-80. When my mother cut the engine, there were a few seconds of silence as we listened to the rain rapping on the ceiling. Then my father said, "We'll wait with you at the bus stop." So we dashed across the steaming asphalt to the plexiglas shelter. The rain sizzled down and cars and trucks swooshed by, and we stood there. Maybe someone said something.

I was thinking about how that fall everything would start without me at Lincoln Middle School. In a few days, everyone I knew would be meeting their new teachers, and the accelerated math class would be starting geometry, doing proofs. In June, we had gotten a letter from the Iowa Department of Education, offering to send me to a new school they were starting called the Peterson School of Math and Science. The year before, they gave a standardized test during homeroom, and everyone who scored in the top half a percentile got a letter. They gave me a talk about whether I would miss my friends or Mr. Reynolds, my math teacher.

I told them I would go. I didn't think about how weird it was going to be, waiting for a bus with my clothes in bags. The kids at school would remember me as the kid who never talked, who drew weird pictures and always wore the same clothes, and cried when he dropped his lunch, who was supposed to be really good at math. . . . Whatever happened to him? Where did he disappear to?

The bus pulled in; a man got out and checked the fistful of signed forms I held out to him, then threw my bags into the compartment that opened in the metal side. My parents hugged me, and I climbed the steps into a warm darkness that smelled of strangers' breath. I walked unsteadily into the dimly fluorescent-lit space, glimpsing faces passing in rows, until I found a pair of empty seats just as the bus roared and pulled out of the parking lot. I remembered to look for a last glimpse of my parents watching me leave, then we surged up the on-ramp and into through traffic. Suddenly I hated the sopping morning and the impersonal helpfulness of my parents, always a little held back, as if they were afraid to know me; and I was glad to be gone, glad to have no part of them, to be where no one knew me, away from the quiet of their house, their self-restraint. I had a dim inner vision of myself rising up in flame.

We kept driving through the slate gray morning that grew slowly brighter, although the rain kept up. Most people were asleep, and every twenty minutes or so we would stop to pick up another child, another one of us. Most of the kids must have gotten up at three or four in the morning to meet the bus as it crossed the state. Everyone was drowsing or sleeping or staring out the window. I slept a little myself, although it felt strange to be dozing off among all these strangers. No one talked, but there was a faintly intimate process taking place among us, a bond forming out of the shared unfamiliarity of the trip. We wouldn't forget it. For all of us, it was the start of a new phase of our lives; a group identity was taking shape out of the rainy morning and the engine noises and forty-eight dreaming minds.

For the first few months we had to sleep in the gym. The student dormitories hadn't been finished properly, and they flooded and had to be rebuilt. Sheets were hung for privacy. We congregated at 9:30 p.m. and were led to the bathroom in groups of fifteen, and there was the funny feeling of seeing kids from your math class again in their pajamas, each holding toothbrush, cup, and toothpaste, being herded sleepily to the line of sinks. We were seeing one another the way only our family had seen us. We'd get back, each to our sleeping bag, to stare up at the moths fluttering around by the ceiling. At 10:15 exactly, the big overhead lights audibly went out, and a chorus of whispers would rise. It was hard to fall asleep in such a big room—your ears picked up how big it was. The girls slept in the library, laid out among the shelves and study tables, but I never heard how that was, although I tried to imagine it—quieter, sounds vanishing instead of bouncing around.

Things like this became normal, became the way we lived, waking curled up on the cool, hard gym floor, having slept the night away just inside the three-point arc. Cold sun streamed through high windows, and voices echoed off bleachers and the rafters painted blue, a few kids already beginning to shout and run around. Some had Walkmen and listened to pop music long after lights-out.

The classes themselves were little different from the ones I had taken at public school. The other students were perhaps more advanced, but the same classroom dynamics seemed in place, as if determined by some underlying law of the adolescent educational condition. Jocks were jocks, cliques were cliques, and students who were popular were popular again. Nothing had changed; I couldn't really imagine it changing, except that I now ate silently in a dining hall, instead of silently with my family.

Thinking about that time is thinking about another person. How every day I was going to be smarter and better. I was strong, proud, as sharp as glass, and I was never going to be any other way. I took top honors in the Junior Putnam, the Westinghouse, and, believe me, I was just starting to accelerate. Walking into the computer lab, into the smell of coffee and plastic and the hum of the fluorescents, I was like a prizefighter smelling sawdust and sweat and hearing the crowd.

I didn't cultivate friendships, just a nerdy camaraderie with the top few science students. But I was the usual combination of petty arrogance and abject loneliness. I was ashamed of my desperate eagerness to please, and unable to control it. Why should I be singled out from other people as uniquely gifted, and uniquely worthless? I ate my lunches alone, and it's a small blessing my diaries were destroyed.

Junior year I won a Ford Grant for summer study. I'd already decided not to go home that summer, and the Ford was a lucky excuse. I very much didn't want to see my parents. I was already hoping to make myself into someone else, a person who had nothing to do with their house or their soft-spoken way of talking, or what I belatedly recognize as their kindness.

I was bright, but no one suspected how bright I would become. Prodigies are an old story, and everyone levels off after a while. Or do we? I may not be smarter than I was last year, but I know more. And I'm certainly no stupider.

So I wasn't always this way. I went to a good school. I wrote lengthy short stories about my hapless infatuations; one of them was even a runner-up in the school magazine. All about the girl I saw in the dining hall, at the party, in the hallway, but never spoke to. I wasn't very much different from a lot of people. Except that I was.

Once you get past a certain threshold, everyone's problems are the same: fortifying your island and hiding the heat signature from your fusion reactor. My first subterranean lab was a disastrous little hole underneath a suburban tract home. One morning, two unsmiling men in leotards appeared on my doorstep and demanded to see what I was working on. I said, "It doesn't do anything." They didn't say anything. I showed them inside. I kept my back to them while I worked my fancy locks, but who was I kidding? The one in white had that look people do when they have X-ray vision. Like you know they're seeing just bones.

I had been as careful as I could be, buying equipment through a dozen aliases, some of them legitimate government agencies. Waste heat was going into the aquifer, and there was enough background radiation that no one should have caught anything I was doing. But obviously I'd hit one of their trip wires. We didn't say anything on the way down. Up close, these two weren't especially reassuring. The white one's eyes were set too far apart, and he only breathed about once a minute, rapidly, in-out. I didn't get much on the black guy, except that in the silences I could hear faint tinny voices and bursts of static, as if a cybernetic component in his chest were inadvertently picking up short-wave. It was vaguely embarrassing, like a fart.

It was my first underground lab, and it showed. It was still too hot because of the reactor, and it looked like shit. I hemmed and hawed and started up a little dimensional viewer I had been tinkering with. The Gateway flickered into life, and through the cloudy window we could see dimly the great misshapen head of one of those alien leviathans trawling the ether like a whale in the depths. They looked bored. The black guy, Something-tron, gave me a speech about meddling in things I didn't understand; it was obvious they were peeved they weren't getting a fight. When they left, they had me tagged as just another back-

yard inventor, but I'd made my mistake—I was in the system. They'd
seen my retinas.

Wearing a cape doesn't do much for your social life. There's a standing,
unspoken, and utterly unreliable truce among enhanced criminals, the
robot-army, hood-and-mask, good-evening-Mister-Bond set. My peer
group is largely a collection of psychotics, aliens, and would-be emper-
ors. The result is I meet people like Lily.

Lily was born in the thirty-fifth century. She's what your sort of
person might call a supervillain, although she might quarrel with the
definition. When you first meet her, you look twice—everyone does.
She's not quite invisible, merely transparent, a woman of Lucite or
water. When you get to know her face, she has that long-jawed look
people start getting a couple centuries from now, a hollowness around
the eyes. You recognize it when you've been up and down the timestream a few times, and seen a few of the far-future possibilities—the
Machine Kings, or the Nomad Planet, or the Steady State, or the Tele-
phony. When we met she looked right past me, just another monkey-
man, but I have more in common with her than I do with most of the
people I meet.

Lily was born in New Jersey at a time when the Earth was dying. Only
200,000 humans were left, wandering among the empty cities and
grasslands that were once the civilized world. She grew up with a thousand square miles of grassland and forest and highways for her backyard. She could drive for days without seeing anyone, up and down the
old I-95, now cracked and overgrown in places. Later, she told me about
the decaying bridges over the East River to the lost city of Brooklyn,
where the towers of Manhattan loomed in the distance. She would find
a stone embankment and eat lunch, down where the warm wind stirred
the stagnant ocean that was slowly rising, year after year.

Her time line was simply a dead end. She told me about the spreading
blight, the dimming, dying sun that she could look straight into without

blinking. The only aliens who came left without saying good-bye. In her future, the new ruler of the Earth was going to be a particularly successful strain of algae that had spread in a supercolony up and down the northwest American seaboard, choking rivers and canals and blooming for miles out into the sea.

Lily was trained to be a hero, humanity's long-shot solution, rigorously screened and genetically engineered. A team of desperate scientists worked for decades, racing against humanity's decay to put her in place to save them. She was the best of them, and they trusted her.

A crowd of tense, brave faces was the last thing she saw on the day she left. Brave Dr. Mendelson, strong-jawed and gray-haired, shook her hand once and then gave the countdown, and the world faded from view. The machine that brought her back in time could only work once. The logic was obvious: She had a list of targets, a suite of weapons layered into a smartmesh leotard, and a mission to save the world. Nearly invisible and devastatingly strong, she succeeded easily.

Years later, when she managed to rebuild her machine and return to her own time, it was all different. The Earth she had known, and everyone on it, was gone, and in its place was a world of happy strangers—the blight had never happened. And she realized she missed the quiet, and the gentle, mournful quality of her thirty-fifth century. So she came back to our time, and after a few months she started hitting high-tech and infrastructural targets. She's still at large, still sabotaging the world in search of the chain of events that started the blight in her version of history, the invisible thread leading back to the vanished ruins of her home.

My other best friend is the Pharaoh, a supervillain, and he's an idiot.

Today was the official last day of fall. There was an early frost last night, and the chill seeps into the stone here. Most inmates don't go out in the yard anymore—no one but me and a few die-hard smokers, idly kicking the dirt, huddled together against the cold I haven't felt since 1976. The wind kicks up dust in the yard, blows leaves through the barbed wire.

Our uniforms flap in the breeze. The trees past the fence are bare now except for the oaks. I can see beams from the security net bouncing around in the infrared and ultraviolet, and the KLNJ antenna is pulsing out low-frequency stuff over the hill.

Somewhere out there, the snow is falling on Lily's base. I can't say where it is, but this late in the year it's pretty well covered. I used to tune in to the perimeter cameras just to scan around the woods. It's buried deep now—a layer of snow, pine needles, frozen dirt, then crushed gravel, concrete, water tanks, and then titanium.

I last saw her six years ago, in a bar. She was smoking. I remember how the match flared and glistened liquidly on her glassy skin, still scored slightly where a chain gun once caught her. She set the cigarette to her lips and drew smoke delicately into her throat, to curl in her lungs like a genie in a smoked-glass bottle. She would only meet me in a public place. I guess we had trust issues.

I went to a lot of trouble to set up that meeting. I tried to think of a way to tell her to come back. I've never been that good at this kind of thing, even before I went into hiding. I tried to think of a reason she would have, a really good argument. But even supervillainesses would rather date a hero. Sometimes I wonder if there really are just two kinds of people in the world.

To be a supervillain, you need to have certain things. Don't bother with a secret identity, that's a hero thing. Not that it wouldn't be convenient to take off the mask and disappear into the crowds, the houses, the working world. Perhaps too convenient—why become the most audacious criminal mind on Earth (or at least in the top four), only to slink off in the other direction when things get difficult? It wouldn't mean as much if you could just walk away. When I'm arrested, they read the litany of my crimes at the trial, longer and gaudier each time. I've been tried for crimes on the Moon, in other centuries, other dimensions, and I'll be damned if I won't put my name on them.

Besides, I never wanted to go back to the way it was before. Heroes have that weakness, not supervillains. When you become a villain you cut your ties and head for the bottom. When you threaten to crash an asteroid into your own planet just so they'll give you a billion dollars or substitute your face on the *Mona Lisa,* there's no statute of limitations. So you have to have the courage of your convictions.

You should have a nemesis. Mine is CoreFire, an imbecile gifted with powers and abilities far beyond mortal man's. If anything can hurt CoreFire I haven't found it, and don't think I haven't looked. I've got others—the Champions, disbanded now but no less dangerous as individuals. Damsel, Stormcloud's daughter, and her ex-husband the gymnast, and that alleged elf they got from somewhere. I've fought dozens of heroes over the years, but CoreFire is the toughest. After all, I made him myself.

You need an obsession. The zeta beam, key to ultimate power. Secret of CoreFire's might, and the fire that scarred me, and made me what I am. And you need a goal. Viz, to take over the world.

And you need . . . something else. I don't know precisely what it is. A reason. A girl you couldn't get, parents slain before your eyes, a nagging grudge against the world. It could be anything. I really don't know what it is, the thing that makes you evil, but it does.

Maybe I should have been a hero. I'm not stupid, you know, I do think of these things. Maybe I should have just gone with the program, joined up with the winning team, and perhaps I would have, had I been asked. But I have the feeling they wouldn't have wanted someone like me. They'd turn up their noses or just never quite notice me. I knew some of them in high school, so I know.

I learned what a villain was by watching television news broadcasts of the big fights in New York and Chicago. I could tell who the villains were because they always lost, no matter how good their ideas were. I don't understand how or when the decision was made for me, but whenever it was the moment is lost now, gone away as far off as Lily's home Earth.

There are moments in life you just can't take back. In the terrible slowness of the accident, I got halfway across the room before realizing what I'd done. I had time to look back and read the controls, to see the glass begin to bulge and craze before it shattered, time to notice the sound of my foot scuffing on the floor, and an urgent musical whine from one of the generators sliding up the scale.

A dozen people have gotten themselves killed trying to replicate the effects of that explosion. I turned and saw my future crystallizing out of a volatile green compound, written out in invisible ink. All my life, I'd been waiting for something to happen to me, and now, before I was ready for it, it was. I saw the misadjusted dials and the whirling gauges and the bubbling green fluid and the electricity arcing around, and a story laid out for me, my sorry self alchemically transmuted into power and robots and fortresses and orbital platforms and costumes and alien kings. I was going to declare war on the world, and I was going to lose.

CHAPTER TWO

WELCOME TO THE TEAM

Four years ago, I decided to start calling myself Fatale. It's my superhero name. I chose it from a list they supplied me in the clinic, and at the time it seemed like the perfect symbol for my dangerous, sexy new self, a cybernetic woman of mystery. Admittedly, I was on a lot of painkillers.

Before this, I was an enhanced operative in an NSA-style spook show. When they fired me, the government techs said I was having an adjustment disorder, but I prefer my term for it. I'm a superheroine, gifted with powers and abilities above the norm. I'm superhuman, one of the good guys. One of the chosen.

I got my powers by accident, a random tourist mishap in São Paulo. It wasn't a fancy accident, just a runaway dump truck on the Rua Augusta that plowed into me and scraped me forty feet along the side of a building. I was on life support for four months and unconscious most of that time. I'm going to be in a clinic for three weeks this year, and the next, and basically for the rest of my life.

Why I was in Brazil, or even who I was there with, I don't know. That went in the accident and the surgery that followed, taken out when armor plate and dead reckoning and a prototype microwave projector went in. I've looked at travel guides to try to jog my memory—was I there to see the architecture? The zoo? I don't even speak Portuguese.

But yes, I did it to myself. I signed the papers, medicated and supine in a hospital bed, scrawling an illegible name with a fuck-it-all panache, knowing vaguely that I didn't have much of a shot otherwise. The press release was of course bullshit, not that anyone bothers to look at my web site. They wrote it while I was still in recovery, all about cancer and a miracle cure. I never even learned all the made-up details about my grandmother and the old house, and how I wanted to be an astronaut. The real story is much more complicated and stupid and isn't a thing I could explain fully, not even when I had all of my original brain tissue.

Protheon approached me in South America. The corporate doctors came to see me several times during my conscious intervals; polite, friendly men, in suits and in lab coats, to talk to me about a proposal they had for me. I was the one-in-a-million accident they had been waiting for, and they were my last option. They explained about the super-soldier program. They told me I was going to be the forerunner of an army of people who looked and fought like me. I said okay.

The Brazilian clinic had contracted the advice of a Swiss designer of artificial organs, three American software engineers, a German military contractor, and a Thai plastic surgeon famous for sex-change operations, but the main design and modification was the work of an unknown party.

Forty-three percent of my original body weight is just gone. Mostly on the left side, ground into the pavement or discarded on the operating table. Muscle, nerve tissue, bone, and skin. Hair, fingernails, cartilage, an eye, and a good deal of brain tissue. A lot of my guts are plastic, too.

That was the unlikely beginning to my career as a superhero, enhancile, trans- or super- or metahuman or whatever other term you like to use to describe it. What I am now, and will be for the rest of my life.

I can see myself reflected in the curving metal walls of the Crisis Room, a patchwork woman of skin and chrome, souvenirs of a bad day in São

Paulo. I lost a lot of skin, and gained four inches of height and a metal skeleton.

I'm in Manhattan, on the forty-eighth floor of a midtown skyscraper, sitting down with the seven most powerful heroes in the world, and I'm lucky they even asked me to be here. A month ago I was spending my daytime hours watching television and listening to the police scanner. It's hard to make it on your own as a cyborg—we have serious overhead, maintenance and supply issues I'd rather not explain.

I check my reflection again to make sure I've got the look exactly right, a silver-haired, high-tech Amazon warrior, hair drawn back in a long ponytail, a gleaming technological marvel. I was going to be the next generation of warfare.

The past few hours are a blur. Flying up from Hanscom Air Force Base, where it took me three hours to get through security, a private helipad. A crowd of reporters stood around the Champions' headquarters shouting questions about CoreFire, but no one so much as recognized me. Then another long security check before I could get a visitor's badge.

Even though I was running late, I stopped in the trophy room outside the Champions' Crisis Room to gaze at the old memorabilia and the old group portraits of the finest superteam in the world. Two of those faces are absent now, two empty places at the table. Nobody says anything, but it's obvious whom I'm here to replace. Galatea's sculpted face beams down from the glamour photographs, a metal angel.

So I'm the last to arrive. Nobody looks up—the meeting's already running. Being this close to so much power is a vertiginous sensation. The heroes pop out at you, impossibly vivid, colorful as playing cards but all from different decks, a jumble of incompatible suits and denominations dealt out for an Alice in Wonderland game. A man with the head of a tiger sits next to a woman made of glass. The woman to my right has wings. This is where I want to be—the players.

The Champions have money behind them. A marble table the size of a small swimming pool, arched ceilings, a dozen instrument panels blinking global updates. There's a charge in the air. This is where the greatest heroes in the world sat—their portraits ring the room, images of the heroes they were ten years ago. Except two of them, Galatea and CoreFire, are missing.

"Whatever this is, it's global. The tides are off, and there's a temperature drop in the deep ocean. And CoreFire is still missing." In the Crisis Room, Damsel tells us the world is ending. We sit in a half circle, like children. A U-shaped table spans the room, and Damsel hovers at the open end before the wall of monitors.

Her force field flickers a moment, green and then indigo, over her skintight red-and-purple costume. Her face is familiar from a thousand interviews and magazine covers; a slender, pretty brunette, nondescript save for the odd little markings on her throat. She has the glamour of a film star, but her power is no illusion.

Damsel's father was Stormcloud, the mainstay of the old Super Squadron, so Damsel is that rare thing, a superhero by inheritance, her name a half-serious play on her father's vocation. His weather powers may not have been genetic, but his strength and speed are there. She wears a pair of swords to compensate, wire-wrapped hilts coming up over her shoulders.

Behind her, a wall-size video monitor flickers, showing weather patterns, locations of recent superhuman crimes, profiles of a few at-large supervillains. The eight people scattered around the conference table are some of the most famous superheroes in the world. People like Feral, Rainbow Triumph, and Elphin. The air is thick with power. These are people who have, quite literally, saved the entire world.

"Honey, we haven't seen a serious threat for almost a year. I've been almost bored."

This is Blackwolf. He doodles on a BlackBerry and twirls a combat knife in the fingers of his off hand. Former Olympic gymnast, millionaire, and onetime scourge of the underworld. Technically, he doesn't have any powers at all, the paragon of the bare knuckle and gadgets style. His lack of a real superpower emerged as a point of pride—any powered hero who cared to make a remark soon found himself challenged to a friendly sparring match, and Blackwolf never lost. He's also Damsel's ex-husband.

Her field goes white for a split second. Then the cat thing, Feral, huffs a sardonic laugh. "Maybe you should be back at work, then. Spend some time on the streets."

Damsel cuts him off. "He should answer his hail at least. He has the same fail-safe signal device as the rest of us."

"I know," Blackwolf replies. "I designed it."

"Could he be off-planet?" I ask.

"Not without saying something. He and I have a deal about that," Damsel says. I look for some sign as to whether this was a stupid question.

"You honestly think there's something behind this," Blackwolf says, as if I hadn't spoken.

"I, too, have felt it. An emanation of the darkness." We all turn to look. Mister Mystic's voice is heavy with portent, and even in the sunlit boardroom the shadows seem to fall heavier in the corner where he stands. He wears a tuxedo and crimson-lined cape, like a cartoon of a stage magician, complete with a wand tucked into a sash at his waist. Rainbow Triumph rolls her eyes. I would laugh if I hadn't seen news footage of him high above Colorado, crimson energy curling out of him to hold a falling satellite motionless above a Denver suburb.

Outside, the East River flashes in the sun. A pile of bagels sits untouched at the center of the table.

"Darkness? Crime, you mean." Feral's voice is a growl distorted by jutting canines. He's a mutant, a genetic metahuman. Massive, he cat-crouches in one of the office chairs—how could someone just be born like that? It must have been a genetic program, but officially he's an accident. He has a long feline tail, and it's lashing, thudding against the mesh back.

I know these people—everyone does. They started the Champions in the early eighties, just as the old Super Squadron started to retire, people like Go-Man and Regina. They were younger and sexier than their predecessors, the seemingly immortal heroes of the postwar boom, with their statesmanlike demeanors and bright costumes like the flags of strange countries. That generation had been compromised by the alien-war intrigues of the seventies, and these people became their newer, slicker replacements. If the Super Squadron were the golden age, they were the silver.

Some of them don't even wear masks anymore. They don't have secret identities as working-class chumps; they date movie stars and attend celebrity charity events. Even their powers are cooler—fast, fluid, nonlinear. Monumental blocks of muscle have gone out of fashion, and these new powers seem to emerge as pure style. The team roster changed every few years, but these were the core, the ones who had been there for the big breakup nine years ago.

I take a few stills out of the camera in my left eye in case I never get this close again, catching details you miss in the magazines, the precise way the light glints off of Lily's skin. If Damsel looks almost ordinary, Lily never could—the daylight miracle of her skin is always there. I can't believe they asked her here. No one is talking to her. Even Blackwolf keeps a wary eye on her.

"I don't want a high-profile event. I'm not talking about getting the team back together, okay? I thought it would be smart for a few of us to just look into things. Informally."

Blackwolf shifts in his chair. "This is CoreFire we're talking about. The big guy can take care of himself."

I watch him unobtrusively, aware of those preternatural reflexes. His hands as he holds the printout in front of him are strong but graceful. I can see scars and calluses. Hands of a pianist turned prizefighter.

"We've got some new faces here, so let's make some introductions. I'm Damsel." The famous face is carefully neutral behind the mask.

They all know one another, but we go around the room anyway. I can't help but feel it's a courtesy to me.

"Feral." It comes out as a breathy cough.

"Blackwolf." He nods, looking just like his *GQ* cover. In costume, his black bodysuit shows up that perfect musculature. Almost forty, he looks twenty-five. Genetically perfect.

"Rainbow Triumph." Rainbow Triumph's is a bright chirpy cartoon of a voice.

"Mister Mystic." Mystic's is baritone perfection, crisp and resonant. I wonder if he used to be a professional actor.

"Elphin." A child's whisper but somehow ageless; the voice that once lured naïve young knights to their doom.

"Lily." The glass woman. Her name brings an unmistakable tension into the room. She worked the other side of things for a long, long time. She's stronger than almost anyone here, and some of them know that firsthand. Now she's come through the looking glass, into the hero world. I wonder how she got here.

When it gets to me, Damsel says a few polite words about my work on the sniper killings. No mention of the NSA. I stand awkwardly to say my code name, conscious of my height.

"Fatale." There's a digital buzz at the back of my voice that the techs never managed to erase. When I sit back down, one armored elbow clacks noisily against the marble tabletop. I don't wear a mask, but I fight the urge to hide my new face behind the silver hair they gave me. Most of it's nylon.

They found me in Boston, living on the last of the reward money from that sniper thing, plus a kill fee from the NSA when they voided my contract. Becoming a superhero doesn't happen all at once, and by that point I was working the bottom end. Spending nights lurking in Allston, or Roxbury, or Somerville, senses open to the police bands and 911 lines, sprinting to be there before the authorities. Supposedly, I grew up around there, but I didn't remember these neighborhoods. There was no particular money in it or even superhero glamour, but I needed to be working. I was lucky to find that sniper thing.

Damsel was just there one day when I got home, standing on the shag carpeting in front of the television. She gave me an appraising stare. I knew who she was, obviously, and apparently she knew me.

"You must be Fatale." She glowed a little. She was being projected here as a hologram, the superhero phone call. Her left foot wafted through a thrift-store coffee table—there hadn't been much room to materialize. I wondered where the transmitter was.

"Damsel?" I ducked a little to come inside.

"I'm here to offer you an opportunity. Part of a group effort we're putting together. If you're willing, there's a meeting coming up at the Manhattan facility. I understand you're temporarily at liberty."

"Uh, right. Of course. Well of course I'm interested. And no, I'm not, uh, engaged right now."

"Excellent. Details will arrive by courier. We'll expect you." She winked out. Whatever level of technology they used, it was pretty far from anything you'd see on the street.

I noticed she didn't promise anything. And she didn't use the word *team*, like the old Champions were. They'd been more like a family, even before Blackwolf and Damsel married. No one expected that to happen again. They wanted an available hero who could be a technician, like Galatea was, but they weren't pretending it was going to be that relationship again.

I could picture the conversation that led to my selection.

"So who can we get? Somebody who does machines."

"Dreadstar?"

"Eh."

"Calliope? Argonaut? The Breach?"

Chorus of shouts: "Not the fucking Breach!"

"Who, then? We've got no psychics, nobody technical . . ."

"Please, just find somebody who's not going to be a total disaster. Have the computer give us a list."

They'd looked at my schematics, and my references had checked out, and Damsel was dispatched. The official invitation came later in a heavy envelope of crisp, velvety paper. I was to report to their headquarters for the informational meeting two days later. They sent me a plane ticket along with. I'd never flown first-class before.

Talking about CoreFire, they fall into old rhythms. They used to be a team—once; they did this for a living. They all seem rusty at first. Damsel's just a part-time crime fighter now. For all her power, she spends more time fund-raising for groups like Amnesty International. Elphin has a line of beauty products. Mister Mystic works as a consultant, to an odd and exclusive clientele.

"All right, say he's missing. Now what?" Blackwolf's natural charisma seems to make him cochair of this meeting.

"Who saw him last?" Damsel asks.

"I did." Blackwolf answers her levelly. "He looked fine." Blackwolf holds the distinction of being the only human ever to knock CoreFire unconscious. He still patrols in costume, part-time, but it's mostly publicity for his corporate holdings.

"He always looks fine," says Feral. He's one of the few heroes on this level still working the streets, still busting up drug deals and foiling muggers. "Damsel? I know you two kept in touch."

"I haven't seen him in a year. When we took down Impossible together last time. He was on form. Untouchable as ever."

I follow the conversation, feeling useless. I've never met CoreFire. I've never even seen him in person.

"He always had that vulnerability to magic. I saw an arrow go right into him one time. Some kind of magic arrow thing."

"A magic arrow is not an object you understand, Blackwolf," Mister Mystic responds. "In my current pursuits, I seldom traffic in such things, but I will inquire."

"The forest realms say nothing," Elphin offers wide-eyed, wings rustling.

Damsel takes a deep breath.

"Look, this is what I'm proposing. CoreFire's never failed to answer a hail before, and if he's over his head, this is going to be serious. If this is Doctor Impossible, it's the moment he's been waiting for. We're setting up a . . . group. People from the powered community. You people are the short list."

That makes them think. The Champions meant a lot to the community before they split, but the core members haven't all been in the same room since then.

As a group, they seem to have trouble keeping still. Feral paces and lashes his tail. Damsel rewraps the cord on one of her sword hilts while she speaks. Elphin flies up to perch on one of the computer banks, her long eldritch spear held lightly in one hand, the barbed metal tip nearly touching the curved ceiling.

Rainbow Triumph taps one foot, glances over at me or at the ceiling, and drums polished fingernails. She was an obvious choice, a high-profile hero with great approval ratings and generous corporate backing. The invitation had probably been cleared through Gentech, and her agent. I'm a little surprised to see her still in the field. Child superheroes so rarely turn out well—look at the Impkin now; look at poor Theodore Bear.

I rub one arm at the line where the steel alloy bonded with my skin. No seam at all—it's like two layers of Neapolitan ice cream, flesh and alloy, some protein voodoo they managed mostly by luck. Underneath it's a lot uglier; wires run everywhere like bad kudzu, and there's still a lot more human tissue in the right half than anyone thinks. Only the Protheon team knows for sure.

Blackwolf watches everyone else, eyes flicking to elbows and knees, all the weak spots. He puts a lot of time and thought into working out exactly how, if it came to it, in a fight, he could hurt the person he's looking at. It's not personal. It's the only thing he's good at, and it's amazing he's survived this long. He was diagnosed mildly autistic before he was a superhero.

Only Lily keeps utterly still, in a chair a few places down the table, a sculptured plexiglas form. She raises one crystalline arm.

"So . . . why do we think it's Doctor Impossible? Isn't he still in jail?" Lily's voice sounds carefully neutral. Damsel answers, looking straight at her.

"I don't, personally, but who knows what he's capable of? And something this big doesn't happen without his knowing."

"Do we know where he is?"

"That setup near Chicago, locked down tight."

"Look, if you're so worried about him, why not just ask him yourself?" Lily looks almost amused. She and the Doctor were an item back in her not-so-distant villain days.

"He knows us. He won't talk to us. Unless you think you could do better?" Blackwolf's tone is even, genial; he's watching to see how she'll take it.

"I was hoping that between us we'd have a few leads, Lily." Feral holds her gaze, tiger face unreadable. They say he has a drinking problem now, but he's pure havoc in a fight.

"I don't have all my old connections, as my presence in this room ought to tell you. CoreFire has a lot of enemies. Any one of them could have found that stuff he hates. The iridium."

"We scan for that. Always," Damsel shoots back.

"I'm just saying, there are a lot of people trying to figure out how to do this. And you haven't been watching. You've been out doing . . . whatever you've been doing." Lily watches their reaction; this part, I now realize, is her job interview.

"You have, maybe. I do my job. I always have," Feral rumbles, and leans back in his chair.

It's an uncomfortable silence. Too many heroes in this room, and too much history.

Most of them are naturals, superpowered since puberty or before. Powers that came on their own. Naturals are the wild talents that form out of the ever-churning soup of the human megapopulace by accident or fate. Once in a hundred million times, a lifetime of factors align, and at the right moment something new coalesces out of high-tech industrial waste, genetic predisposition, and willpower, with a dash of magic or alien invention. It started happening more often in the early 1950s, and no one knows why—nuclear power plants, alien contact, chlorinated water, or too many people dancing the Twist.

A very few of us got this way on purpose. Manufactured, treated with chemicals, surgically altered. Sheer force of will, or radical educational measures, or a willingness to take insane gambles for power. Blackwolf, for example, is little more than a superbly gifted athlete.

His father, legend has it, taught him most of what he knows in their backyard with only a baseball bat, a German shepherd, and an old rubber tire hanging from a tree. I've been snubbed before, for doing for myself what destiny did for others. But it may be a nobler thing to claw one's way up, to seize by an effort what others had handed to them. What they were born with, or what dropped from the sky one calm summer night.

Damsel breaks the silence. "If someone out there has figured out how to beat him, we need to know it."

"We owe it to the man, don't we?" The question hangs in the air. Whatever had split them up made that an actual question.

"He was one of us," says Elphin with finality, in the clarion tones of an Amazonian warrior. "If he truly has fallen, we cannot let him go unavenged."

Elphin sits to my left, looking around with a disturbingly avian stare. We rode up in the elevator together. She's not a teenager; she only looks like one. According to her press kit, she was born in tenth-century England. She's a fairy.

They say she's the remnant of an elite fairy guard, a warrior woman, one of Titania's picked few. When the rest of the fairies departed this world, Titania asked her to stay behind. Where her friends had gone, no one knew. All those years, she'd lasted it out with no word from her own people, sipping tea from acorn cups and hunting the shrinking forests of England with flint arrowheads, fairy tech, while the centuries passed.

And then she'd come out of hiding to battle the enemies of humankind. That's if you take her word for it. I admit she looks like a fairy. She's around five feet tall, with ethereal blond hair, big bright eyes, high cheekbones, tiny breasts. And she acts like you'd think a fairy would act—cute and flighty, blond and haughty. Merry without projecting anything much like happiness. Pretty, but only approximately human.

Her wings look about right; long and iridescent, they whir like an electric fan when she's in flight. She shouldn't be able to fly at all, but *should* can't be depended upon to mean what it's supposed to when she's around. I don't like to look at the place where they join her back, where the insect anatomy joins the human, where the whole thing gets touched with horror. She carries a long spear or pike, a shaft of pale wood tipped with a barbed curlicue like a corner of spiderweb. In her hands it's like a willow wand, but I've seen her punch it through the door of an armored car.

I don't know what she is. Sometimes she acts like the heroine of an epic fantasy novel and sometimes she acts like she's about nine years old, which might be cute if she didn't kill people. But if you tried to make up a list of reasons why a person would look and act like she does, "fairy" would be about the least likely. Maybe it just suits her to say that—better than "wacky elective surgery" or "spy from evil wasp-persons," or whatever it is that made her this way. God knows, my story is no better than hers.

I had four major operations, the longest lasting seventeen hours. The bones and armor went in first, to support the weight of the rest of it. I gained 178 pounds overnight, most of it lightweight alloy steel, bonded by an electrochemical process they wouldn't explain.

For the next six days, I wasn't allowed to move, not that I could have easily. I lay on my back and watched movies and healed. The worst part of it was my skull and jaw. The way it runs across my face like a stripe of silver paint, that took getting used to. My jaw too heavy, my tongue fumbling against metal teeth and cheek, like a strange metal cup always at my lips. At that point, it was all dead metal, like a suit of armor that wouldn't come off.

Next came the first muscle enhancements, basic nerve grafts, and the power plant that would run it all, light as they could make it but still heavy and bulky in my back. Don't ask how they made room for it. I can feel the warmth of it all the time, hotter when I'm working hard. I had to be strapped down most of the time while I learned to access the motor functions of a new set of skeletal muscles.

For months, I walked like a drunk staggering in a high wind. You learn to think and move with it. You have to accept that you're not the same person. It doesn't work if you try to be. You move, then it moves, and then you've gone a step. When a situation's happening too fast, when a gun goes off or I'm hit from behind, the machine takes over and executes everything for me—by the time my regular brain catches up, I've already returned fire, already thrown an elbow, rolled forward, come up in cat stance, and my HUD is showing me half a dozen options. After a while you start to like it.

Everything afterward was refinement. Enhanced senses gradually layered in to include light amplification, infrared. Reflexes, sped up bit by bit over four weeks so I could adjust to the idea of superhuman speed, think in smaller units of time. The arsenal of gadgets that line my arms, legs, and torso—grappling hook, sonics, aqualung, dozens of tricks to get me out of any situation they could think of.

Sensation isn't quite what it was. It feels like half of me is standing in another room, one where there's always a warm, soft breeze blowing. Sometimes I wake up in the night and panic, thinking half of a department-store mannequin has gotten into bed with me. At least I don't get my period anymore.

I'm not complaining. They did a good job. My enemies call me "Tin

Man," which would be less offensive if I had an actual boyfriend. Maybe I had one before the accident, but if I did, he can't have been a very good one. He ought at least to have sent me flowers while I was having my body replaced. Good riddance. Or maybe he doesn't know I'm still alive.

And, wait, what exactly was the Tin Woodman's problem anyway? I can't remember, except that he had a magical ax that chopped him up, limb by limb. Someone must have put a curse on the ax, and there must have been a third person—a tinsmith?—who put him back together again, who stuck on tin parts as the living ones came off. But who was so mad at him in the first place? Why didn't he throw away the ax and get another job?

The joke of it is, there never was a super-soldier program, not one that appears in any Pentagon budget. The Protheon Corporation disappeared without a trace—it was just a front, rented office space. Somebody put a lot of money into making me what I am, then disappeared, leaving me feeling a trifle rejected, if you must know.

That's the part not even the Champions know, my own secret. One of them anyway.

The meeting breaks up into several private debates that sound like they've been argued a hundred times before. Lily pushes her chair back and walks out; I stay and try to catch Damsel's eye, but she's caught up in a back-and-forth with Mister Mystic. I get the impression that the real decisions get made behind closed doors, just the old crowd.

Blackwolf gives me directions to the guest suite, and I wander off down the brushed-steel corridors to the brushed-steel room. We're way too high for the street noise to come in, but I lie awake anyway, thinking about the apartment waiting for me back in Allston. Even at home, sleep doesn't always come. I can send my onboard systems into standby if I want, but the rest of my brain does what it likes.

Sleeping, I dream about my cyborg half, that it's a monster that has half-devoured me, its teeth sunk in the right half of my body. Or it's a forest I've wandered into, and I'm lost amid its mazy pathways, deep pools, strange trees whose long fronds brush my shoulders. In the center there's an enchanted well I can never quite reach. Night falls and the sky shows strange new constellations. When I wake at night, the world glows in wireframe.

Tonight, I have a whole long dream about a list of assembler instructions and their possible uses and then about the team that wrote them, a bunch of engineers in the 1980s. It turns out to be obsolete documentation that got left on an install disc for a chip series three generations before mine, made by a Protheon-owned company out in New Mexico. Just before waking, I catch a glimpse of red earth and a storefront office window in an Albuquerque strip mall, the smell of air conditioning and bad office coffee, the glass door swinging shut, as if whoever made me has only just left the building.

CHAPTER THREE

RIDDLE ME THIS

The guards wake me at about one in the morning, three hours after lights-out. They seem nervous. The scan isn't the usual once-over; they bustle around me for a full half hour, testing the seams on my jumpsuit, checking my teeth, two of them always standing beyond arm's reach.

"If someone ordered a pizza, I don't have any change."

"Shut up. You've got visitors."

When they're satisfied, they shackle my hands behind me with a heavy piece of metal, and a doubled guard leads me down the hall and through a security checkpoint, down a flight of stairs and into a part of the prison I've never seen before.

We pass through a pair of heavy security doors, moving a few rings outward in the high-security onion. A uniformed pair of men check IDs, fingerprint me, nod to each other, and turn keys in unison. Our destination turns out to be a white cinder-block room with a two-way mirror along one wall. The ceiling is paneled, perforated with tiny holes, and has a single square of fluorescent bulbs behind plastic. It's furnished with a metal table and a metal chair.

There is a brief halt, a muted conference among my captors; then they motion me to sit in the chair. My hands are loosed briefly, one of my arms fed through the back of the chair, then remanacled.

The door closes behind them and the bolts shoot home. I can't feel what the restraints are, but they're stronger than regulation handcuffs, which I can snap in a moment. This is a thick, solid metal tube, seemingly cast in one piece, with two holes for my wrists. I test it without much hope. They pretty much know how strong I am, and they're bound to be watching me if I try to get creative. It's hard to estimate what a person of my intelligence is capable of, so in prison it's *Gilligan's Island* rules—they'll always wonder if I can make a radio out of that coconut, or a stun gun. And maybe I could if I had one, and enough copper wire. But not with my hands shackled behind my back.

So I wait there for around twenty minutes; then two superheroes walk into the room.

I don't know them. They're startlingly young, even younger than the so-called Champions. For all I know, they may have gotten their powers while I sat in prison. There's a new generation of superheroes, people I have to fight whose names I don't even know. But you can learn a lot by watching. Superheroes carry their stories around on their bodies.

They're also small for heroes, both under six feet. Coordinated outfits, expensive tailoring, latex and nylon. One wears an orange half mask, and a leotard with flamelike designs in brown, gray, and orange. Whatever else he had done, he has a retractable blade grafted into each forearm, energized metal alloy with a pinkish sheen on it. It must be a new implant; he can't stop testing the edge with one thumb, and the skin is still red with secondary infection where the metal went in. It looks like he paid a lot of money for it, so he probably had more work done under the skin. I'll have to watch him.

The other one is a different matter. Blue traceries glow under his skin. He has a startled look around the eyes, no hair or eyebrows, and no pupils at all, solid blue. Alien technology. I guess him for having informational powers, one of the human calculator types, my opposite number in a way. Smart, without the taint of evil that seems to come with genius. Stupid in a certain way, then.

They look as if seeing me is a little bit of a letdown. They've finally met Doctor Impossible, the Scientist Supreme, and he's a middle-aged man in prison overalls stuck in a metal chair.

Blade Guy takes the lead. He's really happy about those new blades. He could probably cut right through the prison wall, given time.

"This is Bluetooth. I'm Phenom. We're the Chaos Pact. Don't bother introducing yourself; we know who you are."

Jesus. How old is this guy? Twenty? Twenty-two? I can tell it's his first time doing this.

I don't say anything. I just watch. Rich kids? The orange guy might have been. They could be childhood friends, following through on a pact they'd sworn in seventh grade. I wonder if Phenom paid for their implants. I can see they don't know much about me, just what was on TV. They aren't afraid of me.

What happens now? It's a standoff. They keep their distance a little, just common sense. They're nervous—this is their big break. They can't believe they're interrogating *me*, the terror who held the Super Squadron at bay for a decade. A guy who stood in the Oval Office and told the President of the United States to call him Emperor. And now I'm inches away, chained. This is their shot at history.

They're probably hoping I'm going to make it easy for them. That I'll cringe and snarl and make speeches and give everything away. I've made that mistake before. But I don't see any reason why I should make this easy for them.

Again, Phenom breaks the silence. "Been a long time in here, huh? Two years. Not much to a guy like you, though. Bet you're pretty much running things from inside, huh? Pulling strings. Guy like you has a long reach, huh? Mastermind . . ." He chuckles. He has an easy charisma.

I stare back at him. I don't know where he got the idea I'm some kind of boss on the inside. The Prism talks to me sometimes, zaps in through the glass when no one's looking, but he's not making much sense these days. Spend too much time as a rainbow and you lose your grasp on certain things.

Suddenly the absence of chairs is making them look a little stupid. No one knows what to do with their hands. Except me, of course.

"You know why we're here. It's the big guy. Word is, you know where he's gone."

CoreFire! The penny drops. This has been on the news for a while. He's been away for a little longer than normal, eight weeks or so. People are starting to talk. I keep my face carefully expressionless.

"You fought him, right? He was like your nemesis? You guys were archnemeses. Last seen with your friend Lily, I'm told."

We fought once out over the ocean. I had jet boots on, trying to fly like he does. He was wearing that stupid leather jacket, hair falling across his glowing eyes. I lost.

Phenom prattles on. "No sightings. No messages. What could happen to a guy like that? Psychics say he's just gone."

It's actually a good question, and I give it a moment's consideration. But I don't see who could have killed CoreFire, or even how. He isn't supposed to be able to be killed at all, as far as anyone knows—we all thought he was going to be flying around rescuing kittens and putting people like me in jail forever. I've never seen him reach his limits, not even that day on the Golden Gate Bridge, when for a second the whole structural weight of the thing came down on his slight frame. If he can't knock a thing over he can wear it down, the way he slowly pulled Deimos into its new orbit away from the Mars station. You could say he's my greatest invention.

The last bit of whatever iridium isotope can stop him got hurled off the planet decades ago, like a baseball hit over the fence and across the street. To make more, you need lots and lots of heat and pressure, like at the center of a sizable star, or in the Zeta Dimension. Like where he gets his power from.

"He put you away last time, didn't he? When exactly did you see him last?"

Idiot. Damsel beat me last time, not that that's any better. Another pause. Bluetooth looks on, impassive, a human hard drive.

"Not much to say, huh? I get that. Not gonna break that easy. I can deal with that." He snaps one of his forearm blades in and out, fast, giving me a good look at it. And it does look good. Things have come along a bit since I went inside. I wonder what the rest of the heroes are sporting, and if my tricks are old hat by now.

"Just give us a piece of it. You want to end up on a table in a government lab? They do that to people. We could figure out what makes you so smart. Think about that for a while, supergenius. You know what we can do to you in this room?"

Jesus. The same stuff, I assume, they can do to me outside of it. Their friends have already done it to me a dozen times already, so I don't imagine my being in custody is going to make anyone squeamish.

The guards are gone. They figure the heroes can handle themselves. And I don't like those blades at all. They aren't legal in most states, as if that matters. No superhero gets an implant like that, unless he doesn't mind killing people.

What do they expect from me? A full confession?

"Look. If it isn't you, then it's a friend of yours. I know you guys talk to each other. If you can finger the right guy, maybe there's something in it for you."

As interrogations go, this one is already starting to lag a little. Phenom lacks the conversational expansiveness of the truly gifted torturer, but I can see they aren't leaving. It was probably a lot of work to set this up, and they won't want to walk out empty-handed. They want a clue, a story to tell, a memory of how they stood up to Doctor Impossible and he cracked.

"Come on. Was it Bloodstryke? Was it the Pharaoh? Was it your old girlfriend Lily? Come on, Einstein. Talk."

He's talking right into my ear now. His breath is hot, ruffling my hair a little.

"Supposed to be smart, right? Can't hear me? Hey, loser! Hey, stupid!" Suddenly we're nose-to-nose.

"I. Am. A. GENIUS!" The words bubble up out of me before I've thought about what I'm saying.

They glance at each other for just a split second. Then something brushes my cheek. The world jumps and I'm sliding across the floor, one cheek against the tile. Phenom is fast, I'll give him that. I never even saw it.

Three or four seconds have passed. I'm still shackled to the chair. The side of my face is numb. With one arm between the bars of the chair back, I manage to get to my knees.

"Boom, bitch!"

Phenom's pacing, making little half jogs, jabbing the air like a boxer. Bluetooth heaves me and my chair back to upright.

"Dad said we shouldn't . . . ," he says, speaking for the first time.

"Lighten up. It's Doctor Impossible. No one cares."

He hits me again, and this time I almost feel it. It's been a long time since I felt much of anything. Other side of the face this time, and I slide all the way to the wall and stop with my nose up against it. Bluetooth stands me up again. I'm starting to get a little dizzy, but at least the blades haven't come out.

Phenom is back on form. "How long you want to keep this up? You don't have a lot of powers besides that brain of yours. Things get physical, you fold up pretty fast. You want to start losing teeth?"

I spit. "You won't be laughing when I move the—" I start to say, the plan I've concocted in prison on the tip of my tongue. Why do I always tell people my plans?

I look at him and then at Bluetooth, and just for a second I see something else. I'm on my back again, but in another room. A big room with a tiled floor. I land on something soft, which has smeared, soaked into my pants. People are looking at me.

I can still hear Phenom's voice. "So what's it going to be? Look, you've got nothing in here. No gadgets, no gimmicks. You're just a guy in an orange jumpsuit. How long are you going to last?"

But then something strange happens. The scene shifts and I'm back at Peterson. Jason is there, a junior, his class representative. He's in the crowd that afternoon, eating his lunch on a tray, peering over the heads of the younger students—the skinny kid who would later call himself

Blackwolf, and Damsel, tall and quiet. I don't remember them sticking up for the weak and powerless that day.

"Think you're smart? Think you're smart? Wanna show me how smart you are?"

What's happening? Then I put it together. I'm no stranger to psychic attack. Bluetooth isn't a computer; he's a telepath. They're a little more sophisticated than I thought. They came in with a plan. Phenom would pound on me and feed me questions while Bluetooth rummaged around in my mind, pulling up whatever memories were there. I missed it before under the fluorescents, but that circuitry under his skin is starting to pulse.

"Come on, Blue. Ninth grade, man, remember?"

"He's uh—wait. I got something," Bluetooth says. He has his hands on his head now.

"Stick on it."

When the next punch comes, it's a thunderclap. This is probably about as hard as he can hit. I can tell this isn't heading in a good direction. I have to do something. Say something. When you're under psychic attack, the only thing to do is try to take control back.

"Listen. Kid." They stop and stare. "You want to know what happened to CoreFire?" My voice is sort of mushy—my lips are swelling up. I try again.

"Come here. I'm going to tell you a story."

"Shit. This better be good." Phenom lets his hands drop for the moment. They both stop and listen.

"Once . . . once upon a time. There was this girl."

Nonplussed, they exchange another glance, but they're listening. Bluetooth stands me back up again like a fallen chess piece.

I keep talking. Bluetooth is still working on me, and if there's one thing I still have, it's my secrets. I have a plan for when I get out, and a real name, although for all I know, it's public knowledge by now.

Memories scroll by. I thought it would be different at Peterson, but it wasn't. I see myself spending long afternoons in my single room, not very different from the one I live in now. I read and I filled my notebooks with drawings and ideas, crazy stuff. Once when I built the time machine that took me back to the Punic Wars, I couldn't resist stopping to peer in my own window, looking in on that crucible time, of a genius that didn't know itself.

I keep talking. "This girl who was supposed to spin straw into gold. They put her in a jail with a lot of straw in it. And there was a little dwarf who came in to help her."

Phenom hits me again, and I really feel it this time. There's no way for me to roll with these punches, and I'm not feeling especially invincible right this second. Bluetooth checks the window, but I don't think it matters. Even if they kill me they won't be in that much trouble. Maybe none at all. I wonder when he's going to try out the blades.

"Only she had to know his name. Nobody knows. She doesn't know. King doesn't know. Villagers don't know."

"Whatever. Step it up, Blue. This guy's not going to give us anything."

I can't remember how this goes, but it doesn't matter. I'm trying to keep my voice from shaking. I actually don't know how much more of this I can stand.

"So he just keeps showing up and asking her, 'What's my name? What's my name?' "

Phenom shifts, restless. "Okay, Doc. You want to mess with the Phenom?"

Phenom brings out his blades, sliding them from their housings, one in each forearm, each a foot and a half long. He makes a show of it, performing for his friend a little. Bluetooth gives the observation window another sidelong glance, but nothing he sees there seems to bother him. It's coming soon now; I can feel it in my altered blood.

"Finally, she just asks him his name, and he says . . ." Is this how the story goes? I can't remember.

In a flash, Phenom has his face pressed up against mine, one forearm against my chest, blade to my throat. I can feel the chair's front legs come up off the floor. I ready myself to go out like a supervillain. "Fucker fought my father!"

"Listen. The little dwarf says . . ." I just want to get this out.

"Jared, he's . . ." Bluetooth has a hand out, but he's too far away. Phenom's half-turned to look at his friend. The chair is at the tipping point, and then it starts to go over. All I can see is the ceiling.

Why is it always like this? I'd forgotten about this stuff. Let myself get complacent. Images of Peterson get confused with the present day. In another room with a tiled floor, they stand around jeering while I face the urinal. I leave, face blank, in a trance of shame. Somewhere in that darkness, I wedded myself eternally to science and genius and anger. How had I forgotten that?

"Rumpelstiltskin!" I shout. I bend my legs and then drive one heel up and into Phenom's chin as hard as I'm able. It would have broken an ordinary man's neck and jaw, but Phenom's skeleton is mostly metal. He can take it.

I roll to one side and get my knees under me while Bluetooth stares, aghast. Here's the dangerous part: While Phenom is still sprawled out, one arm conveniently extended, I lean back and gingerly bring the metal restraint down on that next-generation titanium blade. I put as much weight on it as I dare, and after a few seconds, the edge bites and goes in. The metal parts, and I'm a free man.

I half-stand, one arm still hooked through the chair, and bring the whole business up and then down on Bluetooth's bald head, restraints and all. In the tiny interrogation room, it sounds like a bomb going off. I hit him again, and the chair falls to pieces.

How had I forgotten this? When life gives you lemons you squeeze them, hard. Make invisible ink. Make an acid poison. Fling it in their eyes.

Phenom is on his feet again, a little wobbly but still game. He's got his hands up, blades extended. Either of those things might take my head off like a dandelion. I duck between the blades and lodge my shoulder in his solar plexus. I wonder, fleetingly, if I'm too slow now. I'm fighting my old enemies' children now. I wonder what they have now that I don't know about. I get one arm around his waist and drive him to the wall.

He's young and healthy and full of biotech modifications, but he doesn't seem to have any combat training. I've got him pinned. His helmet comes off and clatters to the floor. He's blond, younger even than I'd thought. I can smell his shampoo and his cologne. An alarm is going off. He tries to pull away but I'm too well braced, and he doesn't know how to break this hold. He's cursing me out under his breath, thrashing. In a moment he'll get one of those blades free, and then it's going to be over. Bluetooth's clattering around behind me, struggling to get up.

I duck under one of his arms to get him in a submission hold, and with his head between me and the wall, I make an end of it, not particularly nicely. The arm will heal. Guards crowd to the window, horrified. I mostly don't like an audience, but just this once it's gratifying. This is what they were warned against, over and over. They probably had to take a whole class in metahuman containment, never thinking it would matter. I can just see them thinking, God, we're in trouble. We so blew it! Far off, concentric rings of security doors are slamming shut, trapping them in here with me.

I can see myself in the two-way mirror. My nose is bleeding a little, but I don't look as bad as I thought. I put Phenom's blade into the door lock, then kick it out. The guards scatter. A few of them make a stand, but in the hallway I can take them three at a time, swinging the shackle like a club, a wolf among sheep. Sometimes it's good just to work with your hands.

I fan out the prison blueprints in my mind, sharp and clear in three dimensions. I memorized this place years ago, against the day I'd be seeing it from the inside. The cinder-block walls are backed up by a cube of solid titanium plates, laced with heat, motion, and pressure sensors. I know the exact nature of the trap I'm in.

But I have leverage. Dragging Phenom and Bluetooth behind me, a heel in each hand, I make my point to the whey-faced guards manning the security checkpoints: Do you really want to see these heroes die on your shift?

A few minutes later, I can smell fresh air. A shotgun takes out the safety glass, and then I'm out under the floodlights and the black sky, heroes abandoned behind me, broken-field running toward the fence. It's shockingly cold out, and the guards are firing at me freely, snipers in the towers. I take one between the shoulder blades but it doesn't matter. They're only bullets.

When I reach the courtyard wall a roar goes up from the tiers that seems to shake the whole prison, drowning out the sound of gunshots, helicopters, alarms, the whole pandemonium of it. I put up a hand to acknowledge it, make a slight bow. It's my twelfth exit from federal custody.

A mad dash to the outer fencing, across a drainage ditch, and I'm gone, out into the freezing darkness and a long night evading pursuit in the Illinois farmland. In my mind, the new scheme is already falling into place. Overhead, the moon is waxing, innocent of my plans.

They'll be scrambling fighters at the nearest air force base, but they won't catch me. CoreFire is still out there—I'm sure of it—and Lily, and all the rest of them, but I've got tricks they haven't seen yet. When they caught me the last time, I was working on something new, something different. During the long prison stay, it has germinated, and tonight it begins to flower.

I'm cold and free and the smartest man in the world, and this time they're going to know it, I promise you. I promise you that.

CHAPTER FOUR

SUPERFRIENDS

Three days later, I get e-mail from admin@champions.com. I stop before opening it, knowing what it has to contain. I think of half a dozen things to do first, knowing that yesterday was a momentary aberration and that back at home in the apartment it's not going to matter. That the spiral I've been in for the past three years has way too much momentum to stop now.

Even when I finally shame myself into looking, I stare for a few seconds before I can make myself read it. But I'm in. It's temporary, probationary, provisional, but I'm in. I have an ID card waiting for me that can walk me into the White House, or Cape Canaveral. You would think I would whoop or dance or something, but instead I just stand there with my eyes closed for almost a minute. I honestly thought they'd taken my tear ducts.

I get a glass of water and sit down to read the e-mail in earnest, taking my time with it. They list the team, everyone from yesterday's meeting. Technically we don't have assigned roles, but I can see now how we fit together. Damsel is team leader and resident powerhouse, although, should it come to it, Lily is at least as tough. Blackwolf is a master tactician, and in a fight his talents put him on a level with just about anyone. Elphin's a born warrior and bona fide mythological figure, well able to handle herself in a fight and with access to weirder sources of power. Mister Mystic handles his own spheres, the supernatural and extraplanar; most of his powers we have to take for granted. I do tech and surveillance, and bring my own enhancements to the table. Feral's an associate member, with muscle and street connections. Rainbow Triumph is a minor, so she's assigned to Blackwolf as a sidekick.

The e-mail says I get a residence at their headquarters for as long as I want it, which is when I really realize I'm leaving. I'm not at all sure what this is going to be like, but . . . I have a vague image of missions against devilish opponents; tense, earnest conversations held in the private jet; in-jokes and raucous training sessions. Victories. Teammates who'd give their lives for you. Anything but taking bullets for former frat boys; anything but staying home and listening to the police scanner and trying not to put my hand through the drywall and into the apartment next door. Anything but what I have now.

I throw some clothes in a duffel bag, and start to pack some boxes for Goodwill, before giving up and leaving most of it on the sidewalk. I haven't accumulated much new stuff since leaving the NSA, and I really don't care what happens to most of it. I can come back for the stupid car, and suddenly I can barely stand to be there another minute.

I take Amtrak this time, four hours riding south with my knees against the seat in front of me, enduring stares. With my long silver ponytail I'm a fantasy princess, until my mods register, my height and the glint of metal at the wrist, the jaw, under my hair. At least I always get a seat to myself.

Arriving is a relief. I breathe in the stale air of Penn Station, then walk all twenty blocks north and east to my new home, striding among the pedestrians like a native. People look at me here, too, but now it's Manhattan and it's all right somehow. Here I'm just part of the show—I even keep a lookout for any crime I can stop, just in passing. I've always wanted to live in New York.

"Name?" It's a different receptionist than before.

"Fatale."

A blank look.

"Fuh. Toll." For the millionth time I wish I'd been "Cybergirl." It was right there at the top of the list.

I hold up my sheet of printout; he takes it and looks it over, barely glancing at me. The gray metal door behind him is heavily shielded, locked down so hard none of my senses can get a grip. Must be Black-wolf's design—I'm impressed. He hands me a laminated card without a word.

I slide my temp ID through the slot in the elevator, and the button for the Champions suite lights up. I don't know what kind of welcome to expect at the top. When I was an enhanced operative, I worked alone, a deniable asset. I was the cavalry, a cyborg enforcer who stepped off a helicopter and cleaned up the mess of an operation gone wrong. It was my job to be nobody. I don't have fingerprints, and most of my cowork-ers weren't even cleared for my code name. Even my EEG signature has been masked. I was very good at it, at least for a while.

I almost panic on the way up, worried that it's not going to live up to expectations, or that it's all a mistake. But Blackwolf greets me as I come out of the elevator. He's in full costume, like always. He's maybe an inch shorter than I am; we shake hands firmly. In a way I'm relieved that it's him. It's nice that somebody else here is, well, human.

"Welcome to the Tower." God, he's got a good smile.

"Thanks."

"I'll show you to your room. First strategy session isn't until tomor-row, so you've got time to look around."

He leads me through a kind of reception hall to the residential wing. Trophies hang on the walls, half-familiar from the headlines of ten or fifteen years ago. Some I recognize—the gemlike core of a rogue AI, and Doctor Impossible's mind-control helmet, the one he'd used on the Russian ambassador. Others I can't identify at all—the head of a robotic gorilla. I knew the Champions had money, but it's just sinking in how much.

"We've got eight floors here. There's a training room, library, meeting rooms, apartments. There's also an emergency hideout in Hawaii, and another one on the Moon."

"You've got to be kidding." Is he? I knew they had access to alien technology, but still . . .

He smiles and winks. I'm used to ranks and procedures, but super-teams are more about personalities. How does mine fit in here? We pass CoreFire's old room, a reminder that one of those personalities is missing now. The group drifted apart since the mid-nineties breakup, but everyone kept in touch with CoreFire. Even after he started holding his own press conferences, like a bitter NFL quarterback.

"Here you go. Room's keyed to your ID."

"Thanks."

"Rest of the team's out, but they'll trickle in toward evening. Dinner's whatever you can find—I've got patrol."

He leaves me alone to unpack. My room looks like a hotel—whoever lived here before me didn't do much decorating. Then I catch on—this must be Galatea's old room, the famous living robot. It figures.

I don't like robots. I hate meeting them socially, even the smart ones that can paint pictures and talk about religion. I met XCathedra once, at a Washington reception connected to the high-tech industry. She was there, schmoozing with cybernetics executives who crowded around her like dwarves around Snow White. She was painted in white racing stripes for the occasion. I found myself looking at her shoulder joint, wondering whether we had any technologies in common. When our eyes met the feeling was uncomfortably intimate.

I never met Galatea. It's strange to think of sleeping in her bed, brushing my teeth in a bathroom that belonged to a legend. Not that she ever slept, or used a bathroom. She was an android, a very sophisticated one. One that cried and laughed and allegedly fell in love. Everyone loved Galatea, and even I can see why—those wide green eyes, the perfect figure, the meltingly soft voice. She looked designed to be adored—even her weapons were pretty. Looking in the mirror, it's clear that whoever designed me had other things in mind.

It's late afternoon. There's time to walk the halls a little and just breathe in the smell, the gleaming fixtures, the glamour. It's like a luxury hotel suite and science fiction headquarters in one, and I never want to leave. Up on the roof garden, where fliers can come and go, I watch the sun set along the skyline.

The kitchen, though, looks just like any dormitory kitchen. Damsel is standing at the counter, shuffling through old case files, when I come in looking for coffee. In sweatpants and a T-shirt from the Yale Law School she looks a lot smaller, smaller than I am, and I don't see her iconic swords anywhere. The force field pulses a soft, steady amber. It hums a little in the quiet.

When she hears me come in, she jerks her mask down before turning around.

"Sorry," I say. Sort of.

"It's no big deal. There's tea on the stove."

"Thanks." I'm not really a tea person, but I pour myself a little.

"You moved up here from Boston?"

"That's right. Near B.U."

"Nice." Not really, I think. I remember she's seen my apartment. The hardwood floors that clunked and creaked under my weight. The landlord made me put down carpeting and sign a dozen disclaimers, and practically begged me to wear a mask. Superheroes aren't popular tenants.

"Well, we're glad to have you with us. I've never worked with a cyborg before." She touches her mask, making sure it's on straight. She still has a secret identity somewhere.

"Just don't ask me to program your VCR and we'll be fine."

Polite half smirk, but the corners of her mouth don't really move. She doesn't smile a lot. I'm good at noticing these things; we machines are.

"Is that for tomorrow's briefing?"

"Just going over some of the old players."

"Anything I can do? I'm feeling a little useless around here."

"You'll do fine. We all get our start somehow."

I guess we do at that, although some people get born with flight and a force field, while others get ground into the Brazilian pavement. Funny thing.

I'm walking back to my quarters when Lily stops me.

"Come on. The real action's down in the gym."

Everyone seems to have gravitated there. I watch through the glass as Rainbow Triumph runs her workout. She was too young to be in the original Champions—famous as she is, this has got to be a coup for her. She has a complicated fighting routine, training on three heavy bags at once; at her fastest, she's a blur of color.

Lily watches with me.

"Settled in?" she asks.

"I guess. People aren't exactly forthcoming around here."

"Trust me, you've got it easy."

Rainbow thumps the bags in a regular rhythm. She's faster than I am, I realize. Lily shakes her head.

"That bitch. Those fins on her gloves have razor edges."

"How do you—did you guys ever fight?" I ask.

"That one didn't make the TV. Come on, let's go in."

The gym is packed with custom equipment designed to challenge the superhuman physique, supermax weight arrays and a laser-monitored obstacle course. It smells like leather and sweat in here; it's the only room that looks like people use it. Most of the action is on the mats. Blackwolf and Feral are sparring, and even Damsel stops to watch.

At six three, Blackwolf is overmatched by a foot and a half, but it doesn't seem to bother him. He looks like a masked Beowulf against a hairy Grendel. He gives ground thoughtfully, cutting once at Feral's eyes with stiffened fingers, almost as an afterthought.

Feral doesn't just dress up as a monster—the hair and teeth aren't a costume. Being a big cat doesn't seem like much of a power at first, but he moves spookily fast for someone so big, dropping to all fours a few times, once bounding fully over his opponent. His claws leave pin-pricks in the matting.

Feral has spotted his opponent a weapon, a frayed length of cord with a blunt metal hook tied at the end. Blackwolf dangles it absently from his left hand. His posture is loose, offhanded. He is supposed to be thirty-eight if you believe his publicist; but if age is catching up with him it doesn't show. There's a little maneuvering, keeping distance; then they close. There's a flash of movement I can't follow, and Black-wolf is actually off the ground, one foot braced in the crook of his oppo-nent's knee, groping for a hold on Feral's long left arm.

Feral throws him the length of the mats, but he rolls smoothly out of it and comes to his feet again in an easy fighting stance. They trade a few barbs, the usual "You're getting soft, old man" stuff. He pays out cord now, swinging it in long, slow arcs. You have to appreciate the artistry of it. Feral can lift a car, or leap half a city block. His fingers end in claws, for heaven's sake.

Feral tries a wild slash, but Blackwolf just folds away from it. The hook arcs up lazily, and Feral bounds forward under it. Blackwolf lets the hook whip around in three quick motions, once around Feral's throat, and it's over. They say he thinks these things out eleven moves ahead, a high-speed chess player. Feral taps out, shaking his head.

Elphin catches my eye, an invitation or a challenge.

She gestures to the mat, like she's not sure I'll understand English. I don't know what she thinks I am. A knight in patchwork armor? I won-der if they've explained it to her—the accident, the operations, the rest of it.

I shrug. "Bring it on."

"I would not hurt thee." Christ.

The others are clapping now, getting ready for the show.

"Fresh meat!" barks Feral, his fangs mangling the consonants. "Let's see what the feds taught you."

"Yes, let's have a look at you." Blackwolf's watching me carefully, with a techie's concentration. He wants a systems test. He touches a button on the wall and some of that equipment retracts into the wall to give us more space, clearing the floor for a battle royal. I see a video camera switch on overhead.

I don't like this. It feels too much like a tryout, and I thought we were going to avoid all of that bullshit. Is this what it's going to be like on a superhero team? Am I going to have to fight all these people?

It's not that I'm scared. I'm pretty good at this; I've just never fought a world-famous superheroine. I've never fought someone with her own pinup calendar and herbal tea brand. The truth is, I was halfway hoping for a shot at Damsel herself. There are tricks you can try with a force field.

The others have stepped back and watch with frank curiosity. Damsel has seen tapes of me, but the others are waiting to see the new guy's moves. Lily is leaning against the back wall. I glance at her and she gives me an encouraging nod.

Okay. I shake out my hair, then pull it back in its ponytail. I set up on the mats in a modified karate stance, left foot leading, right leg powered up to compensate for all the weight. I'm way too heavy for these mats. I'll never get used to the feeling of my prosthetics powering up for battle. I can feel the power drain deep in my gut as the whole system downshifts to handle the new demand. My legs get extra bouncy, super-charged. This is what they built me for. I've had a couple of specialists tell me even the government doesn't have anything on my tech level, but no one with enough clearance to be believable. I was probably hidden in somebody's black ops R&D budget, disguised as foreign aid to nowhere.

Internally, I set a switch that tells it we're in training mode, so I'll pull punches a little. On full power I can kick through a brick wall, and Elphin looks a little more delicate than that. I could snap that narrow waist of hers with one hand.

The super-soldier program did a lot of work on its onboard tactical assistant, the computer in my head that's always guessing what's going to happen next—plotting trajectories, predicting enemy movement, picking up on what I'm trying to do and doing it better.

Elphin stands opposite, spear held loosely in one hand. Her body is pathetically thin. This is ridiculous, I think. I'm fighting an anorexic in her nightie. But when she moves, she looks light and heavy at the same time, and there's a shimmer. Despite the air conditioning, I seem to catch a whiff of summer nights in the forest, and the fluorescent bulbs project something a little too much like moonlight. She's Titania's warrior, if it's true, and nine hundred years old to my twenty-seven and change, not all of which I remember too clearly.

Time slows down as the computer cranks up my response rate. On the tactical display, static fizzes around her spear. Whatever it is, my camera eye doesn't like looking at it, and it's making a hash of the combat projections. The computer can't decide where it thinks it is. There's no way to tell it I'm fighting a fairy. It probably thinks I'm facing off against a pygmy holding a long stick. I'm already big for a woman, but up against Elphin I tower.

Elphin's not bothered by any of this. She minces forward for an experimental jab that clangs smartly off my left forearm, metal on metal. My riposte stops just short of her snub nose—I show her I'm not as slow as I look. I reach for that spear shaft but end up holding air. She's fast, too.

I close the distance on her again, but she's got no reason to grapple. I block the spear point again and lunge for her wrist, working my superior reach, but she spins away and slips behind me. My fingers brush the trailing edge of her blouse; then something glances hard off my skull plate. I turn but she's already out of reach, rubbing her knuckles where they hit metal.

Cheering from the sidelines. Elphin twirls that spear, looking like she'd appreciate a little more support.

She dances clockwise, keeping her eye on me. If I could close and grapple with her, it would be over in an instant. The truth is, I really do want to beat her. I want to beat one of the Champions. I try to remember anything I can about fairies. I wonder if she's allergic to iron, or is it silver? My databanks don't have anything, but there should be something back in my biological brain at least—superhero lore, or some tidbit from a college English class. What is a fairy, anyway? Am I fighting Tinker Bell? Or am I the foolish knight who follows a woman into the forest, doomed to wake up hundreds of years later. *La belle dame sans merci.*

I check the sidelines. They're taking it all in avidly. And I don't know why in hell I should hold back against this waif-chick, with her anachronistically chic hair. I've got sonics. I've got a grappling hook. I've got tear gas. And I have a gun. I always have a gun.

In the big leagues, you're supposed to be able to eat a couple of bullets and not worry about it, and anyway I have rubber bullets loaded today. The barrel comes down out of my left forearm, which is why it's so thick. I let her think I want to close again, then spray her with a two-second burst, easy as thinking it. Welcome to the twenty-first century, girlie. In the closed gym, the report is shockingly loud. More applause, I think, but I'm half-deafened by the sound.

In a blink she's gone, faster than even I can track. Most of that burst hit the safety glass behind her. Where the hell is she? The close air stinks of gunpowder. I start to backpedal, and the computer is flashing an arrow to show where she went, where I'm supposed to be looking. There she is up by the ceiling, rubbing a welt on her thigh, an angry, pouting fairy now. Touché. Scattered applause from my teammates. Leisurely, I raise my arm for another shot. No way to miss at this range.

She flips forward in the air, and when she comes out of it, she's not holding her spear—too late, I perceive it as a throwing motion. And I'm realizing this on my back, because that's where I suddenly am, and I'm trying to get up but I'm pinned somewhere. I've got a screen flashing static, and Blackwolf's hand is on my shoulder, warning me not to stand. Behind me there's applause, and it isn't for me.

"Let me get it out," he's saying over fairy laughter, and I realize what's happened, although it's a throw she couldn't possibly have made.

The spear did only nominal damage—I could patch it myself. It passed straight through me at the midsection, just a cut in what no one's supposed to know is fake skin and insulation. Titania's Moonforged weapon didn't bother to notice the armor plate, rated to withstand depleted uranium. There's no way she could have aimed it like that, not unless she knew what she was doing. And she can't have known that anyway, because she doesn't even understand what I am, what a cyborg is.

I try to pull myself up the shaft, face red. Everybody is laughing at the rookie. The blade is stuck through the mat, standing out from the concrete flooring underneath. I pull it out and heft its heavy length. The blade is cold and seems to reflect a cold light that isn't in the room. Close up, it has writing, but just before I can make it out, it gets yanked out of my hand, and Elphin's walking away with it, laughing her silvery laugh. Feral slaps me on the shoulder with a fuzzy, clawed hand.

"Welcome to the show, primate!" he barks, out of his psychotic-looking tiger face.

And just then the red lights come on, the ones connected to alarms at the Pentagon, the NSA, the Department of Metahuman Affairs, and NASA. The red light I used to dream about when I was tapping 911 calls just to get a lead.

We all sprint up to the Crisis Room, where the computer is already up and talking, and this part is just like I pictured it. An official from the Illinois facility is already on-screen, explaining how, in a nutshell, they let Doctor Impossible get away again. We're finding out about it forty minutes before the press does.

It's still a strange feeling to stand next to world-famous superheroes. The faces and characters stand out in relief; it's impossible not to notice I'm in a room with a lot of people wearing masks. Damsel's cat's-eye mask and her bitchy self-control; Blackwolf's goggles and his languid poise, one muscled forearm draped across a packing crate. He sees me watching.

"Okay, did anyone not expect this?" Blackwolf is in a good humor.

"What's this Chaos Pact?" Damsel takes charge, the loudest voice in the room. "Friends of yours, Feral? They fucked up. Lily's boyfriend is out again."

"He's not my boyfriend."

"Language, please." Whenever Mister Mystic arrives, he just materializes when you're not looking. I checked it on a security camera once, but it came out static.

Feral shrugs as best he can. "Those guys . . . I owed them a favor. I've worked with them before; I thought they were up to it. The Doctor was a little much for them."

"Huh. You think?" Team or not, this was going to be Damsel's show, I could tell. "We've got our suspect now. Is everyone fully up to speed on the Doctor Impossible file? Original sighting in the first bank job, then a classic evil genius development cycle. Almost textbook."

"Is he as smart as he says he is?" I blurt this out without thinking, newbie question.

Blackwolf answers. "He could be. He's been to other stars, other dimensions. He's solved robotics problems, materials problems that no one else has ever touched. If he were a normal person, he'd be Einstein. At least."

"He always hated Einstein," Lily says, thoughtful. I didn't think anyone hated Einstein.

"He's also insane," Blackwolf adds.

"It's called Malign Hypercognition Disorder. He's an evil genius. It's a disease." I can't tell if Lily's joking, but then she winks at me.

Feral brings us back down to earth. "He's just another criminal. We've beaten him before. Some of us have even beaten him solo. Damsel got him last time."

"CoreFire was there," she notes primly. "I suggest we get some sleep. He'll be deep underground by now. If he moves according to pattern, he'll start his next scheme almost immediately. We'll see movement in two or three days. Probably in your area, Feral."

"Smuggling. Petty theft."

"He'll need money and materials. You know what to do."

They all seem to know this guy. To me, Doctor Impossible was always a television villain, too big for me to care about. He was always in another league, out on some island or in outer space, scheming with crazy mind-bending technologies, while I collared drug dealers and Third World militia. But maybe that's an advantage here. Somebody needs to know how to do police work, how to trace a credit card or a shipping container. What it's like down on the ground with the humans.

We all retire for the night, but no one goes right to sleep. I know, because the interior walls here are thin enough that at night when I crank my senses through the right spectra, I can see right through them. I feel a little guilty, of course, but I can't resist. I've heard so many stories and rumors about this crowd, a tight group for so many years. The actual facts are odd, and a little disappointing.

Rainbow Triumph has the room below mine. When she comes in, she lets the door close behind her and stands for a moment with her eyes closed, breathing deeply. She walks to the bathroom and shuts the door, locking it. She opens a metal briefcase and begins opening pill bottles and boxes, until fourteen pills, capsules, and dietary chews are lined up on the edge of the marble sink in front of her. She does it every twelve hours. She's probably been doing it since she was seven; maybe it's to fix whatever was wrong with her in the first place. Part of it's probably to keep her body from rejecting whatever they've put inside it; I took those, too. She also spends a lot of time on the phone.

Underneath my feet, Blackwolf washes his hands for a full five minutes before popping three or four painkillers, which explains a lot. Then he pushes the little room's furniture to the side and puts himself through a series of calisthenic exercises, handstands and one-arm push-ups, slowly and with no sense of strain. Then he watches television for exactly ninety minutes, then stretches out on the floor to sleep. Damsel and Blackwolf have separate rooms now, and I wonder how it worked between them back when they were married. I guess her force field really must turn off.

The building quiets down. Mister Mystic retires back to wherever it is he lives, no doubt to contemplate the infinite. Feral drops to all fours when he's alone, and sleeps curled in a ball. I think he has back problems from trying to stand on two legs all the time. There's an object inside Blackwolf that transmits when he's sleeping. In the bathroom of her suite to my left, Damsel goes immediately to the toilet and vomits in a neat, businesslike fashion. Not that she needs to worry about her figure, but I guess that's her affair.

I know what it's like. Your powers are what you always have with you. It's one piece of knowledge we all share here. No matter how many dossiers the government keeps on you, no matter what data your enemies have collected, no one knows your powers the way you do. Everyone has seen them on TV. For everyone else, it's a momentary fantasy. They don't have to take them into the kitchen, the bathroom, and the bedroom. Or wake up in the night in flames, or sweep up shattered glass in their apartment, or show up late for work with a black eye. No one else knows where they itch or bruise you, or has tried the things you've tried with them when you were bored or desperate. No one else falls asleep with them and finds them still there in the morning, a dream that won't disperse upon waking.

I'm outside the team locker room next morning after a workout on the practice dummies, trying to reproduce a few of Rainbow's moves. The voices inside stop me.

"I told you this would happen." It's Blackwolf.

"Until CoreFire comes back from whatever this is, it's our best option." Damsel sounds tired.

"You're going to let them wear the uniforms?"

"Jesus, no, fine. We'll let them wear what they want, okay?"

"This was your idea, Ellen. God knows, as far as I'm concerned Jason can solve his own problems."

"Please don't bring that up again."

Something beeps inside my chassis and the voices stop. Damsel brushes past me and out of the changing room.

Blackwolf is still suiting up, and I can see his body is as perfect as they say, muscles defined but not bulging—still beautifully in proportion. This close, I can see scars, and a little salt-and-pepper at his temples. If the rumors are true he's become quite the lady-killer since the divorce, not that he's given me a look so far.

I don't have a special costume beyond some custom shoes to handle my weight. My physique is distinctive enough by itself. I'm wearing my usual working outfit, sweatpants and a gray NSA T-shirt. I've stenciled a Champions logo onto the biggest patches of exposed metal, my left thigh and back. I didn't have anyone to do my back for me, so I think it's a little crooked.

"Sorry. What was that about?"

"Don't worry about it. We went to high school together." He bends down to lace up his boots. Up close, I can smell him a little. "Were you on a team before?"

"Not exactly. I had government jobs. Then I was solo." I don't know why I'm talking like this. I guess it's been a while since I've talked to a man I wasn't beating up. I actually start to blush. "Spideractive probably recommended me. We worked on that sniper thing in Albany."

"I remember. You had some nice moves out there against Elphin. What enhancements have you got?" He turns to look me over, and I blush a little. I'm not used to being looked at.

"Vision. Strength—you know, arms and legs. Onboard tactical computer. A couple intrinsic weapons, different kinds. Armor plate, obviously. Grappling hook. Um, fire extinguisher." He's got my file, so I'm sure none of this is news to him.

"You can't fly, can you?" He does a slow side kick, up over his head, and holds it without a hint of strain. I wonder if the rumors about his parents being part of a breeding project are true. It could explain their disappearance.

"No."

"Me, neither." Everyone knows he doesn't have any powers, apart from being perfect. He starts to do a little warm-up routine now, stretches and handstands. You can see that he really does have a kind of power, even if you can't put a name to it.

"Can I ask a question?"

"Sure."

"There are other heroes you could have picked. Other cyborgs, if that was what you wanted."

"Actually, it was Damsel's call," he says. "When she went out to meet you . . . she just thought you'd fit. Said you reminded her of the old days."

"And she's going to be leader?"

He shrugs. "She's good at what she does."

"Must be weird, taking orders from someone who . . ." I trail off. It's weird to share a moment with someone I've only read about before. He laughs for the first time, a different laugh from the one I'd seen on camera, then shrugs.

"It's for a good cause. There's something else Damsel mentioned. Your file said you went on psych disability."

Here it comes. "I got sick of being treated like a Sharper Image gadget. Is that a disability?"

"What'd you do before that?" He really doesn't know about this, and I'm not ready. I'm sitting there with a billionaire genius crime fighter who thinks I can wear the same uniform as he does—I'm not about to correct the mistake.

"I'll tell you later." I can feel him looking as I walk out.

They didn't exactly write me a glowing recommendation.

The last mission before I left, we'd subdued a drug gang and torched a coca field and were just about back over the border. Most of it I did myself, scaring the piss out of sixteen-year-olds with AK-47s who probably thought I was Damsel.

The NSA trained me to fight, rappel down a wall, read people their rights, perform basic first aid. I was always hoping I'd get to solve mysteries like the FBI agents on television, unravel a story, find a secret conspiracy. But that wasn't what they used me for—most of the time, they threw me on a case just as it was all going to hell. I was shock troops—my job was to soak up bullets for the regular agents and strike terror into the enemy, usually illiterate guerrillas who had never even seen a metahuman, let alone faced one in action.

We were waiting for extraction, and it was one of the rare occasions when I've had a drink, which is really advised against in the manual, but I hadn't been sleeping well lately. South American missions bring back a little of the day before the accident, and it's not a good feeling. And I'd spent too many missions bailing out rookie agents, college kids who'd stare at me behind my back and speculate on exactly what parts of me the clinic had replaced.

I have augmented hearing, too, not that they were being too careful. I had a quiet talk with a few of them, nothing that would put them in a hospital, but nothing they'd forget in a hurry, either. I paid attention in my NSA training, all of it.

I was quietly put on a routine leave, which became an indefinite suspension. They don't even recruit female cyborgs anymore—they're considered too high a risk for psychiatric problems. Go figure.

Two days later I'm up in Boston, clearing the last of my things out, when I get a call on my intrinsic cellular phone, the one I can't turn off. It's Damsel, calling from one of the team jumpjets I'm not allowed to sign out yet. I'm to meet her in thirty minutes. I wonder why she picked me for this, and not one of the others. Blackwolf was free, last I looked.

We're going after known enemies first—anyone CoreFire fought three or more times. It isn't a very long list—most people who've fought CoreFire twice aren't that eager for a third go-round. The ones who are tend to be stupid, like Kosmic Klaw, or crazy, like Nick Napalm.

It's 5:00 a.m., so I dress in street clothes and wait for the meet on a snowy bench in Boston Common, hood up, trying to look inconspicuous. One guy stops and stares at me, but I ignore him.

Obviously, I don't have a secret identity—I look the same all the time.

There's a rubber half mask I can fit onto the right side of my face and neck if I want to make a try at looking human (the effect is grotesque, but with a hood up it basically works). I might have looked more human if I'd wanted, but I hate the store-mannequin plastic feel prosthetics have, the Band-Aid-colored flesh. So when they showed me a whole binder full of pastel swatches, a world of browns and pinks, I finally told them to leave the metal exposed. I save the half mask for emergencies.

She meets me only forty-five minutes later. She wears a long coat for appearances, but it doesn't look like she feels the cold. In the dawn light, she looks different, more ordinary. She has the same markings as her father, faint blue lines on her cheekbones and her neck, but in this light they look painted on. I wonder if she looked this way on Titan, where the dawn comes once every sixteen days.

"I think we have a real lead this time. Police in Providence say they picked up Nick Napalm last night. He says he knows something about Doctor Impossible."

The jumpjet is grounded at Logan, so we drive my old Toyota Tercel all the way down to Providence. Damsel spends the whole drive down looking out the window and ignoring me. I realize, more vividly than before, that I don't know these people at all. They were a team for almost fifteen years. They went to the stars together with Stormcloud. They'd traveled in time, fought alongside Roman legions when Doctor Impossible went back to fix the Punic Wars for Carthage. And they'd all seen Galatea die, under the rings of Saturn.

CHAPTER FIVE

FREE AT LAST

When I get out of here—I thought it a million times when I was in prison. Now I'm lying on a bare mattress with the television on, thinking about nothing. It's the middle of the afternoon. I paid for the room with cash stolen from an ATM I dragged out of a convenience store. I carried it into the back parking lot and tore it apart; then I ran as fast as I could. Not my finest scheme, but these are trying times.

The apartment is three small rooms and a gas stove, and cooking smells drift up from the floor below. Outside, a woman with a bruise on the side of her face is arguing with an elderly man. He looks like a homeless guy.

I've probably seen this building before, overflew it in an orbital plane or drifted over it in the dirigible. The exterior is a grubby pink stucco. I never thought about what it would be like to rent a room in it, with cash and no references. I paid it all up front, six months. I'd walked for eleven hours along the highway, going west until I found a town and a change of clothes. Then I rented a car and drove east, careful to drive the speed limit all the way. I discarded it a couple of hours ago. I need a place to stop running for a while, somewhere they won't be looking.

It's time to start again. There's a scheme already boiling up inside me, a good one. I worked it out in prison, sketching the angles in my mind while staring at the blank white walls. But I'm starting to feel I've been here before.

How do you take over the world? I've tried everything. Doomsday devices of every kind, nuclear, thermonuclear, nanotechnological, gadgets that fit in a shoe box and that were visible from space. I've tried mass mind control; I've stolen the gold reserves in Fort Knox, only to lose them again. I've traveled backward in time to change history, forward in time to escape it; I've stopped time altogether to live in a world of statues. I've commanded robot armies, insect armies, and dinosaur armies. Fungus army. Army of fish. Of rodents. Alien invasion. Interdimensional alien invasion. Alien god invasion. Even a corporate takeover, Impossible Industries, LLC. Each time, it ended the same way. I've been to jail twelve times.

Give me where to stand, said Archimedes, and I will move the world. It feels like I've stood everywhere, the center of the Earth and the top of the Eiffel Tower and on the surface of the Sun.

Though never, up to now, in room 316 in the Starlight Motel in Queens. I've operated out of sinister casinos, accursed castles, diabolical fortresses. Caves. This is somehow worse. The smell of disinfectant comes off of everything, and a brown substance is sweating out of the pale yellow walls in the bathroom. Plaster instead of brushed steel; plastic wood-grain sheeting, pressboard instead of blinking readouts. Seventeen-inch RCA color television with three channels of pornography, instead of forty-foot-high monitors; remote control bolted to the night table, instead of voice-activated command protocols. Instead of robot servants, Debbie at the front desk.

On CNN, the heroes are having a press conference about my disappearance. Blackwolf is making a windy speech about justice. They're asking me to give myself up.

They're running the file footage of my last capture over and over, first a zoom-lens shot, probably from a helicopter, showing me at the bridge of my dirigible, cape streaming in the wind. Then, cut to handheld video of me sprinting down a Manhattan avenue, Power Staff gone, zigzagging between cars, turning around to spray knockout gas to slow them up. You can see the sweat stains. My costume wasn't designed for long-distance running; that cape is as heavy as velvet. Cut to me again, in chains and titanium leg fetters, helmet off, still groggy from the beatings I'd taken—that's the image that ran in the newspapers the next day.

Four years ago, I stood a thousand meters above this spot in Queens, looking down at the world, at the scum. I was planning how I'd exact my tribute, which cities I'd rename in my honor.

"People of Earth!"

The sound of car alarms drifted up from among the buildings. The dirigible glided forward a few car lengths. I looked down to see its long oval shadow swallow Main, Lansing, Dean, and Church.

The battle-blimp was an expensive gamble, but there's no doubt it put me on the map. The sun gleamed off the brass railing; the wind ruffled my imperial robes. I didn't just want their money. I wanted them to look into the sky and see me—something extraordinary, something menacing and grand.

I built the air sack to collapse in a matter of hours and fit inside a couple of shipping containers, so I could appear and disappear virtually without warning. No one knew when I would be looming above them at the wheel of a colossal airship, laughing maniacally through a loudspeaker. No one would forget the sight of it. It obliterated the sun and cast its shadow a country mile, over banks and traffic lights and schools, libraries and police stations.

In the bathroom, the handle on the toilet comes off in my hand. Part of me never adjusted to the super-strength. A profound biochemical change inside me, an inner fire. And a cottony weightlessness in my arms and legs that told me I would never feel quite so acutely again.

This far into my career, that first morning is a moment I can scarcely recapture in memory. Dust sifted down over me, after the moment of heat and pressure was over. I was on my back. I could see the stars. The laboratory was in ruins, and the emergency teams had come and gone without finding me. No question, my graduate study was basically over. It was the last the world knew of me, a fifth-year grad student with a degree nowhere in sight. A clumsy lab assistant come to a tragic end, the beginning of Doctor Impossible's long, impossible doctorate.

Disappointingly enough, I couldn't fly. I couldn't go invisible, or move objects with my mind, or shoot lasers from my eyes. I couldn't communicate with my mind or read other people's thoughts, not that on the whole I wished to. The night wore on, and I exhausted every variant on heat and cold, growing and shrinking. After a lengthy series of hops, half gestures, and brow-furrowings, I satisfied myself I didn't have any of the more recherché talents.

I was fast, though, my reflexes seemed to run on oiled casters, and the world would almost freeze in place when I focused my will. I haven't dodged any bullets yet, but I've come close.

As my eyes adjusted, extra wavelengths seemed to flower slowly into being. The night colored with deep infrared and earthy radio tones, and the unearthly sheen of the frequencies above the violet. The world took on new patterings around me. I wasn't quite human anymore. I was strong, really strong. I could do whatever I wanted. Be a sports star, some lame jock. I imagined what would happen if anyone messed with me now. I imagined it carefully, in slow motion. I wasn't a civilian anymore, I had superpowers. I was a super . . . what? But really, I knew. When you get your powers, you learn a lot about yourself. My professors called me mad. It was time for me to stop punishing myself, and start punishing everybody else.

It all unfolded in my mind, plans and inventions that formed faster than I could name them, chemical, biological, metallurgical, cybernetic, architectural. This is what they had held me back from. This is what had lain dormant, what I had suppressed, that had been like a bomb going off underground, over and over. That last failed experiment had done something. I was strong enough, yes, but this is what my empire would be founded on, on raw computation and rage. A shadowy design was forming. I stole clothes from a laundry room in a nearby dorm. Wearing jeans and a too-large sweatshirt, I walked until the sun came up.

The midwestern dawn was gray and the bus station was gray, as well. I had slept a little next to a dumpster behind a supermarket. I had cracked open pay phones with my hands until I had enough for the bus ticket and a Milky Way bar. I was exhausted and broke, young and evil and superintelligent, somewhere in America.

When it came, the bus was nearly empty. I took a seat two-thirds of the way back, on the left, and sat looking out the window. The roads and houses and gas stations rolled by, and I knew that not one of them was a place I could live or work. My ticket was for Reno, Nevada, bought at random.

I knew I needed to go someplace emptier, preferably with a desert where I could start building underground. Working with my hands if necessary, I'd truck in concrete and generators and electronics. It would be bare-bones at first—the soaring archways and gleaming metal would come later. For now, I'd lay out circuitry on wood and metal frames and make the supercomputer I had already designed in my head. I'd build up power gradually, computing power, electrical power, super-power. Soon I'd be working with teraflops and running off fusion power. For a long time, I watched the world change from green fields to rocky scrub, and the clouds darken and burst up in the mountains. Raining somewhere else maybe, but not here.

I remember those nights, planning technologies that didn't exist yet, outsider science, futurist dreaming, half-magical. The things I could do outside the university setting, now that I didn't have to wait for the pompous fools at the college! I was building another science, my science, wild science, robots and lasers and disembodied brains. A science that buzzed and glowed; it wanted to do things. It could get up and walk, fly, fight, sprout garish glowing creations in the remotest parts of the world, domes and towers and architectural fever dreams. And it was angry. It was mad science.

You don't become a world-class villain overnight. I wandered for a long time before I became Doctor Impossible. Leaving the country for the first time was a revelation. I was opening myself up to new influences, changing myself into a new person, someone exotic and dangerous. All the best villains have a whiff of the foreign about them, something of the Orient or the depths of Transylvania. There has to be mystery.

In those years, I found my way into many strange places. I walked for three days through the northern Sahara, hauling water and dozing in the shade during the day, until I reached Khartoum. The solitude was immense; heat sheeted off my altered skin. At night, I'd dream of pharaohs whispering, of huge spirits prowling the dunes by night.

I fought for prize money in unlicensed hero fights in Bangkok, brawling in basement rooms lined with mattresses, sweating under the lights. It was the bottom end of the hero trade—local talents and wanted fugitives, oddballs with nothing going for them, just a taste of power to set them apart. An American in homebrew armor fought three Australian pigmy shamans; a karate specialist fought a French sorcerer, a Russian who'd come out of Chernobyl. Small-timers, grotesques and rejects, one-on-one or in groups, late into the nights, while the crowd screamed and jeered so loud you couldn't think; you wouldn't feel it when you'd taken a bad cut or a burn. I fought as Baron Benzene, as Count Smackula, as whatever name they put on the marquee. Smartacus. Doctor Fiasco.

I learned basic lessons, how to throw a super-powered punch without falling off your feet, and how to take one. How to spot the telltales of power: the stutter-step of a bad nerve operation, and the alien hybrids, Altairian eyes and Enderri hands. How to look at the way superheroes walk, or their eyes, or their hands, and see what happened to their bodies, once upon a time. Most of them had paid a price for their power, and for most of them it turned out to be too high. If you knew what to look for, you could see it in the first few steps they took in the arena.

I fought three or four times a week, waking up on off days bruised or singed, steamy rainy mornings in Bangkok in an apartment over the market a half-dozen of us rented together, Pharaoh and Shylock and a rotating cast of down-and-outers. I'd be stretched on a mattress on the floor; somebody with an insect's head passed out on the couch.

It was where I met the Pharaoh, and the first time I met anyone at all like me, ones who had found power but said no to the mask and cape, to the role. Of course, most of them were nothing like me—criminals with no advanced degrees, some of them hadn't even been to high school. But like me, they'd said no, and they hadn't found anything worth saying yes to. It's the closest thing I've felt to belonging.

I remember the night Argonaut showed up incognito and fought all comers to a standstill. The night Colony was killed in the ring, and what came out of him. I remember holding a stranger by the hair, one arm raised to the crowd; the alcoholic celebrations on prize money that sent us reeling through the streets, heartsick, swearing drunken vows to one another, our nameless common ethos of silence, exile, and the long defeat.

And I marveled that no one else ever appreciated how serious it all was, the things that were happening to us, the change that had happened to our bodies, the destinies that were slowly beginning to work themselves out for these wastrel ninjas, Martians, exiled sorcerers who would one day have to find their myriad ways home. One night, after an evening when I'd been badly beaten by a magical stone creature, Pharaoh and I sat by the ocean, the strange waters of the Gulf of Thailand. Ribs cracked, I swore inwardly that I would never quit, not ever.

I worked as a bodyguard for a drug cartel in Hong Kong, standing in a dark suit night after night behind a drunken narcotics magnate, the skinny *guailo* who could stop bullets and outwrestle the strongest man. Until one night a group of our competitors came through the door, too many to stop. I walked into the Hong Kong night, carrying three million dollars in a briefcase, Armani suit soaked in blood. The next morning, I was on a flight back to the United States. I was ready to show the world my real face.

At least there's a telephone here. Thinking of those days puts me in mind of my contacts. There's a loose web of acquaintances out there;

even if they didn't visit me in prison, there's still a network. There are things I need if I'm going to get started. I can make some calls. But who? With all the fuss about CoreFire and the Champions back together, it's a bad time to be a villain.

I start making a list. A lot of people are gone, hiding or in prison. Psychic Prime is out there, useful when he's sober. There's Nick Napalm, too, still out of prison. One of them will tell me where people are meeting up these days, maybe even do a little job for me. Lily, I'm not ready to think about.

Then there's the Pharaoh. He'd be useful if only I could find him. Not the real Pharaoh, the one in the Super Squadron, but the other one, the two-bit villain. He had a magic hammer he liked to wave around, that he said made him invulnerable when he spoke a secret word. He'd made a suit of armor and spray-painted it gold, then drawn on it with a child's idea of hieroglyphics, all eyes and wavy lines. He claimed to be a re-incarnation of Ramses, although he used to get the *a* and *o* backward in his own name. The hammer was a big stone thing, the thirdhand hammer of somebody retired. He called it "the Hammer of Ra." I wanted to take it apart to see how it worked, but he never let me.

We were friends in the half-collegial, half-suspicious way villains can be friends. Once, we had to hide out for two days together in a leaky shed in New Jersey while heroes hovered in the sky above us. We whiled away the time telling hero stories and boasting about our big scores. He knew Lily, too. I tried to share a few jobs with him, but the partnership never gelled.

He never amounted to much as a villain. One afternoon in down-town Chicago, he'd driven Serpentine all the way into the lake, and knocked Blockade unconscious. If he'd cared enough to make anything of it, he could have been big. The real Pharaoh never even bothered to hunt him down over the name thing.

But he's gone, too, got out of the game a while ago. He was never that serious about it to begin with. Crime is a serious business, damn it. I told him that.

The name occurred to me during my first real job in the U.S. It was a long ride up the New Jersey turnpike, four hours in semidarkness, squatting on the wheel well. I drowsed a bit—it was strange to be driven along by a robot I'd built, and the gentle rocking motion brought back sensations of childhood road trips. I was dreaming of the zeta effect, flickering red field, its tantalizing mysteries. I woke, to stare into the molded plastic faces of the robots swaying beside me in the long, bare compartment, a row of drowsy crash-test dummies.

I felt us come out of the Holland Tunnel and into the stop-and-go traffic of downtown. The robot in the driver's seat was a good one, convincing enough to pass as human on casual inspection. It only had to drive and pay tolls and smile blandly at other drivers. It would never get out of the van at all, whereas the four in back would go with me into the bank.

The bank was in midtown, a small one, but adequate to my needs. I had gone as far as I could go on ingenuity and petty theft. I needed capital. And I needed contact with the world; I needed them to know about me. I felt the robot smoothly taking its lefts and rights on the way to the target, even honking the horn at a truck blocking the road up ahead.

I powered up the robots. Smart and tough, but they weren't about to fall in love or apply for citizenship. They checked their stun guns; I checked my equipment. I crawled back to the rear door and seated myself. The van cut over to the curb and double-parked squarely in front of the glass double doors.

I kicked open the van's rear door and stepped into the street. A light snow was falling, frosting the edges of things and darkening the asphalt. I had spent months designing and assembling the robots, sewing the costume, fabricating the equipment hanging from my belt. And now I was standing in the street in midtown Manhattan, squinting in the sudden light, midmorning traffic swerving around me, the crowd just beginning to react. It was 10:30 a.m. on a Tuesday, late January, and in the skyscrapers overhead office workers were just halfway through the morning's work, rustling papers and chatting at their desks. I was twenty-four years old.

A burly man wearing a uniform was staring angrily at me through the window and pointing as if to say, Go away! There was a second of vertigo, a sick moment of nightmarish embarrassment. What was I doing? I ought to be up there with them; I ought to be at work. I was wearing a costume; I was a publicity stunt, an overgrown out-of-season trick-or-treater, or a schizophrenic. This was the moment of truth, worse than any crime fighter or secret weapon. My insides clenched.

I forced my legs to take me forward toward the bank's heavy plate-glass facade. Behind me, the robots were raising their concussion pistols, and my earplugs cut in automatically. The man standing just inside put up his hand, gesturing at me to stop, go away. That was the moment. I shook my head. Stop? Go away? No. Absolutely not. I felt an unfamiliar smile take hold on my face.

He raised his gun, too late. Because I didn't have to stop. I grabbed the door and pulled so hard, it came off one of its hinges and hung there. I wasn't going to stop and I wasn't going to pay any damages and I wasn't going to say sorry, because I wouldn't have to do what anyone else said, ever again. The sonic went off behind me as I went through the door, and after that there was a whole lot more I wasn't going to be paying for.

"Kneel!"

I pointed to the floor, and in a second the crowd was on its knees. Most of the bank crowd would be deaf for the next thirty seconds or so anyway, but I needed to look like I was giving orders. I looked up, to see I was holding the unconscious bank guard aloft by his shirt. I tossed him into a potted palm. It was only hours later that I got home and realized he'd shot me square in the chest. There was a bang as they breached the vault. Two robots were brandishing their pistols at the crowd while the rest shoveled bricks of currency into sacks. I had nothing to do but stride around the lobby looking menacing and in control, but it felt like an eternity.

I went on shouting. I screamed, although I don't know what I said to them. I declared myself Emperor of Manhattan, America, the world. I was shaking. Outside, traffic had stopped. People across the street peered in at me.

I could hear sirens now, but the final phase was already in progress. I'd dug the tunnel weeks before. I motioned two robots to the front of the bank to engage the police. The others were already loading the money into the shaft. After my escape, they'd collapse the tunnel behind me.

Only one thing left to do. I turned to face one of the security cameras. It was time to let them know who I was, what I'd known for years. I'd planned something—I forget what—but something else rose to my lips. The humiliations build up, and you know you'll never get back at them, even though somewhere inside you're better than they are. The real you is somewhere else, someone invisible, unknowable. Someone impossible.

"I'm Doctor Impossible." I shouted it to them. "Doctor Impossible!" They would know me now; they had to. I turned and climbed down into the shaft.

The tunnel had an exit point, miles south, and a rented truck was waiting for me. I changed into civilian clothes. On the return trip, I had one last moment of weakness. There was no turning back now. I wasn't just a missing person anymore, or an eccentric inventor. I was a super-villain. For heaven's sake, I'd just robbed a bank in broad daylight. I pulled over to the side of the road. I felt like I was going to be sick. What had I done? There was no way to hide this. Why had I thought this was going to work? These people could fly. They could see through objects. They would run me down like an animal.

I thought about turning myself in, giving it all up. If I gave everything back, all the money and the gold, they couldn't do that much to me. A few years and I'd be out. I could go back to the labs. The robotics work I'd done in the past eight months would win me a research grant and help mend fences at the university. I'd be able to go on working, even do some research if I cut the right deal. Having powers didn't mean I had to do this stupid stuff. This ridiculous little incident could all be forgotten, the stupid costume, the name. Just drop it all here.

I put my hands on my helmet, ready to lift it off. And . . . what? Walk into the police station? Call the FBI? Go to prison? Even if I turned myself in, it wouldn't change anything.

It wouldn't make me one of them. I knew that when I got my powers, but really I knew it before then. I learned it as a child on my first day of school, on the warm rainy streets of Bangkok, and in college. If you're different you always know it, and you can't fix it even if you want to. What do you do when you find out your heart is the wrong kind? You take what you're given, and be the hero you can be. Hero to your own cold, inverted heart.

It's time to start again. Maybe this time it will be different. I've learned from my mistakes. With CoreFire gone, I may never get a better chance.

I think I'm going to be staying on here in my suite at the Starlight Motel. The ruins of my old base are going to be too hot for a while. I've checked all the hero traffic I can monitor, and I think I got away clean. There's a RadioShack one street over, plenty of copper wire, and all the take-out food I can eat. I've got plans now, ideas I worked out in prison. In a few weeks, free, someone like me can accomplish a lot.

I do a little sketching, but the kernel of the new plan is a simple one. To take over the world, I need four items—a mirror, a book, a doll, and a jewel. It's a trick, a hack I worked out back in the cell. Four objects no one particularly cares about, sifted out of all the clutter of the world, but combine them in the right way and they mean everything. I still don't know where they are, and I need to get them without being caught. And there are still so many variables: Where is CoreFire? What if he returns?

I'm careful. I wear sunglasses even at night, and speak in an affected voice. But the Arabic man in the pink button-down shirt at the convenience store has seen me. The attendant at the laundromat knows me by a different name. The two who work the front desk at the motel know me, the old man who owns it and the teenage girl, with her acne and her dull stare. And the take-out delivery boy from the Chinese restaurant. I don't know what they think I am. Anyone could guess my secret.

All night long the traffic moves outside my window. I've pushed all the furniture to the corners of the room, and the new, improved Power Staff is spread out on a sheet laid over the carpet, a skeletal frame clogged with wiring. It's just a metal frame now, with circuits and wires, but I'm expecting packages. Nick Napalm will fetch me what I need, things you can't buy at RadioShack. I redesigned it in prison, working in my head in the darkness while the guards paced back and forth outside.

I recall the last time but one, the battle-blimp listing, belching black smoke into the clear air as I strapped myself into a suborbital flight suit. My hands shook filling the tank, the stink of rocket fuel still in my nostrils. It was the last of five escape plans, the bottom end of a flowchart I'd put together back at the base.

And there was CoreFire, teamed up with the massive Battalion, two and a half tons of metal impossibly adrift on the summer breeze, uncanny. I'd thrown everything I had at them, and CoreFire looked smooth and unscarred, crisp as if he'd just stepped off a yacht. Underneath us, Queens spread out a little too close—I was losing altitude. My eye was already picking out places where it might be safe to fall. Soon I'd be going back to prison for term number ten.

"Give up yet?" he asked.

"Never!" And it is never. I've dreamed for so long of the day one of my plans will actually be fulfilled, the last step in place, executed to the last detail, the last ball rolling down its ramp into the last cup to pull the last lever in the grandest Rube Goldberg machine of all. When the doomsday device is unveiled, the launching laser built, the weather-controlling satellite finally aloft, the skies dancing to my whim. Sunny days when I wish them, dark, crackling storms, or late-afternoon drizzle. All these years underground, I dreamed of a land where I could live in the weather I wished.

"Surrender or be destroyed!"

On the bridge of my battle-blimp the wind rises, carrying a new scent. Autumn.

CHAPTER SIX

THE GAME IS AFOOT

Windows are shattered for blocks in every direction. The television news this morning shows Nick Napalm battling, ringed with flame. They evacuated the area early this morning, and an eerie calm has settled on the neighborhood. Damsel and I pass the first perimeter—she flashes some identification at the policemen on the barricades, who stare at our costumes as if we were brightly colored poisonous fish.

Damsel walks ahead, ignoring me. They direct us to a warehouse three blocks in, where they're holding him. Walking through the streets in costume, I feel like a visitor from another planet. Footfalls ring in the silence. Empty facades gape, blotched with scorch marks; the air seems to hum with the impact of punches on hardened bodies. There are fire trucks parked outside the warehouse.

I start to show my temp ID again at the door, but Damsel brushes past them, and I follow. "The new girl's with me," she mutters. Nice of her to mention it.

Inside, the scene has a familiar look, the hasty ad hoc containment protocols that spring up around a hostile metahuman capture and have nothing to do with normal arrest procedure. Nick Napalm is lying facedown in a cleared space in the center of the concrete floor, hands cuffed behind him. A policeman is holding a hose on him, just standing there soaking him continually to keep his flame out.

They've marked out a circle sixteen feet around him in red paint, and eight or ten policemen in body armor stand watching him from behind a ring of stacked-up tires. They look exhausted and pissed off. They've had a long and dangerous morning, all because two superpowers decided to have a night on the town. A couple of marksmen lounge up on a catwalk, leaning on the rail.

He lies right in the puddle, which is draining into a grating in the floor. Nick Napalm is a smallish man with dark hair and olive skin, wearing a full-length orange-and-black robe. It must have created an impressive flowing effect when it was dry, but now it just looks like wet laundry. He isn't moving. I can see the side of his face is heavily bruised.

Nick Napalm is just what he sounds like, a human flamethrower. He gets these fits where he goes out and burns things. His eyes and his voice have a blank schizophrenic gloss, but when he's not on one of his pyromaniac tears, he's fairly sensible, and he needs to make a living, like anyone else. The native canniness of the insane, I guess. He's escaped plenty of fireproof holding cells over the years.

A few of the police look up at us when we arrive. They don't seem particularly friendly, but there is a note of relief when they see the costumes. We're used to the weirdness, they think. We'll take this mess off their hands. A junior officer conducts us past the wall of tires.

"Nick Napalm. He had an all-night fight with Bearskin last night. A diamond got stolen, two guys fighting over the take. We brought him down around six this morning. Word came in to call you."

Damsel seems used to these kinds of interactions, remaining gracious but distant. "Thanks. What happened to the gem? Any word?"

"No sign of it now. Where were you guys last night?"

"We had other business." She was having another shouting match with Blackwolf, actually. I could hear it all the way down the hall.

We step inside the magic circle and walk out to where he lies. No one follows. I kneel down to talk.

They keep the hose on him, and I'm getting a little wet just crouching there. He still hasn't moved. This is what people like this come to, all that talent and ambition.

"Nick," I whisper.

"Tin Man." His voice is a little distorted by the bruising and the way he's lying with his cheek on the cement. He's been awake the whole time. "Get me out. They're gonna kill me. Heard 'em talking about it."

It isn't that implausible. They can always say he tried to escape. No one is going to miss this guy.

"We need to ask you about CoreFire."

"Get me out of here first. Special. Special detention. I know you can do it."

"Why should I bother?"

"I saw him. Doctor Impossible. Four days ago. Tell you where."

"Fuck." I give Damsel a look. What do we do here?

"Do it. We'll walk him out." She's impatient.

"The cops are going to be pissed off is all."

We do it. The police sergeant starts to say something, but Damsel gives him a look. He's playing out of his league, and he knows it. But I can't help feeling the gaze of those marksmen on the back of my head. I'm not like Damsel—a bullet in the right place will finish me off, just as it would anybody. Damsel doesn't seem to care. She's been a superhero all her life, and it's obvious she couldn't care less what the civilian police think.

I pull Nick to his feet, making a point of being rough about it, and walk him through the perimeter, nervously aware of the complete absence of due process. He's not helping this look any more legitimate, leaning on me like a drunk and whispering in my ear.

"I know what's inside of you, Tin Man. I can see it burning. It burned in him, too."

CoreFire.

"We can't take him in the car," Damsel says, sounding bored. "Can you call Blackwolf on that thing?"

"Sure."

"Tell him to come get us in that ship of his, and that we've got a passenger. Sometimes his toys come in handy."

I spend some time in the Crisis Room learning the computer system while Lily looks on. The display looms above me, casting white light onto our faces as I slide windows and data around, looking for a pattern. Blackwolf stands behind me, pointing out features. It's a customized mainframe Blackwolf's company built to his own design.

"They let on like they're loners, but these people know each other." Blackwolf is lecturing me, Supervillains 101. He only does his Clint Eastwood routine in public; in private he's got a higher voice, almost geekily nasal.

I wonder how he knows this stuff. Blackwolf was left behind on a camping trip with his brother and sister in New Mexico when he was eight. He wandered off and he was in the wilderness for five days, and they found him just sitting on a rock somewhere. He never went to school—he was diagnosed autistic. I suppose wearing a picture of an animal on his chest helps him with that.

"A villain like Doctor Impossible makes ripples. They build things; they use custom equipment. Even someone like Doctor Impossible can't do everything by himself. You don't build a hundred-foot-tall robot out of nothing. They need people to fly things into orbit, or make a molecule-perfect cut, or translate ancient runes. There's rumors and gossip, trace evidence. There's a shadow economy out there, where these things get done."

This is something I actually know how to do. It's a lot like the world of drug lords and arms dealers I dealt with as an enhanced operative, just much stranger. I watch Doctor Impossible's influence extend through the money markets, smugglers, small-time powers-for-hire like Nick. Somebody called him about stealing that diamond, and somebody showed up afterward to take it off him.

"I am here."

In a warehouse in Chicago, Mister Mystic materializes out of the darkness, trailing that cape he wears. I stare behind him, straining to see where he could possibly have come from, but even in ultraviolet, the wall behind him is in total shadow.

We've been loitering here for at least an hour. It was a break-in at a warehouse. Feral was listening in over the police band, and heard it was laboratory supplies. Damsel is squinting with curious intensity at something too faint for me to see. Is there anything she can't do?

She answers Mystic without turning around. "Great. Microvision isn't turning up anything. Check the place for resonances."

"Emanations."

"Whatever."

Mystic closes his eyes and stretches out his arms, fingers twitching. I don't see anything else happening, except his amulet glows a little. He looks like a child playing Marco Polo. I look over at Damsel, who is waiting for his response, perfectly unsmiling. "Yes, there was a presence here. A very . . . difficult mind."

Feral growls. "It was him. I know it. This is all geek stuff." He doesn't meet up with the superpowers much. He doesn't fly. He hides on rooftops, and traces drug shipments. For all that he's been to the Moon, he still kicks knives out of people's hands night after night. He just really hates crime.

I can access the manifest from here. Nothing's missing except a set of precision-ground optical diamonds. We interviewed some of the security personnel, but they don't remember a thing, not even showing up to work. Nick Napalm did this, but he wasn't alone.

Lily leans against one wall. "God, is this really what you people do? Just stand around in a group? We thought you had computers or something."

"Actually, we do." Blackwolf looks up from whatever he is crouching over. "Fatale, can you run this tread print through your database? I don't think it's standard." Supervillains tend to build from scratch, since their technology is way beyond what's commonly available. So everything's a little off—screw sizes, voltages—like when you go to Europe. I take a scan and run it through my onboard records, but there's nothing.

Feral isn't taking this well. "So it's another wasted night? Doctor Impossible is out there working, people, and the five most powerful people on the planet are standing around in a warehouse." I know how he feels. We all want to hit something.

"Look, we're all frustrated. . . ."

"Lily." Feral's ears lie flat now. "The man was your lover, was he not?"

"Sort of," Lily says. She looks bored with this already.

"There must be things you're not telling us."

"Look, I've got amnesty, all right? Ask Damsel if you're not satisfied."

"Really? 'Cause I don't remember signing anything."

They stand like that for a moment, frozen except for Feral's tail lashing back and forth. Blackwolf makes the tiniest of motions to step forward, and Damsel, again almost without moving, gestures him to stop. Then Feral leaps, claws outstretched, and at almost the same moment Lily takes a quiet step to her right and deals him a precise blow on the side of the head. He staggers, reaches for his stance again, then she clips him across the chin. He's out.

"Poor kitty," she murmurs.

No one else says anything for a moment. Lily looks straight at Damsel for a moment, maybe daring her to kick her out on the spot.

Damsel shrugs. "Point made, I think." Blackwolf glances at her and cocks an eyebrow. Is she hiding a smile?

On the jumpjet ride home I get the seat next to her.

"I can't believe you did that."

She lets a breath out, then laughs a little.

"It's the tail thing. He does it three times, and then he jumps. Doctor Impossible told me."

I play the scene back later on video and she's right. I'll remember.

Five superheroes walk into a bar in Green Bay, Wisconsin. It's me and Damsel again, with Rainbow Triumph, Feral, and Lily. The bar is Mephisto, a nightclub with a reputation for attracting black-market moguls and the hipper, sketchier side of the powered community. I was here once before and was not, I am mortified to say, let in.

We land in a vacant lot a few blocks away. I can already sense the others getting into character. Damsel briefs us on the way over, mostly for my benefit.

"In and out. Don't start anything we can't finish."

"These guys are mostly wannabes," Blackwolf adds, checking the fit of his gloves.

"Ohmigod, I totally used to go here," Lily whispers in my ear, starting to giggle.

Two massive bouncers are watching the door, but at a glare from Damsel they step aside. Inside, the room goes quiet right away. In the past few days, it's been easy to forget that Damsel's a worldwide celebrity, especially among this kind of crowd. It's dark inside, but of course that's no obstacle to me. I'm already getting traces of radiation, a couple of different particle emissions, maybe even a whiff of sulfur.

Damsel steps into a cleared space under one of the overhead lights. I have to admit she exudes a sense of confidence and authority better than any force field. Years of being untouchable, godlike, and the daughter of one of the most powerful men on Earth. She wears that costume like a uniform, not a disguise. You can just tell her mom's a princess.

"Take it easy. Nothing to worry about. We're just here for a drink." Her voice carries to the end of the room. She has a celebrity's easy smile, but she gives the room a good hard stare. Everyone knows about CoreFire. There's a second reaction when Lily steps into the light, a faint hiss that comes from nowhere. Someone over by the pool tables whispers, "Judas."

There must be forty or fifty people in here, way too many to keep track of. A big man with tattoos covering one side of his face gets the idea of stepping into my path.

"Hey, girly-bot," he grunts, or something like it. He scans funny, enhanced, of course.

And of course they would key on me as the unknown, the one they can intimidate. It's a familiar moment, familiar to my old self in bone-deep memories of being five and a half feet tall, overweight, a dishwater blonde, the least noticeable person in any room. I slap him, hard, back-handed; the sound is like a handful of heavy ball bearings thrown against a wall. He stumbles back into his chair and I step forward to finish it.

A few people get to their feet, and I'm suddenly conscious of the weak points in my armor plate. I look around for a pillar, anything, to put my back to. A clawed hand falls on my shoulder.

"Easy, Fatale. Any real powers here?" Feral's voice brings me back to reality. We're the superheroes here; they're the criminal element, a cowardly and superstitious lot. And I've got teammates.

I throw my senses open; the room goes white and green in my left eye, with gashes of pink and violet energy spikes. I feel my hard drive spin up as all the faces in the room are fed through a facial recognition program I got off a contact in law enforcement.

Half a dozen names come up in the metahuman database. One is Psychic Prime, one of Doctor Impossible's old colleagues. I spot him in a corner booth and give him a hard look. He's wearing a powder blue jumpsuit, uniform of whatever far-future training academy he claims to have gone through, and with his bald, domed skull, he looks like an out-of-work *Star Trek* extra. He can't be stupid enough to make a move on us. He holds up his hands, one of them with a drink in it, and toasts me in mock surrender.

The rest of us fan out through the crowd, looking for our man. No one's having a conversation anymore. They seem almost cowed by the reputation of a legendary team. Feral wades through the crowd, looking down from an ogre's height, nodding to the occasional contact. Lily is putting a brave face on things, but she hangs back by the exit doors. This has the potential to turn nasty for her.

There's a scuffle at the far side of the room, somebody pleading. It's Rainbow Triumph bullying a disheveled man in a purple velvet jacket; he has the look of a hippie who's fallen into shady company. She gets his lapel in a quick under-and-up move and lifts him one-handed. She's doing it like in the movies, holding him off the ground, arm extended, smiling like an evil schoolgirl. I've picked up and thrown a lot of people, and you don't do it that way, even if you're strong—you use your hips, your shoulders. She hoists him higher, and I can hear the sound of cable twanging inside her. I've seen a lot worse, but somehow watching this makes me ill. She's so thin, I think she's less human than I am.

His name is Terrapin, and he swears he doesn't know anything. I, for one, believe him. He's a low-level exotic arms dealer with minor energy emission powers. The crowd's looking on, growing restless. There's only so much humiliation they're going to take before things get ugly. Most of these people had nothing personal against CoreFire. Who would, really? Only Doctor Impossible seemed to have that persistent grudge.

We head for the exit, the crowd slowly parting for us, and when we get to the doors, Blackwolf stops and turns again.

"Anyone here sees Doctor Impossible, anyone knows where he is, get in touch, if you know what's good for you."

There's an answering murmur now in the crowd. Someone yells out, "You'll never get him."

"Come on. We're done here." Damsel gestures us out.

I go last. I'm almost out when someone tries to break a beer bottle across the back of my skull. A stupid idea anyway—the metal plating is an inch thick. There's a built-in reflex that stops things like that, so my first warning is feeling my body twist into action, my left arm coming up automatically to block the bottle and seize the arm in a submission hold, while my right is already raised, ready to strike and shatter ribs, to punch through armor plate.

But as it turns out, my attacker isn't even strong for a human. Lily's cool fingers close on my wrist just in time to stop me from killing Psychic Prime.

On a cobbled street in Irkutsk, the snow settles on my chassis and melts—it's getting colder. I'm on a rooftop, crouching on tar paper and gravel. Lily kneels next to me, apparently oblivious to the weather.

Psychic Prime talked—it didn't take much. Someone hired him and Nick Napalm to steal the diamond, a two-bit Russian smuggler, a middleman. But who was the middleman working for? Lily and I have been sent here to find out. The others are off on what I assume are more important errands. I'm feeling a little nervous about screwing this up, and I wish Lily talked more. She doesn't seem nervous at all.

"You ever been to Russia before?" Lame, but I'm trying. She's supposed to be a teammate, after all. I'm used to working alone.

"I guess. I was all over, back then. You know."

"I was here a few times. Maybe more. The NSA didn't always tell me where I was."

A pause.

"Did you, um, really grow up in the future?"

"Uh-huh."

"Wow."

"Yeah, it's a long story."

The three targets are in a bar across the street. I'm holding a recoilless rifle jacked into my weapons system; the camera on the gun sight goes right into my video feed. I get a pale green light-enhanced image of cobbled streets, and past the other rooftops the silhouette of a cathedral. Awareness.exe is on, tagging the world's heat sources, metals, and fast movers, chattering away. Cars are fountains of information, driver bios and state-by-state itineraries. Power cables run like ley lines through the park.

In infrared, the three people coming out of the bar read like a bonfire on the cold night. A woman and two men, her breath steaming in the display like she's breathing smoke and fire. I aim the rifle and zoom in, just to see. I can hear them laughing and talking in the quiet night, oddly far off; their magnified image looks close enough to touch. A little box on one side of the screen is spewing numbers and text—distance, wind speed, and the computer's broken-English translation of their drunken conversation.

A shot rings out; it's what I've been waiting for, intrigue at the far fringe of Doctor Impossible's supply chain. Maybe they worked out that Psychic Prime talked to us. One of the men staggers, but the other half of my new brain is already crunching numbers, running its own little Zapruder film and drawing a straight line up to a window in the building opposite.

"Wait here." I hand Lily the rifle.

I sprint down the fire escape and across the street, and a few minutes later I'm standing in front of a metal door. I brace and kick it in, my fighting form motion-captured off old Bruce Lee footage, Hong Kong perfection transposed into steel. I'm throwing a side kick from the summer of 1972, pure digitally recorded magic, every time. The door splinters at the lock and slams open.

The sniper was set up in someone's living room, a high rise on the west side of the street. There was a space cleared between the house plants and a coffee table, with a tripod among the dust bunnies and bits of old Lego. A row of clips was laid out on the hardwood floor. He knelt and smoked their cigarettes while he waited for the shot. I'm through the door and across the room before he can get the barrel around. It's pure science fiction, a blaster rifle, Buck Rogers fins and a curving, ornate shoulder stock in red and gold. Doctor Impossible might as well have written his name on it.

It's a long flight home in the jumpjet. It's a plush high-tech affair, a prototype from one of Blackwolf's aerospace start-ups that never went into full production. Lily settles in companionably next to me, while Feral takes a whole row to snooze, his feet dangling in the aisle. Mister Mystic studies a leather-bound book, seat belt fastidiously in place. Blackwolf and Damsel sit up front as pilot and copilot, neither one speaking.

Damsel knows where we're going now. She was there exactly two years before. Strapped in by the window, I think about how it must have been for them on Titan, the alien army surging around them, tens of thousands of aliens, each one bred to be the perfect warrior. Galatea gave her life for them, glowing like a star. When they got back to Earth, nothing could ever be the same.

CHAPTER SEVEN

ENEMY OF MY ENEMY

I find my uniform in a safe-deposit box, left there under an assumed name. When I finally settled on this identity, I had two dozen suits made, to my own design. This one has been waiting since 1987, and the metallic fabric is cool and clean after its long rest in the dark. Back in my apartment, I spread the pieces out on the bed. Red for the zeta effect, gold for, well, gold. Red tights—trousers won't do, unfortunately. I have thin legs, but the cape compensates. Red gloves, armored and weighted along the fingers, finned along the outer edge like a 1950s rocket ship.

The crested red helmet is made of lightweight alloys and foam rubber, and inlaid with a dozen cybernetic systems, command and control. The tunic has red-and-gold trim and is woven from a material of my own invention, flameproof, waterproof, bulletproof, soundproof, proof against acid and cosmic rays, and gamma and zeta radiation. I settle it onto my head, and feel myself stand a little straighter.

The cape is pure melodrama, a coup de théâtre, useless in a fight but indispensable in making an entrance, worth minutes of tedious oration. No one who sees that broad crimson swath billowing behind me as I step through the breach I've made in their perimeter is going to ask too many silly questions. A simple half mask is enough to keep my identity from public knowledge and fold me into the public persona.

In street clothes I'd just be a criminal. Which I am, of course, but in the costume I'm something more. I wear the flag of a country that never existed and the uniform of its glorious army, spreading forth the dominion of the invincible empire of me. Doctor Impossible.

Once upon a time, in the days of Baron Ether and Doctor Mind, villains conducted their business amid a delicious combination of glamour and danger. A fiendishly clever and unscrupulous fellow could seek out swanky secret clubs in the heart of London, and glittering Chicago speakeasies full of jazz and tuxedoes, where Mephistophelian men and icily beautiful women conducted their scandalous intrigues. That was before everything went computerized, before they froze our assets and tracked our fingerprints in global databases.

But for some kinds of information, there's only one place to go. I put on a pair of ridiculous sunglasses and take a late-afternoon Greyhound bus out into rural Pennsylvania. I'm alone and untouchable. Every hero in the world would love to collar me, and they haven't got a clue. For just an hour or so, it feels good to be a gangster. Back at the motel, my Power Staff is taking shape—Nick Napalm got the job done.

According to my informants I'm looking for a half-built shopping mall, abandoned now, the kind of place where suburban teenagers smoke pot and throw rocks at bottles. This is where we meet one another, and like them, we're always half-listening for police sirens or the sonic boom of a hero's approach. This one has been running about three weeks, so it's due to shut down in a week or two—the heroes will find out from some wannabe on the fringes of the scene. They'll crash in and pick up a few stragglers, but by then there's always a new place to meet up.

Word always spreads, and we meet to trade stories of our latest exploits, triumphs, and narrow escapes. There's always something to pass on—who's in jail and who got out, the inside story on this week's costumed crusader. We get to see new faces, or just masks, after weeks or months in the laboratory or asteroid or submarine. People get drunk, hook up, I suppose. We share the mordant humor of our kind. It's as much camaraderie as we get.

In better days, I would arrive in a radar-invisible helicopter, purring in silent and nuclear-powered, the envy of the underworld. Tonight, I'm on foot. I get off the bus at a Roy Rogers and hike four miles down the highway, my costume in a duffel bag. This could really fix things for me, I realize. There are things I need, which I can't trust Psychic Prime to find. If I can get a line on where Laserator or Dollface is, or even the Pharaoh, that could tip things my way. I've let myself become too much of a loner. I need a cabal, a syndicate, a posse of some kind. The proverbial criminal fraternity.

It's almost dark when I get there. I change outside in the bushes, getting ready for my entrance. The mall's developers went bankrupt a few years ago and work just stopped. It's mostly beams and plastic sheeting, but there are a few sections of functional ceiling. They've set up a makeshift bar, just planks on cinder blocks, and a cloaking device to keep any passing heroes in the dark, and a big light pole in what was going to be the lobby. It has the makeshift look of a movie set, or a campground. There's a gas-powered generator running the lights and a boom box playing Thelonious Monk.

I step through a slit in the plastic sheeting and into the light. It's going strong tonight, thirty or forty of us milling around, the usual assortment of half-brilliant, half-unlucky types sitting in twos and threes. A man made of rock. Something like a demon-woman, horns and a tail. A man clad in metal armor, holding an ax; a pale blue man, translucent. Half a dozen others in bright-colored leotards, some with golden or red auras, or glowing eyes, some displaying symbols of skulls, lightning bolts, animals. Losers and geniuses and Olympic-class athletes, with nothing much in common except the preference above all else to reign in his or her personal hell. And that feeling of menace, that vibe that tells you, somehow, these aren't the heroes.

A few people look up, then pretend not to see me. I hear whispering. My face feels hot. I wish I'd gotten my Power Staff together in time for this. I hear somebody mention the Pharaoh, and a burst of laughter, and it occurs to me that I never particularly fit in at these gatherings. When I was on top of the game, when I was a world power, I didn't bother with this scene. People came to me when summoned, or they read about me in the newspaper.

I've forgotten what it's like out here with the smaller operators, people like the Pharaoh or the Quizzler, cutting deals for a few grains of plutonium or a high-tech crossbow. I'm not a natural mixer. And there's the difference in education. I look around more carefully. Villains fight villains, too.

"Doctor Impossible! Hey, Doc!"

A familiar red costume waves to me. He's sitting at the bar with a few guys I don't know, but I know Bloodstryke from the Thailand days. He's basically okay, for a guy whose armor drinks blood.

"Bloodstryke. Long time."

"Doctor Impossible, everybody."

They nod, three of them in masks—falcon mask, plain domino, and a full-face helmet with glowing eyes. No one seems to feel like giving his name.

"I heard you put Phenom in the hospital." This from the domino mask. He wears a blond goatee and has muscles like a martial artist. Behind the mask, his eyes have a watery quality. Psychic?

"Just part of the job."

"Not like fighting the Super Squadron, was it? Bet you miss that blimp."

"It worked, didn't it?" No one ever lets me forget that thing.

The mask guy speaks up. "You know Damsel just did a press conference? They want you to give yourself up."

"Idiots."

"They want you for CoreFire's disappearance. They got hold of Nick and those guys out in Russia. Word has it you're a marked man." The helmet muffles his voice slightly, like he could use a few more airholes in there.

"Born that way," I reply, rote villain bravado, but they laugh and make a ritual toast. Like the rest of them, I was born in a suburban hospital, a healthy and not particularly fated baby.

"Any of you seen Laserator lately?" I ask casually enough. I wonder if I should tell them I don't know where CoreFire is. Maybe it's better if they think I took him out.

"Harvard, right? Guy had tenure, lucky bastard. One grad seminar in the—" the helmet guy starts to say, but suddenly my four tablemates seem to flinch, cringing away from me, and something jars me half out of my seat, spilling my drink. It feels like a pickup truck backing into my chair.

"Hey." A deep voice, electronically filtered. I can feel cold coming off the metal behind me. Suddenly I'm alone at this end of the bar.

"Who dares?" I demand, rising from my seat. You have to let people know who they're dealing with.

Kosmic Klaw dares. He was a Ukrainian mercenary until he found the Klaw armor in a wrecked spacecraft. It's about eleven feet tall, black iron, but one arm is hugely swollen, a great scythelike claw like a fiddler crab's.

"Damsel just trash the Kosmicar. She say she look for CoreFire. Say she look for you." He stands over me, half-crouched, the claw resting on the tile in front of him.

"I'm sorry, Klaw." I spread my arms. "That's just terrible."

I peer upward, but there isn't much of a face to look at, just the three tiny LEDs mounted on the front of his helmet. It's hard to tell what he's thinking. They say he sleeps in the armor.

"Bounty pretty good, I hear. Maybe I turn you in myself."

"Are you threatening me, Klaw?" I summon all the villainous hauteur I have available, staring up at where I hope his camera is. I can feel heads turning, eager for some mayhem. This is getting out of hand.

"Oh, I not afraid of you, Doctor Impossible. You want go to jail again? Or maybe I just crush you here, what you think of that?"

In an instant, he's got me in that stupid claw of his. The iron is cold, pinning my arms. The crowd forms a circle around us.

"You dare touch me? A man of science?" I wish I were enough of one to know what to do now, to figure the angles with my arms pinned to my sides. Close-up, the iron is pitted and scarred, and I wonder how old it is. I push a little, but it's no contest, and now everyone can see me wriggling, helpless. My hand is inches away from my utility belt, but my fingers can barely brush it. One EMP charge would settle this.

Bloodstryke tries to step in. "Come on, Klaw . . ."

Klaw hoists me higher. "You smart. You think you smarter than . . . Klaw?"

Laughter. Someone shouts, "Do him! Do it for Psychic Prime!"

"Shut up!" I turn and scream at them. "I'll crush you, too! All of you!" God damn it.

My feet are dangling six feet off the ground, and my cape is getting engine oil on it. Finally, he makes a decision and tosses me to the far end of the bar, where I sprawl in a pile of plastic garbage bags. Everyone's laughing now, and I hear a little applause.

"Doctor Impossible, everybody! He here all week!"

I manage a petulant little flourish with the cape and walk off, legs shaking a little.

It's a long walk back to the Greyhound stop, but no one thinks to offer me a ride. I change out of my costume in the bushes outside. Out here under the stars, it's very quiet. Overhead, the new moon is just a thin sliver; I can see the whole solar system turning like a merry-go-round, or a ticking clock. Time's running out.

Baron Ether is old. He lost an eye fighting Paragon, and replaced it with a mechanical device of his own construction. Whatever gave him his original superpowers has mostly faded, except in the elongated shape of his skull and a coal-like glow behind his remaining eye. He's an old man—no one really knows how old—and he's been a villain a long, long time. He started out robbing railroads. He fought Victorian adventurers and American whiz kids, wore a mustache and carried a trick cane whose jeweled head bulged with concealed gadgetry.

In the late 1940s, he came to America and founded the first League of Evil. He fought the Super Squadron long before I did, even cruised the timestream and fought the SS three thousand centuries from now. One time, he threw in with his own alternate-dimensional self to steal a fortune in gold, only to cheat his double out of the proceeds. Classic.

In the fifties, he blazed a trail of infamy. He did it all, robbed the Freedom Force of their memory, swapped bodies with them, cloned himself. Lost one set of powers and gained another, was set adrift in time and spent six years in the Cretaceous before building his own time machine. He came back from that one twenty years younger, a side effect of the chronon particles.

In the sixties, he reinvented himself again as a Mephistophelian master of illusion, and stayed out of prison for a while. As recently as 1978, they thought they'd seen the last of him, when a stolen space shuttle disappeared into the void, outbound from the plane of the ecliptic at a perilous angle. But a year later he returned, only to be defeated again in the waning days of the Carter presidency. But he never lost his panache— by the end, he was using hardware with gears and brass fittings against mutants with fusion-powered hardware.

I should have gone to him first. We've only met a few times, but I guess I consider him a kind of mentor or a kindred spirit. To be honest, I patterned my costume on his. He's a gentleman, a genius, not like those small-timers out at the mall. I guess I made a mistake, thinking they were worth my time. The Baron is the real thing. If anyone can help me, it's him.

He lives by himself in a Gothic house in New Haven. When they caught him for the last time, they let him stay at home, in deference to his seniority. He just can't leave, ever. His old foe the Mechanist is spending his retirement years seeing that he doesn't.

So it isn't easy to get in to see him. The house is screened by a line of oak trees and sits on a low rise, overhung by oaks and elms, a shadowy blot on the neighborhood even on a sunny day. No one mows the lawn. Dull silver spheres circulate endlessly through the grounds, a few feet in the air, watching. I come in high, buoyed by a little gravity generator, hovering level with the treetops and jamming every frequency I can think of. The house itself is a gabled Victorian monstrosity. I alight on the roof, crimson boots scuffing for a second on the sharp peak before I catch myself and swing down into an open window.

I'd heard he'd fallen on hard times, but seeing him is still a shock. He hasn't been out much lately, and rumor has it one of his last experiments went badly—a mutation ray. This is the first time I've seen the results. His right arm ends in an insectile claw, and the skin on the right half of his body looks puckered and angry. At the interface, you can see where his body's metabolism is fighting the effects of a halfway transformation.

I step down from the window and try to assume a dignified attitude. We haven't met lately, and it occurs to me to wonder what he might think of me, arguably his successor in the realm of villainy. It's odd to think that for once I may not be the evilest man in the room.

"Doctor Impossible. I heard you were out of jail." His voice is a gasping wheeze emanating from the depths of the wheelchair.

"Baron Ether."

He fingers his cane with his good hand, thinking. You never know what you're going to get when you meet a fellow villain. People have different styles. I try to keep things collegial.

"I . . . I've always admired your work."

"I appreciate that, Doctor Impossible. It's nice to think one's work is admired."

We're in a study of sorts, all books and globes of different sizes, some of great antiquity, painted with alchemical codes. There are framed newspaper clippings from the glory days, mostly London tabloids: BIG BEN VANISHES; ELGIN MARBLES MISSING; PRINCE ETHER?; HYPNOTIZED QUEEN WEDS SCOUNDREL. In a paparazzi shot, a young Ether (née Kleinfeld), diabolically handsome in evening dress, winks at the camera as he's led away in handcuffs. His clothes are exquisite. Cars in the background date the photo to the 1930s. One wall is given over to a detailed android schematic.

He stands, painfully, and pretends to examine one of the globes. What he could be thinking about, I have no idea—this is a man who claims to have arranged the Korean War. A screen door bangs. Out in the real world, people are coming in for Wonder bread and Diet Pepsi.

Finally, he sits back down and wheels himself around to face me.

"What do you want?" he asks.

Steepling my hands, I reply, "Baron, I was hoping to confer with you on a technical matter."

"You understand the conditions of my incarceration, I hope."

"As well as you do."

"Very well, then."

"I need a power source. Very large output, very compact. I need it in three weeks."

He sighs, and takes a moment before responding. "I'm a bit surprised you would come to me for help, Doctor. I understood you to be a fairly sharp individual."

"You know I do robots. Robots take time. They're looking for me."

He goes on as if I hadn't spoken. "I heard about CoreFire. You chose an infelicitous moment for your escape."

"It's not as easy as it used to be."

"Did you do it?"

"What?"

"Did you do it?"

"I didn't do it," I reply.

"Do you know who did?"

"No. You?"

"No." Glowing red eye.

"Portable?" he asks.

"Well, not necessarily. But time is a factor."

He stands slowly, walks to the bookshelf, and faces it for a long while, but he doesn't take down any books. I glance outside; the countermeasures I set up aren't going to fool the Mechanist forever.

"I'm also looking for a man called Laserator. Do you know him?"

"Laserator. Wore a hat with a kind of . . ." He gestures vaguely.

"Mirror, yes. That's him."

"Retired. Bright chap, turned out to be a Harvard professor. They're holding him up at McLean."

He doesn't turn around, but adds, "Have you heard from your friend the Pharaoh recently?"

"Not for years now. He's out of it now. Why?"

"Just thinking."

Another pause, then a slow shake of his head.

"I can't help you. I'm too old, son. These things"—vague motion toward the window—"they watch me like hawks. I had my best chance, and it blew up in my face." In the dimness, I can't see his expression. "What are you going to do next? Another Power Staff? Going to make yourself invincible?"

"I'm going to move the m—" I start to lay it out for him, but he gestures sharply with the nonclaw hand.

"Don't tell me! Don't explain your schemes. You'll depress me. You worked on that—what was it?—zeta energy? Whatever happened to that? Didn't pan out?"

"Not yet."

"Forget it, son. It never does. They always win, you know."

He coughs and signals for his attendants, and I start to leave. Going to the window, clambering out, I must look like an overage leotarded Peter Pan. I don't have a potbelly, but you can see where one might be starting.

I rise out of the shadows. The houses on their tree-lined streets fall away below me. I touch down a quarter of a mile away, in a parking lot behind an Applebee's, put on my sunglasses, and start the drive home. I'm on my own then. I guess I always knew that.

CHAPTER EIGHT

EARTH'S MIGHTIEST HEROES

I come home to Galatea's suite and find a jumpsuit laid out on my bed, its colors the Champions' yellow and orange. That's how they tell me I'm a Champion. A New Champion, to be exact.

I sit down, hard. I'm a little stunned. No, a lot stunned. I close my eyes for a little bit. I guess something at the back of my mind expected my stint as a superhero to end pretty soon, one way or the other. Not this. This wasn't in the script.

I sit for a while first just holding it, letting the high-tech cloth slide and pool in my hands. It's stiff in places, suggesting embedded circuitry; the stitching is perfect.

I start to change into it but then stop halfway. Looking at myself naked in the mirror is like an aching feeling. You can see every place the damage happened. And you can see all the enhancements, hinted at when I'm wearing clothes, the complete design where woman's flesh melds with plastic and metal. Appreciate the technological sea change that turned crippling injury into something else. What's gone came back in silver and chrome, titanium and silicon, a map of catastrophe.

I try it on, gingerly. The costume is a one-off, cut to work around and complement my cybernetic elements, even the ports on my right thigh. In fact, it shows off the best of my bodywork. I've never been especially slender—even before the changes I was probably no Damsel—but when I try it on it fits me sheer and perfect, the way I'd always imagined.

At the window, I take a moment to luxuriate, Manhattan spread out below me. It barely seems real.

This isn't my usual sweatpants and tank top ensemble; it's a real superhero costume, like Damsel wears. It's unnervingly like being naked, but at least no one will mistake me for a robot.

I stop and look at myself in the full-length mirror, a machine-woman hybrid in a leotard. Female cyborgs are supposed to be wasp-waisted pleasure machines, but the fact is, it takes a lot of structural metal to carry a miniature reactor and this much hardware. I'm six four, taller than most men, with long thighs and broad shoulders. Even with my silver hair down, the impression is a bit more fearsome than tradition-ally beautiful.

The uniform isn't especially modest, baring more skin than I'm used to around the shoulders and above the knees. But the patterning com-plements the silver and peach of my skin tone, and the effect is not unpleasant. You could even call it flattering.

I run a hand down my flank, feeling the cool metal and then the real flesh, thinking of how long it's been. Not since the accident, and how long before that? I don't even know. I only know I'm not a virgin. That's all.

I look again, to see Fatale of the Champions. It's hard not to feel a lit-tle proud of myself. I flip the hair back and do a Fatale pose for an imag-inary photo shoot.

I hear scattered applause as I come into the kitchen. Someone whis-tles. There's a cake with my name on it, and Lily's as well. She joins in with a bemused expression. Everyone shakes my hand. Blackwolf explains: Apparently, the founding members met without us and put it to a vote, and that was it. I've got a new security clearance and an offi-cial ID.

"Is the costume all right? Damsel designed it." Blackwolf plays host, passing out plastic cups of champagne.

"It's perfect." It is. And I'm kind of touched, thinking of Damsel spending so much time on her own, thinking of me.

"They say I have a knack for it. Look. You did good back there in the bar. I hope you'll stay on with us."

"I'd . . . yeah, I'd really like that." Suddenly, I would. I empty my glass. Damsel did a lot for me when she asked me to join. Suddenly, I feel bad for disliking her.

"Look, I know we kind of come from, uh, different worlds."

"I was raised normal, if you didn't know. I didn't get my powers until I was sixteen. Until then, I was the amazing little girl who couldn't."

"But . . . genetically, I thought . . ."

"I'll tell you all about it sometime. The costume's okay?"

"I didn't realize it would be so tight."

"You get used to it. I did."

Everybody's changed their look over the years, at least a little. Elphin still wears her suspiciously Pre-Raphaelite "traditional" costume; she's added an armband to signify her Champions affiliation; Blackwolf hasn't changed, but then he relates to his wolf getup in some way that I'm afraid to ask about. Damsel's looks like a cross between her father's and mine.

We're a team, at least in the clothes department. Officially, it's a response to the CoreFire situation and Doctor Impossible's escape. Damsel herself makes the announcement that evening at a press conference, with the six of us standing behind her. Re-forming the team means notifying the city, the State Department, and the UN. The logo that had been dark for almost ten years glows from the Champions Building overlooking the city. We're an item in late-night talk-show monologues. Calls and congratulations come in from other major superteams.

Tomorrow, we're all going to Doctor Impossible's island, ten hours in Blackwolf's *Wolfship*, to fight a bona fide major villain. If they're right, he'll be there waiting for us, with God knows what wacky inventions at the ready. We don't even have a scientist with us. Or CoreFire.

———

When the party breaks up, everyone goes their separate ways, to the rooftops or the gym. My eyes follow Blackwolf out; Lily notices and carefully cocks a silvery eyebrow, which I studiously ignore.

I linger for a while looking out at the city. I could rest up for tomorrow, but there's something else I've been meaning to do.

Upstairs in the computer room, they have a modest library, including films. I meander upstairs, and, a little furtively, slip the DVD of *Titan Six* from its shelf. It's still in the shrink wrap; I'm probably making a newbie mistake by even watching it.

The documentary came out the year after the team broke up, five hours of patchwork archival video, found footage, and FOIA-obtained government video. No one on the team agreed to be interviewed, but it purports to tell the true story of the world's greatest superteam. It's not quite that, but it's something.

I don't know what I'm looking for. To get to know CoreFire, I guess. They've all met him, and I've just seen a few speeches on TV. I wanted to be a detective, but I'm the only one here without a clue about the missing person.

I put the disk in the player, settle on the couch. A solemn voice-over introduces the three original members, young superheroes at the start of their careers.

Behind the opening credits, archival film from the early eighties shows Damsel's first press conference when she was only sixteen and her powers manifested, her father and the rest of the Super Squadron beaming behind her, and then she's zooming around at her eighteenth birthday party in a white jumpsuit. Then an early shot of her and her mother before she left Earth. The film has a yellow-tinted home-movie quality. There's a gawky adolescent Blackwolf sweeping the opposition at the U.S. gymnastics finals, not out yet as anything but a precocious

Rhodes scholar. And CoreFire in his ROTC uniform, clowning with his dorm mates only a few days before his accident.

After the obligatory origin stories, the talking heads kick in with the much-retold story of their first meeting. All three had, coincidentally, been in pursuit of a particularly nasty drug ring, which had gone to ground in the sewage system, and the heroes followed the same police tip underground on the same night. It must have been a strange encounter in the watery undercity, two men and a woman, all in masks, none over the age of twenty-four. Damsel, crown princess of the super-hero world, her force field glowing green with power, casting deep shadows along the waterway. CoreFire had torn aside the gratings of another drain, lazily triggering half a dozen alarms. Blackwolf crouched concealed in a storm drain, night-vision goggles buckled on across the mask.

We'll never know exactly how the conversation went, or how long it took. I don't even know if they exchanged secret identities then, or later.

A man named Frederick Allen was deputy director for Metahuman Affairs at the time, and he gave the team sponsorship. He was hoping for a group of attractive, marketable young heroes who would prove both popular and pliable to U.S. policy recommendations. Everyone agrees the name was his idea.

Hence the Champions; when the team roster finalized, their ages ranged from twenty years (Blackwolf) to over a thousand (if you believe Elphin). They were very young and a little dazzled by the attention. They accepted his offer and became an official government team.

Why? Damsel, perhaps because of her father; Blackwolf because he needed legitimacy, and maybe (although he'd never admitted it) super-powers on his side. CoreFire is harder to pin down. Because he'd wanted to be in the Super Squadron but it fell apart before he was ready? He had everything else, the perfect superhero life—the mighty powers, the fiendish nemesis, everything down to the writer girlfriend who always needed rescuing. He always fulfilled expectations, as if he'd never had to make a decision at all.

It's nearly ten when Lily drifts in to watch for a while. She hovers a few feet behind me, holding a bag of potato chips. I can see her without turning around—I have attachments for that.

"I brought snacks. Can I watch?"

"Have a seat." She didn't get a costume, I notice, so I ask.

"I don't wear clothes. We worked out some decals, like on a car window."

"Well, congratulations anyway."

"Thanks. You, too." We shake hands awkwardly. On-screen, the heroes are thrashing their first bank robbery together; CoreFire turns over their getaway car, bullets pinging off of him.

"I like your moves."

"Beating up Psychic Prime isn't much of a move."

"Meant against Elphin. It's hard to land a shot on her. Trust me, I know."

"It must be weird being on the team. After all that, well, other stuff."

"All that villainy, you mean? It's okay. Everyone wants to be the bad girl. Just for a while."

A superteam needs certain things, the right mix of personalities, an unpredictable battlefield alchemy, a thing no one can predict, or duplicate. Two of them could fly and stop bullets; the third was the best detective and the best athlete in the world. But they needed to shore up the team.

Allen reached out to the superhero world. The most likely candidates lived under secret identities; some were off-world, or in the hospital. It took months to bring them all in.

The recruitment meeting happens in a meeting room in an anony-mous office building in Washington, D.C. The filmmakers pulled origi-nal tapes and footage of the meeting. Allen has an overhead projector and he ticks through a list of points, crime statistics and potential off-planet threats, making his case. In front of him are eleven young super-heroes, top talent, fully costumed and cocky.

The camera does a slow pan, and Lily leans forward to catch all the faces.

"Look at that crowd. They asked Leapfrog, can you believe that? And Anne de Siècle. What a bunch of also-rans! I should have gotten in while I could. God, we both should have."

"Thanks, but I was six. And I didn't have any of this stuff yet."

She takes in the skeletal metal of my calves, upper arms. "That must have been some accident."

"It was."

Galatea is there, still an unknown—they don't even realize she's a robot. Blackwolf, cocky as ever, riding a wave of celebrity following a spectacular hostage rescue. Captain Kelvin is dripping water on the car-pet, his cooling pipes rimed with frost. No Elphin yet, but Mister Mystic, glaring at the psychic Pontifex, later exposed as a fraud. Some of them I don't know at all: a mustachioed man in chain mail with a sword at his side; a young man with a vampiric look who keeps well away from the windows; a woman in goggles, holding what looks like an Edwardian time machine.

Fred Allen cast his net wide, and the results look like a meeting of the board of directors in Candy Land. CoreFire floats at the back, obviously impatient with the selection process.

"We need to take on these unconventional threats in an organized way. In the face of people like Doctor Impossible, we can't just guess and hope. We need our own operatives in the field." Allen takes a deep breath.

"Under the circumstances, for purposes of public relations I think it best that Damsel be chosen to lead and operate as team spokesperson."

You can see from Damsel's face that she doesn't like the way he's handling this.

A ripple runs through the crowd, glances exchanged. The vampire huffs a little.

"Shouldn't we be making decisions like that for ourselves?" The red-and-white woman, who must have been cut pretty early in the process.

Damsel breaks through the noise. You can already hear the voice that would give Damsel's famous testimony before the Senate.

"I'm not going to order people around. I didn't ask for any of this."

"Yes, but surely you see how it's going to be interpreted," says Allen, temporizing, giving the camera a nervous look, as if he already knows he's playing to history.

"With my military background—" Blackwolf begins.

"Which is, you understand, off the record. You're just going to be Blackwolf on this team."

"Wait . . . what else is he?" Damsel shoots him a look. An odd look, and a familiar one; rewinding, I could swear they've known each other from somewhere, longer than the others. There's another story here.

"You don't need to know that."

"What else don't I need to know? It's supposed to be my team, damn it."

"Look. The purpose of this is to have a superteam with institutional legitimacy again. A team people can trust. Not a bunch of costumed weirdos." The camera cuts from Allen to stock footage of Elphin at a press conference. She's examining a stapler, fascinated.

"There are going to be changes. You've all done most of your work solo up to this point. I'm offering you government sponsorship and all the resources that go with it. Security clearances within reason, transport, and state-of-the-art facilities. Legitimacy. A chance to do a little good, and no more working in the shadows."

"There are those of us who are more comfortable there, Mr. Allen." Even on videotape, Mister Mystic's voice carries its rich resonance. You wouldn't know it, but two years earlier he'd been sleeping in a dumpster behind a Walgreens. A beat, then everyone starts talking at once.

"Does this mean we're going to have to disclose our real names? Because I'm not prepared to . . ."

"Names are power, they say . . ." Mister Mystic begins some kind of point about wizarding law.

"I swore an oath to Queen Titania. I cannot break it. And technically I'm not an American citizen; I'm a fairy."

"I don't have a driver's license. . . ."

"I don't have a real name."

Damsel stands. "Thank you, Deputy Director Allen. Now each of you, if you'll follow me into the next chamber when I call your code name? This isn't an audition, more like an informational interview."

Even then she had good command of a room.

They chose carefully. Galatea's abilities were impressive, and she gave the group a high-tech edge they'd lacked. Mister Mystic was the Earth's foremost sorcerer, the master of mysteries that had been lost for generations. And Elphin . . . God knows where they unearthed her, the world's only living fairy warrior.

An early press conference shows how easily they captured the public imagination. Blackwolf is absolutely magnetic, while CoreFire's power is unearthly. Everyone stares as a scantily clad Galatea floats above the crowd, radiating golden energy. Mister Mystic glares with a mesmerist's dark authority.

Magic and technology, superpowers and athleticism and indomitable will, and a myth brought into the present day. Once Elphin joined the group, they had a genuine fairy paladin! The energy of it was palpable. Here were the people who were going to save the world.

They gave press conferences and made public appearances and trained together as much as their disparate abilities would allow, Elphin sharing Celtic fighting secrets with Blackwolf, Blackwolf acquainting her with the bo stick and three-section staff. At the high end of the power scale, Damsel and CoreFire sparred with earth-shattering force above the Washington Mall.

But it was the big three, that unique mix of personalities and power, who held them together. Damsel's discipline and readiness at command, her glamour and authority; CoreFire's blond all-American image, his geniality, confidence, and all-conquering might, balanced by Blackwolf's unpredictable intellect and dark charisma. They were unstoppable.

From their lavishly equipped headquarters in the center, they sallied forth to fight crimes and right the wrongs of the world. Their uniform was recognized everywhere. After a while, it was almost normal to see them flying back in early dawn after a hard night's work, almost normal to see Damsel hauling a freighter off a coral reef, or Elphin calming a tornado above Oklahoma City.

Team portraits from the era show a happy young group of friends, a perfect ease. I wonder what happened to it all.

Maybe it was the Somali crisis—the Champions had always had government sponsorship, but some anonymous genius at the State Department decided it would be diplomatic and cost-effective to make them a shadow arm of the U.S. military.

The team smelled a rat. There was a team meeting, of which no record was kept, but which was perhaps the real founding moment of the Champions. There, they planned Blackwolf's first infiltration of the Pentagon, skulking in full costume through the most secure facility in the world, while Galatea landed on a U.S. satellite and hacked the computer system from orbit. They brought back the full record of Fred Allen's extended plan for the United States' foremost superteam.

C-SPAN broadcast the hush and then the rising stir as Damsel walked fully costumed onto the Senate floor with the self-possession of the truly powerful. She deposited the full documentation of the episode onto the Vice President's lap as the murmur rose to a roar of approval. Her speech and then the celebrated walkout made it official: They were a dedicated team, not a cat's-paw for the executive branch. The United

States quietly withdrew funding, and it was time to find a new patron, and a new paradigm for the superteam.

But that was only half the battle. They had always lived in the shadow of the Super Squadron, and maybe it was inevitable they would clash. There was always the sense that the heroes of this generation were just stand-ins. It's a charge that dogged Damsel in particular. And it seemed like the Super Squadron would always be there above them. Some of them weren't even aging.

That changed the day Paragon went bad. In his time, he had been a match for CoreFire, maybe more than a match, but the man who burned with a magical fire had finally lost control. We never found out where the Nightstar Sapphire came from—it was the kind of thing that might have been looted from any museum in Europe—but something in it had gone wrong.

He'd gone into semi-retirement a decade before, but there were disturbing rumors. His powers had changed, fermented within him, curdling in their long disuse. His force field used to be invisible, clean, but now it was visible as a blue flicker. When he struck, there was a blue flash and an ozone smell. He found a new costume, called himself Cerulean for a while, then Gaslight. But the change was ongoing.

He was older than he looked. The evil in the Nightstar was coming back to haunt him, change him. Whatever it was he found was so long ago, he could only barely remember it, a nineteen-year-old corporal called upon by the military to test something neither of them ever understood.

By the time the Champions arrived, it was too late for anything but a demolition job, but the Super Squadron wouldn't stand for it. CoreFire sided with them and an all-out fight seemed inevitable, Stormcloud against Damsel, CoreFire against Blackwolf, Regina versus Mister Mystic. At the critical moment, Paragon escaped Mystic's temporary bonds and attacked, leaving them no choice. It was a grim task, but it made the

Champions era official—the Super Squadron's aura of invincibility was gone, and the Champions reigned. But back at Champions HQ, I'm sure no one forgot that moment before Paragon burst in on them. I couldn't help but wonder what would have come next.

On the screen, it's the golden age. In a montage of headlines, supervillains fall like wheat before them. People like Slimelord and the Visage were taken off the streets for a long time.

"You worried about tomorrow?" Lily asks, munching popcorn. Mercifully, it goes transparent almost as soon as she bites down on it. Enzymes in her saliva?

"A little. I'm used to drug dealers. All this weird tech—"

"You're kind of a weird tech person yourself. But I don't think we'll see any action."

"Are you sure? Blackwolf thinks this is the one."

"Trust me. This stuff looks different from the other side."

Even Doctor Impossible lost to them, again and again. His face looms on the screen, imperious in his early-eighties high-crested helmet. Now we're being treated to a montage of Impossible's captures. The caped villain is throwing up his hands in surrender in a sequence of control rooms, cockpits, and city streets. I gather my nerve and ask what I actually want to know for a change.

"Lily? Were you really in love with him?"

She sighs. "It wasn't like that. He's smart, you know? And he made me laugh."

We move on to the third DVD in the set. The fourth and fifth episodes focus on the mature years, when major crises tended to center around individual members. An interdimensional incursion from a demon overlord Mister Mystic had humbled one too many times. An ancient fairy curse. A crime lord from Blackwolf's past, maybe connected to his siblings' disappearance. An alien overlord sought out Damsel, taking revenge against her father for some off-world exploit. And, of course, CoreFire's endless go-rounds against Doctor Impossible.

There must have been other moments, ones the cameras didn't capture. I still feel as if I'm missing something, the real story: the first time they confessed their secret identities to one another; the moment they learned Galatea's real nature, or CoreFire's secret vulnerability. I try to watch with a detective's eye, looking for what's been buried.

When did Blackwolf and Damsel fall in love? Damsel and CoreFire were the obvious couple, matched in power and fame. Early on you see them together a lot, always soaring above the others, chatting, sparring. It's hard not to wonder, especially after CoreFire's girlfriend drops out of the picture. And then . . . am I wrong to detect a hint of unease between the two of them? Maybe it's just the Paragon episode, the way the team split.

I stop and contemplate that famous face. Classically handsome, prominent chin, never a hair out of place. He could always say the right things, always knew what to do. For all that muscle, he was smart. He didn't have Blackwolf's sense of humor or his sense of mission, quite, but he never wavered, always did what was right. With all that power he could have been the worst villain of the age, but he always chose truth, and justice.

Damsel crosses through the computer room from the roof deck. "Are you really watching that thing? God, look at my eighties hair." But she doesn't hang around. I wouldn't either, knowing what was coming.

I feel like skipping the wedding spectacle, but Lily makes us watch every treacly second of it. It was practically a national holiday at the time, but watching it now feels painful, the way the two of them glare at each other. CoreFire was the best man, Galatea the maid of honor.

At least we get to fast-forward through a compilation of painful *Saturday Night Live* appearances—there was no way to make Galatea funny.

The best part was John Belushi in a red leotard and plastic cape, expectorating mashed potatoes all over a gamely smiling CoreFire. I think he was supposed to be Doctor Impossible.

It's all good fun. But superteams are about personalities, and I can't help noticing how over time the team starts to withdraw into its own little groups. Blackwolf and Damsel; Elphin and Mister Mystic. CoreFire and Galatea were more and more often alone.

Then the music darkens. They're getting to the Titan incident, and even the voice-over finally shuts up. Lily may be the only person who didn't grow up with this, but even so, she gets a little quiet.

Damsel ran the press conference at the UN. "This is real; it's galactic. We need the full team here." CoreFire was pulled in from Cabo; Mister Mystic from a shadowy intervention in Khartoum.

The galactic wars we used to hear about from the Super Squadron had come to find Earth. The Pangaeans and the Enderri together ruled about 15 percent of the Milky Way, but they were locked together in a slow, incomprehensible alien war. In the past, heroes from Earth had served on one side or the other, but never with Earth in the balance. Apparently, the Enderri had decided to take us out of the equation.

Damsel showed slides in the situation room, shots from the space probe that had caught a dark mass out by Saturn, where no such mass should be. Magnification and spectrum analysis gave out results too bizarre to believe at first. But confirmation came from off-planet sources, courtesy of old Super Squadron contacts.

By the time the Champions got there the Enderri fleet had been gathering for days, shadowed by the massive planet. They arrived under a diplomatic flag, and there was an audience with the Enderri overlord; the Champions were our planetary ambassadors. Damsel's legendary self-possession held up well, perhaps one benefit of her off-planetary lineage. But it was Blackwolf who discovered and invoked an obscure section of their martial code, and demanded a trial by combat; he was probably the first to guess what it would mean. The six active Champions set down on Saturn's largest moon to face the assembled Enderri ground force. They had a force field that ensured atmosphere and warmth as they stood to watch what had to be their final opponents assemble on the frozen plain.

No one can forget that moment as the five Enderri troop carriers disgorged their entire elite occupation force to face them. One of Blackwolf's remote bugs recorded the event, sending a frame back once every second or two. In the first few images, the heroes can only watch as the alien horror encircles them. The camera pans across a single panoramic frame of Damsel, the powerhouse, squaring up against an army of ten thousand alien warfighters. She stands back-to-back with Blackwolf, who is grimly readying his Special Forces moves to haul the first miscreant out of the crowd. CoreFire's smug air of invincibility is for once checked, those movie-star cheekbones tinted red in the light of the fleet's fusion engines. Elphin, the consummate warrior, utterly unfazed, raises her spear against aliens in powered space armor. Mister Mystic is readying himself for the performance of a lifetime. Galatea's face, unreadable, gives no hint of what is coming next.

The battle lasted only forty-one seconds, but the filmmaker plays the frames back one by one. The Enderri warriors were each eight feet high, seemingly part insect, part machine. There was no way to hold a perimeter against numbers like these. The group was swallowed up instantly, six fighting points in a sea of green and black. The footage shows Damsel and CoreFire sending the first wave flying back into the crowd, but it barely makes a dent. Blackwolf is a blur, kicking out at alien joints, cracking hard shells. Elphin and Mister Mystic have stuck together in the crowd. She's aloft and wreaking havoc, spear point flashing; light blossoms from his hands, his mouth moving in some terrible invocation, already knowing he'll never finish it. Behind him, the Enderri are pulling up heavier weapons.

Then Galatea rises into the air, and the last frame is solid white. Whoever built Galatea included an autodestruct mode, and she knew exactly how it worked and how far the blast would extend. She was gone, and the Enderri departed, beaten and cowed, never to return.

After Titan, the team fell apart into twos and threes. Cliques formed. Damsel and CoreFire worked together, usually with Elphin; but there were a lot of solo missions, too. The Champions Call, when sounded, would produce at best four rather testy heroes, who went about their business with a minimum of crosstalk and departed in different directions. Finally Damsel called a meeting, put it to a vote, and it was over.

The last time they were all in a room together was at the press conference where Damsel read a short statement announcing their dissolution as a team. A few weeks later, CoreFire appeared in his new costume, and the era was over. A few second-tier teams stepped up their operations to fill the void. The documentary spends a little time on the postteam careers, but there just isn't much to say. Damsel left Earth for a while, reportedly in search of her mother, but came back months later empty-handed. She joined up for a while with the Reformers, while the rest went on to solo careers. Blackwolf went back to solo crime fighting, and Elphin enjoyed a brief vogue as the figurehead for a New Age movement.

The divorce was made public five months later, reaching the public as a kind of aftershock. A year later, Elphin, CoreFire, and Damsel reformed very briefly to take down Antitron IV, but there was never serious talk of a new team, not until now. Publishers rushed to offer them millions for the tell-all memoir, but none of them ever cashed in. CoreFire did a few fund-raisers with Damsel, but that was pretty much it.

Lily yawns. "Is it almost over? We have to keep looking for Dudley Do-Right tomorrow."

"Isn't that . . . do they really have those cartoons in your future?"

"Learned it in ancient civ class. I was a whiz."

"You know we're going to that island, right? Aren't you nervous about meeting your old boyfriend?"

"He won't be there. He's too smart for that."

"Blackwolf seemed pretty sure."

"You never go right back to your fortress after jail. He's hiding out somewhere else. Trust me."

Lily heads off to bed, and I clean up the popcorn as the denouement rolls. No one on the team would even talk to the filmmakers, so *Titan Six* closes with a faux interview sequence, video clips rigged up to sound like they're answering questions from the omnipresent voice-over.

Even considering the sound bites come from different decades and press conferences, the effect is jumbled. Elphin babbling about Oberon and the rest of her fairy friends, Damsel's boilerplate truth-and-justice rhetoric, Mister Mystic's portentous nonsense. Blackwolf comes off the scariest—they must have caught him right after the divorce. It makes you wonder how these people ever spent ten minutes together, let alone ten years. Or how they can ever hope to beat the smartest man in the world without CoreFire.

Afterward, I go back and watch a few sequences again, and this time the breakup seems to begin earlier. Well before Titan they had stopped grinning at one another the same giddy way; on second hearing, some of that banter looks awfully strained. I keep coming back to that handsome, enigmatic face. Smiling in team photographs, serious and statesmanlike in an address to the UN, grim and determined in battle, clobbering Doctor Impossible or whomever. That unshakable confidence that saved the team time and again. No one ever lost faith in him; the polls prove it. So whatever happened to the perfect superhero?

CHAPTER NINE

MY MASTER PLAN UNFOLDS

Laserator was a great scientist but his work was wasted on conventional thinkers. There has to be a little bit of crime in any theory, or it's not truly good science. You have to break the rules to get anything real done. That's just one of the many things they don't teach you at Harvard.

I haven't been back since graduation. I take a deep breath and do an equipment check. See that the mask is on straight, the cape flows. I'm dressed for the occasion, as befits the most famous graduate of my year. I never went to any of the reunions, not even in disguise. I never had anything to come back for.

The first phase of my world takeover begins tonight, but you have to do these things slowly or you get caught. Security is tight around the Institute for Advanced Thought. I wait in the alley across the street for security guards to change shifts. I wait for the moon to rise; for the tide to go out and expose outflow channels on the Charles. Then I tense, spring, and catch the bottom rung of a fire escape ladder.

Standing upright on the gravel surface of the roof, moonlight illuminates the whole city. Anyone looking up could see me, but although it's only eleven, the world seems asleep. I recognize landmarks from years ago—Memorial Hall, Thayer Hall. The padlock on the skylight is the same as it was twenty-five years ago, and I reach for my utility belt. I manage to pick it silently, even in gloves.

A campus guard passes below me, and he could see me if he looked up. I pause to wait while a square of moonlight on the floor below travels a few feet to one side. I've been up here before—there used to be a way up from the computer lab. One of the senior CS majors showed it to me, his spot to think or smoke pot unmolested. After he graduated, I would come up here late at night and listen to the sounds of drunken revelry coming up from the dorms on weekend nights, or just cool off during long summer nights of coding.

If there's anyone at all like me reading this, take note: I'm breaking a self-set rule by returning to the scene of the crime. The first time I came here, I had a different mission in mind—when I was in eighth grade, my guidance counselor told me I was a genius. I wanted to know what that meant.

If you think of a genius . . . well, you can picture Mozart, or Einstein. Someone who can do a thing better than anyone else. Not just anything, but a particular subject, like math or music, a specific topic they seem to have been born for.

I waited to find my subject. To see a thing—chess, physics, dance, a painting—and recognize it. I was a stranger in the world. I waited to see something and know it, to say, "This is me." And I would know that it was now, that one day in my life when the fumbling, the false starts, all the little trials and failures, would stop. I pictured the moment, the rush of excitement, the sure-handed swiftness of apprehension, the stunned look on the teacher's face. There'd be silence, and I'd feel for one second that I was standing at the center of the universe.

I read books, biographies of men and women in the past who had actually experienced this. And now I had learned it was going to happen to me. I waited for the moment when I would be picked. I was a shy, homely child. Unless something changed, I was going to grow up into a dumpy postdoc who never knew the touch of fire. I wondered what shape it would take, because I couldn't see it.

But that woman said I was a genius. If only she'd known.

A micro-winch of my own design pays out cable at my belt. Above me, the rectangular skylight dwindles; below, my red leather boots dangle, descending foot by foot to rest on either side of the sleeping guard's body, the only witness to my return. I used to fantasize about being asked back as a commencement speaker and returning, unmasked, to tell them all the Truth.

Parts of the Institute are open to the public. A sign in the lobby announces the current exhibits: "The Genius of Leonardo," "The Magic of Geodes," and "What Makes the Weather?" The café is closed and dark, but I can still see the table where I used to wait for Erica Lowenstein. The smell of this place after hours makes me remember what it felt like the first time. When I was here and had everything ahead of me. I drop a thousand-dollar bill into the "Pay what you can" admissions box and walk in through the turnstile.

My first year was the year of an enormously cold winter. I was a thin, shy freshman, and college was a new landscape to me, brick and dark wood, like an enormous Georgian mansion owned by a distant relation, where I had been left to explore on a long Sunday afternoon. I would eat alone in the dining hall, with my glasses steamed up from the warmth of so many happy, healthy bodies.

I had nothing to say to my roommates. They were charmingly ordinary people, now two doctors and a lawyer who have no idea what their forgettable onetime roommate has become. I'd sleep, fitfully, through whatever social events went on at nights in the common room, fluorescent light and beery laughter leaking in under the door. I'd go whole days without speaking except in the classroom, where my sharp impatience with the other students seemed to disrupt an unspoken patrician agreement not to seem too smart or try too hard, an agreement that I would have no part of. I wanted to blaze.

I sat in on graduate-level seminars and carried twice the normal course load, and there were ripples of awareness of my abilities running through several departments.

At night, I would go to sleep and dream of teaching in a vast arched lecture hall, and great leathery wings unfolded from my back and spread out through the warm, hazy air of the classroom as I spoke of a fantastic heretical knowledge. And I would wake shivering to my own misplaced self, floundering among smug, knowing prep school students.

Jason, I knew, was running a parallel track, only somewhat behind me, his conventional good looks and inexplicable confidence carrying him past the real complexities of the work. His all-embracing good nature even extended to me—the few times we passed in the quad, I was the recipient of his benevolent nod and smile, the not quite focused eyes never quite acknowledging the humiliations of the past.

I won the Putnam Prize without straining (Jason, by some accident, took third, but I still beat him by a respectable margin). I remember the day I took it, the first Saturday of December, having just that morning flunked the mandatory swimming test for the third time, the smell of chlorine still on me. My ideas on the Zeta Dimension were still just a few random notes in a notebook, and as yet there was no shadow of my split with Professor Burke, only a sense of unguessable potential.

Once I'm in the museum area, the security is a joke. A stuffed polar bear and oscilloscopes and obsolete models of the atom loom side by side in the darkness.

Laserator's mirror is kept in the back, in the research section, the high-security wing. I met him once, a midwesterner with a mild expression. He only wanted his theories to be given wider recognition.

I'm taking a risk, but a piece like this is one of a kind. They're not going to figure out what I want it for until it's too late—Blackwolf has some technical training, but they don't have any real scientists. Which is sad, because they'll never truly appreciate what I'm going to do.

Even half-finished, the new Power Staff is a marvel, a magician's wand of solid circuitry, packed with unpleasant surprises. Da Vinci beams down at me from his life-size display, the very image of the well-adjusted, well-meaning scientist. The plaque goes on and on about his contributions to the welfare of humanity, his selfless devotion to knowledge. Sucker.

At that time, I thought I knew everything that was going to happen to me. It didn't occur to me that I might fall in love.

I don't know why Erica started talking to me. Something I said struck her as funny, I guess. She was a junior, and I was asked to speak in her economics seminar about the pure-math ramifications of the game theory they were studying. We walked to her next class as I sweated profusely and expounded on the differences between Dutch- and English-style auctions. She was a political science major, with hazel eyes, a low, throaty voice, and a steady gaze that held mine. It may have been the first full-length conversation I had had since arriving at college.

I read her columns in the *Crimson* and sat near her in the Cabot House dining hall. She would usually come over and talk to me for a few minutes, and then more and more often put her tray down next to mine.

I felt as if I had stepped through a doorway, that for a moment it was possible for me to become a regular person. To step out of the trap, the Zeta Dimension in which I lived. I sensed another chance to change myself, a last opportunity to become a kind of Jason Garner myself.

There was a short time, maybe a semester or two, when we would have lunch in the early afternoons, laughing and chattering together in the dining hall. I listened to her talk about her family, her private school. She was smart, and she had the confidence to spend time with people like Jason. But I fancied she saw through them, that there was something more acute, more critical in her. And that maybe she would see through to me.

Years later we would become a joke, the perpetual damsel in distress and the fiendish love-struck villain. Even other villains thought it was funny. I suppose it was obvious to everyone but me what was going on, but I wasn't part of Jason's circle. I didn't even know they knew each other.

That summer I was asked by Professor Burke, the departmental elder statesman, to work in his high-energy physics laboratory. It was a signal honor—Burke was the department's Nobelist and his advanced particle physics seminar defined the undergraduate elite. I was the youngest student ever to attend it. I told Erica because I had no one else to tell aside from my parents.

I was even permitted to book a little time on the particle accelerator for my own simple tests. I was given just enough access to allow me to discover the Zeta Dimension, and enable the accident that would bring about the end of my academic career, and introduce CoreFire to the world.

When I reach the storage room, I can see something's amiss, the flooring a fraction of an inch higher than in the corridor—pressure-sensitive. I touch a stud on the Power Staff, and rise three inches from the floor. A second touch, and I drift slowly out into the middle of the room. Laser trip wires bend silently around me.

Laserator's device glistens in a wire-fronted cabinet at the back of one of the laboratory rooms. The idiots have forgotten all about it! Light drips and runs off of it; it's almost weightless. They say he could throw back visible light as a solid force, and reflect even gravity. With the mirror in my hand, the first stage of my plan is complete.

In the end, it took the Champions, Battalion, and Stormcloud himself to stop him; the mirror looks just as it did the day when it fell from his hand in the middle of Broadway, just at Forty-first Street. Now it waits forgotten on a shelf, pregnant with brilliance and ruin.

Jason's accident changed everything for me. I was banned forever from the high-energy test lab. It wasn't my fault, I told them; he stepped into the test area. Never mind that the underlying ideas were completely sound—no one, even Burke, wanted anything to do with me. Even though no one got hurt; in fact, hey, someone got superpowers.

It's surprisingly easy to cross over from being a prodigy to being a crank. The zeta beam problem obsessed me, and, determined to solve it, I began failing classes in earnest. Still a sophomore in my seventh semester, I walked the icy pathways of Harvard Yard in the one sweater I owned, muttering. People I'd never met before seemed to recognize and avoid me; Jason was off on his way to stardom by then, jauntily renamed, college forgotten. Erica would soon follow, intrepid reporter/girlfriend to the world's newest superhero.

I was halfway to being a campus legend; people would point me out when they saw me in the windowless snack room on the fourth level, sipping coffee and eating Skittles. I lived in the libraries doing my own research, hunting in the card catalog. Every night the security people ushered me out at midnight, and found me waiting every morning when they came to unlock the glass doors. I lived in the hum of the fluorescents, the muted rustling of paper and rumble of movable stacks. I began checking out older and older books, books whose call slips had not been stamped for decades; books with odd but informative notes scribbled in the margins by undergraduates from the twenties and thirties. It was in this way that I first became acquainted with the name of Ernest Kleinfeld. But no one listed in the libraries of America's oldest, wisest institution had ever answered my questions.

I moved off campus, but not very far. I found a basement apartment in Davis Square in Somerville, I haunted cafés and bookstores. Once, on the street, I heard someone point me out to a group of incoming freshmen as "the Zeta Beam Guy."

At night, lying on my bunk, I felt as if I were lying at the bottom of a river of dark water. Where was all my potential now?

After a while, I was asked by the university to take time off, counseling recommended. I refused. I went down to the library as I usually did, where I studied and read all day. At midnight, the stacks closed, and I sat down on the front steps. The long winter had passed, and it was a warm, misty night in May. Here and there, students were hurrying back to their dorms, laughing and talking about trivial things that I could no longer imagine.

My last stop is in the museum annex across the street, but I'm going to have to hurry. Sirens sound outside—one of the guards must have woken up and identified me. They know they're dealing with a costume now, so it won't take them long to bring in the posthuman element, vectoring in from up and down the East Coast.

And here it comes: Damsel glides above me, black against the sky like a nightmare goddess, uncannily weightless, laser eyes shining in the darkness. The crescent moon symbol on her chest is dimly visible by starlight. The field damper should keep her from spotting me. I clutch Laserator's invention to my chest.

Rainwater is soaking into my costume, seeping through the steel and nylon fibers onto super-hardened skin. I wish I were anywhere but here; I wish I were home. But I'm a supervillain, and I don't have a home, just a space station, or a jail cell, or a base, or a sewer tunnel. I don't have a secret identity; I'm Doctor Impossible just about all the time now.

The annex is just a big warehouse, most of it underground. The fire stairs are at the back, locked, but I crouch down and aim Laserator's device at the sheet metal. Starlight is enough; reflected, amplified, and focused, it burns right through. The aluminum stairway booms as I pound down five flights, arms out, cape flying. I already know where I'm going. Wherever he is, CoreFire isn't around anymore to stop me.

I moved on to graduate study at Tufts, the physics department, squeaking in with a stipend on the basis of early work and the fact that when I tried, I could still do pure math better than anyone. But I remember wandering down to the student center one afternoon to take the GREs, startled at how young all the seniors looked, and how slowly they worked. When I wandered up the aisle, completed test in hand, they asked me if I was taking a rest room break.

My adviser at Tufts was an ancient chemist, a man who didn't expect to understand my research, and didn't ask about my progress. The work was not going well. Experiments produced null results, or random. I seemed on the verge of a thing that would not materialize. Kleinfeld's monographs haunted me, his insights decades old but still out of my reach.

Erica, oddly enough, still found the time for an occasional lunch with me when she came up from New York, where she was already making her name as a writer. But apart from these rare glimpses of sunlight, my human contacts were with lab assistants and systems administrators. Boston is a rainy city that peters out into suburban strip malls and office parks at the extremities, and this is where the high-tech laboratories flourished, at which I found work and enough lab space to push forward with my ideas. I daydreamed on the long bus rides to and from the suburbs.

And no one knew what had been entrusted to me. At night, I stared at the television, feeling the seasons go past at unfathomable velocity. I felt myself growing older and fatter, my power languishing, flickering, while Dimension Zeta grew ever clearer, its red radiation glowing just behind the visible world. At times I felt close to that discovery again, the one that would make my name, prove them wrong. A genius languishing alone and undiscovered.

Down three, four, five flights, into the reserve archives, then past the government seals into the proscribed section—fiddling the locks takes only a few seconds. Downstairs in the stacks, the shelves run endlessly on, mostly cardboard boxes with miscellaneous lots, donated or bought at auction. I'm looking for a piece of a private collection, brought to America and broken up after World War II. Luckily, I know my way around the archives.

It's right where the catalog said it would be. *Tactical Climatology,* 1927 edition in two volumes, Neptune Press, copious illustrations, fair condition. Officially proscribed by a wartime council of generals, senators, and scientists, only four people alive know it even exists, which makes it one of the better-known works of Ernest Kleinfeld, aka Lianne Stekleferd, aka Lester Lankenfried. Better known as Baron Ether.

Inside, beautifully drawn diagrams illustrate what needs to happen; columns of meticulous equations prove their effectiveness. "What Makes the Weather?" indeed. I do, now, and it's going to get a lot colder soon. The book goes in my satchel, two items in one night and I'm halfway there—it's almost too easy. I don't fight fair, not hero-fair anyway, but it's not like I cut corners. Anybody could do what I do, anybody at all, if only they'd do the homework.

By the end, even other graduate students were starting to avoid me. I was older than they were. Our first semester, there was a welcoming party, and I was shocked at how young they seemed. I stood there limply for an hour in my tweed jacket before slipping out and going to a movie. I thought that at graduate school I would finally meet people like myself, but my fellow students looked like ski instructors, drinking and dancing like people on MTV. A few of them even knew who I was, the screwup, the Zeta Beam Guy.

My roommates in college had gone on to become entertainment lawyers, theater directors, physicians. I always thought that being smart would excuse everything—the $11,000 per year lifestyle, the dreary walk-up apartment in Somerville, the deferred hopes.

Maybe there are no other people like me, even in the sciences. I don't know what they want from it, how they can be satisfied with the petty round of grant money, publication, and prizes. Whereas I have always known, deep down.

I spent endless hours in the stacks, looking hopelessly for the one book that would show me the way forward, that would unlock Dimension Zeta. I wanted things I saw only dimly—fluids that glowed, and electricity that arced and danced like a living thing. I wanted science inside of me, changing me, my body as a generator, as a reactor, a crucible. Transformation, transcendence. And so, of course, they called me mad.

They laughed at me, and that I would never forgive or forget. I would, to use the old phrase, show them. I would find it, and not for anyone else's sake. Save the world? I don't think so. I have my reasons. The world was lost a long time ago, and nothing's going to fix it, maybe not even science.

And what if I did find something back in those stacks, way back, a book so old it's not in the card catalog, moldering in the last reaches of the library system, a sub-sub-sub-basement, so old that the title could not be distinguished. I took it from the shelf and sat down on the floor and read. I found it. I looked where no one thought to look. I read a book no one else thought to read.

No ordinary book. A book of leaves, a book of rain, a book of parking lots and college quadrangles and all the long walks and lonely afternoons of my days and nights. What is a genius? I read and read and read, until I saw in that summer landscape of strip malls and parking lots and high school auditoriums a grand design laid out like a printed circuit in grass and asphalt, a strange rune of mysterious import, shining and telling the true story of the slow closing of the last great age.

Getting out is easy. Never guessing my target, they didn't even follow me to the archives. Heroes don't concern themselves with things like libraries and research. Once they've had their origin, they don't try to think anymore, just fly around. Books, inventions, discovery—they leave that to us.

Damsel will be zooming south again to her luxury suite at the Champions' Tower. I steal a car out of a rental lot, my prizes on the passenger seat. The car has tinted windows, so I don't even have to change.

It's another thing I used to do. Driving home from the laboratory late in the night, I would detour onto the highway just to feel like I was going somewhere. The drive takes four hours this time. I stay carefully under the speed limit for most of the way, racing the rising sun at the end, book and mirror on the passenger seat beside me. The master plan is well on its way to completion.

They say you never forget your origin, but most of that evening is gone for me, no matter how many times I return to it. Fragments of it come back to me at odd times.

I'd been having dinner with Erica—I remember that much—and we talked afterward, walking back to my apartment, but most of that night is still missing. I went back to the lab to work late. When I hurried across the road from the bus stop, the air smelled like rain. There was a haze around the street lamps and the car headlights as I waited to cross the expressway. I was still commuting to an office park in Lexington, pulling long hours and nursing along the last of a series of failed experiments.

The rain was pounding the parking lot outside. It was a Friday night, the best time to do my own work, and the parking lot was empty of anything but the lights glowing orange-yellow and the empty white lines drawn on the pavement like a cartoon skeleton. Out beyond the last parking spaces, there's nothing but swamp, bulrushes and tall grass and frogs and chirping insects and the black suburban night of Massachusetts. I stared out at it from tinted-glass windows, breathing climate-controlled air as another deadline slipped away. I was losing my funding. This was my last chance to prove my ideas.

The target solution was a unique fluid. A revolutionary new fuel source, infused with the zeta radiation only I understood, a fluorescent cocktail of rare poisons, unstable isotopes, and exotic metals, it roiled in the beaker, swirling purple and green. *Toxic* isn't the word for it; it was malign, practically sapient. A single drop would have powered an ocean liner for a thousand years. One evening, on impulse, I stripped a glove off and touched a sample. It was cool and luminous, and the end of my finger went instantly numb.

The temperature went on rising. Spiderweb cracks formed on the glass of the containment chamber an instant before the explosion. The pain was like burning or drowning, and it went on and on, unbearable. I wanted to faint, to leave my body. When you can't bear something but it goes on anyway, the person who survives isn't you anymore; you've changed and become someone else, a new person, the one who did bear it after all. The formula saturated my body, and I changed.

CHAPTER TEN

WELCOME TO MY ISLAND

Golden Age, then Silver Age, then Iron. There must be a Rust Age as well, an age when even the base metals we're made of now will have changed again. By what, into what, I don't know. All cyborgs have to think about rust—high-tech alloys or no, the metal parts of me will eventually oxidize. People call this the Information Age, the Silicon Age, or the Nuclear Age, but I think they're wrong. They don't have the temper of it. When the world's metal changes to iron, it changes for the last time.

I sink into one of the leather seats of Blackwolf's custom-built airship, tangible proof that I'm not a small-timer anymore. Below us, I can already see that Doctor Impossible's base has rusted.

Coming in from the air, we see the remains of a shattered grandeur, skeletal arcs of decaying metal soaring into the sky, gesturing at what used to be. In its prime, the base held unsurpassed marvels; now, metal and concrete lie rotting in the sun.

The north beach is dotted with a row of immense concrete pylons, streaked with rust from their internal reinforcements, foundations for a high-energy physics laboratory that went unbuilt. A railway, overgrown now, leads inward to the main facility, a jewel set into cliff and jungle by robot labor. A central dome bulks up out of the trees, only the spines of its four structural girders intact. The curve of the dome itself is still defined by a rotting latticework, but half the panes have fallen in, to shatter on the gleaming laboratory floor below. Moss and vines drip from the holes.

Water has seeped into everything. When CoreFire cannoned through the outer bulkhead, the whole structure shifted off its axis, windows shattered, the sterile shell cracked, and seals popped. The floors of clean workrooms are smeared with windblown dirt and animal tracks, lost to contamination. Thick tree roots have broken through the tile. Iron railings have begun to rust, and stone stairways have cracked and fallen away.

Under the laboratory dome, an enormous spherical mechanism lies frozen in decay. A stray beam of heat vision made a tiny hole to let the moisture in, and the delicate mechanisms, so smooth and finely balanced that a child could turn them with one hand, rusted into a solid mass. And Phathom-5, a supercomputer built to plot the arcs of shattering atoms, is silent; tropical rains now fall into the sterile core, where the tiniest particles of dust were once forbidden. The plasma rifles mounted along the eastern wall are silent, and the particle accelerator is still, pointed upward at a seventy-degree angle, garishly painted and crested with radiator fins. A family of osprey nests in the barrel.

"And they actually called him mad," Damsel mutters next to me.

Lily kicks at a shell casing. Blackwolf shushes them.

Damsel points. "That's where they breached the inner fortress. You were unconscious by then."

"I was shamming," mutters Blackwolf. "I can do that, you know."

Doctor Impossible built this fortress in the late 1970s, at the beginning of his career, that golden time when every six months he was back again, looming giant on the world's view screen. No one knew what to expect—peril from the sky, or an armored robot rising out of Hudson Bay, or a mind-exchanging ray—a stranger among us aping familiarity, peering at the others with hyperintelligent eyes. He'd even gone to the stars, tamed an alien god. No field of endeavor seemed closed to his manifold, questing intellect.

Out there in international waters, he worked day and night. His gleaming citadel would have been visible from space if the light hadn't been bent around it. He'd fought Stormcloud to a standstill, thrown back the Super Squadron, outwitted Doctor Mind on his home ground. His battles with CoreFire dominated the news. And there were rumors of a device, a machine he had conceived and would one day build, that could make him utterly invincible.

Then three superheroes banded together as friends and teammates, and the world had a reigning super-team again. Doctor Impossible had a real opponent, and they foiled his schemes again and again. The last time, they'd brought the fight to him.

A couple of areas are still sealed off. Doctor Impossible dug deep— there are eight or nine levels below ground, living quarters and specialized laboratories. And the scans show shafts running deeper, down below the level of the ocean floor. One of them, we've tagged as a geothermal pipe; the others are anybody's guess. Blackwolf spends a little time looking at them, then shakes his head.

The titanic remains of a late-generation Antitron sprawl across the courtyard and over one wall, an enormous blaster cannon still clutched in its hand. It had fought a desperate fight, but stripped of malign animation, it displays a primitive beauty, a face like an Inca mask. Its chest dimples inward where Damsel's final punch landed.

The eight of us stand there in the shadow of the doomsday device, lying on its side now, partially buried in the sandy ground. What had it been like that day? What was he thinking? The helmet, the cape, the army of mutants. He must have known he was going to lose. He was supposed to be smart, though. He was supposed to have been a scientist.

I shuffle vision modes through infrared, ultraviolet, and a weird sonic ping that makes me nauseous. I can do a kind of ultrasound bounce, a limited X-ray vision. Everybody shows up different on that one. Blackwolf's a baseline normal, an ordinary man; a few bits of metal have lodged in him over the years, and one of his knees got rebuilt. Feral's all organic, flesh and bone, both much denser than normal—and of course he's not human; his skeleton's a morph between human and a Bengal tiger. Damsel shows up all black—the sonics bounce off her skin, just like everything else. Rainbow's insides are crammed with augmentations, cables, floating extra organs. Her technology's a different flavor from mine, more biomimetic, H. R. Giger's dream of a schoolgirl.

We're not sure exactly what the device was. A series of metal-plated globes, one inside the other, multiple shells now broken open and exposed to the air. Sand lies in the mechanism, fatally spoiling its polished smoothness. I remember Doctor Impossible on TV, swearing it would destroy the Earth if he turned it on. Mister Mystic puts one hand to its side and shivers. He says Doctor Impossible's work is too complicated for him to read, that he has a hypercompressed style. But he thinks it probably would have worked.

I've been over and over the footage recorded of the last time anyone saw him, a fragment of news video taken after a skirmish with Embryarch. His face glows vivid in close-up, barred with scan lines. He's walking, talking to someone off-camera, right before it cuts out. A name.

Mystic stands in the center of the chamber, arms out, fingers spread. He's reading energy traces out of the surrounding air. If CoreFire came here, he'll have left a unique signature. Mister Mystic has unusually long fingers.

"CoreFire did come here, but only for a minute. He landed there, and stood for a while. I think he was using his zeta sense. Then he went inside for a few minutes. He didn't touch anything."

"So what?" Rainbow looks bored, twitchy. She's used to fighting in front of a camera.

"We don't know yet." Blackwolf's thinking something, but he's not saying what.

It's getting cold in the shadows. Elphin perches on the outer wall, watching the sun set over a tropical sea like glass, gilding everything and casting long shadows from the towers and the beams poking up out of the ruined portions. The enormous hulk is absolutely silent, absolutely still.

The service door is armored; two feet thick, it's set into the rock away from the main installation. People always think cyborgs can open things, as if carrying a chip in your head made you a magic lock pick. But I see a look go between Rainbow and Feral that plainly says, Amateur hour! so I kneel, tear off a panel, and give it my best. Any 57 percent–replacement cyborg knows a little about military electronics. I hack away for about fifteen minutes, armor heating up in the hot sun, before I hear the hum and click of bolts sliding back. Feral and I haul it open together, his thick, hairy arm reaching over me to pull with demonic strength as I strain awkwardly from a crouch, his breath on the back of my neck. He's as strong as I am, at the very least.

The group spills inside, down a service ladder clinging to one wall of an underground chamber, a rock-walled factory space. Elphin skims down and in, spear shaft held high, feet well off the ground—she won't touch cold iron. God, she even trails her legs behind her like Tinker Bell. Blackwolf slides down with his feet on the outside. Feral stalks in afterward, climbing head down like a squirrel descending a tree. Damsel waits a moment in the sunlight, the last to come inside.

For fourteen years, this was his stronghold, an open challenge to the world. The inside is cavernous, a metal catwalk crossing a deep crevasse, rock walls rising to meet overhead. Light spills in through what might be gun ports, unmanned now. Doctor Impossible built machines to attack the world, machines to make cities cower, and he built to scale. Infrared shows bats nesting above.

"Power's on," I remark, pointlessly. A few shafts of light scar the dimness. Beneath us, electricity once flashed and sparked between towers of metal, now lifeless. Damsel and Blackwolf are talking, barely looking around.

"No, you're missing the point. Just because I can't fly doesn't make it—"

"Jesus, give it a rest, Marc."

But the door at the far end of the bridge shoots open. Blackwolf spots it first, but waits for Damsel.

"Uh . . . darling?"

"What?"

"Contact."

I've never worked with real professionals before, and the response is impressive. Damsel shouts, "Fliers! Get in the air!" And everyone scatters, Elphin buzzing sideways off the bridge. The robots bear the imprint of Impossible's style, metal spiders moving with aggressive intelligence. One of them has lost a leg in the earlier battle. Feral bounds forward, ducking and rolling under the chattering guns. I've seen video of Feral working, but video is nothing. It doesn't tell you what it's like to be close to someone that big who can move that quickly.

I kick into a power sprint to catch up, legs extending an extra foot of metal skeleton, cantilevering out from inside my calves. Blackwolf dodges an initial burst of fire with ridiculous ease, turning an insolently casual cartwheel before vaulting atop the lead robot and yanking at its sensory cluster.

Elphin is already beside one of them, her lance lodged in its side, with a cry of "Titania!" As I plow into Blackwolf's ride, she levers hers off the bridge and into space, while Feral tears at the other's wiring. I'm too pissed off for subtlety, and by the time Damsel and Lily catch up, I've broken this one's back.

"Nice one." Blackwolf gives my arm a playful slap that clunks dully on armor, but inside it I feel it for a long time after that. Mister Mystic materializes from somewhere with a shrug.

The inner door goes quicker than the first. Damsel scouts ahead. I hear a blast, and she comes skidding backward unhurt along the polished metal floor, the front of her costume shredded. I look the other way as she twists it around to cover herself—I don't need that kind of trouble.

Blackwolf stops to help her up, but she snaps at him.

"Don't be ridiculous." I'd swear that behind that mask, he looks hurt. I must be imagining things.

We come out into the entrance hall, built on a titanic scale, the upper reaches lost in arched and buttressed dimness, letting in the sunlight where the ceiling has rusted out. Even Feral seems subdued by its cathedral hush. Elphin lets herself drift upward in the warm air as we spread out across its football-field width, half-waiting for a counterassault that launched two years ago. The air is damp, and a few tufts of grass have managed to take hold in the places where the mud collects.

A thin stream trickles where one of the ceiling seams split, puddling on the floor before draining off to some lower level. Galleries to the left and right afford glimpses of laboratories and audience chambers where the battle raged, leaving blast marks and the shells of shattered robots. A few intact display cases hold some of the Doctor's trophies—a helmet, a pistol, and an odd-looking piece of ancient bone. At the far end, a pair of immense doors hang on their hinges. The throne room lies beyond, where they arrested him.

The upper rooms are still open to the sky in places. The rain has washed dirt and leaves in, and seabirds build their nests in cracks in the monumental statuary. We walk slowly in the metal-walled rooms, listening to our footsteps, unwilling to speak. The walls feature displays of dead television screens and banks of LEDs, red and orange and green, now dull, gemlike nubs.

Mystic concentrates on reading old thoughts, but it's been a long time since Doctor Impossible was here. The rest of us idle around, poking through living quarters and office space. The Doctor used chipboard desks and Aeron chairs, just like a high-tech start-up.

Blackwolf puts a hand on my shoulder for balance while he adjusts his tights. Damsel doesn't appear to notice.

One wing still runs on its own generator. From overhead, I hear Blackwolf saying, "See the control room? I remember from when we switched brains that time," and I follow.

Here the rooms are still bright and clean, humming with life. The control room where we end up looks down on the great domed laboratory. Catwalks crosshatch the upper reaches. The dome's retractable roof has jammed open a little, giving us a sliver of fading sunlight.

I lean over the rail to watch Lily squinting at something on the laboratory floor. "C'mon up," I call. "Looks like we're in here."

Going in I squeeze past Feral standing guard, his loud breathing and his animal warmth.

Blackwolf taps away at a computer but doesn't seem terribly interested in what he's doing. An animated hologram globe shows the Earth morphing from the primordial supercontinent Pangaea through the present day into a future version, a single landmass labeled Pangaea Ultima, ice ages coming and going in between. Colored graphs show temperature and CO_2 levels shifting too fast to follow.

"Now what?" I look over at Damsel.

"Keep looking. He can't hide forever."

In the field, everyone defers to Damsel and Blackwolf, our nominal co-leaders who don't seem to want to look at each other.

Finally, Blackwolf speaks up. "We've got other options. Someone's still got to track down those iridium isotopes."

"I thought you and Damsel got rid of that stuff ten years ago." Feral's back again, apparently satisfied there are no evildoers nearby.

"That was ten years ago; I've thought of a whole new set of possibilities since then. I'm including matter transmutation, and a couple of unidentified ETs. There are magical options." Blackwolf ticks them off on his fingers.

"God, I didn't think of that. CoreFire hated magic." Damsel is looking down at the laboratory floor. She seems to be remembering something, or trying to. I watch Damsel and that famous force field shimmering, and involuntarily I wonder if I could take her if it came to it. Blackwolf glances over, and I feel uncomfortably as if he's read my mind.

"Fucking Impossible." Damsel slumps into one of the high-tech chairs and spins around, looking at the ceiling, her force field flickering blue.

"What happens now? What can we expect?" I ask.

Lily looks at me and speaks the answer everyone is already thinking: "Doomsday."

No one talks on the way back up, even when I waste a clip on a laughing hologram of the Doctor, a rookie mistake. I blush furiously, but Blackwolf winks at me.

Back in Blackwolf's high-tech airship, acceleration pushes me back into my seat, and the island recedes behind us, but I can't stop thinking about it. I used to have a real life; I used to be someone who went on vacation to Brazil. I used to be able to walk down a street without getting stared at, and lie on a bed, and talk to a man who would look at me in something approaching a normal way.

Mentiac predicts that in the very far future, the stars will have cycled through all possible stages of their fusion reactions, from hydrogen to helium and so on down the periodic table to iron. And then there will be a true iron age, when every atom in the universe will have turned to iron, everything transmuted by inexorable centuries to basest metal, even high-tech alloys, even diamonds. Everything. In my imagination, iron stars orbited by iron planets float through an iron galaxy in an iron void. But even then it won't be over. There's always a Rust Age.

PART
TWO

CHAPTER ELEVEN

INVINCIBLE

Dressed in gray coveralls and a sanitary mask, I mop the marble floor of the Champions' lobby and dust the statue of Galatea until I'm satisfied my machines have disabled the cameras. Then I retire to a supply closet and change, stepping out under the domed skylight in full mask and cape. Time for stage two of the doomsday plan, a three-stage plan not counting the actual doomsday.

It's an illicit thrill to walk through the front door in costume. Just another chapter to the legend, and everything is falling into place, almost too easily this time. No sign of CoreFire, and the Champs are off on another useless reconnaissance mission. They'll be gone for hours, and meanwhile the next piece of my device will soon be safely in my possession. Thanks to me, Dollface is finally going to have her day in the sun.

The new Power Staff is complete and for the hundredth time, I test it out for grip and heft. Most of the parts came out of a local RadioShack, but the design . . . only I know how to do that. Molecular circuitry, holograms, pocket MRI . . . I had a lot of time in prison. The power jewel glows a deep red, and I pad silently and invisibly through the corridors, no more than a drift of static on the monitors. I have the floor plans from the place memorized, details culled and inferred from blueprints, satellite photos, fan magazines, even that interminable documentary.

I have to admit it's magnificent. Spinning in place, I gawk like a tourist at the profoundly vulgar piece of architecture. Guy Campbell, the Silver Sentinel, more or less bought his way onto the team by refitting this place as the team headquarters after gutting the telecom giant that built it. He lasted about six weeks, and I think he was just too embarrassed to ask for it back.

Splendid, but the place smells like they always do—sweat and ozone and disinfectant, hospital smells. The ability to stretch your limbs or secrete acids can wreak havoc on the human metabolism. There's a fine line between a superpower and a chronic medical condition.

The heroes left an hour ago, and there's time for a little sightseeing. The entrance lobby is a museum of superherodom, souvenirs from brighter days.

The wedding of Damsel and Blackwolf was the brightest moment of 1980s superherodom, a union of the two founding members of the greatest super-team in the world, at the height of its powers. The added fact that Damsel was Stormcloud's daughter made it a matter of super-hero royalty. They were our Charles and Diana. When Stormcloud placed the Nightstar Sapphire around Damsel's neck, it was effectively a coronation for the Champions, a passing of the torch. Both Peterson graduates, actually—to think I knew them when. Not that they'd remember me.

The rest of us watched from the shadows, wondering what it meant. I was there myself, hidden in the crowd, waiting for my moment. Stormcloud stood in the background, looking almost statesmanlike. CoreFire was the best man and gave a toast even I found funny—someone must have written it for him, probably Blackwolf. When they kissed, Damsel's shield glowed a deep red, then disappeared altogether as they rose into the air. I should have finished her right there, but I was still a little sentimental back then.

———

The Crisis Room. This is where their shifting roster of robots, athletes, madmen, and gods used to get together and talk about me. A U-shaped table points its open end toward a sprawling computer console and three enormous wall-mounted display screens. This is where my face must have looked out at them, threatening, leering, and demanding tribute. I hope they had a good sound system.

To business. Their computer security isn't much to write home about—probably Blackwolf's work, clever but not exactly genius, just self-confident. Heroes like these don't think very hard about security. They assume their own reputation is going to scare people off, and if someone does try to break in, they can just have a fight about it. Great office chairs, though. Picture window looks out over midtown—the feng shui is immaculate. I spend a few minutes noodling around on the broad, flat console before diving in.

I could break it, but I don't even have to. Toward the end of *Titan Six* they show outtakes from a televised tour of the fortress, shortly after they came back from outer space. Damsel's talking to the camera, looking very, very tired. No one seems to be doing any work. It was their greatest triumph, but they seem to be suffering from a group depression. In fact, they're weeks from breaking up.

In the background, Blackwolf is just sitting down at the computer. With the film slowed down and enhanced, you can see Blackwolf's arms moving at the keyboard as he logs himself in, and from there it isn't too much work to figure out where his hands must have been, what he was typing. You only have to do your homework on these things. I key it in now: GALATEA.

Once I'm in the system, it's impossible not to start poking around a little. I flip through staff records, secret identities, powers. Damsel, Blackwolf, Elphin. I already know who they are. I remember some of them quite well, even if they would never remember me. And everyone knows who you are, CoreFire. Jason.

Activity logs. Blackwolf's been online recently, going back through the CoreFire archives. He spent a little time in the media archives—file footage of Galatea aloft in action, wine-colored hair always floating away on an intangible breeze, violet headband above her featureless green eyes. She projected silvery energy from her hands—even I don't know what it was. It hurt like hell, though.

Blackwolf's also been looking at me. The entry under DOCTOR IMPOSSIBLE is surprisingly inadequate. I've never given out much under interrogation, but even so it's surprising how much I kept from them. The file gives age (estimated), place of birth (a short piece on my accent and regionalisms), estimated Stanford-Binet (insultingly low; but then, they haven't seen my best efforts yet). A couple hundred megabytes of shaky-cam video footage, and some rather reductive psychological guesswork.

All those years and they don't know me. There are five working theories as to my real identity, all of them dead wrong. Four are missing persons cases dating from the 1960s. Their photographs all look and sound a little bit like me, precocious intellects with aptitude in math and science, prodigies who performed less and less well in school as they grew older. By eleven or twelve, they'd all displayed antisocial behavior patterns—here, a prizewinning violinist becomes a drug user; there, a national mathematics champion burns down his own school. Three of them show histories of child abuse. All of them went missing between the ages of thirteen and fifteen, vanished out of Portland, Shaker Heights, San Diego, and Bridgeport. Did they all slip out of their neighborhoods early one morning and onto a bus? Did they find new names somewhere? How did each one manage his disappearing act? And what did he become? All I know is, none of them ended up being me.

The last face is Polgar, aka Martin van Polk-Garfield IV. Once, he was the scientist president of an alternate dimension's America. Dethroned and exiled, he went looking for new Americas to conquer, and once in a while he still shows up in ours, dressed in the stars, stripes, and eagles of his native country, eager to accept our throne. I kind of like him, actually. He showed pluck, thought outside the box. Life gave him lemons, and he brewed his own brand of dimension-traveling, world-conquering lemonade. I almost wish they were right about Polgar—it's better than my real story any day.

There wasn't any warning with me, not the kind they look for. My earliest dreams were about my own brain, a cloud lit by flashes of blue and purple lightning. My school file never showed anything out of the ordinary. I quietly watched other children's showy disorders, their early cognitive failures or compulsive aggression, and knew I was something different. Nobody was watching out for me. I rose undetected through the intermediate grades and they confidently packed me off to Peterson, another success for the system.

At sixteen, I would sit quietly in an empty classroom and work out problem sets weeks in advance. The work went as fast as I could write it. I had a system where I did the mental work three or four questions ahead of where my pen was. It was May already, almost the end of term. Outside, the hot Iowa sun was steaming off the previous night's rainfall. They knew I was smart—I would skip my junior year entirely and begin the senior curriculum in the fall.

Another student with this kind of gift might have become popular, sold the answers or traded them, or at least let a hint drop every once in a while. I never talked in class, never helped people with their work. Never pandered.

This wasn't my real work anyway. I had a milk crate in my closet, where I kept my real efforts, a mounting pile of spiral-bound notebooks that sizzled with my jagged ballpoint scribblings. I worked all the time, even during the achingly slow class lectures. I'd mastered junior-level calculus years ago.

So I doodled holes in space, robot locomotion systems, and quantum computing devices. I fit them in around the day's dutiful notes on mitosis or *The Catcher in the Rye* or the Federalist Papers; then I would layer circuit diagrams for impossible machines, mechanisms of gears and pulleys raising and lowering cartoon weights, and dragons whose fish-scaled tails wound over and under, around and through columns of figures and dates of battles, tapering as thin as the fineness of my pencil allowed before finishing in a broad-head arrow point.

I wrote code for computer games I ran on the primitive mainframe the school had, partners at chess, and even a dungeon game, where I steered a tiny swordsman or wizard through endlessly layer-caked levels that spiraled into the earth, sunken ballrooms and throne rooms and treasure houses giving way to caverns, grottoes, and lightless oceans, and still deeper caverns below those.

I extended them as I played, everything getting stranger the farther down I went, from goblins and wolves to giant ants, dragons, and demons, and castles underground. I still play it occasionally, in the off-hours. There was never any sense who had dug that deep, or why, or when I was going to find the real bottom, but I never wanted to stop, knowing a great prize rested there, a centuries-old glittering treasure or hidden revelation, buried fathoms-deep under stone and earth; a relic from the deepest past, precious as life and ancient as childhood memory.

The bell rang for dinner. I gathered up books and papers and hurried down the long, dim corridor lined with lockers banging open and closed, shouldering among the larger kids. As an adult, I'm still a little smaller than average. I wasn't any younger than the people in my grade, but I looked it. Something bounced off of my backpack, a little wad of paper. Hisses and titters as I passed down a hallway. I didn't turn around, but silently I recorded everything.

Later, I'd sit on a toilet lid in our dorm bathroom and cut slowly and deliberately down my forearm. Just a couple of thin red lines, as much as a cat might do. It lasted for a while—for days, I felt the pull of the scabs on my skin when I flexed my arms. I could feel it under my clothes, a secret reminder of who I really was.

One time, I had a different idea. I brought the razor up, to my scalp. A piece of hair came away, and another, leaving bare scalp. The hair came away inch by inch. I nicked my scalp and started bleeding, but it didn't matter. The cut hair covered the floor, and piled up on my shoulders like ash. I watched myself becoming someone else. One day you wake up and realize the world can be conquered.

One day I would show them. Pull a rabbit from my hat. Breathe fire. I picked up my tray and joined the line behind the others. "We're with him," a tall horsey girl ahead of me explained to the lady serving food. Her friends held it for a moment, then collapsed into laughter.

I'm going to put on a mask and scrawl my name across the face of the world, build cities of gold, come back and stomp this place flat, until even the bricks are just dust. So you can just shut up. All of you. I'm going to move the world.

Cough cough. "FAGgot . . ." Titters. Jason Garner, and a couple of his friends. Peterson was the same as middle school had been, only maybe more so. There had to be a way out of this, all of it. In my head soared louder and louder the sad, sweet songs of science.

Oddly enough, there's a second name listed in the computer under recent searches. CoreFire was looking for someone, too.

NAME: THE PHARAOH (2)

Why the Pharaoh? He wasn't much of a supervillain at all, just a crank, a nuisance in a costume. I think he called himself the Mummy for a while before I met him. He pulled a few bank jobs in the late 1970s, claiming to be the reincarnation of the pharaoh Ramses. His most notable feature was that he'd chosen the same name as a more famous hero, but he wasn't important enough for them to fight over it. Some villains make you embarrassed to *be* a villain.

ALIAS: NELSON GERARD.

Nelson the Pharaoh, King of the Nile. I never knew his real name, and I wonder how they did. I'm mildly surprised he has an entry at all. If it weren't for that hammer he'd have been a complete joke.

BIRTHPLACE: TUCSON, ARIZONA.
KNOWN ASSOCIATES: MISS MINDBENDER. EMBRYARCH.
DOCTOR IMPOSSIBLE.

Known associate. I'm not really used to having friends. We could be in the same room without fighting anyway. I don't know the others.

NOTES: POSSIBLE MENTAL INSTABILITY.

Maybe. But he was smart, too, that was the thing. You just wouldn't think it. The irony is, he really did have a serious power in him, more than I ever figured out. I just don't think he knew what he had.

GOALS: GLOBAL DOMINATION; FOUNDATION OF
NEO-NILOTIC WORLD-STATE; AUTOREINCARNATION
AS RAMSES IV.

I used to yell at him about that lack of ambition, but he didn't seem to care. He was lazy, and he just didn't have much patience for the big picture. That business about a revived Nilotic empire, pyramids on the Potomac, was a smoke screen. And as for "autoreincarnation," he never bothered to figure out which Ramses he was the reincarnation of. When we broke into the Boston MFA that time, he couldn't even read his own inscriptions.

POWERS: HAND-TO-HAND WEAPON (HAMMER OF RA).
INVINCIBILITY (HAMMER OF RA).

The telling brevity of that notation. The Pharaoh's invulnerability was just this side of magical, if not on the far side altogether. They never found anything that would get through it, and no one knew how it worked, although I was willing to bet it wasn't the might of Ra. He'd pick up that hammer and mumble a made-up power word, and a second later he'd be one of the toughest villains on the planet. Then he'd yell, "It's hammer time!" just to embarrass me. Bastard.

He wasn't just robust; whatever he had seemed to eat inertia. Bullets didn't faze him; someone like Battalion would swing a girder, or a parade float, or a railway car, and it would just wrap around him, or he'd tear through it. He took a sixteen-inch shell once, the kind fired from battleships and designed to break down hardened fortifications, but it just dug a hole with Pharaoh at the bottom. This is the kind of technology that shouldn't exist, and more than once I tried to get the thing away from him, but he'd only laugh.

What was under all that gold paint he'd slathered on? Was it high-tech? An artifact from the future? The effect looked at least half magical, and followed no logic I could see. But it had made him invincible, or just about. He could come in handy.

SOURCE OF ABILITIES: UNKNOWN.
STATUS: AT LARGE. POSSIBLY INACTIVE.
LAST KNOWN SIGHTING: CANCÚN, MEXICO.

Cancún. I lost track of him, too, but that's not unusual for people like us. We'd met in Thailand, and I never found out where he was from. He talked as if he'd had a little college. Most villains are unusual people, but there's a fuzzy line with real mental instability. He disappeared into a demimonde of junkies and outpatient care, wherever people like that go. But trust Blackwolf to keep track, even of the Pharaoh.

The Power Staff chimes softly—the energy signature from Blackwolf's plane is closer than it should be. Enough kidding around. I do one last search to make sure I'm in the right place. I am. Dollface's effects are still on-site.

If the front lobby is a monument to heroism, the trophy hall is its opposite. I pause a moment, humbled. The hall is crowded with display cases, trophy plaques, and force fields that hold souvenirs of the most twisted imaginations of the century run riot. The Oboist's oboe, the Gentleman's gloves and monocle hang together across from a life-size mannequin wearing the Abomination's armor. An ornate golden key hangs by itself, one section lifted away to reveal miniaturized circuitry of the thirtieth century.

The workmanship here is priceless, and even I can't name it all. A fountain pen, a fedora, a painting whose lurid colors shift as I watch. A dress worn by Anne de Siècle, one of Sinistra's left-handed gloves. I spot one of Baron Ether's old pocket watches and contemplate stealing it back for him. Amulets, shields, ray guns. Malevolent statuary. A tiny castle under glass. A music box. A shelf holds books and blueprints. I could leave with an armload, but that would attract attention.

A decade ago the Champions fought a woman who called herself Dollface. She built tiny malevolent toys—a cowboy, a tiger, a carriage—but the toys worked, and they each did something different. A novelty villain, arguably, but she had a kind of concentrated ingenuity. Why only toys? It must have meant something to her.

They're in back, a dusty miniature carnival behind glass, their creator mislabeled as "Doll Woman." *Sic transit gloria mundi.* Tiny merry-go-round, tiny Ferris wheel, tiny elephants, and tiny calliope, each with its own sinister function. A genius work of miniaturization; they don't make craftsmen like her anymore. They have the full set, but I snap the lock and take only the one I need.

Gravity is many things to many people: a wave, a particle, a force. To Dollface, it was the luminous gaze of a tiny laughing fat man, a tiny ray that could make a person heavier or lighter. Some trick inside it no one ever figured out, not even me.

But in my hands, Dollface will finally get her due. She and Laserator never met, but they're going to make a great team.

A louder chime from the Power Staff tells me I've made a mistake. I cut it too close. I just have time to change back into my cleaning uniform before someone's caped shadow falls into the front hallway from the lobby, long and thin in the afternoon light. There are three of them standing there. Floating, actually. Damsel, Blackwolf, Lily. This is going to be awkward, to say the least.

It's been a long time. Not since that night in the bar. It feels like all the blood is rushing to my chest, and I'm frozen. She's right there. Crap. In two steps, I could reach out and touch her back, just under the shoulder blade.

I don't know what to do. It's unprofessional. I should be attacking while they think they're alone. In another second they're going to see me anyway. Is she going to fight me? In front of her friends?

You can't let these things get to you, not if you're going to get anywhere. It's sooner than the plan calls for, but never mind. I can do this. The Power Staff is charged. I fought their fathers to a standstill in the days of the Super Squadron, and I'll fight them, too. I step out into the light, ready for anything.

But then they aren't looking at me. The television is on in the lobby, so I hear it at the same time they do. CoreFire has been found.

That morning, for an instant, I thought I was in jail again, waking up under a dozen cameras, waiting for the guards to unstrap me. But there was no one there, just the alarm clock and the anonymous charm of the Starlight Motel. It's four days later.

Slowly, deliberately, I dress for the occasion. I'm still not used to street clothes, and the overlapping folds and clasps and pockets of a single-breasted suit seemed absurdly overcomplicated after the economy of my imperial garments. I comb my hair straight back, and trim my beard, a pale, slightly weary Lucifer. I am aging, slowly, in spite of my powers. Finished, I step back to inspect the results. I look like a person I had forgotten about, the shabby postdoc I said good-bye to twenty-five years ago. I look like a civilian. I look like a loser.

Outside in the street, my face feels naked. No sunglasses. I'm taking a serious risk here. It has been eleven years since I walked outdoors in public without a mask on. That long since I've been this close to a civilian who isn't cowering or calling the police. I take the subway across the river, where once I flew. Doctor Impossible comes to Manhattan.

Emerging, I make slow progress up Amsterdam Avenue toward 112th Street. No one bats an eyelash as I walk past the corner where I first landed Antitron. A panhandler stares insolently into my face, and inside the pocket of my trousers, I clench a fist. No one knows me.

When I get there at last, the memorial service is half over, and the crowd is so large, it spills out onto the cathedral steps. Some of them are crying, and many carry signed photographs. Plenty of them are just here to see the most distinguished mourners, to get a glimpse of Damsel or Blackwolf or Elphin, the television-friendly heroes. I wonder if Erica's in there somewhere. She's been in seclusion for a long time, filing the occasional story remotely, still mostly CoreFire material. She keeps her whereabouts a secret these days, which is probably my fault.

I've come a long way for this, but as I edge inside through the sitting and standing mourners, into the dim, echoing interior of St. John the Divine, I'm not sure what I'm here to do. Working my way forward, I can see the reserved section up front, behind the velvet rope. Of course they aren't going to let me up there, but I want to see who came.

I try not to look for her. She would be up on that platform with the capes and masks, up in the riot of forms and mythologies of the VIP area. But in a way, it's too easy—in this light, she registers only as a group of highlights, where the candles reflect. I only have to spot the apparently empty seat.

And there she is, sitting between Feral and another hero, who I don't recognize, a girl with a seahorse on her chest. She's listening quietly, head bowed a little. I stare, despite myself. Who is she trying to kid? I've seen her tear the door off a Wells Fargo truck bare-handed, laughing, dragging a guardsman out by his shirt. I was there when she took the depleted-uranium rounds that chipped and scored the right side of her collarbone. We rode the roof of a D train together out of Manhattan that time, while the Metaman was still scouring Broadway for us, and we leaped off the Manhattan Bridge together when they finally found us. We crawled ashore at Williamsburg, to the cheers of drunken party-goers on a rooftop. In the cathedral half-light, she looks like a shadow among the reds and blues of the do-gooders.

I didn't kill him. But it's bad taste at any funeral to have tried to kill the deceased as often as I have, and taste is very much on my mind. Sooner or later, one of the crew on the podium is bound to recognize the incognito Doctor Impossible, and although I assume it is considered to be in equally bad taste to try to kill me as I pay my respects, taste feels like an increasingly tenuous shield against the planet-wrecking ordnance the VIPs are capable of launching in my direction.

I never understood CoreFire or liked him particularly. I should know how he worked if anyone can, but I don't. I've pieced together as much as I can about his exploits from news broadcasts, hacked computer files, and eyewitnesses. He could fly, which was reason enough to resent him. He didn't even have the decency to work for it, to flap a pair of wings or at least glow a little. He seemed to do it purely out of a sense of entitlement—something about it suggested that the rest of us had simply knuckled under to gravity. I didn't kill him. But I wish I knew who the murderer was, because it was supposed to be me.

The image dominated TV news for days, a column of steam the size of a city block reaching out of the Indian Ocean into the sky. Helicopters and the smaller specks of superpowered fliers hung in misty silhouette, waiting to discover what had struck the water with such heat and force. Hard to tell where he came from. It didn't make sense, scientists complained, that an object large enough to do that had not broken up in the atmosphere. When they brought him up, he looked unhurt, perfect like always. He had disrupted weather patterns for a thousand miles when he hit.

The mayor of New York spoke. CoreFire had a lot of friends in the community. He was faster, stronger, and tougher than almost anyone else. He never failed to answer a call for help, he never did celebrity endorsements, and, as far as I know, he never lost. Even old Baron Ether came, wheeled gently up the handicapped ramp by two of the Mechanist's gunmetal-finish golems.

I stand unobtrusively among the masses, clutching my burden, half-listening while a representative from the State Department recites a litany of good deeds and public services. A middle-aged woman to my left begins weeping uncontrollably. I have plenty of time to sit and tick off the familiar names and faces. I know a couple of them from the Peterson School, which was a real breeding ground for powered types.

Before they shut it down, Peterson alone graduated eleven powered individuals. It wasn't an accident; there was something in the culture there that drove it. Six of them are up there now, at least. It's not as if I feel like talking, but I stare for a while, looking at what we've become, the ones who found power.

I remember Blackwolf, a thin, bright freshman who worked a little too hard to make people laugh. Wrestling team, gymnastics team, electronics club. He published clever sonnets about members of the student government, and became the smallest member of the rugby team. He's here with Damsel and the rest of the popular kids. He looks grave, but he hasn't lost that habit of watching everyone around him. I take care to stay well out of his line of view. They came in when I was a senior. Damsel, too, who attended in her secret identity, but I remember her anyway, a quiet, mathy girl who wore her brown hair long and straight. Debating team, and she ran the yearbook staff.

Jeff Burgess, who became Naga, a vigilante-cum-mercenary. He wears a cheap suit, eyes moving with a fighter's twitchiness. Rarity, tall, with curly hair, bright eyes, and a glassy, confident smile, who went to

Africa on a Fulbright and found the mystical Gemstone Nefalis, and
touched it. And Mechria, a freshman when I was a senior—I see her
again bent over the lathe in metal shop, her wide, froggy face always
grinning over something.

I knew so many of them, then and later, but we're all changed now,
utterly, by industrial accidents, wild talents, gods. We've become psychics and knife throwers, rogues and religious fanatics and clowns, and
criminals. They wouldn't recognize me now, even if they remembered
me. Even if I wanted them to.

When I think about it, I guess CoreFire must have had a story, too,
something better than that a smug, popular jock accidentally became a
smug, popular superhero. No one could possibly be as boring as he
seemed.

At the end of the service a line forms leading to a makeshift shrine.
I join it in good order, and leave my wreath with the rest.

I'm threading my way out when Lily finds me.

"Hello, Lily." The crowd is flowing around us. People are noticing
Lily, of course, but no one looks twice at me.

"You're looking well."

"Thanks." I don't want to think about this. It's not as if they were even
together that long.

People are leaving. I can see Blackwolf starting to look for her. Any
second now, he's going to see us, and all hell is going to break loose.

"Listen, I'm sorry. . . ."

"It's okay."

"I'm . . ."

"It's okay, Jonathan. Go."

I never really had a girlfriend before that, or afterward, obviously. We
met around the time of the Legion of Evil fiasco that Mentiac had put

together, which had seemed like such a good idea at the time. For a few months, the concept had been making its way through a grapevine made up of prison-yard gossip, chitchat over the transfer of stolen goods, low-voiced exchanges in seedy underworld dives, stray psychical transmissions. . . . The idea was attractive; you get sick of seven-on-one battles that always turn bad, of getting the upper hand, just to have some teenage monkey wonder steal the keys to the weapons locker.

I met the original villain team once, the Delinquent Five, when they traveled to the present day to learn the future of their villainy. Their methods were hopelessly outdated, but in their day, they were geniuses! The Sinister Servant of Atlantis! The Diabolical Duplicate Sun! Their schemes are legend now, if only for their scope, their vision, the outlandish expense. It humbles even my own undertakings. But they came here seeking aid from their future selves, the selves they assumed would be wealthy and powerful, rulers of nations. When they found the world still ruled by governments and policed by heroes, they departed in silence, humbled. Maybe that was the beginning of the end for them.

Mentiac was semilegendary in the world of crime. A rogue supercomputer from the 1960s, built by a prescient trio of graduate students whose work went a little too far ahead of the curve. Mentiac got away from them, legend had it, suborned a forklift, and made his way into the labyrinthine sewer system underneath Chicago. He put down roots, and has been growing ever since, stealthily manipulating criminal affairs through phone lines. There's a miniature cult of hackers and hardware enthusiasts that buy him cooling fans and RAM.

Both Lily and I were contacted—I received a phone call over an extremely private line, Mentiac's circa 1977 speech synthesizer quacking out the time and place for our meeting. It was held in rented office space in a downtown L.A. high rise. It was a curious concatenation of the obscure powers of the world, a dozen maniacs, menaces, and underworld bosses, standing, sitting, or perching on bits and pieces of office furniture left over from a defunct talent agency. Of course nothing was agreed on, not even who had the right to speak first. No one

bothered to offer a name. Two of them turned out to have the same villain epithet ("the Infamous . . ."), and violence threatened to break out.
Mentiac's managerial skills were far from adequate, and the afternoon
wound down as one crime lord after another stormed out.

I kept staring at Lily. She stood with her back to a line of windows
facing west, the L.A. skyline behind her, blue sky shading into gray and
brown at the horizon. The colors deepened as the afternoon wore on
and the light grew orange and purple. It warped and rippled as it came
through her face and body. I'd heard of her, of course, mostly a bank
robber, pound for pound one of the strongest out there.

I could never tell when she was looking at me. Her eyes are like the
rest of her body, clear glass marbles, featureless as a statue's. I once
pointed out that she should be blind. Transparent eyes shouldn't work;
an optic nerve needs to reflect light. She made a rude noise.

There's a photograph of her charging a line of Paris cops, punching
her way out of a bank robbery. A blue-and-red défense de stationner
sign shows, distorted, through her midsection. She's in motion; her
right arm is a little blurry, just starting to swing. You can see the police
beginning to give way at the spot she's aiming for. She was never that
careful—she didn't have to be.

The last of the Napoleons of Crime had left, and we were alone, the
room darkening into shadow. It seemed natural to have a drink, once
we found a place that would serve us. So the Legion never materialized
as such, although a few of the robots later came back as the Machine
Intelligence Coalition, which I guess still has its asteroid somewhere.
And I met Lily.

We had dinner that one night at the fortress. We ate in the main control room, inside the long arc of the command console. Electricity
swirled overhead from the big generators I'd put in—it was my last
doomsday device but one. I lit candles anyway, and everything glinted
with the unaccustomed warm illumination. The robots cooked us a
sumptuous meal; afterward, I programmed them to do this funny
dance I had thought of, and we almost fell out of our chairs laughing.

Lily and I had a whole plan put together. I could outthink anyone they could throw at me, create byzantine schemes, and craft devices beyond imagining. She was all but unbeatable in a straight fight. She seemed to want it as much as I did.

I was deep in hiding when I heard about her and CoreFire. It was in the papers, how they'd been seen coming out of one of the hero-style bars in London, England being one of the countries where, it turns out, she's still legal. They'd been together a few weeks. He had always had a kind of loner, hero-on-the-edge appeal, and I guess that was part of it. And maybe it was her way of getting out of it, coming in from the cold. There was no mention of me; no reason why there should be.

I guess she got bored with me. Some nights on the island, it's beautiful—tropical constellations, jungle sounds, and luminous fish. But when it's five in the morning in the hideout and you can't sleep, and CNN's stuck on another economic summit, well, that's another feeling. You're blacked out and can't work because some hero team is trolling the South Seas, the heat is unbearable, and it's an hour until dawn, the slow tropical sunrise over the lagoon, and you're thinking about how far you are from home, and that this whole thing was maybe not such a brilliant idea after all, but there's nothing you can do about it now.

My style of work takes a lot of preparation. I build things and test them out. I have to order parts, or cast them myself. I have to pull all-nighters to debug my robots' pathfinding routines before an invasion. It isn't that interesting to other people.

I leave just as the trucks begin arriving. They're burying him in a nuclear-waste facility, I'm afraid, taking no chances. No one understood what kept him going all those years, what exactly was inside of him. Something might become unstable, burst underground. You can't put that class of object in Arlington National Cemetery.

I wonder who did do it, if it wasn't me. I pick my way down Amsterdam, among the mourners, walking faster now, until I'm lost among the thousands there, lost among people who can't fly or teleport or turn to water, just going their way, until I could be one of them. She'll tell them I'd been there. She's in that world now, and I suppose I understand. Those are her new friends. They could come after me, I guess, but it doesn't matter—I'm good at escapes. Maybe into the sewers, like the old days. It doesn't matter. You keep going. You keep trying to take over the world.

CHAPTER TWELVE

SAVE THE WORLD

He's gone. We've lost Earth's strongest, fastest, and probably just its best superhero. The man who defined the term, practically. The funeral is odd, surreal. I sit in the VIP section, feeling like an impostor in my New Champions outfit, a version of the same uniform he used to wear. People who really knew him cried; I just sit there, feeling like a tourist. In the pictures they clutch, CoreFire is still smiling his boyish smile, the man who never expected this, not in a million years.

I sit in front with the team, but I've never felt less like one of them. They've seen CoreFire shrug off surface-to-air missiles, dive unprotected into lava. You just didn't worry about CoreFire. You counted on him to make it through, to soak up damage the rest of the team couldn't handle.

It's a part of their lives I can't touch, and it makes my full membership feel like a joke. I think they broke up after Titan partly because they couldn't stand losing anyone else. Then losing him to Doctor Impossible, who they'd beaten before, who they thought was evil but at least a known quantity, that just makes it worse.

It hits them all differently. Blackwolf sulks, silently angrier than I've ever seen him. Elphin goes fairy-solemn, the closest to stillness I've seen in her. Feral is unreadable, but he smells of liquor. Damsel recedes even further into her lonely-leader mask.

I leave as soon as I can, brushing through the mass of reporters to one of our hired cars. A few shout my name, hoping for a picture; a couple even pronounce it right.

The day after the funeral, the old guard arrives to give us a briefing. Stormcloud and Regina, the surviving members of the Super Squadron, Damsel's father and stepmother. It's 11:31 a.m. by the digital clock that never stops blinking inside my left eye. There's probably a way to turn it off, but that knowledge vanished with the rest of the Protheon Corporation.

Blackwolf bristled when the call came in. These guys are supposed to be letting us run things our way now. Damsel speaks privately with him for a few minutes when he arrives, but her response to Regina is visibly cool. I don't know what happened to Damsel's real mom, but it doesn't look like the stepmom was much of a replacement.

It's practically a state occasion. I've never seen the Super Squadron up close before. Damsel and Blackwolf are famous, but these people *invented* us. Stormcloud hovers motionless, toes slightly pointed, resting solidly in air, as if encased in glass. A lot of people don't know how to hold themselves when they're flying; their legs just go everywhere. I don't know how it works—there is no ground effect that I can see, no radiation, nothing. Regina is another thing entirely—like an animated chess piece, she hefts the Scepter of Elfland, the weapon that can vanquish any mortal foe, if the stories can be believed.

We sit around the U-shaped conference table while Stormcloud glares out from the center, sometimes turning to gesture at the display screens. He has almost no perceptible body language, only a wave of the hand here and there to reinforce a point he's making. His hair is white; and his costume is a white-and-silver leotard with a simple blue-and-yellow logo on his chest, a diamond inside a circle, which must mean something profound to the cosmic types he runs with.

Regina stands next to him in full regalia, feet on the floor but radiat-

ing a queenly authority. Damsel's distaste is almost palpable. I wonder if
Regina wore that crown around the house.

Super Squadron members don't often come out in public. Stormcloud spends most of his time outside the solar system. Once, they
had the monumental quality of the large-scale scientific projects of
the period, like fission reactors and Saturn V rockets. Like the Cold
War–era science that spawned them, they've gone into eclipse.

World War II saw the first public superheroes, government-
engineered and packaged by a U.S. Army agency sifting tens of thousands of recruits for certain qualities. There were rumors of men pulled
out of their boot camp into special programs. They adapted to peace-
time life as crime fighters and government spokesmen.

But Pandora's box had been opened. World War II jump-started a
dozen new technologies and set off the widespread ransacking of the
Old World. People changed. Some of them were servicemen, the outcome of super-soldier programs on both sides. A few stranger and more
terrible things came out of the devastation of Europe and the Far East,
things formed in that crucible or driven from hiding as whole cities
were flattened and populations relocated.

There hadn't been anything like the Super Squadron before. Pharaoh, the first one, an archaeologist turned crusader. Lightwave, an
energy being, barely human after being translated into radiant information. Stormcloud, the all-American athlete turned living tornado, and
Regina, mystic powerhouse. Go-Man, the fastest man alive, and Paragon the Living Flame. They were hastily repackaged as an all-American
team, and sent out to defend the American way of life.

As the 1960s took off and their powers matured, they became larger
than life. These were men picked for loyalty, men without a lot of imagination, but they couldn't help but be changed by the things they'd seen.
You could see it in their faces. Laughing sorcerers from kaleidoscopic
dimensions, seductive alien princesses, far-future civilizations . . . their
training was eroding. They seemed eternal, archetypal, cosmic. It was
like watching the Beatles go from *Revolver* to *Let It Be*. They were seen

less and less in public; by 1976, nothing less than a full-scale threat to reality could draw them out.

Seeing Stormcloud is just another reminder of how far down the power scale I really am. He's impervious to any scan I can perform, his body registering solid white to X rays, like a black hole or a force field. Nothing I carry could even scratch him. The best efforts of twentieth-century biotechnology are nothing to him, mere cleverness, a gadget, gewgaw, half woman, half cuckoo clock. He's practically a god.

Behind him, Doctor Impossible's face looks down at us from three view screens, a close-up shot that must have been taken during one of his public tirades, his dark hair swept up and back.

"You've really done it this time. Wherever Doctor Impossible is, he's a menace to everyone and everything on this planet."

He goes on and on in his immaculate news anchor's baritone, citing patterns of attack, points of origin. Blackwolf talks back to him a few times, defending our efforts, and there's something a little gallant about it—this must be worst for Damsel. Lily slouches next to me in the back, arms crossed. Stormcloud doesn't look at her at all.

The room strobes and shimmers as I slide my vision up and down the spectra. In the higher spectra Stormcloud gives contradictory readings, ultradense but radiating energy, coruscating, celestial.

Outside, the sky shifts from black to a brilliant white, banded with red and blue.

I look around the room, and for the first time I notice something: Lily isn't truly transparent to all wavelengths of light. I know lasers go through her, and even microwaves, but my sensory range is very wide. No one's paying attention to me, so I scroll up and up into the higher bands until she stands out, opaque and solid, like anyone else.

I'm one of the only people who's ever gotten a good look at her face. With her transparent features, she's a glittering, half-seen menace. But in my altered vision, she's actually a rather ordinary, not unpleasant-looking woman, with a pretty, roundish face. I take a picture and save it.

When the lecture's done, we file out. Damsel heads to the roof, Blackwolf to the gym. We've all got some thinking to do. If we're going to be a real team at all.

It's 12:19 a.m. at the Champions Building, but I guess superheroes are supposed to stay up late. It's resident members only, plus Mister Mystic, who is favoring us with his absurdly dignified presence; apparently, he keeps odd hours as well. It's not a real meeting; everyone just ended up in the kitchen and started talking.

And this is how I pictured it, you know, a few brave souls staying awake to rescue the world from disaster. The overhead lights make the room look warmer. Lily and I are on stools; Mystic stands. Damsel's perched on the counter eating ramen noodles, talking fast. It's close in here; the steam from Damsel's noodles condenses down the side of Lily's arm. Lily's opened a bottle of wine.

"God, that was grueling." Blackwolf balances one of the steak knives on the end of his finger before testing it for throwing balance.

Damsel shrugs. "At least you don't get it at Christmas."

"He always hated me. He's a powers snob."

"Let it go, hon."

"Do you think he's right?" I ask.

"If he is, what can we do about it? He's too good at losing himself. He's out there somewhere, probably half a kilometer underground. Laughing his freaky laugh. Talking to his robots."

Feral looks up. "This was a revenge scenario. Villains aren't that complicated."

"I disagree." Damsel waves her chopsticks expansively. "He hasn't been sitting still. He's clearing the ground for something."

Lily says quietly, "If it's him, he's doing something new. He has to be. Otherwise, he couldn't have . . . you know."

"This is ridiculous. He's an evil genius. We're not going to second-guess him. Remember the space monster? No one saw that thing coming. Remember the fungus army?"

"He is indeed a most puissant foe. He seeks power, does he not? Land and serfs." Elphin perches on the counter like an oversized cockatoo. Silence falls.

"Elphin, what exactly do you think Doctor Impossible is?" Blackwolf asks.

"A magician? A villainous king, or . . . Fine. I do not know."

"There's gonna be a theme. Frogs. Hats. I don't know."

Lily raises a hand. "I hate to be the one to say this, but there's still no proof Doctor Impossible is involved."

Blackwolf stands. "This wasn't some purse snatcher; this takes genius." Lily's on her feet, and Blackwolf is, too, that knife suddenly back in his hand in a fancy three-fingered grip.

"Well, um, he was in jail the whole time. How do you explain that?" I jump in, not wanting to be part of a Lily-Blackwolf throw-down, not in the kitchen anyway.

"He might have left a trap for CoreFire," Damsel observes. "That's not out of character, is it?"

"And CoreFire just, you know, walked right into it?" Lily's pacing now.

"Well, he wasn't exactly Doctor Mind," Damsel says, and almost manages a smile. "But you still haven't told us how he did it."

"All right," I say. "Let's assume we're him, just for a minute. How would we do it? Take down CoreFire." I steal a look at Blackwolf. If anyone has an answer for this, it's him.

Blackwolf's almost too eager to tackle this one. "The autopsy gave us nothing, right? I had half the powered community in to scan it. We went over X rays, microscopic traces, iridium—nothing."

Damsel starts ticking off options. "You couldn't burn him. You couldn't crush him, cut him. He was too tough. I could have taken him down. Maybe."

"I did it once." Blackwolf says it quietly. It's not a boast.

"And you're lucky you have an alibi."

"What about the Enderri?" I ask.

"They don't come into this system. If they do, we know about it."

"What if he's hiding in the past? Killing our grandparents?" Feral muses, staring at the ceiling.

"We should be so lucky," Blackwolf mutters.

Damsel snorts. "Time travel makes me throw up," she notes.

"Everything makes you throw up," Blackwolf says, getting to his feet. "No, Impossible would want it face-to-face. He's nothing if not predictable. Besides, that wouldn't leave a body. I saw Jason's, and there was no mark. Nothing. CoreFire's the toughest thing this side of a black hole. It's provable."

"Well actually, I have some bad news for you on that score."

"Psychics? Something with his mind?" I'm trying to treat this like a murder, any murder.

"The guy was immune," Feral says. At least they're taking me seriously.

"But he managed it," Blackwolf goes on. "He did the impossible."

"And now with CoreFire out of the way, he's going for the whole thing."

Blackwolf's looking at me, holding my gaze. "I know the science as well as anyone. He's trying to solve conventionally impossible problems by unconventional means. What does that point to?"

Then he glances sideways toward the corner by the sink. Mister Mystic steeples his hands. He's been standing there this whole time, watching us and listening, waiting for us to get this far.

"You know what it means."

Even though it's late when we break up, I can't sleep. Blackwolf and Mister Mystic and Damsel and Elphin talked for an hour about magical artifacts, demons from other planes, demigods they have fought or had drinks with.

In the end, we made a list on a napkin. There are only so many items lying around that give the level of magical kick we're talking about and can still be carried around: Durandal, the Nightstar, Fortuna's Eye, the Flux Emerald, the Scepter of Elfland. The ones so powerful that with the right eyes, you can see them from orbit. What you'd have to have to kill CoreFire. We thought we knew where they were, but one of them must have gotten loose.

Find the artifact and we find Impossible and put him out of commission. Elphin and Mystic seem right at home with this new development, but for me it's a complete unknown. Mutants and machines and aliens may be weird, but they're still science. You can deal with them without upsetting anyone's belief systems too badly. But I fundamentally don't belong in the same room with something Guinevere is supposed to have touched.

I pace in my room awhile, then out in the corridors, data unfolding across my vision—maps, spreadsheets, case files, dates of last sighting, and lots of numbers, estimates of their capabilities, supernatural auras spelled out in ergs and kilowatts. A couple are grayed out, presumed lost or destroyed; a few others are colored red or blue, indicating curses, or, in a few cases, sentience. I let my machine brain assimilate it all—it's better at it, and the knowledge will be there when I need it.

Blackwolf is waiting for the elevator, kitted out for one of his nighttime patrols, canisters of nerve gas or whatever slung from his belt. We haven't really spoken since the funeral.

"Hi, Fatale. I have a couple of things I need you to crunch the numbers on later."

"Fine. I mean, that's fine, but . . . I just wanted to say I'm sorry. About CoreFire. All of this. I wish there was something I could do." I stumble over it, even though I'd been rehearsing it a moment earlier.

I reach out to touch his shoulder but then stop. He's Blackwolf, after all. Scourge of crime. The stylized wolf mask looks back, snarling like always.

"You didn't know him," he says, looking away.

"I'm sorry," I say after a moment.

"I appreciate it, but . . . you didn't know CoreFire."

"I know. And I know I can't really know what you're going through, but . . ." But what?

"It's really okay," he says, which is about the worst thing possible, and I actually start to get angry.

"No, it's not okay. Look, I'm not Galatea. I'm not a robot, is that clear? In spite of what everyone seems to think. I'm your teammate."

"I . . . No." Blackwolf's voice is frigid, angry.

"No, what?" I wait for him to go on.

"What I meant was, CoreFire was a jerk."

The elevator doors open and he steps inside.

"Blackwolf, I . . ."

"It's okay. Leave it," he mutters as the doors close between us.

I go upstairs to the Crisis Room and go back through CoreFire's records. Somehow, it can't be as simple as this. I think about what Lily said, that maybe it isn't Doctor Impossible. In fact, if there's anything we know about Doctor Impossible, it's that he hasn't had any luck against Core-Fire. From that perspective, he's practically the last person on Earth you could suspect.

CoreFire emerged from a laboratory accident with his full slate of powers; accident unrepeatable, of course. Problem is, you could accuse practically any villain out there of wanting him out of the picture. And, just as problematic, none of them had a way of doing it. If you look up his powers, you get "invincible," a word that occurs a spare handful of times among over fifteen hundred cataloged metahumans. Granted, there's an asterisk there for the iridium, but that approach hasn't led us anywhere so far.

Invincible. It's what everyone wants to claim they are. Not just tough, but downright invulnerable. Damsel is, nearly, and Lily's about equal, but either of them would fall after enough pounding. It's happened before. I'm well armored, but where I'm not metal I'm an ordinary woman.

They've got practically everything ever written about him. No way to go through it all, even for a machine like me. I run a computer search for the word—who else in the powers database qualifies for that ultimate accolade? Only one—the Pharaoh, a one-joke supervillain with a silly hat. I go back to CoreFire's file, looking again for anything unusual. The man was so damned uncomplicated. That bland, big-chinned countenance. Life had dealt him such a good hand, you couldn't even suspect him of cheating.

CHAPTER THIRTEEN

NEVER SURRENDER

I sit in a coffee shop in my funeral suit, my briefcase at my side. A risk to be out here, but information security is one of my fortes. My face isn't well known, and I've got my trusty sunglasses. No one knows my name. I watch the pedestrians go by—old people, homeless people, other people in suits, people with jobs. Paper cups and candy wrappers, and the sidewalk spotted with old chewing gum. It just seems unbelievable.

I close my eyes, for a moment. There are days when you just don't feel all that evil.

"Hey. Um. Honey? I think that guy over there is Doctor Impossible."

Shit.

This is how a superfight starts. Everybody has them, and you have to be ready. For a lot of people, these fights are the main thing, the main point of the exercise. Smashing things—this is what their powers are for. It's what I built the staff for, but to tell the truth I'm more about the science. If the science goes right, no one should ever get near me.

I stand up too quickly, knocking over the latte in front of me. It's nearly full, and the sound it makes as it slops over the table edge and onto the floor is unnaturally distinct. A little of it splashes onto my new slacks.

Blackwolf is standing in the doorway and staring right at me, talking rapidly into the communicator on his wrist, keeping one eye on me. A few civilians near me are picking up on what's happening. Shit shit shit. Obviously he knows who I am now. This will mean the Champions, and here I am, out of uniform. Lucky day, for them. I'm going to get pounded. These are the times when I wish I could fly.

"Who was the first person to hit you?" That was one of Steve the therapist's questions. But I don't know who he was. I was on my way out of a bank, calling for my escape helicopter; then I was picking myself up half a block away, and the side of my head was numb. Looking back, I saw where I'd skidded across the snowy sidewalk, hit the edge of a pillar on the front of the bank, broken off a section of the marble plate. My ears were ringing a little. Passersby were pointing; my cape was torn and muddy along one side. I'd gotten punched.

He was coming toward me, joking to somebody over the shortwave, getting ready to wrap this one up. A weekend hero in a home-brew exoskeleton cased in dirty yellow industrial plastic. The hydraulics whined as he trotted forward, a fancy long-barreled rifle slung across his back.

He stopped when he saw me getting up off the sidewalk. I can't describe the next few seconds too well because I don't remember much except that I was on him before he got the rifle up, and then he was flying backward through the bank window and into the lobby. Thinking back I must have already hit him a few times, because I could smell insulation burning, and the armor was having trouble righting itself. I'm strong, remember.

He tried for a roundhouse and connected a little, but he obviously didn't have full power. I could see his eyes and a bit of his face through the plastic helmet. He knew he was out of his depth. I knew it, too.

I braced a hand on his shoulder, got a few fingers under the rim of his helmet, and tore it off. He looked about forty-five years old, dark brown hair and a mustache, some firefighter on his weekend hobby. He looked terrified, and angry. I could hear sirens, but I stayed on him, held him down with one foot while I tore the armor off him piece by piece, taking my time, feeling the straps part, tearing wires out. So this is a hero, I thought. I told him what I thought of the workmanship on his armor, because I could tell he had built it himself, and then I left.

But that guy was an amateur, a fading sports hero with an engineering degree. These are the Champions, or what's left of them. They're world-class. They have communicators and a headquarters and VTOL jets. I wish Psychic Prime were here, and sober. Or Lily. Lily was so good at this part. Well, I'm a professional, too, or so the newspapers claim. I grab a napkin out of the dispenser and keep it over my nose and mouth while the civilians clear out. Always protect your identity.

No need to stand on ceremony. I snatch a mug from the table next to me, and with no windup throw it as hard as I can at Blackwolf's head. He sees it coming, of course, and it shatters harmlessly on the wall next to him. At least it gets him out of the doorway.

Christ. Okay. They must have been nearby, beating up on a small-timer, maybe, or just out shopping for more leotards. Police are probably already stopping traffic for them, setting the stage for my demolition. I have sixty seconds at most. I'm trying not to panic. Villains are supposed to be able to improvise. For a mask, I stick the napkin to my face with a roll of tape from behind the counter, then kick out a clear area in the middle of the tables.

It's not as bad as it looks. I'm wearing part of my costume under my clothes, and I've got my emergency kit. I open the briefcase, take out the Power Staff, and begin to piece it together. Zeta-powered of course— twenty-five years old, and still the best power source you can carry in one hand.

I peer outside. At least this isn't the whole team, just a few of the core members. And they aren't really a team at all anymore, although I haven't been following the soap-opera details. They fan out on the sidewalk in an arc, just like in their old publicity photos.

Blackwolf, "the Ultimate Crime Fighter," twirling one of his throwing knives. Damsel, "First Lady of Power," hovering three feet off the pavement. She'll be trouble. Feral, "Savage Streetfighter," barely keeping formation. Elphin, "Warrior Princess," imperturbable as ever, hefting her silly spear. Where did they get her, again? Rainbow Triumph, "Teen Idol with an Attitude." Christ.

But there's something a little off about it. They haven't been a team for quite a while, and to my professional eye they look . . . ragged. Damsel and Blackwolf used to fight next to each other, but they've put Feral between them in the formation. Feral seems even more manic than usual.

Beatable? Maybe.

Damsel borrows a megaphone from one of the cops. "Doctor Impossible! Is that you?"

"Who dares!?"

"You know us, Doctor Impossible. We're the Champions." Rainbow says something to her. "The New Champions."

"Fine. It's me."

"You're an escaped felon. We're giving you a chance to surrender quietly. This doesn't have to be a fight."

This sort of offer is a mere formality for a man with a Power Staff and a napkin taped to his face, and she knows it. I'm sweating, wishing I had my helmet. I promised myself once that I wouldn't go down in street clothes.

"You didn't think prison would stop me, did you? I'm back, and I'm going to take over the world."

"It's five against one, Doctor Impossible. Same odds as last time. Final offer."

I could bring up CoreFire, but I won't. They're shorthanded and they

know it. I'll get out of this, and I'm destined to rule this world.

"Come on in."

A brief pause ensues, a twitchy moment, like the beginning of a gunfight. It's always chancy, facing down one of these people. No matter who it is, you're going to be dealing with the end product of a long, improbable story, of a person so strange and powerful that he or she broke the rules of what is ordinarily possible. Whoever you're facing is guaranteed to be special—an Olympic wrestler, a radioactive freak, the fated son of somebody. They're winners. Taking a red arrow or a sea horse or the letter G as their symbol, they sally forth to make your life difficult.

Rainbow Triumph steps forward. One of my most popular enemies, posing in all her teen-idol glory.

"I know what you're going to say," I begin.

"You're under arrest." She says it like a bossy eighth grader, like "You're in my seat."

Blackwolf mutters, "By the numbers, people." He's got that twitchy autistic look he gets in a fight, his odd neurology hyperaccelerating, problem solving in real time.

But they've forgotten how fast I am. My wrist flickers, one of my sonic grenades. The heroes scatter. Damsel leaps to shield her ex-husband, but Feral is a sitting duck. It goes off with a boom, shattering windows down the block, setting off car alarms for a quarter mile. Feral flies like an oversized plush toy and I can count him out for about a minute. He'll be angry when he gets up. Dust rolls over everything.

And then Rainbow Triumph socks me in the stomach, and I fold up like a paper bag. She's the daughter of one of Gentech's top executives, and they've been working on her for years, ever since she was seven years old and they found out she had a degenerative bone disease. An experimental treatment saved her life, but the price was that she became, over time, a permanent inmate of their research and development division. After the first round of implants went in, they kept layering in new technology, more every year. Then the marketing department got its hands on her.

They've been grooming her as a superhero since she was eleven, starting her on search and rescue work, then moving up to crime fighting. She looks great on the news videos, but when you stand up close to her, you can see there isn't much human tissue left. I took a blood sample once when I was holding her hostage, just to see. It looked wrong, more orange than red, and it stank.

Say what you will about Gentech and its publicity practices, that girl can hit, and those fins on the sides of her gloves are razor-sharp. Stupidly, I'd been watching the show outside, and now a teenage girl is going to beat me senseless. She hits me again and I fall down. She doesn't weigh much, but she has this trick of bracing herself against the ground to get leverage. So much for the world's smartest man. I scramble around for a second under a table.

She comes on in a fighting stance, gorgeous wing chun stuff, her face set, with those scary eyes unblinking. She moves like speeded-up stop-motion animation. I'm strong, but let's face it, I'm not the fighter she is, not toe-to-toe. It's just not my métier. I pick up a chair and toss it at her, but she catches it, twists it out of my hand, and smashes it against the floor. I swing again, stagger her, but she pulls off an admirable spin kick to my chin. The world tumbles, and then I feel pavement against my back. I'm sliding out into the street, legs in the air. A news helicopter overhead is catching the whole thing.

Who's next? Feral's coming to in a furry heap of brick dust and broken glass. I wobble to my feet, staff in hand, barely in time to meet Feral's rush, an enormous man with the head of a tiger. He's over seven feet tall, prodigiously strong, like a pickup truck with claws. He's never killed anyone that I know of, but he's not particularly careful not to. He's ended careers before, plenty of them. I've never had him in the lab, so I never found out if he was a hyperevolved feline, or a gene graft, or a particularly nasty piece of veterinary surgery.

I step up to Feral and swing two-handed with the staff, catching him full in the face. It feels like I'm hitting a concrete wall with a baseball bat. His counterpunch bowls me over. I fly ten feet before grinding to a stop on the asphalt. I change tactics, the Power Staff sprays sleeping gas, and Feral staggers, falls.

If you haven't been this close to superhumans, you don't understand what it's like to fight them. Even when you've got powers yourself, the predominant impression is one of shock. The forces moving around you are out of human scale, and your nervous system doesn't know how to deal with it. It's like being in a car accident, over and over again. You never feel the pain until later.

Everything slows down. Lightning flickers overhead, then thunder. On one knee, I raise the staff just in time to absorb it. Damsel. The Power Staff's now in its fully powered state, force field humming and vibrating in one hand. Someone's in the shadows. Lily? Mister Mystic? I don't have time to think about it. Out in the street, it's going to be sheer murder.

Who's next? Damsel charges out of the smoke. I tear a parking meter from the sidewalk, wield it, keeping the Power Staff in the off hand. I keep her at bay and sort of manage to jab her in the eye. She takes another pass and I swing it at her. I'm faster, but she parries it with a forearm. She grabs me one-handed—I can feel the new suit tear as we swing around and into a brick wall. I'm staggering forward like a drunk, one sleeve hanging off my jacket, and she swoops in at me, but I sidestep and manage to plant a wad of plastique on the small of her back. She's clawing for it when it goes off, sending her backward in a long arc the length of a football field, over the shops and parked cars, to land with a distant crunch and tinkle of glass. Who's next?

Elphin, coming down out of the storm. A laser beam shatters off her spear point; then she hefts it to jab. The spear rings off my Power Staff with a bell-like clang. I hit her with the pocket sonic disruptor and she staggers.

Glancing around, I see the storefront is in ruins. When did that happen? A boom rattles windows up and down the street. The sky above us is darkening, thunderheads looming over Manhattan. My staff unfolds like a conjurer's trick and begins to glow. Bolts of power form a cage around me.

It's raining. Traffic has stopped for blocks everywhere. The force field is fading, raindrops sizzling off of it. Damsel is back, and blue fire blooms around us as we grapple, fingers intertwined. I can't keep this up much longer. Feral has a car up over his head, arms straight, the thing balanced on the midpoint, a pretty nice sedan. The thing creaks, and something in the trunk shifts, but he keeps it there long enough to brace for a throw. There're too many of them. The light around Elphin's spear point is getting brighter, and I back up. Even I can feel that heat.

The battle comes to a halt momentarily, like the instant of silence in a crowded bar. Elphin raises her spear as high as she can over her head. Then a blinding flash. Lightning strikes once, twice. Rain smell, steam, the summertime reek of hot asphalt. My Power Staff absorbs the charge, but the noise and shock are shattering. The sidewalk underneath me cracks, blackened.

Time to stop thinking about a clean win. There's a submarine waiting for me in the Hudson River. If I can make it a few blocks along Eighty-third, this will all be behind me.

I glare back at my assembled foes; then my staff belches a concealing smoke. Stooping, I heave a manhole cover out of the street, then drop down into the sewers. A beam from my Power Staff welds it shut above me. That will hold them a moment. The staff's charge is almost down to nothing.

My eyes adjust, and I can make out the ancient tile on the floor and ceiling. I've been down here before. It's startlingly quiet, and you get used to the smell. You wouldn't think it could be so quiet in Manhattan. There's an inch or two of water in here, but mercifully it's fairly clean. A few blocks away I'll find daylight, and freedom.

"What happened to CoreFire?" Blackwolf's quiet voice carries through the tunnels. Of course it's him—I'd missed him in the fight overhead. Who else would have charted the battle ahead of time, known the sewer map, come straight here, and waited? He steps into view, cracking his knuckles theatrically.

"Jesus, Blackwolf, I didn't do it! You've got the wrong guy." I wish I hadn't blown up his ex-wife just now.

One of his knives ricochets off the tile, right into my head. I aim the staff and try to blast him, but he saw it coming a second ago. He's already in the air, swinging off a ceiling pipe, covering the ground between us much too fast. The kick takes me in the chest.

I know he doesn't have any powers, but he's scary as hell, so graceful that even now it's hard not to stop and watch. I wonder what makes him this way, what primal, originary scene branded him with an obsession that makes him dress like an animal, and helps him fight. Who does he see when he looks at me?

I try to stand again. My legs don't feel all that firm, but he gives me time. He's just standing there waiting for me.

"How'd you do it?" he demands. "How did you kill him?"

He hits me twice before I can answer, or even move again. I'm supposed to be fast, but the man's like a demon. It's just the two of us in the sewers, no TV cameras, and he isn't going to hold back. He's one of the ones who enjoy this.

"Was it the iridium?" he snarls.

"I don't know! It wasn't me!"

I lunge for him, but it's as if he's seen this movie before. His hands close on my wrist and he swings me around into the wall.

"Was it a black hole? Was it magic?" He kicks me in the head again, and I flop over into the muck.

Another kick, this time in the stomach, and pocket change fountains from my trousers. He can spot any move before I do it. I need to throw him off his game, if that's possible.

"Ask your wife." It comes out in a gut-punched voice, but he hears me.

"What?" He freezes a moment, graceless for once. I kick the legs out from under him, then grab an ankle and twist. Desperate, I'm strong enough to lift him, spin, and smack him into the wall. I think he's stunned.

I stagger on, splashing through garbage, hoping to God he doesn't get up and run after me, but too tired to do anything about it if he does.

This is why I'm not ready. This is the part I always forget about until it's too late, the flaw in the plan, the part where they hit you again and again. A less reflective man might have missed the point but, as I keep telling you, I'm a genius.

The last phase of my plan is coming, the one I haven't figured out yet. I need to be invincible, and soon. By the time the moon comes into position.

I spot a set of rungs set in the wall, scrabble up them and out into the fresh air, gasping on my hands and knees on the sidewalk. Only two blocks left. Pedestrians stream around me, like they don't even know I'm in a fight. Then they all look up.

My feet leave the ground, and the breath goes out of me. Damsel has me this time, clutching my lapels in her fists, dragging me up. We climb, story after story, out of the chasm of Broadway. I can feel the warmth of her breath on my forehead as we shoot up past the highest rooftops, and for a moment I hang above the city grid, bathed in the midafternoon sun, bright as any hero ever born.

Then the shock of it wears off, and I realize my hands are free. There is a capsule on the inside of my mouth, containing a tiny sample of gas I bought from an alien visitor, the atmosphere of an ocean planet forty light-years away.

I grab her fists in mine, bite down hard, and nerve myself to kiss her on the lips. The last trick, one I've held in reserve for years. She's astonished, openmouthed, and my poison breath passes into her.

She falls away, fainting, and I hover on the Power Staff's diminishing charge. In ten minutes, she'll have recovered, but I'll be miles away. Lazily, lucky for once, I drift, and the breeze takes me west and down over the rooftops of Columbia students, over the trees of Riverside Park, and into the Hudson River.

I sink toward the dark water as my submarine surfaces underneath me, and I'm already charting my next destination. Next time, it won't be so easy. I take one last look at Manhattan, sketch a bow, and descend.

CHAPTER FOURTEEN

AT LAST WE MEET

Lily and I have been up for hours, combing through the debris of yesterday's fight for clues about where Doctor Impossible came from, or what he's going to do.

I'm up here as penance for having missed the event while running down a false lead in Monongahela, Pennsylvania. Lily managed to miss it, too—vacation day supposedly—and no one knows where Mister Mystic was. Damsel's in a foul mood. Everyone has been, since the funeral.

It would help if the rest of the team would talk about what happened yesterday. Most of what I know, I got from newspapers. As far as I can tell, Blackwolf bumped into an out-of-uniform Doctor Impossible and called the alert. Ritual banter followed, after which Doctor Impossible proceeded to thrash the lot of them on national television and escape via means unknown. Blackwolf got bested in single combat, and Damsel, our resident powerhouse, went down on some vulnerability that's not even listed in the central computer. Feral's going to be in the hospital for weeks. They're killing us in the press.

With the rest of the team licking their wounds back at HQ, Lily and I do a slow walk-through of the rubble. Neither of us has done this before.

I try to start us off. "They sure managed to break a lot of windows."

"That's what I got, too."

"I feel stupid for hanging around here. We should go to the zoo or something." Yesterday's freak storm has passed and I'm starting to overheat.

The whole block is cordoned off with yellow police tape, and the police are watching me closely as I walk around in the middle of the street. They must be wondering why the Champions wrecked this block, let Doctor Impossible slip away, then sent a notorious villain and somebody they've never heard of to figure out what happened.

I cycle viewing modes in the hopes something exciting will come up to justify holding back the cleanup crews this long.

I give it another try. "So. Blackwolf bumps into Doctor Impossible. Calls the Champs . . ."

"Except the ones who are out of town, and it's totally not their fault," Lily adds.

"Where were you?"

"Robbing a bank, thanks."

"So . . ." For all I know, this is a test, and Blackwolf's watching us from somewhere. In the coffee shop, Rainbow Triumph's pointed girl-size shoe prints square off against the marks of the supercriminal's loafers.

"He leaves the Starbucks . . ." Lily prompts. Residual trace of some zeta energy leading out the front window.

"What's he doing in a coffee shop?"

"Genius is mysterious."

"And there's a . . . fight." I gesture uncertainly.

Outside, the pavement has buckled and heaved under blows of incalculable force. The energy traces here are more distinct: Damsel's slashing track through the air; yellow-green where Elphin managed one of her weather tricks; Doctor Impossible's staff leaving a riot of colors and shapes.

"A big fight. Five against one." Lily can't see the energy traces, but it's pretty obvious what was going on. The Champions' collective energies focused on one man who wouldn't go down.

"And I guess he got away here."

The Doctor's energy track leads to a manhole cover. Classic—no wonder they're so upset. Lily lifts it up one-handed.

"Ech. Mister Mystic skipped the fight, too. Why doesn't he go down there?"

"I'll go. I can do some spectroscopy on the fight scene."

"Show-off."

Street noise cuts off abruptly when I lower myself in. The city's been through here already to check for structural damage, so the scene is probably worthless, but it's a relief to be offstage for a minute.

"See anything?" Lily calls from overhead.

"Hang on."

There's a lot of cracked tile where Blackwolf and Doctor Impossible met up. The Doctor caught him off guard somehow and threw him into the wall. A chip on the wall shows where Blackwolf threw one of his knives, and I have a lame impulse to find it and hand it back to him, before I remember he's a millionaire.

"I think your boyfriend beat up my boyfriend," I call back.

"He's not my boyfriend."

"Fine."

"And you're not going out with Blackwolf. He just talked to you."

"Okay!" I'd told her about it, what Blackwolf said. Who else could I tell?

"Any clues, Madame Detective? Are we done? The police are looking at me."

"I guess we're done."

Just then, my radar pings on another object, small and cool and metallic, just under the water. There's a handful of loose change, an old-fashioned subway token, and a motel key with a tag that reads *Starlight Motel, Queens, New York*.

Cold entrances are dicey when you're talking about a metahuman living situation. There's no real way to guess what weirdness you'll find, anything from genetically enhanced cockroaches up to a pocket black hole. For a second, I think about getting the others.

But it's worth the risk for the chance of catching Doctor Impossible alone and making that collar. Forget the newspaper headlines—the look on Damsel's face will be more than worth it.

The key goes in and turns. I open the door as quietly as I can, feeling a little foolish—for all I know, he's standing right on the other side. What will I say, exactly? But the lights are off and the living room is empty. I wait for a moment in the hall, hoping this isn't one of my bad decisions. It's 6:59 p.m.

It's warm inside, quiet and dark, and I stand in the doorway, letting my organic eye adjust. I can make out shelves and a couch, and garbage on the floor. A white plastic telephone sits on an end table that looks like it was salvaged from the curb outside. It has one drawer, which hangs open, displaying a jumble of circuit boards, slabs of coarse-grained green plastic laced with metal. Loose objects crowd the shelves—a doll's head, a lumpy piece of pottery, a plastic figurine from a Japanese animated show.

The room is coated with a layer of dust, which has gotten into everything. In the corners, power cables and network cords lie half-covered in it. The walls are painted with the bumpy, gooey white paint endemic to cheap apartments in New York, and it laps onto the edges of doorknobs and light switches and windowpanes. The air smells of sweat and decayed food and a burned odor from the radiator.

I step inside. A plastic bag hangs from the doorknob in lieu of a garbage bag, spilling over with take-out containers and used paper towels, a bare concession to the idea of housekeeping. Someone ate and slept here for a few weeks at least.

To my left, the last of the sunlight filters through dirty windowpanes and onto carpet fragments scattered on the floor and grimy linoleum tile. Ahead of me, a short corridor ends in the half-open door of a bathroom, and what must be a bedroom door on the left. Living room first, I decide. On the carpet, a polished metal tube, outsized, oxidized at one end, as if it had once been part of an immense engine. The surface has a crazed patina that looks superheated. It must have come out of one of the Doctor's rocket planes.

The couch has a faded plaid upholstery that looks as if it had spent a few weeks outdoors. On the floor, almost buried under cardboard boxes and packing materials, is a robotic hand almost four feet across, three jointed fingers and a thumb, painted a carnival blue and red. Where the wrist should be, it trails long wires, as if torn from its owner with immense force. I touch one broad, cool finger. The door sighs shut behind me and cuts off the street noise outside. Overhead, a neighbor paces around. A toilet flushes elsewhere in the building.

In the sudden quiet, I hear cooling fans, and the whir and the chirp of hard drives read/writing. I follow the sound down the hall, and in the bedroom, green and red LEDs spangle the dusty air like fireflies, next to a futon laid out on the bare floor. I'm conscious of being at the heart of something.

He must have come here as a last resort, when the money for castles and islands ran out, when they found the last of his offshore accounts and buried caches. And he was here not too long ago.

I look over the tangle of circuitry, careful not to touch. He must have started with five or six off-the-shelf PCs, but none of it looks stock now. Some of the wiring is plainly stuff that's never been done before, inexplicable but obviously intentional rewirings, chips sawed in half, or soaking in solutions in Burger King glasses. I'm looking at a supercomputer. He probably bought everything at CompUSA and wired it all together himself on his hands and knees. It's easy to forget how smart he is.

I should have called in by now, but I want to know what he's doing. I sit down on the futon and look for a port on the back of one of the computers that I can jack into. Even my plug sizes are getting out of date.

The data sheets down across my display in blue-white ASCII, a hugely complex piece of engineering, all shear forces and rotational inertia. Diagrams show the Earth wrapped in an interconnected web of lines of force, thousands of tiny vectors. Something big and complicated is being simulated or controlled from here, but I don't have the math for it. Most of the minds that can understand this kind of thing are on the wrong side in the first place. Half a dozen lines crisscross and connect at a symbol or diagram sketched in, what looks like a lightning bolt. He's got a question mark next to it, too—something he's still working out? The words "More power! Invincible!" appear, underlined.

Pages and pages of orbital schemata, asteroids, planets, comets moving around, columns of figures, stranger things: A fat man? A jewel? Stars and governments, heroes and villains are connected by dotted lines extending through space, time, and other dimensions. This must be how a mastermind sees the world. I see Damsel and Blackwolf, and the others are scattered around. I don't see myself there, unless I'm the letter F? Would he know about me? Do I want him to?

I download it all, always listening for a footstep in the hallway. But I don't think he's coming back.

It's on the way out that I see it. There's a twin to the enormous robotic hand lying on the kitchen counter, but this one is human-size, intact, with a cunning ball joint where the arm would go. Where my arm would go, actually, because this time I recognize the workmanship.

Back at the Champions', this time I'm the one standing at the giant screen in the Crisis Room. I lay out what I've found—the key, the motel, the diagrams. I throw the Doctor's calculations up on the big screen, page after page, while they listen to my analysis.

Blackwolf scribbles notes frantically as I talk, but he's not looking at me. I tell them everything but that last thing.

When I'm finished, Blackwolf and Damsel are talking fast, overlapping each other's sentences.

"It's good work, Fatale," he says, barely glancing up.

"Really good. This is going to do it." Even Damsel is smiling for once, wickedly. "It's confirmation. He's going magical."

"And he's desperate. We've got a time limit."

On the screen, spheres rotate around one another, and around the Sun. There's a critical window of time coming in a few days.

"Fine, but what's that?" I point to the lightning bolt.

"Whatever it is, we don't want him to have it."

Lily asks, "What did it look like? The room."

I shrug. "I don't know . . . evil impoverished grad student?"

She doesn't look happy. "You're right that he's desperate. I think he's going to try to take over the world."

Blackwolf stands unnaturally still in his skintight black leather, his lips moving silently every minute or two. I look closer. He's saying "Doomsday."

He's contemplating a white board scribbled nearly solid with over-laying diagrams in red, green, blue, yellow. It's not all that dissimilar from what Doctor Impossible was working on, and I wonder for a second what Blackwolf would have been like as a villain, and what kept him from going that route. I remember the Doctor's squalid surroundings, the smell of spoiled food. When Blackwolf speaks, it's in a grim monotone.

"No villain ever beat CoreFire. But what if a hero could?"

"You know the cataloged powers." Damsel looks bored. "I could have done it. You could. Who else?"

"Lily."

"No. I'll vouch for her." Damsel sounds sure of herself. I wonder why.

"We need to expand this list."

Damsel stands. "Say whatever it is you're saying."

"What if it's the Scepter of Elfland?" Blackwolf licks his lips before he says it. I've never seen him nervous before. There was a bit of silence after. A taboo subject. Damsel's expression is, as always, hard to read, but if I had to guess I'd say she's appalled, and at least two other things. Apprehensive? But maybe a little bit grateful to Blackwolf for coming out and saying it. Maybe she'd like to take a swing at that stepmother after all.

Any mortal foe.

I know Blackwolf keeps a lab somewhere upstairs. It's already a late night, but I wait until 2:30 before I go looking. Everyone is asleep and the whole building is quiet, so I just wander around until I find it. There's a keypad lock, but, as I said, I'm good at things like that.

It's cold inside, and pitch-dark except for bright halogen bulbs illuminating the work area. He's in shirtsleeves and a mask. I can see wine purple bruises from yesterday's fight.

"Fatale." He doesn't even have to turn around. He's going over tapes of the fight, frame by frame, on a big flat-screen monitor. Elphin's frozen mouth open in a silent battle shout.

"Yeah. Hi."

He goes on working, paging forward frame by frame. Doctor Impossible is zapping someone off-camera with his walking stick.

"Look at that. It's not the same staff he had before. He got a new one."

"Sorry I missed out."

"Not your fault."

Outside, the city looks asleep, except for a few late workers twinkling in the office blocks around us.

"Look, I don't know how to say this. . . . I need you to take a look at my enhancements."

"Sure. You having a hardware problem?"

"Kind of."

"Just step up on the scanner. Ah, can you take the costume off? It's shielded."

"Okay."

I set down my bag and step onto a glass-topped dais, a kind of walk-in MRI. There's a lot about my body I don't like people to see, but I guess I asked for this. It takes a minute to get the costume off. I strip down to the tank top and panties I wear underneath and take a breath. LED indicators run up my side and down one leg, glowing brilliant in the darkness. The air on my skin raises goose bumps. He can see just about everything that's been done.

"Galatea helped build this when she was here. Just hold still for a couple of minutes."

He does something at the keyboard and the scanning element swings over soundlessly on two long arms and gently encircles my midsection before doing a slow transit up and then down. The results come up on two of the big monitors.

It's a full-body scan. I haven't seen this view of myself since Protheon closed. I can see my skeleton—everything they did. On the screen, my fusion plant pulses like a second heart. A cascade of cables and jewel-like points descend through me. When I move, it moves. Looking at the screen, Blackwolf is looking at me in a way no one has ever looked at me, with power or without.

He gives a low whistle. "You're a piece of work."

"I'll take that as a compliment."

"I'm not kidding. This is brilliant work. Totally unconventional. Somebody wasn't kidding around." I'm blushing, furiously, but the monitor doesn't show that.

"Yeah, well, that's kind of what I wanted to talk to you about. I think . . . I think I found out who the somebody is." I take a breath, then reach into the bag and toss him the metal hand I've been carrying around all day. "This was in Doctor Impossible's motel room."

He turns it over and over, his long fingers feeling the joints, spreading the fingers. You can see the same configuration in my own arm, right up there on the screen, and I can almost feel his hands on me. There's a long silence. I can hear the air conditioning, a couple of machines beeping, the thrumming of hard drives.

No one knows much about Blackwolf's own origin. Why he's so good at things. A lot of people, including me, think he's the outcome of a government breeding project. But that doesn't really explain the crime fighting, the obsessive behavior. I want to ask, but I don't.

"Has anyone else seen this?" he asks.

"Just you."

"He made CoreFire, too, you know. That's the rumor." He takes my hand, the real one, turns it over, feeling the metal bones. His hands are still warm in the cold laboratory.

"What if there's a bomb? Or a microphone, or a tracking device?" I feel excited just saying the words, and I'm not even sure why.

"The NSA must have checked you over. I'll look myself, but you're clean, I'm sure of it."

There never was a supersoldier project. I must have been part of one of his schemes, and not even one of the good ones. There was never going to be another one of me, unless we were going to be superhenchmen robbing banks for a malicious idiot in a cape. But I'm not even that; I'm a discard. Or am I?

I step off the platform and snatch my hand back. "Get it off the screen."

"Fatale . . ."

"Just get it off. Get rid of it."

"I really don't think it matters."

"Maybe I'm one of them." I'm whispering now. "Did that ever occur to you? It doesn't have to be a bomb. I could be a traitor. It could be written in the code."

I'm making this up. Doctor Impossible probably doesn't even know I'm out here. But maybe he does, and I'm under his control. Maybe this is all part of it.

Blackwolf widens his stance a little as he listens, one foot feeling the floor. His pupils dilate behind the mask, and his breathing changes. I can see him waking up, noticing me in a way he'd never done before. As a threat.

"I could be the one. He could have planned every bit of this. I wouldn't even necessarily have to know about it." I take a step toward him. I know I'm right, and it feels powerful in a way I haven't known before.

"Fatale . . ." He doesn't go on. He's trying to figure out how to beat me. I honestly don't know what will happen next, but something has to. I take another step, and reach for him.

He moves so fast, he's an afterimage on the cameras. Somehow I never thought of him as dangerous. He reads human to all my senses, just bone and meat, like the rest of them.

The world slows down. I'm moving into fighting stance, arms coming up, but it's too late. He doesn't hit me that hard, but he gets just enough leverage behind me to knock me off my feet, all 450-plus pounds. By the time I hit the tile, he's pulled an extensible police baton from somewhere I didn't see. He's straddling me, one hand pinning one of my arms back, the other holding the baton cocked, trembling. I'm ready to unleash some seriously nasty countermeasures, but he's stopped. It's a submission hold, and if I were human, I would be in agony, but I'm not.

It's as good a chance as I'll ever get. I could punch him through the ceiling, but I lean up to kiss him. He's breathing hard. It's been a while since my nonmetal days, and I've kind of forgotten how this goes, but I bet I can figure it out. My artificial nerves are lit up, even better than I thought they would be. I can feel the taut muscles in his forearms, even the tremor of his skin, but my hands are as strong as his, stronger even. I'm steel maybe, but I'm not dead. I'm getting a lot of error messages from my onboard systems—they don't like having anybody this close. They keep wanting to electrocute him or break his wrist, and part of me is busy stopping them.

Our lips touch, and for a second it's everything I thought it would be. The metal in my jaw is awkward but somehow exciting, and he kisses back. I pull him down to me, get his weight against me. I'd forgotten what it was like to want something this much. He reaches up under my shirt, and the feeling is so good it makes me want to cry. Nobody but a surgeon has touched me there for a really, really long time.

Then I make a mistake. I reach for the mask, and he catches my arm, ready to break it. His jaw sets, and I'm dealing with Blackwolf again. It's like watching a different personality take hold, and I get a glimpse of what he's always holding back, a terrible, unappeasable mourning. Something really god-awful must have happened to him at some point.

And the only woman he'd chosen was the closest the world could produce to an unbreakable girl. I'll never be anything but an also-ran, half invulnerable, half twentysomething nobody. Metal alloy and flesh are nothing compared to Stormcloud's daughter.

Before he can do anything, I catch him under the arm and lift him off of me as I get to my feet. I could break bone with the grip I've got, but I set him down.

"I'm sorry," he says.

"Forget it," I say, grab my costume, and slip out. The early-morning corridors are pitch-dark, but not to me.

CHAPTER FIFTEEN

MAYBE WE ARE NOT SO DIFFERENT, YOU AND I

The way people talk about it, you'd think anyone could build a doomsday device. Like it's not a power at all. But you have to remember everything, catalog everything, and realize how to fit it together in a new way, a way that solves or destroys or takes everything apart. If it were so easy, they would have figured out what I'm doing by now.

This is the last piece, the jewel, the one I've been putting off. I didn't want to come back here, and I didn't want to do it this way. I'd hoped for something subtler, and a fresh invention. But then, I'd hoped for a lot of things.

I'll have to hope nobody sees a miniature submarine come whirring up the Charles River by night. They've been one step behind me for a week, Elphin and Damsel and the cyborg whose name I keep forgetting, skimming over the coastal waters. But I'm shielded from their vision, and it holds, this time.

The physics building used to be my second home, and slipping in a window is nothing to me. No one guards this stuff anyway; there are just a couple of padlocks to keep students out, and I shoulder my way through them with barely an effort. Practically my last work as a legitimate scientist, but it might as well be a stuffed polar bear.

Inside, the air gets dustier, staler. How many years has it been? I'm in front of the last door, and beyond it I can see the silhouette of the familiar apparatus, shrouded in dust cloths.

But there's a dark figure leaning in the doorway, poised and elegant. This is the one I should have foreseen, the logical adversary. The most dangerous of the New Champions.

Mister Mystic has the pencil mustache and jet black hair of a cartoon stage magician, with high cheekbones and a long, handsome face. He stares unruffled into the barrel of my homemade plasma rifle as if it were a bouquet of flowers. He smiles and tips his hat, defiant yet elegant.

"I know what you've come for. But they've set me to guard it, you see."

In his long, graceful fingers he flourishes a long black-lacquered wand, with an inch of white tip. He invariably appears in full evening dress—a tuxedo, dazzling white gloves, and a cape made of a cloth that flows and drapes itself with impossible elegance, regardless of local atmospheric conditions. He's older than most of us, at least in apparent age.

I step forward and swing, and the fight is already over. He folds up at the first punch like any civilian, slumps to the floor, his cape settling over him. I prod the cape with my foot, half-expecting it to be empty, but there's a warm body, and it's him. He just lies there, breathing.

But Mystic has a way of wrong-footing you. I step over him and through the doorway, and everything ceases to make sense. Instead of the lecture hall beyond, I'm in a small room with identical doors on each wall. God, I hate fighting magicians.

Mister Mystic has always kind of bothered me. The Champions' personnel database lists him as William Zard, a failed stage magician and petty crook. None of this explains why he thinks he's a superhero.

The true history of William Zard is hardly one to strike terror into his foes. No college education—he barely finished high school. For two years, he traveled with the Merchant Marine—Europe first, then India, then the Far East. He jumped ship in Hong Kong, and there's a notation from the American embassy concerning vagrancy. He must have made his way inland, wandering through Tibet, learning from a little-known group called the Seven, a semireputable New Age cult. He popped up again in the United States almost four years later, under the name Mister Mystic. Then we have the first record of his crime-fighting adventures.

At first, we thought he was just a hypnotist, one of those quiet, liquid-voiced masters of men. Eyewitnesses were vague, or they couldn't remember meeting him at all, even when placed at the scene.

He still used his fists as much as his voice. Hypnotism was a show-man's flourish, window dressing for old-fashioned fisticuffs and detective work. But he never abandoned the elaborate accoutrements of the stage magician—the final phase of an arrest would be an elaborate coup de théâtre, a curtain jerked aside to reveal the culprit already chained up, the stolen goods already back where they belonged. He had a showy knack for staging his own apparent death.

I back out, suspicious of what will happen next, and find him still there in the hall, collapsed.

I don't like magic. I think I've said that. There are too many frauds mixed up with it; it reeks of old-time vaudeville and stage shows and con men. It's shadowy and psychological and too much like hypnotism, and nobody likes what it implies about the world. It goes against the whole premise of my—well, my whole thing. That we live in an ordered universe. That the stars and planets swing around one another according to laws. And that a smart-enough man, a man who is very, very smart indeed, can apply these rules at the right time in the right way, curving one orb just a few hundred feet closer to another, and thus make himself their master, and master of all. If Mister Mystic thinks he lives in a world different from that one, I have to prove that he's wrong and I'm right.

Mystic's adventures take place in other dimensions, or concern legendary artifacts whose existence flatly contradicts the most basic understanding of the historical record. He seems most comfortable in his own milieu, up against werewolves or Indian fakirs—I don't know these people—mystical menaces that never even crop up unless he's around.

What are his powers? Depending on who you ask, he's a player on a cosmic scale, or a skinny man in a cheap tuxedo. But I know for a fact he has gotten out of situations that should have killed a normal man. I myself saw him enter the Mayfield Sanitarium before it collapsed, and we all know how badly that situation ended. If he is a fraud, he must be a very brave one.

I tie him up in his own cape, then shake him awake.

"Magic's not going to save you, Zard. Fix whatever you did to the hallway."

"It's not magic, exactly. Not the way you're thinking of it."

That punch didn't bother him as much as I thought it had. He lies there bound and blindfolded, but from the sound of it, you'd think he was holding *me* captive.

"Tricks, then. Whatever it is you've done."

"You want to get through the door, don't you? Go ahead. Try. After all, you don't even believe in magic."

I look back toward the doorway, then nod. I can't stay here all night. I grasp the cloth of his cape and pull him easily across the floor behind me. Whatever's in there, he's going to meet it, too.

A second room, as before. Then a third, and a fourth. I count footsteps. We should have been in the lecture hall by now. We should be outside the building.

"Be reasonable, Zard, or Mystic, whatever you call yourself. It's the twenty-first century. Now where are we?"

"When you were in the eighth grade, your guidance counselor told you you were a genius. Remember that?" He ought not to have known that. His voice rises and falls in a seductive rhythm, the voice of a hypnotist, but I know about such tricks.

"So . . . so what?"

"Well, mine did, too," he says, laughing a magician's stagy laugh. And then the spell precipitates out into the warm air, a pattern of frost and mist like a huge snowflake gradually becoming apparent, etched into the pavement. The charge in the air feels like the third act of a play, or the light on a playground a moment before sunset.

The cape lies empty on the tiled floor, still tied.

Never mind. Teleportation isn't necessarily magic. He thinks the ordinary rules don't apply to him, but they do. They apply everywhere, even at Harvard. That's what science is. But when I step through the doorway, it's not the same building. It's not even Cambridge.

This is wrong. I've seen this place before, but only from the outside. It's Mister Mystic's house, an ordinary, square-shouldered brownstone by a back corner of Prospect Park in Brooklyn. Faded purple velvet curtains veil the dusty windows. Outside, tufts of grass grow in the neglected yard; plastic bags have snagged on the low wrought-iron fence facing Ocean Parkway. I'm breathing the exhausted air of the city's late-summer evening.

And it seems to have been abandoned years ago. From the front hall, I can see into the sitting room and the dining room, and the staircase leading up to a second floor. A feathering of dust lies on the coffee table, the Victorian ornamentation, the ashtrays.

Tricks with time, I suppose. I try to remember when it was I left the submarine. But what am I afraid of? Ghosts? Witches? Ridiculous. But there is documented evidence of strange heroes who came from Europe in the war years, out of Dresden and Warsaw, things disturbed out of their long rest. Men who could dissolve themselves, heat metal at a distance, shriek loudly enough to shatter buildings. But I'm obliged to ignore such things until they're proven true. That's science.

A flicker in the dimness—he's here. Taking no chances, I pull the trigger on my plasma pistol. But the beam strikes nothing but air and glass. The mirror shatters, and I'm alone in the darkening house. Where are his teammates? That half-alien woman, that cyborg who replaced Galatea, those are people I understand.

I wave my flashlight across a line of bric-a-brac, souvenirs from Europe and the Far East. Maybe he brought something back, some trick or device I've never heard of. How much space can there be back here? A stuffed tiger looms in the angle between two hallways. I watch it carefully for a minute, but it doesn't move.

Sitting rooms, smoking rooms, a library, a music room. I lose count of the stairways; they go up and down in threes and sevens, according to no plan I can detect. I listen for traffic noise, but there isn't any.

I stop in a paneled hallway by a bust of Schiller. I need to draw him out.

"Why not make this a fair fight, Mystic? Because you know you're a fake. You have to hide and play tricks! I know your secrets! I know about the Seven!" My voice sounds weak, lost in all this darkness.

But he calls back, the voice coming from anywhere and nowhere. "You think I found something. You think the Secret Seven gave me something, some device. Is that your theory?"

"A gadget, some trick. You're not a magician, Zard. It's not possible!"

"Relax, Doctor. Enjoy the show. Didn't you ever want to believe in magic?"

His voice is a perfectly refined baritone, a theater voice, nothing like what you'd expect from a petty crook from the suburbs. It sounds noble, and a little sad.

I follow it into another darkened room. I'm starting to lose focus—a drug in the air, in the candles? Am I back at Harvard now? Or still under the ocean in the submarine? I grope for the submarine's steering wheel, then remember. I'm in Mister Mystic's house. It's dark outside now.

"I can see in the dark, Doctor. Did you know that?"

"No. No, I didn't," I reply under my breath.

"You think you have secrets from me. But I can see in your darkness, too, down below the dungeon you once built. The fire beneath the world, and the magical winter. The snake that ate your heart."

Lights come up, blinding for a moment; then I see him in front of me. I'm just in time. He's on the pocket stage of the old lecture hall, the one where CoreFire was born. The lecture hall is an enormous domed room, empty for years. Breathing in the dusty air is like drinking in memories.

Old-fashioned footlights illuminate him from below, and he's set up what appears to be a little magic act. A chalk line forms a circle around him, and a small folding table displays the accoutrements of a children's magic show—a hat, a deck of cards, a birdcage. And inside the cage, glowing from within, the Zeta Gem.

"Ladies and gentlemen, our show begins." He gestures and a phantasmal audience begins to appear, holograms perhaps. I even see myself as I was in college, standing before the zeta beam device, waiting expectantly for my cue. Almost a caricature in my glasses and lab coat; nearby stand Erica and Jason himself, looking on, just as they did in my memories.

Enough. I draw my pistol and hold it on him. "Give me what I came for."

I gesture with the gun, advancing on him, and the phantoms vanish. "Last warning."

He shakes his head and covers the birdcage. I fire at him point-blank, but the plasma bolt stops short in midair above the chalk line. Impossible.

"This is a magic circle." He gestures at the floor.

He taps the covered cage with his stick.

"This is a magic wand."

He whips the cover off of the cage, and it's gone; in its place, a dove explodes into the air. When he turns back to me, his eyes seem enormous, black.

"Look deep into my eyes. . . ."

I can't help myself. I do, and when he looks back, his eyes are unnervingly clear and deep. A magician's eyes should be heavy-lidded, misty, and deceptive, but his eyes seem to see to the bottom of things, and catch something that I missed. He laughs his hysterical booming laugh one more time. A laugh that knows something.

He gestures, his cape swirls so close to my face that I blink, and then I'm back in the old physics building, alone. I look around and step through the door again, alert for the next trick, but nothing happens. At center stage is an enormous device, like a telescope, or a laser gun, mounted on a rotating platform. At one end, it bulges to contain a red sphere the size of a softball, the Zeta Gem itself. My first creation and greatest mistake. Everything is as I remember it, untouched.

I should have known it. Magicians are all talk.

I didn't ask to have a nemesis. He chose me. CoreFire was a Peterson student, too. I remember him, of course, as Jason Garner.

I didn't know he was my nemesis then. He was just Jason. All-state track, basketball team, editor on the *Peterson Star*, class speaker his junior year. He looked almost the same then as he did in his last public appearance. He never seemed to get much older after the accident.

He had started at Peterson a year earlier. The impression he made was instantaneous, a warm, genial, all-encompassing presence. Where I had to strain to be understood, his voice seemed to fill the room, audible and distinct even at the other end of a crowded corridor. Long before he got any powers, he seemed to walk through walls. Before I ever saw a human being glow, he seemed to.

At first, Peterson seemed like a new start for me, but Jason and his friends set me straight very quickly. Certain details I will pass over in silence, but, most unforgivable of all, they didn't notice me. They didn't care who I was. I was nothing to them, just another target.

I don't remember seeing him behave with intentional cruelty. He didn't so much participate in bullying as sanction it, skate over it. It was the norm there—he wasn't the only one. Damsel and Blackwolf were there, a few years younger than I was, faces in the hallway that I noticed and cataloged, although it never occurred to them to learn my name. Heroes, even then.

Oddly enough, when Jason and I were alone, I became just another buddy of his. We sat next to each other in advanced math and biochemistry, and we even exchanged an offhanded friendly word or two, as if nothing had ever happened. He had a certain rote ability in the sciences that he parlayed into a decent GPA. We endured pop quizzes and extra problem sets together. The two of us were at the top of the class, rivals even then.

"We're screwed now, huh, buddy?" he'd say.

"Got that right," I'd reply in a voice I'd never heard from myself before or since, a voice I conjured suddenly for this new temporary moment of geeky camaraderie. "We're sunk!"

Because I actually did like him a little. At least he treated me like a normal person. Of course I knew it was cheap coin—the whole world was Jason Garner's friend; I just happened to be the part of it he was sitting near. Once or twice maybe I wondered whether I had a special place in his cosmos; whether he thought, in his private moments, If only I knew him better. If only we were closer. But if that were true, no sign of it ever came.

I studied him as I would an anomalous particle or a stellar fluctuation. I had always taken my unpopularity as a sacrifice, the price of my intelligence, but he seemed not to have to make that bargain. There was something he knew about the world, and I tried to learn it.

When he graduated, the school forgot about him—there were others to fill his place. But I never did. We met again at Harvard, and again much later on. By that time, we'd both had our accidents, and we were both wearing masks.

———

For Jason, Harvard was a steady march along a course that seemed already to have been prepared for him; he moved smoothly through the expected programs and girlfriends and collegiate chums toward a waiting career. But for me, it was a slow, inexorable drifting outward from any definable center.

We might as well have gone to different schools. On weekends, I caught up on my extra course load in the Science Center; I knew all the free hours on the campus mainframe, and how to sign out an oscilloscope. He knew . . . what? Parties and cheerleaders, I suppose. He cut a figure straight out of an admissions brochure.

Jason enrolled in physics, and at the beginning of each term I cringed to find his blue-eyed smiling face waiting in the seminar room, my fair-haired double. We still competed for the top of the class, he with his plodding intellect and I with my eccentric brilliance, sudden leaps and bursts of calculation that carried me alone into unknown planes of speculation. We paced each other—the oaf didn't have the sense to give up, or even comprehend how far behind he was.

I might have stood it from a peer, or a new acquaintance. But I despised the idea of sharing my new life with someone from Peterson, the place that knew me as the lunchroom pratfaller. He would nod to me if we passed each other on the quad, recognition of a shared history. There was still that bond that—perhaps I should admit—I myself was unwilling to sever. Maybe because he had treated me as a friend, however briefly, as a member of that other world I had never known entrance to. Maybe he was still the standard for me, the one person I had to prove myself to. Maybe I knew even then that I would never have humbled the world until I had humbled him.

Jason's accident happened in our junior year. I wish to be clear: The zeta beam was indeed of my own conception, and I can document that whatever Professor Burke says. I ran the simulations myself on campus mainframes late on Friday and Saturday nights when everyone else was out drinking, laughing, and who knows what else.

At first, I thought it was only a previously undetectable form of radiation. It would be years before I understood that it was a dimension, a literal space you could go to. But I had found a primitive way to channel that energy and project it.

At stake was the Whittier-Feingold Prize for Undergraduate Science, and an interview with Erica Lowenstein, raven-haired reporter for the *Harvard Crimson*. Of course I had met her by then, and my infatuation was in full flourish. He and Erica knew each other, I eventually discovered. Naturally, I suppose, they were attracted. People are.

Absurdly, Jason actually took the time to try to read and even review my work. I think he raised some churlish objection about Calabi-Yau manifolds. It was one of our last conversations, and in retrospect, perhaps I should have listened. That was probably the last time when I could really have done something differently. He'd done some calculations—feeble, but he'd worked on them—I might at least have looked. But I was intent on the moment of my triumph, and there was no way I'd let him undermine me. Not when Erica was involved.

"This is science, not one of your rugby scrums," I snapped. The fool.

The day of the demonstration arrived. The hall was packed with milling students, faculty, and the media—the *New York Times* sent a reporter, as did *Scientific American* and *Nature*. The Department of Defense had sent half a dozen people. Jason was there, I suppose on the strength of our old friendship, resplendent in his ROTC uniform (years later, I found out he was a scholarship student). And Erica herself, right there in the front row, her gray eyes only on me.

Professor Burke gave a brief introduction on the theory of zeta power, while I sat at the control console in my white lab coat, playing my role of protégé to the hilt. Both of us were in the shadow of the enormous zeta apparatus. For once, I was the center of attention, and Jason sat in the audience, unrecognized. The lights dimmed. I activated the controls with a theatrical flourish, and a buzz arose in the hall as the three-spoked zeta attractor began to move.

I wish to make it clear that, positioned as I was to monitor the machinery, my back was to the crowd. I couldn't possibly have prevented the accident. If the shielding proved inadequate, if Erica wandered into the path of the zeta particles, if human lives were at stake, I had no way of knowing.

And if Jason hadn't been there, I'm sure someone else would have stepped in to save her. He just happened to be standing there, right in position to play the hero and push her out of the way. The zeta beam caught him full in the chest, and he was silhouetted in a shimmering golden haze of particles, penetrating his body, infusing him with the limitless power of zeta energy. They made a big deal of it, but really, it could have been anybody laying down his life like that. Me, Professor Burke, anybody. And then someone else would have gained the power of CoreFire. Someone else would have won her heart forever.

I have never asked him what it felt like, that thunder-crash moment when the zeta energy entered his body. The last thing I remember is Erica lying in his arms, their faces close together, tinted red in the glowing light of my parallel dimension.

It was the last time I saw Jason as Jason. He had been young and likable; now he could fly and lift a bus. His strength was matchless; he had bland, predictable good looks, and a bland, predictable mind. He was the perfect superhero; he even had heat vision. It was a short trip from Harvard to international stardom, propelled by forces I alone could have summoned.

And I? The one who made him what he was? His buddy, arguably, yes. His pal from way back. I was a footnote to the legend, the goofy lab assistant who happened to be at the controls. At best, the Zeta Beam Guy.

Imagine my surprise when, years later, CoreFire turned up on my doorstep. No one knew my identity as Doctor Impossible; so as far as I knew, there was no one who knew of the link between us.

He looked different but also the same. The accident hadn't changed him much—even behind that stupid domino mask, there was no mistaking Jason Garner. He wore a brilliant white leotard and a gold cape. Blond hair and square jaw. The leotard was tight, outlining every curve of a musculature I can only call perfect. He could fly. He drifted through the air like a wisp of smoke, but he was, I knew, the most solid thing to be found on this Earth.

"Looks like I've come to the right place," he observed to no one.

He walked through the grand entrance hall as if he owned it, footsteps echoing off the marble. He cocked an insouciant eye at the enormous Art Deco statuary—myself, triumphant, one foot resting atop a submissive globe. Yes, I'd had plans, dreams, just like anyone else. It was the first time my mind had run absolutely wild; everything I had ever scribbled in my old notebooks had sprung to malevolent life. In the lower caverns, I had found DNA traces of unprecedented antiquity. I was shattering paradigms monthly, my robots were getting better, and in the basement labs there were hints of greater things, other dimensions, interstellar travel. Thoughts so brilliant, it was criminal just to think them.

I was a supervillain, a supergenius, and I couldn't see anyone stopping me. I was going to be another Alexander the Great, Fu Manchu, Professor Moriarty, all rolled into one. I issued my very first global threat, demanding obeisance. And in response, CoreFire arrived.

There I was in my control room, a glass and steel wonder built into a cliff side, overlooking a snowy Arctic landscape. I built it myself. I had given some little thought to defense. I knew, sooner or later, the authorities would get tired of just fighting me off and would come looking for me. I'd be ready.

But no one told me it was going to be like this. Bullets bounced off of him. He walked over trapdoors like solid steel floors. Robots shattered themselves on him. He punched through doors, melted walls with his eyes. His body absorbed radiation like a black hole, or reflected it. If anything, he seemed to get stronger as he went on. It was a blowout.

Did he know who I was? By the time he tore the doors off of my control room, I already had my mask and helmet on; there was no way he could have recognized me. My costume then was a powder blue one with red trim. Red utility belt, red helmet. Red fins on the forearms, and a long red cloak. On the chest, my old symbol, the imperial crest I had imagined for myself, a red planet ringed with gold. For an instant, there was something mortifying about his presence there, an uninvited guest in the room where I ate my lunches and dinners alone.

But when our eyes met, a moment confirmed what I had thought. He didn't know me.

"Stand back, villain!"

That close, his physical presence was even more impressive. The zeta beam had done its work. My powers are good, but they aren't my primary asset. CoreFire was an M-class being, and I'd never seen that before. Up close, he was unearthly, crystalline power in the depths of those eyes, waiting to explode outward. A smell in the air, ozone, a storm coming.

The truth is, my plans for this stage were a bit sketchy. I hadn't figured on anybody getting that far, and, well, I did think the freeze ray was basically infallible. I never worked out a coherent vision for what would happen at this moment. Always so busy; just like I never got around to finishing that throne.

Three basic contingencies for this scenario. Unfortunately, he'd already walked through the first of them, the electrocution field, in essence a superhero bug zapper, without noticing it. My finger hovered over the button that would turn my command console into a rocket-propelled escape pod. In just about fifteen seconds, I could be a dot on the horizon, on my way to a cover identity in the Azores. But no, I thought. Let's try this. I've got powers of my own. How bad could it be?

"Your reign of terror is over, Doctor Impossible. You're coming with me." It hadn't been that much of a reign, actually. Maybe more of a stewardship.

The Impossiblaster was my last chance. It was the nastiest thing I could build that still fit in one hand, absolute small-arms hellfire. I held it on him for about five seconds as he walked toward me, the flames washing over him, and he didn't flinch. I could feel the reflected heat of it.

"Nice try, Impossible!" Jesus. I waited until the overhead light came on, then threw it at him.

And then there was nothing to do but to put up my fists, which looked about a third the size of his. I have long fingers, meant for control knobs and test tubes, not striking things. I'm a scientist, I think I should remind you. But I had decided not to go quietly. I would see this through.

"Take that!"

We faced off a moment in silence, and then he reached for me. He put his hands on me, a scientist! I recall there was a brief pursuit around the command console. I may have flailed at him once or twice. I managed to inform him, before passing out entirely, that he hadn't heard the last of Doctor Impossible.

I came to in the air, dangling by my cape as he flew me back to the authorities. Hanging limp, face averted, I pretended to be unconscious the whole five hours until we arrived in Ottawa. And I kept the mask on.

The trial was mercifully brief. Bank robbery, racketeering, blackmail, countless zoning and regulatory violations. But they didn't discover my original name. My fingerprints are long gone, and even dental records can be faked. I didn't stay inside long—they weren't prepared for me, that time.

After that first outing, the game was afoot. The next time we met, he and I were old enemies—nemeses.

The thing of it is, I actually liked Erica, even afterward. Even after the headline HERO THWARTS WOULD-BE WORLD CONQUEROR appeared over her byline. She was a sharp writer, although her book of short stories never got much attention.

I didn't see her much after that—she was swept away into the bright lights of the superhero world and the society pages. But I followed her work later on when it appeared in the *Sun,* all her Champions stories. Good work. She even broke the news of Lily's origin.

And yes, I took her hostage a few times—just in the early days, to draw CoreFire out. It never failed to get him moving. I would snatch her off the street and roar off in a supersonic aircraft of my own design, then tie her to the columns in my laboratory as the doomsday machine powered up.

And if my eyes behind the mask seemed to gleam with a special, yearning intensity, waiting for her to look, to recognize me, I don't think she took any notice. Something about my approach just failed to attract her attention.

In later years, true, we drifted apart. You can't just take the same hostage every time. Not that my dating techniques grew any more sophisticated in the meantime. But she must be out there somewhere. I'm still waiting for that interview.

The Zeta Gem lies cool in my hand, the last piece of the puzzle. It looks like glass or a ruby, but I know how to build a machine that will tap its energy, enough to move the planet. I shake my head, still fuzzy from Mister Mystic's routine, but it clears as I walk unseen back through the Yard and through the side streets down to the Charles River. In three days, I'm going to conquer the world, but I've lost my chance at him. CoreFire will go down in history as the man I couldn't beat.

It's hard not to feel a little sorry. Perhaps it's only professional pride—I made him, after all, and I like my creations to last. And we did have a score to settle, he and I. The world thought it began in Nova Scotia, but it had a deeper subterranean history stretching so much further back. It's even possible that he knew it, too—what if we were both pretending up in Nova Scotia, each for his own reasons, and then forever afterward?

We'll never know. I was going to beat him, and on the day I beat him, I was going to take my mask off and stare into his face, and let him know that it was me all along. The whole world would have known Doctor Impossible beat CoreFire, but most of all, Jason Garner would have known that I beat *him*. To a pulp. But now he never will.

CHAPTER SIXTEEN

SECRET ORIGINS

I knew this would happen. That this would end in some awful screwup, and that would be it for me and the Champions. New Champions. Whatever. I knew a hundred fancy uniforms wouldn't make up the difference between them and me. I wonder if Doctor Impossible's island is where I should be now; maybe he'd even take me as a henchman. Maybe Lily can tell me.

Damsel must know something's going on. Blackwolf's acting normal, just ignoring me, but I blush every time he walks into the room. You'd think being part machine would have some advantage in that area. Maybe if I really were a robot. Thank God Elphin manages to ignore it, or more likely is blissfully oblivious to anything unrelated to her weird fantasy life.

To make matters worse, Doctor Impossible is nowhere to be found. Every day we don't find him is another day for him to figure out how to beat us. Every day we expect to hear him announce that our pitiful world is doomed, that the Earth will soon be his. He is doing something diabolical, somewhere; that much is certain. I wonder what it will be like to meet him.

The hunt for magical devices is in full swing, and the idea is to split into subteams, which comes as something of a relief. Blackwolf is in Los

Angeles, Feral is handling Prague, and Stormcloud has come out of retirement to sit up at the Phantom Satellite. Lily's seeing a villain friend. But no one's thinking about those possibilities. They're thinking about the Scepter of Elfland, a piece of fairy-tale logic escaped into our world. Damsel will go all the way to Angkor Wat this afternoon, but before she leaves she gives me the mission.

She is back in full ice queen persona for the briefing in the Crisis Room. She hands me a stack of printout. She knows. She must.

"I want you to search out every one of these magical artifacts. Confirm they're in place and not tampered with, and warn the owners that Doctor Impossible is on the prowl for a power source. Can you do that?"

I nod, not really trusting myself to say anything, or even look her in the eye.

"Good. I'm sending Elphin along to look after you. You can have the ChampJet if you want."

Great. I don't ask where Mister Mystic is—apparently, no one's ever supposed to ask what he's doing. I just hope there's somebody I can beat up at the end of this trip.

There's no further comment. The Scepter of Elfland has been placed, diplomatically, at the close of my list, without comment, and I wonder about that. Am I being sent to face our worst foe? Maybe, but it's like a secret between Damsel and me. I'm going to meet the woman who raised her after her mother left, and that's an odd little intimacy, especially in light of recent events. For the millionth time, I wish I understood how superteams work, what the dynamic here is supposed to be. Am I supposed to end up fighting Damsel? Are we fighting already? And who's winning?

The rest of the list turns out to be people on the magical fringe of superherodom, most of them in Manhattan itself and the outer boroughs. Apparently, magical superheroes don't quite do it the way the rest of us do, and we get a tour of the least likely places you could think of to find a superhero. In fact, I have only Damsel's word for it that the whole thing isn't a joke or a hazing ritual. We interview a psychic healer in an inappropriately slinky dress, and in a corporate boardroom, a voice speaks out of a brazen mask. We meet an improbably muscled man wearing a bright red outfit, living in a garret, and a private investigator with hooves. All shake their heads—no sign of Doctor Impossible.

In Newark, I visit an actual magic shop, a dusty antique store that looks like an empty storefront from the outside. Inside, it's bigger, and full of old clocks; tapestries; mannequins and dressmakers' dummies; gowns and tuxedos and a ceremonial saber that might have been swung in the Crimean War. An old man comes out from behind a curtain in the back, just a piece of patterned fabric tacked across a door frame. I get the sense that it would be a very bad idea to make a deal with him. I flash my ID, and back out once he tells me everything is okay.

Regina herself turns out to live in Phoenix. It makes sense now that Damsel would choose someone else for this, but I can't tell if sending me is punishment or a sign that she's beginning to trust me. I have to admit I'm curious—Damsel's family life has long been a subject of speculation.

I make the call to Phoenix myself to tell her we we're coming. Her real name has always been a big secret, but this late in the game, they're letting me in on some of the classified files, files that go all the way back to the Super Squadron.

She called herself Regina, and she fought crime until the early 1970s. She was the first of the Super Squadron to retire. A tall, dark woman with a commanding eye, she wore a crown and robes that gave her strength, and fought with a mystic scepter that cast a ruby ray that had power over evil minds, and could perform other feats, as well.

Or so she claimed. She also claimed to be the surviving member of a band of children that had acquired monarchical power in the feudal government of a pseudomedieval civilization of a dimension populated by humans, elves, and talking animals. The difficulty arose because this was, in fact, the plot of a popular series of children's books called *Four Children in Elfland*. It was as if she expected to be taken seriously as law enforcement on the strength of an acquaintance with Winnie-the-Pooh and Christopher Robin. She wouldn't be the first major hero to succumb to mental instability later in life.

Not long after the Champions formed, she retired into her secret identity, which she had gone to great lengths to protect. Then she just disappeared from sight, as superheroes do, except for a controversial interview conducted in great secrecy and later published in *The New Yorker*. The Scepter of Elfland is still on the books, a class-A magical artifact.

I park the rental car in front of the house, which is in a quiet suburb of Phoenix. Elphin's been chattering aimlessly since we flew in, about Titania and fights she's been in and the weather here and about different kinds of trees, which she seems to pay a lot of attention to. Our training duel on the first day is a forgotten thing for her.

It's the middle of the afternoon, and the lengthening shadows are just beginning to cross the roads. A couple of newspapers are lying around on the front lawn. But Regina said she'd be home, and there's a car in the driveway.

Elphin looks around, puzzled. "Is she not a queen? I do not see her attendants." I was afraid of this.

"Um, I was thinking you could wait in the car. To, you know, keep watch." As a social being, Elphin is perfectly pleasant, but only as long as you're not invested in the conversation going in a particular direction for very long.

I leave her there humming to herself, her spear leaning awkwardly into the backseat. She's got a communicator, so she'll listen in and beep me if there's a problem. My weight snaps a flagstone going up the front walk.

It's like visiting the school bully's mother. I'm going to sit down with the woman who raised Damsel, the most famous female hero in the world. With CoreFire gone, the leader of the Champions may be the biggest hero in the world, no exceptions. I wonder again why it's me—I guess because I never worked with her before.

I think about Paragon going bad, how they found him. What am I going to find here? I scan the house with every faculty I have available. One human female inside, flat normal to anything I can pick up. Still, I brace myself for anything. I press the doorbell, and she answers.

She looks older out of costume. Softer, a princess grown fleshy and middle-aged. Is this really who Damsel was so afraid of?

I used to be a fan of the *Elfland* series myself, and maybe I was thinking she'd look more like the girl they cast for the movies. There's a photograph that circulates on the Internet, supposedly from the earliest case files, of four children wrapped in shiny foil emergency blankets, grinning like maniacs. She might have been one of them grown up, black hair and pale skin, but much older. Her real name is Linda.

I step inside. Meeting the Champions was one thing, but the members of the Super Squadron are a step beyond, something closer to myth, their origins in the stars or among the gods. But her living room looks like any middle-class suburban housewife's, and I'm surprised to find I'm a head taller than her. She glances twice at my face, the metal hand I extend to grasp hers. She lights a cigarette without asking.

"Can I offer you anything? Cocktail?" she says.

"Um, no thanks, ma'am. My metal half doesn't like it."

"Damsel must have sent you. You're Fatale. The cyborg."

"That's right." I actually wasn't sure she'd remember me from her visit.

"We didn't used to have them, you know." The conversation grinds to a halt there. Maybe I should have brought Elphin along after all. I take a breath and get to the point.

"We need to know, well, about the Scepter of Elfland. Whether anything's, well, happened with it lately."

"Then you don't know?" she asks. I sit forward. Maybe I've got something here after all.

"Why don't you tell me."

"I guess since I'm no longer part of their little fantasy club, it's all right for me to talk about it. It's not as if anyone ever believed us anyway." She takes another drag from the cigarette. I've spent enough time around superheroes to recognize the look on her face. She's going to tell me her origin.

"It's hard to remember details now. I've had to tell the story so many times now, what I remember is a blur of therapy rooms, my years in costume, and then maybe, way at the back, what I remember may not be anything more than a glimpse of lights shining in a dark forest. It's been thirty-four years since then, most of it in offices, entering sales data into computers. That's what I do for a living now. My secret identity."

She tells me the story of her journey to that other world, the story from the children's book. How she'd stumbled into the other world one morning with her brothers and sister, and had adventures uncounted in a magic land beyond imagining.

"We came to what thousands of people have searched for since, a standing stone five feet high, marking a path we hadn't seen before. It had writing on it, a message we didn't bother to read; and maybe it was important, but it's lost forever now. We turned down the path without much comment, expecting any moment to come out in someone's backyard and turn around. We walked for ten minutes, and there was at some point a change that afterward we all remembered differently—to me, it was a shift in the quality of the light, but nothing I've ever been able to describe. And the forest grew darker and then lighter as we walked, and then we met the first of the fairies, standing there real as a policeman."

And then one day, they stumbled back. She gets up and paces the living room as she speaks, mixes herself a drink, something strong-looking. She gestures a lot when she talks, and she doesn't really look at me.

"I'm not saying it was a game, and I'm not saying it wasn't a game. All anyone knows for sure is that we were gone for eleven days, long enough for the search to become national news. No one has completely explained where we were, or how at the end of it we showed up again in that field after volunteers had searched every square foot of it, in the midst of all those dogs and reporters and emergency personnel, dressed the way we were, and obviously happier than we had ever been in our lives. We certainly weren't twelve years older than when we had left, although a moment before it had seemed that way.

"It was raining the day we came back. We had set out riding that spring morning, the four of us, to look at what the flooding had done. The footing grew uncertain and we tied the horses and walked ahead. We began to hear faint helicopters and engine noise, and the whiff of exhaust, and I think we all realized what was happening at roughly the same time. It was exactly like waking up out of a dream, and the exact moment when you realize you're waking up is the moment after which you can't possibly get back to sleep. And then the noise broke on us all at once, and through the trees we could see the bright colors of tents and windbreakers. One of the rescue workers saw us and yelled, and then people were running toward us with blankets.

"I remember two things the most vividly. One was the recognition on Sean the High King's face. I think he may have known first, having lived the longest time at home. The other was Wendy, who in the moments before they reached us tore off the amulet she had won from the White Queen, snapping the chain, and threw it as hard as she could back into the trees. We never found it, or Sean's hammer. Nothing except the clothes we wore, and my scepter. Sean always claimed the rescue workers took them, but they would never admit it.

"I still thought we were going to give brief explanations and good-byes, and set off back to the kingdom. It never occurred to me or any of us until later that something so real and concrete could vanish forever into a group of trees so thin, you could see the back of a house behind them."

Years of therapy followed, and explanations piled on explanations for what had happened to them—hidden caves; a drop in the water table; drugs.

"There are still things that need explaining. The clothes we were wearing. The sounds that were heard in the woods that first night we were back. Wendy had a whole new way of speaking, and she looked straight at you instead of ducking her head. And I had the long scar on my inside right forearm, which my mother claims was already there, but I will never believe it, ever, until the day I die.

"People couldn't resist the charm of the whole idea, and it snow-balled once that clinician went on NPR. Then there was *Four Children in Elfland,* the case study that became the children's book, and those sequels that the other guy wrote. And then we were on T-shirts. I changed my name when I turned eighteen, and again at twenty-three. People dressed up as us and ran web sites and held conventions. They all hate me now, too. I'm sorry, but I'm a little tired of defending myself.

"We did try to go back, you know. The first time was only a week afterward. And on the one-year anniversary, we spent a whole day there, combing the wet grass for any sign of the marker stone. I must have gone back a dozen times alone or with David, whenever we were feeling especially depressed or bored, or felt like cutting school. I know Sean camped out there for two weeks one summer. But time runs much faster in Elfland, and it must have run a long time there by now."

I can see the last cocktail taking effect, and she keeps going, gesturing a little more broadly. The eldest had been a king or emperor of something, and he tried to take control of the group. They fought end-lessly; not all of them even agreed on what had happened, or if any-thing had happened at all. There was a lot of talk about the gifts they'd received, and whether Linda had stolen one of them. In the end, they vanished together, leaving Linda under a somewhat farcical "decree of exile."

And what could she do then? Linda reemerged in her public persona as Regina, Queen, Crusader of Elfland, one of the first and most suc-cessful female superheroes. She'd married Stormcloud after Damsel's mother left, and retired from active life.

"I wouldn't even be in therapy if I could just forget about these things. The court dances, men and women crossing the pink-and-white tile of the ballroom on autumn nights. Going out onto the terrace to cool off, the night air icy on my face, and looking up at the Moon to wonder if the Earth were real at all. Stopping one morning for an hour by a wooden bridge while David and Sean argued over whether we had lost the way. Wendy and I sat and played a game with a pattern in the carvings on the wooden railing. I would know it if I saw it tomorrow. I could draw it now. Believe me."

"But the staff?" I ask. I can't resist. "The Scepter, I mean. It works, doesn't it? I mean, that's proof. That you went."

"Agatha's wand. Sometimes I don't even know if I saw it in Elfland, or if it's something from a game we played afterward, or a dream. Here, I'll show it to you. I keep it with the costume."

She disappears, then comes back with a small wooden case, maybe twenty inches long.

"It was weakening on my last adventure. It had become something else, just a stick, or maybe that's what it always was. The ruby doesn't even look like a ruby anymore. Just colored glass.

"Maybe it's the curse. Or maybe it's Sean's fault; maybe his silly decree actually did something. Doctor Impossible won't be coming here if he knows what he's doing. Tell Damsel I'm sorry."

Out of its case, it looks like a stage prop, and I wonder if it ever was magical. It must have been . . . I guess. I'm out of my depth here. I thought the Super Squadron was the one thing you could trust, the real heroes, if there are any. Now it's just us. I wonder how long Damsel has known that.

I thank her and walk quietly down the walk. It's dark as I leave. As I start the engine, I see her on the front step, looking down at us, peering to see Elphin through the tinted windows. I press down on the accelerator and we pull hastily away before I even notice that Elphin is weeping, tears pouring unheeded down her face. I manage to pretend not to see as I drive us back to the airport, and the waiting ChampJet takes us to our next mission.

Blackwolf's scheme isn't working. It's 6:14 a.m. by that ever-blinking clock, and none of us has slept all night. I sag in my harness, tired of clinging to the museum roof. The Nightstar sits untouched in its leaded-glass display case at the Institute for Advanced Thought. Doctor Impossible didn't come. No one is coming. And Blackwolf has managed to direct the whole operation without speaking to me once.

Disgusted, Blackwolf tears off his hat and tosses it in the trash, walking away from his role as a fake security guard in a lifelike rubber mask. In a few minutes, the regular staff will get here, and we'd rather be gone.

The rest of us are concealed around the chamber. Lily, cast as a fake statue, lowers her arms with a loud sigh and follows him, brushing plaster dust from her face and hands. The rest of us keep to our places and watch them go, sensing a showdown.

Sure enough, their conversation gets louder and louder, until we can hear Blackwolf from the lobby.

"Wait. You say you saw him?"

"I'm sorry I told you any of this. What did you want me to do?" says Lily.

"He is a wanted criminal. This is exactly the reason your membership is probationary."

"He wasn't doing anything!" I look at Damsel, still in her own place as a carved Madonna. Elphin, probably the only convincing-looking art object among us, is still posed by the door, watching curiously.

"Except gloating. Except laughing in our faces," responds Blackwolf.

"We just talked for a second. It doesn't always have to be a super-fight."

"He would have surrendered."

"With Phenom there? And Salvo? It would have been murder."

"CoreFire was murdered. He could be coming for you next. Did you ever think of that?"

"You don't know any of this for sure. Doctor Impossible was in jail."

"But you weren't, were you? Where were you before CoreFire disappeared, anyway?"

"For the millionth time, I had nothing to do with it."

"This would all be easier if we could establish—"

"Bullshit! I know who CoreFire was looking for, and it wasn't Doctor Impossible, I'll tell you that much."

"He escaped right after CoreFire disappeared. He hates CoreFire; we know that. And now he's trying to take over the world. Just what is missing for you?"

"You ever think about what you look like to us? You're just a gang of high-tech thugs and bullies and . . . and weirdos."

Blackwolf, for once, is silent.

"Just don't follow me." I can tell from her voice that she's already walking away, heels clicking on the polished floor.

Blackwolf comes back, a uniformed silhouette against the arched doorway. "I told you she was a mistake."

Damsel, Lily's plaster double, looks after her thoughtfully. "I wonder whose?"

Lily is gone when we get home. She must have visited the tower on her way back—she took off her transponder and left it in her room. I find it sitting on what was CoreFire's old bed.

I guess I thought we were going to be friends, and now I don't know what we are. Do we have to fight now? Has she gone back to Doctor Impossible? She could have been tipping Doctor Impossible off for weeks, I guess—that's what Blackwolf thinks. But then how did we surprise him at the funeral? I can't really believe it.

I go back to the computer, hoping for some detail here that I missed before. If CoreFire wasn't looking for Doctor Impossible, then who? His old girlfriend, maybe?

I'm browsing through early file photos when I see the thing I shouldn't see. CoreFire's only a year or so out of college, at a black-tie fund-raising dinner. He's wearing his costume, a little incongruous-looking, but it's the woman next to him I notice, a raven-haired woman in glasses, smiling and directing a sly-seeming remark to the hero over an expensive-looking steak as he grins into the camera.

She's smartly dressed and wearing glasses but even under the makeup, I recognize her. Solidly visible, and a good seven years before she arrived from the future and committed her first crime. Lily.

My communicator beeps and Damsel cuts in.

"It's happening. Turn on NPR."

I do, and immediately I hear Doctor Impossible's voice. He's surfaced at last to make a public statement, and they're rebroadcasting it all over the country. Probably the world.

It begins with "Greetings, insects!" and goes on from there, and I don't listen to the whole thing. Not exactly a prose masterpiece, but the message is clear. He's found whatever it was he needed to find and he's going to be taking over the world soon—surrender or be destroyed. I guess he didn't need the Nightstar after all.

The tower hums with tension; I can hear the jumpjet revving its engines over my head.

Everyone's calling for the Champions to save them, and it's giving me a funny feeling in what's left of my guts. He's been a step ahead of us the whole time. I bet he planned this entire thing.

I haven't had time to think very much about what this means for me. I wasn't joking with Blackwolf, I really could be a spy, or a traitor, or a bomb, and I might not know it.

I wonder if this makes Doctor Impossible my nemesis, and what exactly I should do about that. Maybe Doctor Impossible will know— he's had nemeses before. In fact, he should be in the market for a new one right about now. I wonder if he'll know who I am, and whether we met before the operation, if we talked at all. I'll have to ask him about it if I get the chance. He may be the last man in the world who can tell me who I am. This could really turn into something.

It makes me feel better, having my own reasons for being on the island. I picture our big showdown, brain against brawn with the rest of the New Champions looking on in awe. When he's at my mercy, I can demand things, tell him things, make him explain. I should probably start working on my speech, just in case.

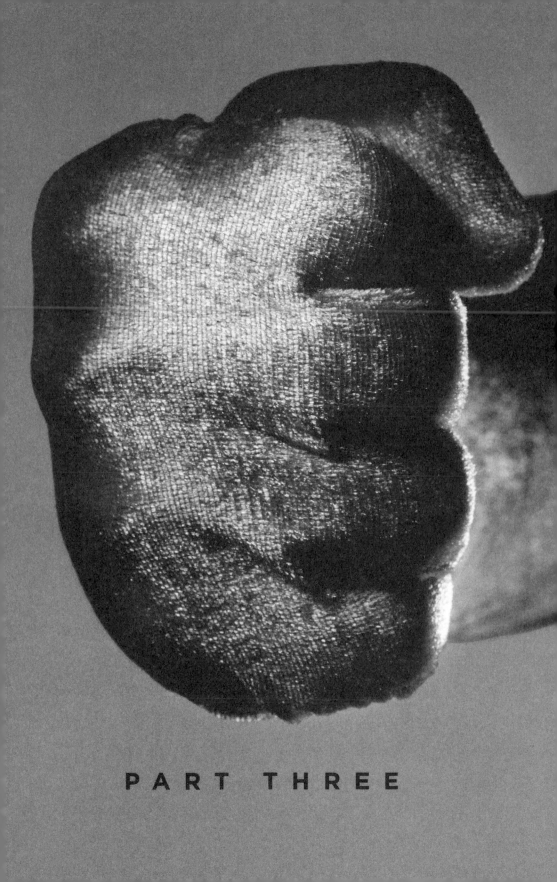

PART THREE

CHAPTER SEVENTEEN

JOIN ME AND WE CANNOT BE DEFEATED

Two days now. Two days before the world falls beneath the heel of my red patent-leather boot. The New Champions know it and I know it. The game, as they say, is afoot, and I must return to my island, or what's left of it.

Forty thousand feet over the Pacific Ocean, a red-and-gold flier sails silent and radar invisible; the sun is setting beneath a perfect sea of clouds. Alone in the cockpit, I can take a minute to watch my island come into view. Below, invisible, a homing beacon wakes to guide me in, spiraling down into the dusk.

My flier comes to rest in the ruined courtyard, and I step out, smelling the familiar smells of jungle and burned oil. This was my home.

Looking around at the devastation, I can still feel the aches of when they brought me in last, two years ago. The last battle was a messy one, but even so, I can tell they've been back here. The footprints make it plain—Blackwolf's athletic step, like a dancer's, next to that cyborg's metal tread. One of mine, I think—a promising idea, but one of the software people I hired ratted me out. I got her out of the hospital any-way; you'd think she'd go easy on me.

And Lily's been here with them, picking through my things with the rest of the heroes. I wonder if she thought about the last time she'd been here, when I flew her in after her Paris fight, and watched the coverage on CNN. I wonder if she showed them my control room. And I wonder where she is now.

Sighing, I begin checking over systems. There's a little power left in the reserve generators. The front entrance opens to my touch, and I step into the entrance hall. There's a musty smell. A lot of water got in during the rainy season, but it's still impressive, if only the scale of it.

This was the one I built first, and the one I came back to. Before the space station, before the blimp, before anything, I was younger and hungry for recognition, with just a handful of minions and my first billion dollars in a Swiss account. We set down by helicopter, flattening the wet grass. As the rotors spun down, I stepped out into the warm, moist air dressed in full regalia, cape and helmet. A group of young technicians scrambled out afterward, toppling crates of equipment out onto the forest floor.

At the first encampment, robots began digging out the foundations of my fortress, the centerpiece of my great empire of crime. The first holes we dug filled with water, and the jungle got in everywhere it could. But slowly the towers rose, far from the shipping lanes, in a tiny footprint where the satellites never crossed overhead. Tropical birds circled among the girders.

Walking there now under the shattered ceiling, the moment comes flooding back, all the romance of one's first truly historic crime. One never forgets it.

The centrifuges whirled day and night, performing the slow alchemy of genetic modification. The sharp tang of the preservative chemicals; the coolness and hush of the sterile chamber; the daily ritual of decontamination. Keyboards clattering in the early mornings, test after test, ranks of green CRT screens displaying collated data.

The laboratory never ceased to be a place of mystery for me. Science blurred into religion, into necromancy. I worked long into the night, feeling at times as if the whole of the Earth had fallen away outside, leaving only the darkness, the work, the endless questing into the past. Then the first stirrings of life.

They beat me that time, too. But I came back.

The doomsday device is spread out on the laboratory floor, ten thousand square feet of world-threatening ingenuity. It isn't my largest outing (unless you include the Moon), but surely my grandest (*especially* if you include the Moon).

Dollface's work is the heart of it. The little fat man shines his gravity ray, only barely strong enough to pin a G-man to the floor, or loft a few bars of gold out of a vault. But Laserator's lens catches, magnifies, and focuses it upward—240,000 miles upward. The bulkiest part of the apparatus is the power source, a new version of my old zeta generator. I lack Dollface's gift for concision, but I feel I give things my own flair—arching buttresses, arcing bolts of electricity, tubes and flashing lights. It doesn't have to look like that, but it works, and I like it. At least you can see what everything does.

The Moon is full tonight, very full, and the tides are unusually strong. As the Moon grows heavier, it distorts the Earth's orbit ever so gently. This is where the math comes in, the equations Baron Ether worked out decades ago to prevent the stress from tearing the planet apart or any similar nonsense. The net result is that I control the motion of this planet everyone is standing on.

As has been shown (cf. Kleinfeld, 1928), tiny adjustments in the Earth's position in the solar system can have far-reaching climatic effects—it won't take long for Earth's leaders to get the message. It's Kleinfeld's math, but it took Doctor Impossible to put into practice. Doctor and Emperor-elect, I should say.

But—and I stress this—it's not enough. You can be as smart as you want to be, you can be the smartest man in the world, but if you try something like this, a Special Forces reject is still going to rappel over the wall and punch you in the stomach. And then you're going to be the smartest man on the floor sucking wind. You need to prepare for this stage—I know that now. Hence my return to Baron Ether's humble home.

"Yes, I made her. Didn't you ever suspect?" He's lost in the past, making some point I can't follow.

"Baron . . ." I try to interrupt, but Baron Ether's mind wanders as he potters around in the dark corners of his study in the old dark house in New Haven. I try not to fidget. The top of my helmet nearly grazes an enormous mobile depicting an antiquated conception of our solar system. A reminder that the planets are still moving, and time is running out on my plan.

"She was my finest creation. Those emerald eyes . . . Oh, the methods are lost now. You can't get pure ingredients anymore. She was built to explode, you know. Just not on Titan."

"Baron. You know what happens now. There's going to be a fight, and I need protection. I need power."

"Powers. Of course you would. A bit late now to fall into a vat, you know, something nicely irradiated."

"Yes, a bit." I try not to snap at the Baron, but I'm feeling inexplicably tense.

"There was a magic ring somewhere, don't you know. Prophecy, if I can just think of it. I'm sure I can find the reference. . . ." He makes a shuffling motion in the direction of one of the bookshelves, but I cut him off.

"God damn it, Baron!"

He freezes. No one talks to Baron Ether like this, I guess, especially not pissant upstarts who weren't even alive for the bulk of his career. Who'd never known the days before the Super Squadron. Outside, I can hear children yelling and playing kickball out in the street.

"We're better than this. In two days, the Champions are going to show up and smash everything I've built, my priceless scientific inventions, just like they've done to you. How many times is it going to happen? How long are we going to be under their thumbs?"

I wait for him to reach for his cane, to press the ruby stud or the diamond, but instead he answers me.

"Yes, of course. Living like this . . . one forgets." The Baron's accent is unplaceable. Not quite Germanic. Somewhere in the Balkans, perhaps. His eyes are lost in the darkness, in the unfathomable past. "I had my reasons once, too, you know. They cast me out. All because of my work. The galvanic principle . . . But I returned."

His right hand, the insect one, clenches. "I showed them their master."

For an instant, I can see the anger that once cowed the world, and it's frightening, even to me. Wherever Baron Ether came from, it was probably a lot worse than the suburban Midwest. He falls silent again.

"Baron?" I venture. "Is there anything else? Something you've got left over. Even a death ray would help."

He seems to emerge from his reverie. "Yes. Yes, a letter came for you."

"What do you mean?"

He wheels himself over to where I'm standing and closes the window. "It was on the table one morning. I don't know how you people keep getting in. I think the Mechanist must be a bit out of date."

He shows me the envelope. The outside simply reads "Doctor Impossible." I hesitate, but the Baron has already opened it. Inside, there is simply a card with a precise latitude and longitude, and a name: Nelson Gerard.

A sudden hope—maybe the Pharaoh is coming out of retirement! Maybe he heard I'm back in the game, and wants in on the action. He might be useful in the crunch, properly directed. Doctor Impossible and the Pharaoh. Back-to-back in the arena, we'd been a force to be reckoned with. I'm surprised at how much I've missed him—maybe I'll even give him Egypt once we've conquered the world. It would be good to have company for a change.

But it isn't his handwriting. Underneath the numbers is written another message:

Good luck.
   L.

Doctor Impossible and the Pharaoh, together again, in an arena fight to beat the world. Could it happen?

I never managed to piece together all the rest of the Pharaoh's story. CoreFire's search records helped, and Baron Ether filled in the rest. Ambling down through Mexico, he'd fetched up at a surf shack in Costa Rica. An invulnerable man can afford to take his time, sleeping rough and hitchhiking. When the Pharaoh went missing, no one came looking for him. The Pharaoh's Return? The Revenge of the Pharaoh? No one cared. No one gave a damn.

The coordinates in the note are precise, but once I get close, it's obvious where he died, even from a thousand feet up. The sea is frozen solid out to a hundred yards from shore, spreading out from a cave in a cliff face.

I still don't understand it. Superfights rarely go to the death, very rarely—even Feral holds to that line. This one had, and unleashed something strange.

As I get closer, the temperature drops; inside the cave, it is the Arctic. When I find the Pharaoh, he is sitting on a chair of ice, his flesh blue-white. The hammer has cracked, fused—the explosion must have been lethally intense, but the air was unnaturally cold, well below freezing, chilled by the magic emanating from the weapon he still holds. Even I can smell the power in it.

He used to have these cheesy sayings, things like "By Ra!" or "Isis preserve us!" like he was really an Egyptian king, who just happened to speak English. His hieroglyphics looked like they'd been copied off a cereal box or a King Tut T-shirt. And he used to sing that Steve Martin song under his breath during a fight, call out "He's an Egyptian!" at the wrong moment, and I'd crack up just when I was defusing a bomb or breaking a particularly tricky lock. And that idiotic headdress, like a giant papier-mâché television antenna.

It must be the hammer. Cracks show on it now—whatever kept him alive all these years finally failed him at the critical moment. But here he sits, sole monarch of a strange and fanciful realm, enthroned at last. His flesh is ice-cold.

Now I know why I'm here. The hammer is still glowing faintly. Gently, I slide it from his frozen hand. I've seen what this hammer can do, and I've got a use for it. Someone's going to pay for what happened here, oh yes. I'm starting to have a tiny suspicion who that is. I return to the island, my doomsday device complete.

The heroes are on their way here in a supersonic jet, and I'm staking everything on a magic hammer. The Pharaoh would have enjoyed that, but frankly, it ticks me off just a little.

Professionally speaking, it's no way to work, staking one's plan on an object that occasionally whispers secrets no rational person can accept. Truthfully, it goes against everything I stand for.

My world is a sphere of rock that circles an orb of nuclear fire, and science and I are setting our backs against it, and it will move. That much is clear. In my island fortress, I keep an elephant tusk, 32,000 years old, incised with a few scratches marking the phases of the Moon, made by the hand of a Paleolithic supergenius, the progenitor of that universe and my distant forebear. He, or she, knew something of what I am about to do. Maybe she dreamed of it.

And so even if I'm forced to admit that science isn't all there is, I don't like it. Every couple of years, another one gets unearthed, one of the old things that's come down to us out of the forgotten past. A gem or a rod, or a magic shoe. Out of Troy or Atlantis or Lemuria, or the dark forest between here and Grandmother's, something that doesn't play by the rules.

I don't know if finding Durandal or Aladdin's lamp makes those stories true, or if the stories just attached themselves to the objects. The objects themselves get handed on so many times that they lose their significance, become just tools. Once upon a time, they meant royalty or holiness to somebody, a priest or hero of ancient times, but after all this time, they're just an old joke. But the power—that stays around.

All I can conclude is that the deep past is a strange place. These things are found and lost again, and when you find one, your life changes forever, like the Pharaoh's did.

I think again about Mister Mystic's laugh, and what the Baron said, before I left, as the shadows lengthened in his suburban kitchen and SUVs wound home through the darkening streets. Years ago, a boy found an ancient magic hammer and learned the word that would change him into something invincible, a king or emperor. A pharaoh. A nonsense story, a fairy tale, but now I hold it in my hands.

It was dark by the time he finished. At the end, the Baron whispered the word itself in my ear.

"It won't work," I said.

"Maybe not. But it might do something."

I put my foot on his windowsill, but he stopped me again.

"Doctor Impossible?" His voice was scarcely more than a croak.

"What is it?"

"Do it, boy. Beat them hollow."

Now the superheroes are coming over the horizon. My instruments picked them up an hour ago. Drumming my fingers on the golden railing of a balcony, the highest tower of my fortress, I watch. They're flying in a V formation, low across a tropical sea as smooth as glass.

Two hours ago, I hijacked four major communications satellites to issue my proclamation of universal sovereignty. In effect, I conquered the world. Wearing my old robes, sitting on a refurbished throne, it might have been the glory days. No one could see the blast marks on the wall just outside of camera range. Now I just need to make my proclamation stick.

The mirror array seems to be working. The signal loss is as near zero as it's possible to be. Once I had it in my hands, it was easy to copy, but only Laserator's work could have reflected so truly, golden, perfect. He got a rotten deal.

Overhead, the Moon is full. I had to wait until it passed directly overhead. The Moon itself is a kind of mirror, a very dull one. I peer into the reflector, and two and three-fifths seconds later, my image reaches the Moon, enormously magnified. Then I put the laughing fat man in his place, Dollface's tiny creation. At a touch, his eyes will light up and his chin will move up and down, and the Moon will grow heavier. At my direction, the Earth will be pulled gently off of its course, nudged outward from the Sun. The math is hard, but it's just math; Baron Ether did it years ago. As the Earth grows colder, my power becomes apparent, and the nations submit.

This isn't the first plan I've had, or the tenth. I would have been in Brooklyn with Lily if things had worked out. And I know how this must look—the hidden fortress, the helmet, the cape, the army of robots. I'm smart—ungodly so, to tell the truth—and the question still surfaces. When they ask me, I don't know what I'll say. What could I have been thinking? How did I end up on the side of the monsters?

Camera twelve shows them touching down, Damsel and Elphin descending to touch the ground as softly as angels in a Renaissance painting. The others emerge from the landing vehicle, Blackwolf performing a neat little combat roll out of the cockpit. He wears a full-body stealth costume, grays and blacks, and it's like the Peterson class reunion none of us went to. I brace myself for Lily to follow him out, but she doesn't.

Damsel gives them a pep talk before they split up. The parabolic microphones catch a little of it.

"You're all professionals. You're all heroes. I know we don't have CoreFire, but you know what? Doctor Impossible is just a scientist. These guys always lose it in the end."

At least now I know what they think of me. "Lose it in the end"? Nice. At the control console, I grin at her and shake my head. He who laughs last laughs longest, and I happen to have a really good laugh.

They split up to take me on, but the cameras track them—Rainbow Triumph heads off into the jungle, while Damsel and Elphin take to the air. Blackwolf skulks off through the wreckage of my airstrip, and the cyborg heads in the other direction. Mister Mystic walks into shadow and just fades away. Something shimmers on camera nine; then it's gone. A secret weapon?

I start pressing buttons and the console lights up, flashing mostly red, with spots of green. They couldn't destroy everything last time, and I've had about forty-eight hours to walk around making repairs—traps, robots, sensors.

It won't stop all of them, but it doesn't have to. I finger the hammer, heavy and satisfying in my hand. I want to say the word and test it, but I don't know how much of its power is left. I had a little time to inspect it—it's damaged but not dead. Some of what the Pharaoh had is still in there, whether it's the power of Ra or Mickey Mouse; it used to work for him, so maybe it will work for me.

It's time to go and face them. To prepare them, as we say in the trade, a proper reception. Welcome to my island, assholes.

CHAPTER EIGHTEEN

AND NOW FOR THOSE
MEDDLING CHILDREN

"Um, did we win?"

*My dear "Champions." Welcome. By the time you hear this, I will have taken
over the world. Please do not be alarmed.*

This is not a good sign. I hear speaker hiss, and Doctor Impossible's
now-familiar voice comes to us with plenty of reverb. It's a recording.

My ears are ringing. I think a shrapnel fragment must have bounced
off one of my cranial plates. My artificial skin has that fried feeling like
after a grenade detonates nearby, but I can't remember when that was.
My left knee joint is frozen. I'm leaning against a metal wall in a room
somewhere, and I'm trying to put the whole situation together again,
but I'm dazed and my RAM is patchy. I'm having a cyborg moment.

There's a diagnosis and repair routine that I do, which they drilled me
on every day during rehabilitation. I'm not a technician—there's no
way I'm going to understand my body—so they gave me a long check-
list. It starts with the head. The hard drives check themselves; I just have
to check the tubing and the cameras and whatnot, which means getting
inside.

On reflex, I turn to the wall to hide how the faceplate swings out, and
you can see how deeply the metal impinges into my skull. There's a cav-
ity where the fan is, the size of a golf ball, and you don't want to think
about what came out to make room for it.

"Yeah. Lucky he was totally unprepared." Rainbow's voice.

"Is Fatale awake yet?" Blackwolf's.

"Still booting up." Rainbow again, dull-voiced.

"I heard that," I say. "What happened?"

I must be the last one to wake up. Seven separate cells, ringing the perimeter of a circular room cut into the rock. About fifteen feet of rock separates each cell. The last one—intended for Lily, presumably—is empty. At least we can see one another. There's a public-address system, over which Doctor Impossible is making an interminable victory speech. It's too far away to smash.

Each of our cells is different. Mine is fenced in front with ordinary bars, but when I walk up to touch them, there's something, a lock in my software, that stops me. My arms and legs seize up, there's a queasy moment when I seem to be trying to step out of my own armor, and I nearly fall before the gyros right me. I couldn't walk through it if my life depended on it, which, ha ha, ironically it does.

> I congratulate you on your usual fine showing. However, as you must by now have realized, none can defeat the might of Doctor Impossible. By means of a scheme so brilliant only I could have devised it, I have taken control of our planet's orbit.

"Has anybody got their communicator still?" Rainbow's voice again. Silence as everybody checks. "Jesus."

It all began so well, eighteen hours ago. Feral was still in the hospital, but Rainbow Triumph was there, itching to come along for once. Her mood was infectious. We'd piled into the jumpjet, fired up and armed to the teeth, everyone with their own reasons for wanting to smash something big and delicate. No more vague conspiracies, no more poking around in bars and prisons and magic shops. Even without CoreFire, we were the greatest heroes in the world. All we needed was a fair fight.

The island looked the same, the same ruined base, but now sprinkled with a few functioning lights. He'd started things up again, underground where the heroes hadn't reached all the way in last time.

We split up to take him, the classic approach. The last I saw of them,

Blackwolf was firing a grappling-hook gun with perfect accuracy, preparing to scale the outer cliff, with Rainbow Triumph following up the line. Damsel tore the cover off an accessway, and Elphin flitted off down the main hallway. Mystic vanished as I watched, flashing his enigmatic grin. Left alone, I waded into a sewage tunnel to find a way up through the septic system. It wasn't hard—most of Doctor Impossible's traps are pretty transparent to my vision—trapdoors, lasers, shifting walls all show up clearly marked when you look with the right frequencies.

The place was enormous. After about an hour and a half, I heard the sounds of what could only be the decisive battle. I sprinted through one metal gallery, then another, until I found the central control room. We had him cornered, and it was all over. He's only a technician, after all. He looks like he weighs 120 pounds.

I took a film of the last battle as it happened, taped out of my left eye. I run it back, reliving the moment—as I came into the hall, I could see the battle unfolding about 150 feet away. The Champions had cleared a circle in a swarming army of cybernetic minions, and they were throwing down with the Doctor. I was the last to arrive. And I could see right away that I was the world's last hope.

I stopped for maybe three seconds to watch. Damsel was closing in on the Doctor, looking quite simply like the wrath of God. Whatever my feelings about her, I never quite considered what it would be like to have her angry at me. Watching the tape, I saw Blackwolf dodge a first and then a second energy blast, twisting his body, banking on sheer athletic ability. Mister Mystic was whispering alien syllables, his low and resonant voice carrying through the chamber.

And the Doctor beat them. It was barely even a fight. Rainbow went down before I could even power all the way up and start my sprint. It reminds me of nothing so much as footage of CoreFire dispatching some helpless nobody.

Doctor Impossible looked happy. No, he looked like he was having the best day of his entire life. He had a new weapon, a hammer held in his left hand; Mister Mystic conjured an eerie walking shadow, but it shattered like glass when the hammer touched it. Bullets, punches, bolts of energy—nothing could touch him, and he seemed a hundred times as strong. By the time I got there he was using its handle to pin Damsel against the wall by her neck, holding her off the ground like a naughty puppy.

Blackwolf looked genuinely shocked, angrier than I'd ever seen him. He managed a fancy duck and roll that carried him past the blaster fire and almost to Doctor Impossible himself, who then clubbed him to the ground one-handed with the butt of a ray gun, not even seeming to think about it. The blaster was in his right hand; he spun it in his fingers, then sprayed shot after shot at Elphin, who dodged madly, faster than a hummingbird, her cutie-pie face drawn with concentration.

He let Damsel drop, choked out, then managed to grab Elphin's spear just behind the blade. That's my cue, I remember thinking.

The room blurred as I accelerated to my top speed, pounding across the cavernous room, dodging robotic minions like a broken-field runner. Everyone else slowed down as all my systems kicked up to their highest level. I ducked a cybernetic ogre's swinging steel fists and bulled straight through a crowd of smaller scrimmagers with a sound like a refrigerator dropped from a crane. Chips of metal, plastic, and glass sprayed from the impact, but I didn't slow. A proximity alarm beeped and I reached one arm back to shred a diving drone helicopter with depleted-uranium slugs—no rubber bullets this time. For good or ill, this is what I was made for. The next generation of warfare.

Sixty feet away, and Elphin had lost her spear, the last heavy hitter still standing. I knocked Impossible's last defender to the floor, stepped over Blackwolf's prone form, and made ready to settle this for good. Elphin had fallen to her knees, stunned by a right cross; he yanked her off the ground. She was fading.

I was thirty feet away, then fifteen. Even Elphin stopped to watch when she saw me, mesmerized by this oncoming disaster. I was coming for my maker. Tactical computer sized up the fight, estimated a five-second outcome. Half a dozen bone-breaking combat scenarios scrolled across my onboard display. I cracked my knuckles theatrically.

"Doctor Impossible," I growled. "This ends now."

He looked up from his work as I started my leap, left ankle pivoting as my hips cranked around, ready to deliver a digitally calibrated, fusion-powered titanium-alloy side kick like the crack of doom.

At the last instant, his gaze flicked up to me and he saw me distinctly for the first time. He was still holding Elphin off the floor left-handed, but he found just a moment to pluck an oblong piece of plastic off his belt and point it at me. In playback, it looks like the little black remote you get with your car keys. He pressed the button and it was over. My little home movie ends in an extreme close-up of the laboratory's scarred marble floor. He's a professional. He knew exactly who I was and how I worked, and unlike me he came prepared. He took me down in less than a second, frozen like the Tin Woodman in the rain.

My first act will be to demand the surrender of all the governments of Earth, via the United Nations Security Council. You have no alternative. Legal details of this process can be found on my web site.

Across from me, Elphin sits in her own special cell, a low stone platform three feet on each side, her arms hugging her knees. Apart from the platform, the room is cold iron. A wooden cross hangs on each wall, the door, floor, and ceiling. Her spear is outside, propped against the wall with Damsel's swords. She looks around without speaking, her huge eyes all pupil.

"What's the plan? Does anyone have a plan?" I ask.

Blackwolf shushes me, points at the walls. Listening devices.

But at this point, I don't care much. I glare at him. "I thought you said we could beat him!"

He shrugs. "This was way outside the usual parameters. It may not have been him, you know. Could've been a shape changer."

"No metamorphs. I saw hard skeleton in there. It was him."

"He is no warrior," whispers Elphin, sullen. Another quarter heard from.

A deep thrumming comes through the rock, engines turning in the depths. Would he actually throw us into the Sun? How crazy is he, exactly? And how exactly do we get out of this one?

Two doors down from me, Mister Mystic is bound and gagged. Beyond him is the empty cell, fitted with reinforced manacles.

Whatever those machines are doing, they're running at a fever pitch. Damsel is sleeping on the floor, curled up in a corner, bathing in the amber lamplight. Rainbow Triumph stares straight ahead, not moving. Every few minutes, she swallows, as if trying to get rid of a nasty taste in her mouth.

"Anyone hear from Lily?" I ask, breaking the silence.

Blackwolf shrugs awkwardly. "Not since her little walkout. Not unless you have. I put her up on the usual lists, but you know how she is. Just about invisible when she wants to be."

"Great," Rainbow chimes in. "And who asked her to join, again?"

Blackwolf's neck is in a simple collar welded to the wall. No lock to pick, or chain to break. He can't even sit down. It's like Doctor Impossible's making fun of his lack of powers. Any of the rest of us could have broken it in a second.

"Who said 'split up'? Was that my idea?"

Blackwolf strains at the collar for a second, then gives up. "That's it. Now I'll never avenge my brother and sister. Fuck!"

Not moving, Damsel looks up. "Give it a rest, Marc. We're all in the same boat here."

"That's fine, Damsel. You rested now? You want to break us out of here?"

She doesn't answer.

Rainbow takes something from a pouch at her neck and eats it.

"What? It's my meds. I need them every twelve hours. Basically in seventy-two hours I'll be dead, if anyone cares."

Silence reigns. We must be way under the ruined laboratory by now. I can hear the ocean, faintly.

Across the hall from me, Elphin still isn't moving off of her little platform.

"What are you looking at?" She must have caught me looking. But I have to ask.

"Well . . . why doesn't Elphin do it?"

"She's a fairy." Even Blackwolf sounds a bit on edge.

"I cannot break the bars, Fatale. These symbols restrain me, nor can I touch cold iron. I'll never fulfill Titania's mission."

"What mission? What was it? Why didn't you go ahead and do it, if you've really been around for centuries?"

"It isn't time yet. And I'm not . . . I'm not entirely sure what it is."

"So those crosses are really holding you back? What about a Buddha, or a Star of David? Would that bother you as much?"

"I heard Doctor Impossible was Jewish," Rainbow puts in.

"Seriously, how much would it hurt you to break out of there?" I want to push her. Just once, I want her to behave like an ordinary person, drop the act and get us out of here.

"I cannot," she says flatly.

"Is it, like, a phobia? Are you afraid?"

"I am of the Legion of the Western Sidhe. I do not know fear. But I'm governed by our law."

Damsel wearily intervenes. "Fatale? Let it go."

"No, I'm not going to die because a fake elf won't cross an imaginary line. I know what's holding me, and it's not something I made up."

"You don't know what you're talking about. Why don't you walk out of here yourself if you can, clockwork lady."

"It's a software lock! It's electricity and metal. That's what I am. I'm the next generation of warfare."

"And I am twenty generations of war. What is it you're so proud of, that makes you walk about and twitch and strut that way, like the bronze guardsman who strikes the hours on the clock at St. Clement's?"

"I'm a super-soldier!"

"You're no one!"

"Fatale, just shut up," Blackwolf adds, helpfully.

But I'm on my feet now, and I turn to the rest of them. "She's not a fairy! She's just not. She's a genetic experiment, or an alien. And it would be nice if Tinker Bell here dropped the pretense, just this once, before Doctor Impossible, you know, throws our entire planet into the Sun."

Group silence. I can see I don't have everyone's support in this.

Having accepted your surrender, I will begin the launch of the new Ice Age, the Age of Doctor Impossible. An era of science and marvels and, of course, my total domination of the world.

"God, when is he going to shut up?" Rainbow sighs. She isn't looking so good.

I try to change the subject. "Blackwolf? I thought you said he needed a power source for this."

"He could be bluffing." He doesn't bother looking at me.

"He didn't look like he was bluffing when he beat the crap out of you." Rainbow won't leave it alone.

"Jeez." Blackwolf mock-cringes. "Thought you were my sidekick."

Silently, Rainbow gives him the finger.

"He had a new weapon, damn it. Did anyone else see that hammer he was holding?"

"We all saw the hammer. Nobody knows what it is."

"It looked magical."

"That's what Mystic said before he went down. The Doctor took him out first."

"Forget it," Damsel says. "We couldn't even save CoreFire."

Our fearless leader. In the amber glow of an overhead light, Damsel sits at the back of her cell, her knees up. She's loose in there—I can't see anything restraining her. He took her swords, but otherwise I can't see any reason why she doesn't smash her way out. I'm too embarrassed to ask what the problem is. Without the swords, she looks like a different person—a slight, greenish, surprisingly young brunette. She has the cell next to Blackwolf's.

"This was such a mistake. The military would have prepared properly, instead of just jetting off after lunch. This should have been a ground assault."

"Come on, Ellen. You've seen what Doctor Impossible does to conventional forces. We're the logical counterforce."

"You mean CoreFire was. Without him, Doctor Impossible's beaten us twice this week. The first time, he didn't even have his costume. Let's face it, the New Champions was a stupid name, and kind of a stupid idea. We shouldn't have tried it." Damsel punches the wall hard. It should crack the concrete; it should smash it to powder. There's just a dull smack.

"That's easy for you to say, Miss Stormcloud. It's not as if the rest of us had anywhere to go."

"And I did? Didn't you ever wonder why I didn't join the Supers?"

He holds up a black-gloved hand. "Don't start."

"I can't believe you never figured it out. CoreFire knew; I guess he could sense stuff. The one date we had, he worked it out. After that he wouldn't go near me. Fucking racist."

"Maybe you shouldn't have slept with him then." Blackwolf's tone is low and bitter. He's smart; he knows we're listening. Maybe he doesn't care.

"You remember what happened to my mother?" Damsel sounds like she really wants to know.

"Your mother?"

"You know . . . the alien princess?" she says, her voice acid now. "Remember her? Stormcloud's first wife. It was one of those superhero marriages—he saves her planet; she goes back to the stars."

"I know. But . . ."

"Think about it. She wasn't human, even if she looked a little like us. She wasn't even a mammal. No one even thinks about the fact that I look human. My hands are a little big, see? And my ears, that's why I wear my hair long.

"I shouldn't exist at all. Her people have an advanced gene science, and my mother's father donated his expertise as a wedding present. I'm mostly a clone of my father—they switched the gender, probably so it would be less obvious. They managed to include a few of my mother's traits—my biology is less human than you think. Why do you think I throw up all the time?

"I know my nervous system reads funny, and my blood type's irregular, a one-off. I'm red-green color-blind. Did you know that?

"My father did his best to hide it. They raised me human, but my mother was always an alien. Green skin, of course. Her breath always smelled like cinnamon. Her eyes were huge. Cold hands, and she loved to swim. She went back when I was nine, when she succeeded to the throne on her world. We spoke English together when we could, over the hyperwave communicator. I never learned her language, only a few words. It's difficult for humans to learn, but I thought I should.

"At first, they thought I didn't have any powers. My father raised me pretty strictly. I was in private school under a secret identity, God, until eleventh grade. I hated it. Then on my sixteenth birthday, I walked out onto the Peterson quad and screamed. I broke windows. Fucking Regina was pissed.

"After that, at night I'd be flying above the city in a blaze of light, but I'd retreat afterward into my secretary job. And afterward, after the Champions, there was nothing to stop me from being Damsel all the time. And the reality was, I had no idea who Damsel was, not really. Not when she wasn't saving people. All I wanted was to be in the Super Squadron.

"I still have my title. I'm even still a princess. My mother rules an ocean planet somewhere; it's in my passport. But the Super Squadron wouldn't take off-worlders. And I failed the goddamn blood test."

"It doesn't make any difference. Not to me," Blackwolf says. He looks calmer than I thought he'd be. Like he's finally understood something, a missing piece. CoreFire must have seen it first, with those eyes of his.

She gestures weakly at the overhead lamp. "Her sun's radiation takes away my powers anyway. That's what the lamp is for, smart guy. I guess Doctor Impossible knew it, too. Face it, I'm a mistake."

Yes, in the coming era I shall rule your puny world, as is my right. I will be just but fair, and above all, scientific. It will be my pleasure to keep you alive to witness your total and utter defeat.

And Elphin stirs on her platform and makes the longest speech I've ever heard from her.

"You know how they found me? I was starving and I passed out. A couple of hunters—they thought their luck was in."

"Jesus," I say. She flinches at the name. "Sorry."

"I was born in the twelfth century of your Christ, and I am the last fairy in the world. When the Fair Folk left the world of humankind early in the seventeenth century, I was left behind—Titania could not or would not explain why. But there I stayed, the lone fairy in all the woods of England."

She crouches in her cell and tells the story.

"Year by year and century by century, the game thinned out, acorns lost their flavor, and the spring dew grew less and less nourishing. Alone, I walked the forests, empty now of knights-errant and loitering maidens, while the long nineteenth century stretched on. And the twentieth. The forest diminished into odd patches of undeveloped land, crisscrossed by dirt roads and power lines, overflown by airplanes three times a day. I began hearing cars zoom past on the expressway, where once cool forest had stretched hundreds of silent miles in every direction. I grew used to hearing them pass, always behind the next stand of trees. Squirrels replaced deer; wolves were a distant memory. One day, a young boy in a red anorak saw me in full daylight as I crouched drinking from a drainpipe.

"I waited for Titania's plan to become clear. I hiked farther north as time went on, and then farther. I crossed the roads late at night, asphalt stinging the soles of my bare feet, to get to the next square of land. I was lamed once when a car struck me. I'd taken wounds before in Titania's service—I knew the burn of cold iron, and once the flash and hot thump of a lead musket ball—but this, the blinding light and the force of it rolling me over and over, it was like nothing I'd ever felt. I flashed away into the brush before the shock had worn off, and lay there shaking."

I look around and the others are listening silently. Blackwolf has heard this before; he must have. Rainbow clearly hasn't. But Elphin is speaking to me.

"I began to starve. I grew thin, thin even for a fairy, a creature of long nails and silvery skin stretched over hollow bird bones. The fish were gone. I munched nettles and drank tainted water from streams, and in winter I raided squirrels' granaries. On summer nights, I sat and gazed at the few stars visible beyond the light of the cities, and dreamed of old hunts. It was 1975, unfathomably late in the day to be a full-blooded fairy in England. I wandered dazed in the forest, moonlight shining through my flesh. I was fading.

"One morning in early spring, I collapsed and lay for hours at the bottom of a culvert, until a sudden rainstorm washed me down out of the hills. The hunters were up from Berwickshire, making a day of it. They found me stretched out in a streambed, unconscious in full day-light.

"It was noon, and they were already a little drunk when they found me, a tiny woman in a nightdress, four and a half feet tall, inhumanly graceful even in sleep. One of them handed his buddy his gun and went to get a closer look. He must not have noticed the wings, or the nails.

"According to a police report, I was later seen walking along the expressway around noon, naked, blood splashed over my face and body. I did not know what had happened. But when, after three hundred years, one of the Fair Folk walked barefoot up the center line of a main road, it was a Catholic priest who recognized the gravity of the situation.

"He bundled me off the street and found me clothes, and a room with no crosses or cold iron. He called his superior, who found a scholar at the Vatican archive who specialized in such things. The Catholic Church has what you would call a very fine institutional memory. The last man to have been in this situation wrote in twelfth-century Latin and told the protocols, modes of address for speech between fairies and Christian men. And it remains in effect, Vatican Two notwithstanding. The priest repeated the language they gave him, and, dazed, I replied in the language of the ancient compact, words I had learned under Henry the Second.

"I have been charged with two tasks, to uphold the honor of Fairy and to fulfill the task that has been laid on me, when the time is right. But those who made the covenant knew nothing of the world I found myself in now, nor did Titania.

"I was a nine days' wonder. The press grew tired of me—I could not be featured forever on your talk shows and in your magazines. I could not go back to the forest, to graze on highway median strips. I did not know how to rent an apartment, or work in a trade, or live in a city. I am a fairy, but I cannot be Titania's knight anymore.

"But Damsel found me and offered me a job, one that made sense of my life again. I could be a superhero."

"How about you? How'd you get started?"

For once, Damsel is looking directly at me, but the amber light makes it hard to read her features when she asks me the question I've been waiting to figure out.

"You guys don't want to hear about it." I'm not ready to talk about it anyway.

"What'd they do to you?" She says it in a tone I've never heard from her.

And for a full minute, I can't answer, a minute before the thoughts start to come again.

"I was a superhero, too, for a while, but the NSA was just easier. It's not like how they tell you it will be. It's hard to make it on your own as a cyborg—I've tried. I weigh almost five hundred pounds. I can't find clothes that fit me. I can't ride a bicycle. I can't eat in a normal restaurant, or sit in a chair not reinforced for my weight. I need special foods; I need medication to keep my body from rejecting the implants, and then I get sick too often due to a depressed immune system.

"And those are only things I know about. I have systems nobody understands. It's not like I'm a car that can be recalled if one model out of a million fails—there's only one of me."

I don't want to tell them this stuff, but I'm sick of being the only one who knows. It all comes spilling out.

"When they told me they weren't going to take care of me anymore, I thought I was dead. The Ohio facility that maintained me shut down overnight; I went in one day and found a bare office. And when I went to try to trace their assets, I found out they never existed."

It's about as far as I can go, but there's more I can't even put into words. I still don't have a boyfriend. I can't even have children—that's where the fusion reactor went in. I know it's crazy, but I thought Doctor Impossible was going to take me in, or maybe he would fix me, put me back the way I was. I know that's crazy. But I hate this piece of metal that I had them put inside me. God, I hate it. The way you can only hate a part of yourself that you made.

I leave you to ponder the error of your ways. The error of opposing . . . Doctor Impossible. Ahahaha hahahahahahaaa!

Damsel actually looks a little better now, but that light is still shutting down her powers. She and Blackwolf are talking in low tones. They've been in tight spots before.

Blackwolf sees me looking. "It's all right."

"How is it all right? We're starting a new Ice Age and the entire Earth is now ruled by the angriest dork in the world. So tell me, how is it all right?"

"I've actually got a backup plan. We've got reinforcements."

"Backup? Who is it—is it Stormcloud? Is it the Super Squadron?" But he shakes his head.

"You really are new to this, aren't you? There's no way he was going to stay down for long."

The speakers crackle, and Doctor Impossible starts up again; he's recorded his speech, and it's starting to repeat.

My dear "Champions." Welcome. By the time you hear this . . .

"God, what an asshole." Blackwolf curses with sudden feeling. Amazingly, Damsel starts to smile, and then giggle a little. Suddenly, we're all laughing, almost like a team again. Then, far off, I hear the thunder.

CHAPTER NINETEEN

BUT BEFORE I KILL YOU

"Well, well, well. CoreFire." I've waited more than half a lifetime for this.

CoreFire slumps, arms manacled to a central set of pillars. He's doing that stupid thing of pretending to be asleep, like we're at summer camp. Well, let him. But I wish for once he would at least look up and see this, because frankly, it's another tour de force. Spectacular.

I keep talking, but my mind is elsewhere. I've got to concentrate on conquering the world.

"Now that you are lying helpless at my feet. Now that your finest efforts have proved futile. Now that you are totally in my power.

"Now that there is nothing you can do to stop me. Now that you are thousands of miles from help. Now that there is no possibility of escape. Now that you have, finally and irremediably, lost."

Even though my experiment was a failure.

"Now that the armies of the world are helpless against me. With my lasers. And force fields. And my army of robot soldiers. With their force fields. And their laser eyes."

Even though I never got the girl.

"Now that your defeat is total and abject. Now that I have crushed you, comprehensively and without qualification. And I will reign supreme forever.

"Now that I win."

Even though I'll never be you.

Yes, he faked it. I don't know how yet. I'll have to make him tell me.

The generators are just the hub of a network of forces I've set up, stretching well past the orbit of the Moon. Gravitational generation, and perfect reflection of energy. There's no one who can see the whole of it except me, the scale of the project, a vast and shadowy galleon putting about infinitely slow, infinitely ponderous in the high seas of the ether, dragged at by innumerable threads and sheets.

It can't be done all at once, only by a slow, steady application of impetus. It was a fantastic piece of mathematics, a baroquely extended word problem of novelistic proportions, a shifting matrix of angles of incidence, rates of spin, shear strength.... To manipulate an unthinkably heavy mass of rock and clay, oceans and seas, buses and grand pianos afloat in space, was like an ant pushing an ocean liner, a tail wagging a million-ton dog. Behind me the machines rise up, tier upon tier, to the cavernous ceiling.

I might have managed this years ago if that experiment had been completed. Those meddling fools! If only I'd written my dissertation properly. If only I'd gotten to finish. But I still needed you gone.

The tendrils of energy whip out and charge the five subsidiary poles, and the whole apparatus begins to turn, ever so slowly, massively, nudging the Earth off course without breaking it apart. Slowly, almost imperceptibly bringing the whole ponderous business, the whole cosmic clockwork, to heel. For a second, I stand at the fulcrum point of creation.

God I'm so unhappy.

When the Nemesis Alert went off, I could scarcely believe it. I set them up a long time ago to scan for objects that were superdense and fast-moving and human-size. In other words, for him.

I should have guessed it, with all the publicity, that maudlin spectacle. I wonder if there was anything in the coffin at all. There must have been a few people in on it, laughing up their sleeves at me. And to think I fell for it, I, Doctor Impossible! Tricked, by one of these mental pygmies. And it was so obvious, exactly the kind of almost clever idea these people come up with, like pretending you've been knocked unconscious. Like the secret identity thing. As if we don't know what you look like.

Maybe he wanted to draw me out. No one would fight him anymore—maybe he was bored. He changes things just by existing. Nothing about him is normal. His senses alone make a difference to what you can try when he's on the planet.

I had about ninety minutes' warning, ninety minutes to recalculate everything, my enormous intelligence working at full power. But it's better this way—the Champions were always in a league below him. Beating them without CoreFire is almost cheating.

But you have no idea what it's like to face one of these people. One of the absolute unstoppables. He's strong, much too strong to bother shooting at. You may as well shine a flashlight on him. CoreFire has only gotten stronger over the years, and the world of solid matter must be like fog to him now.

You need layers. And there needs to be a trick. I used to fight Go-Man, the Super Squadron's speedster with a carefree disregard for atmospheric friction and inertia and a few other things we rubes understand to be the laws of physics. I'd rarely see his actual body, lost at the center of a perpetual whirlwind like a hummingbird's wing or a helicopter's rotor, invisibly rapid.

I first met him in Berlin, and built a whole new class of defenses to deal with his class of ability—trip wires, gases, immobilizing foams, areas of the complex that could seal off instantly if I even suspected he was inside them. Then I'd pour in everything I could think of—poisons, sonic vibrations, mutant bees—until something worked, until he fell unconscious and stopped moving, precipitated out of the air like a spirit.

CoreFire poses these threats and more, and he's seen my older tricks already. It's not like I can just set off a smoke bomb, duck into a hall of mirrors, and run away cackling. I don't think there's anyone who could beat him in a straight fight. There's nothing else like him now, not on Earth anyway.

He set down lightly in the ruined forecourt. There was no one waiting for him. Henchmen are no use in a situation like this. Don't get me started about henchmen.

"Wow. Time to fire the maid." Imbecile.

I left it quiet for a few moments, waiting, silent, then hit the lights. If it spooked him, he didn't show it. He spent a little time looking around. He could have tunneled straight to me if he'd known where I was. He could have been running through there at a hundred miles per hour if he'd wanted, but he was going to play this out, just like I was.

He'd gotten lazy—that, I noticed. He didn't even x-ray the place, it's been so long since anything could hurt him. The first mine went off, shuddering through the complex like distant thunder. On camera, CoreFire was unruffled, but he spoke for the first time.

"Nice try."

I leaned in to the microphone. Time to talk some trash.

"You didn't think your prisons would stop me, did you? You knew I'd be back. I . . . Doctor Impossible!"

It passed the time.

All heroes have an origin. It's a rule, right? Flash of fire, a miraculous accident. But what could have made something like you, CoreFire? So ungodly powerful, so perfect. You've barely aged, you know. You might live a thousand years. Some people think you're an alien; some people think you're Cain, condemned to wander the Earth, untouchable. Maybe you came from the future? A broken future, like Lily's, here to fix the past. But no, I've been to the future, many futures, and seen nothing like you except you. I've seen futures where you went bad, went to my side, and futures where you reigned as king. I've seen alternate realities where the accident that gave you powers happened to Erica instead, or Professor Burke, or the kid standing next to you, or me—but not the real me.

It's one of the hardest puzzles. I was there, and I've tried everything to solve it, to work out the mystery of your accident, the secret inside you. It's been a long time since Professor Burke's seminars. But you never were much of a scientist, were you, Jason? Has everybody forgotten about the zeta beam? Because I didn't.

"Hmm . . . I sense a trap." He poked his head into the entrance hall.

The doors sealed shut, and the room fogged with an acid mist. Of course it was a trap. It was all traps, all the way. In the corridor beyond, cutting lasers lit the place in lurid greens and reds. Then sonics, then microwaves. He watched it all with an appraising stare, and pushed the next door open.

"That all you got?"

I often wonder what Einstein would have done in my position. At Peterson, I kept an Einstein poster in my room, the one that says "Imagination is more important than knowledge." Einstein was smart, maybe even as smart as Laserator, but he played it way too safe. Then again, nobody ever threw a grappling hook at Einstein.

I like to think he would have enjoyed my work, if he could have seen it. But no one sees anything I do, not until it's hovering over Chicago.

All the rooms were traps, but he came on like a hero out of legend. I froze him in a block of ice, and he melted it. Lava he cools with his breath, and shatters. Electricity, poison darts, voodoo skulls. I try everything, just to be sure. The lasers left red tracks on his skin that faded after a few seconds, an odd little secondary effect. He was getting impatient. We'd done this part before.

Then he was through the last door, brushing off some electrified wires. I'd had an idea about a Taser that didn't quite come off.

And now there's nothing between me and him but air. I'm only sixty feet away, sitting on the throne you've seen in my broadcasts.

"Hello, CoreFire. Did you think you were being clever?"

"You'll never get away with this," he snarls.

"Oh, come off it. I already have. You just missed it while you were playing the dearly departed."

"I'm going to break you."

"All right, then. Go on. Hit me. Go on."

In an eye blink, he's speeding up the steps to the dais, half flying, readying a blow that would have shivered diamond. It passes noiselessly through the hologram figure, and, on cue, laughter fills the laboratory.

"Sorry. Couldn't resist."

Lights up on the real throne. I get my hands up just in time, and then he's on me.

We've fought so many times—underwater, in outer space, in burning control rooms and crashing spaceships and ancient temples, on Mars and at the center of the Earth. And I lost, every time.

Not that I haven't come close. But whatever he's got powering him is tough, very tough, some freakish zeta vortex that I never quite solved. He behaves as if he were superdense and as light as a soap bubble, simultaneously. It drives conventional physics crazy.

Our earliest battles were all robots and lasers, big ones. I piled on the iron and the lasers, thinking sooner or later I'd hit his limits. But he smashed it all into scrap, victims of a mistaken conception. I could build anything out of metal, but he'd always be stronger than any metal.

In the seventies I grew more sophisticated. I used psychology. I took hostages, stole sidekicks and women and dogs. Erica and I spent some more time together, on trains, in caves, but the mask never came off, and she never guessed. I learned that CoreFire could be confused, by mirrors or drugs or insane twists of logic. He could be fooled by android duplicates, holograms, telepathy, and mind-switching devices.

But only temporarily. Sooner or later, he'd cut through the fog, and I'd feel his fists on me again.

In the eighties, there was magic, and the new cybernetics. I always fell at the last, beaten into unconsciousness. I'm tough, but there are limits to it if you just keep on hitting me. But if my career has a meaning, it's that in the long run, I'm better than people like him.

I lose the scepter in the first second, slapped out of my hand. It goes spinning across the marble, no big loss—it was zeta-powered, useless against him. I throw a punch, but he catches it, and the counterpunch rings off my helmet. The robes are hard to fight in, but I swore I wasn't going down in T-shirt and jeans. I draw the blaster and zap him with it, just for old times' sake. I hope it stings.

I know he isn't untouchable. I've seen him bleed, and the time that alien gladiator came to Earth to challenge him, he had a black eye before he finished that fight. Once I think I broke his nose.

He catches the blaster and crushes it in his hand, grabs my collar and throws me twenty or thirty feet into the wall. I land hard and it's a moment before I can breathe again. He looks a little confused, a little resigned, as if to ask, Why are you making me do all this? But he comes on again.

It comes down to bodies. A blurred, panting moment when we wrestle, power on power, his breath on my cheek. It always comes to this, at the end, despite all my precautions, the layers upon layers, the deceit. I taste the familiar mixture of blood, sweat, and defeat.

He's still the strongest hero I've ever fought. He reaches to catch me in a headlock, but I slip out, cape going over my head, and we're apart again. I drop a couple of flashbangs to buy time.

I jab him in the eye, but I'm punching marble. His head barely moves. "Had enough?" he quips, ever the wit. He isn't even mussed.

He smiles, then blurs, and I barely see the punch before it lands. Then I'm on my hands and knees. The room doesn't quite spin, but it slides a little as I get to my feet. The scar he once left on my face is starting to hurt, which means I'm under a lot of stress.

His eyes change color for an instant and my outer robes start to smolder. I tear them off and square up again. He reaches for my throat, but I catch his arm and throw him on his back on the carpet. It gives me time to get the Hammer of Ra out.

I shouldn't have waited. I knew when I first touched the hammer what it could do. It's broken, but there's just enough power left. For a few minutes, I can be invincible.

I whisper that unrepeatable, unpronounceable word, and power flows out of the hammer and into me. I feel light and quick; the world slows down. I flex one hand, and feel the power of a mountain in it. It's so good; it feels like cheating. For a few minutes, I'm CoreFire. I'm better than CoreFire—I'm Doctor Impossible.

I swing and hit him on the chin just as he's getting up, and he pinwheels around and back into the floor. The shock sends echoes through the room. He looks a little surprised, like he didn't think I had it in me. He's won too many times before to have expected anything new. But he's not scared yet.

"Nelson Gerard says hello." Hopping down a step, I brace myself and hit him again, harder. *Ka-tham!* Echoes bounce off the vaulted ceiling. I know what he's feeling, because this is what always happens to me, two minutes before I go back to prison. He's dazed now, trying to shake it off.

"Wh . . ." It's like he's starting to form a question.

"Feel that? Who's invincible now?"

I hit him and he actually flies through the air to the far wall. His face is getting a puffy look I've never seen before. I must be starting to get through to him. He's learning something, just as I once did. And I'm learning, too. I'd been stupid, trying so many elaborate devices, when it always comes down to a punching match. Boom! The heroes had been showing me all along exactly how it's done. Why hadn't I paid attention?

He's barely on his feet now. He starts to put his hands up, trying to form fists. I set it up again, taking my time. One, two, three, boom! Who was the first person to hit you, CoreFire? It was me.

I hit him and hit him, knocking him all the way out into the front courtyard. The charge runs down eventually. He blacks out near the end, just like I used to. And for one utterly still and perfect moment, I've conquered the world.

I drag him back to the main laboratory, and chain him to a pillar. There doesn't seem to be anywhere else to put him.

Waiting, while the machinery powers up, I doze. There's still a lot I don't understand about that long-ago night. Memory doesn't work the way it ought to, reeling off like a movie. Pieces come back sometimes, fragments of the insoluble mystery of the past. Erica again—we were doing laundry together—the buzz of fluorescent lights and the thrum of the dryers seemed unbelievably loud. The air was warm and stale in the basement. She cocked her head, inclined just fractionally toward me, and something in the air changed. I thought for a second she was going to kiss me. I flushed. This is it, I thought. I thought I felt her lips already, warm against mine, parting. This is how it happens, how you become another person, how you get to grow up.

Then the timer buzzed, and she looked up, startled. Now I'm in the old lab again. It's time to check the mixture. Down the long fluorescent-lit corridor, with that faint acrid laboratory smell, half nauseating and half comforting. That's how it began. Then the explosion, and the long, long, long, long mourning afterward.

"I know you're awake."

You'd be surprised what it takes to restrain an entity with his capacities. It took a while.

"Fine. Pretend. In just a few minutes, I'm going to become the greatest supervillain of all time. I thought you should watch. Open your eyes at least. I'm standing right here."

Finally, he does.

"It's good, isn't it? I actually think it's my best one yet. You should appreciate my work more, you know. You're the only one who gets to see it."

He doesn't respond.

"Nothing? Oh well. I tried."

He heaves a deep, exasperated sigh, like I'm boring him terribly. In a low voice, he asks, "Look, will you at least tell me what this is all about?"

"What it's about? I'm so glad you asked." I steeple my fingers and touch them to my lips. I can't help myself; it's just good to be a villain, every once in a while.

"Like you, I had powers. I could have gone your way. I didn't, but you know, I can almost imagine what it must have been like. The first time, as you waited for the sun to go down, not until eight o'clock maybe in the summer months. You'd wait in your room, doing a few stretches while the streets cleared. You were in your apartment, maybe, in New York.

"Then you opened the window, pushed it all the way up. Set your left foot in the sill, poked your head out, and stood. Leaning out a little bit, one hand still hooked inside, you let your body extend and hang a little. The night air smelled like a forest; the wind slipped under your T-shirt. The moon was almost full, lighting up the night, an invitation to climb. And you did, fingers finding gaps in the facade, up the side of the building like a ladder. Nothing to it.

"Up on the rooftop, you could see the city, smell it. The air was like a warm bath; the wind was sour and salty coming off the bay. You jogged back and forth a couple of times, then sighted in on the building across the alley. The gap was fifteen feet, and five stories down; without giving yourself time to think, you sprinted, springboarded off the low wall, did a lazy somersault in the air before you hit, arms extended, not even a wobble. Perfect. The accident that gave you this power never took anything away—you were still strong, quick, muscles like spring steel and skin like Teflon.

"Soon it was a rhythm, ten steps and release, moving downtown. Once or twice you'd had to catch a ledge and hang by your hands, or take a few hops to the left or right, but in the end, you'd gone half a mile without touching pavement. In the slanted light of the setting sun, you were golden.

"You'd go all over the city at night, Harlem, SoHo, Wall Street. Lurking around neighborhoods and waiting for a drug deal or a mugging. Then the feeling, as you stepped from the shadow of a stairwell. The criminals thought you were just a kid with something on his face. They were laughing, and they didn't know what was coming. Then the cries of 'Oh no,' the priceless look on their faces. And the victims' gratitude. That thanks I never got, for all my scheming.

"But of course it wasn't like that for you. You could fly. You just rose up from the rooftops and into the warm night air. Then you swooped around a little until you spotted some hapless evildoer. It must have been awesome. God, to have all the world love you like that. And for what? For joining the winning team. So easy. But not this time . . . Jason."

For once, I provoke a reaction.

"What? How do you know my name?" He's a little nervous, even. He'd better be. I savor every syllable.

"Oh ho ho . . . Well you might wonder. Did you never think about what happened to your old friend? The one who made you, made you what you are, and your greatest enemy. And you never guessed, after all these years."

He gapes. "Who? You're not . . . Professor Burke?"

Fuck. "No . . . who *made* you, Jason."

CoreFire is nonplussed.

"I don't really understand what you're talking about."

"What about this? I'll let you go, and all you have to do is tell me my real name." Nothing. And now it comes.

"Maybe . . . *this* will refresh your memory." I take off my mask and let him see me, all the better to look at his blank, mild, staring face. Finally. It feels like it's been a thousand years.

He clears his throat nervously. "I'm sorry?"

"From college. You know. From Peterson. The one who followed you, looked up to you. Created you. Beat you. Right? Right?"

Slow, uncomprehending shake of the head. Nothing.

"Fine. Fine. Doesn't matter. After all, when I rule the world, they'll know me. And worship me. Even . . . Erica!"

I let the name sink in. I know it's not original. I know it was a long time ago.

"Who?" he asks.

"Erica." I try to pack some meaning into the name, but I have to admit he looks a little blank. "Um . . . you know. The writer."

He shakes his head a little apologetically. "I guess. I mean, I remember who she is and all, sure. But, um, why, do you know her?"

Jesus. It's not as if I expected an apology. Fine. That's great. Super, in fact. My life's ambition wasted. I guess it doesn't matter after all. If you'll just wait there, I'll go and destroy the world with this machine I've built.

"We're screwed now, buddy," I mutter. I throw the main switch. Behind me, the mammoth engines go into overdrive, shifting their hum another few steps up the scale. For the first time, I think he might look a little scared. I keep talking as I work.

"Doctor Impossible. My name's Doctor Impossible. You could at least have said that. Well, too bad, Jason, you've blown your chance to save the world. There isn't going to be a next time, Jason. I hope you've noticed the Moon's a little bigger. I'm going to scrawl my name across this puny planet. My real name, Doctor Impossible.

"I'm taking over the world, and you're going to watch. . . . Hahahaha . . . ahahahahahahaha!"

I laugh, but the mechanics of total world conquest are enormously vexed. You'll notice that if you ever try it. Conventional house-to-house and nation-to-nation pacification is unwieldy, to say the least. It's particularly hard to keep track of all the islands. There's mind control, if you've got the means, but it's awkward. There's no fun in waking everybody up in the morning, every day, and telling them to brush their teeth. You can do it by proxy, stealthily infiltrating major world governments, but then who gets the credit?

Probably the most foolproof method is to come up with a way of destroying the world, and then just let everyone know you have it. And then you sit on it for as long as you can, knowing that in the end somebody's going to knock you off your perch, whether or not you have the guts to pull the switch.

This is going to be different. This is one thing they didn't foresee. I don't have to destroy the Earth, just cool it down a little. Soon we'll see temperature drops of ten or twenty degrees Celsius. Ice creeps down from the poles, and the Earth's whiteness starts reflecting more heat back into space, cooling things down further. Global warming becomes a fond memory.

This is the Ice Empire scenario, one of the Baron's better concepts, but I'll be the one to pull it off, ruling from an enormous city of ice, each year the Earth's potentates begging me for a few more degrees Celsius. They'll need my zeta technology to survive, a collateral bonus, and I'll finally be able to tell that wretched Nobel committee what to do. And then the charm of the conceit, a huge aesthetic upside. Ice castles rising above now-frozen cities. Underground caves, fed by thermal vents. Cross-country skiing, pine forests, and I'll clone off some mammoths and wolves for effect. Every year a white Christmas!

And things won't have to be all that different. A few parades, maybe. New York will be Impossible City. Or Impossibleopolis. Maybe a few Ethergrads here and there. And I can always swing the Earth's orbit in a bit for the occasional sunny day. It's not like I'm going to be a jerk about it.

I give the Champions a short little speech in their cells, then glance over at the figure slumped in despair between the supporting pillars. Who knew that it was all so easy?

It feels so good, I just have to say it:

"So much for CoreFire. And so much for those wretched Champions!" Then, right behind me, someone clears her throat, and I freeze. "Well, almost."

I don't know how she got in, but then Lily's always been hard to see. CoreFire revives a little to see her, his gallant rescuer.

"Hello, Jonathan," she says. "It's nice to see you."

"Lily. And what a lovely outfit." I try to keep my voice steady. I'm not ready for this yet. She's still wearing her New Champions regalia. I make a sardonic bow, hoping I look at least somewhat composed. She shrugs, then takes a step toward me.

"Don't move!" I try to put some steel in it. I draw the blaster again, not quite pointing it at her.

"Fine." She puts her hands up in mock surrender. "Should I just wait here?"

"Whatever. Just don't think you can stop me."

"Yes, I know. Nobody can stop you, Jonathan."

"It's Doctor Impossible to you. Don't try to free him. I'm warning you." It's a standoff for the moment. The fact is, I'm not really sure I could stop her. I've never had to try.

"So is this really you now? These people?" I ask. I nod my head at CoreFire, chained. Seriously, she could at least be embarrassed about it.

"Come on, Jonathan."

"That's Doctor Impossible. What do you think you're doing here, Lily?"

"Oh, I don't know. I just thought I'd see what was happening. I quit the New Champions two days ago, for your information. Why, what exactly are you doing?"

"Taking over the world, actually. Eternity of snow and ice. Myself the only source of power, that sort of thing. Everybody swears fealty or death. You included." CoreFire is watching us like a hawk, waiting for one of us to make a move.

"A new Ice Age? Huh."

"Something wrong? Feeling a little . . . chilly, perhaps?"

"I'd hoped for something more imaginative. Wasn't that one of the Baron's ideas?" she asks.

"Shut up! It's the Ice Empire, and it's totally going to work."

"Well, it isn't now, I'm afraid." She takes another step. I point the blaster at her again, not that she seems to care.

"That's right, Impossible," CoreFire snarls, emboldened. "You're finished!"

Lily doesn't even turn around to answer him. "You shut up, fuck-head. I've got your number."

I trace an imaginary line on the floor with my foot. "I'm not kidding. I could throw this planet into the Sun at any time! If you get any closer I mean."

"Look, don't take it personally, I just don't want to live the rest of my life in your Ice Age thing. By the power vested in me by the New Champions, I'm hereby saving the world. Step away from the machine."

I wave her back with the blaster, one hand on the lever. "Don't cross that line. I'm serious. It works." Why is no one afraid of my blaster?

She advances another step, taking her time. I touch the Hammer of Ra at my belt, but it's cold and silent, just a rock on a stick.

She puts up her fists.

"You really want to do this?" I ask, giving her my "Stay back; I'm crazy" look. "Last chance. I'm tougher than you think."

She crosses the line. The rest doesn't take long, and I'd actually rather not describe it. Let's just say I have the sense to fold up after a couple of rounds, and she leaves me tied to the pylon next to CoreFire's. I wish he hadn't seen that. She's not even breathing hard.

Then she turns her attention to the machine. With a little admiration, I like to think, a little regret. Both of us watch her.

I try to delay the inevitable. "Are you hoping you'll get a medal? Maybe you'll get your boyfriend back."

She ignores me. She's thinking of something else, and after a moment she starts to speak in a low voice. I'm not even sure who she's talking to at first.

"You must have wondered what happened to me. Didn't you? I thought you were supposed to be smart."

She sounds almost upset. Her back is to us as she tries to figure out what to break first. She starts yanking out wires in strategic places. The turbine hum starts running back down the scale in a cosmic diminuendo. I can smell something burning.

"It was that time Baron Ether teamed up with the Living Diamond. I was still writing, but it was a dead end for me. My stories sucked, and I was writing too many superhero profiles to pay the bills. I'd become just CoreFire's girl. I needed a new angle.

"Just by chance, I found out where the two of them were hiding—they called for CoreFire, and I answered the phone and got the address. I followed them to an abandoned chemical factory and crept inside with my camera and sensible shoes."

She spots Laserator's reflecting lens. Crash, tinkle.

"It was the chance I needed, a real story I could break, but I went a little too far and they caught me. I ran for it, like always, and I tripped and fell, just like always. Toppled right off a catwalk and into a vat of some vile liquid they'd just mixed up together.

"I went home and showered, but already I felt a change, a stirring in my blood. A power. I went up to my room and stood there, looking out an open window at the street outside, white houses. It was early spring, and the breeze blew in. I thought of Jason and whether I should call him, but I didn't.

"I stood in the center of my room. It kept building until I was white-hot. My hand set the curtains on fire; I seared bare footprints into the carpet. Naked, I made my way very slowly down the hall and through the sitting room, then out onto the lawn.

"I looked at myself, changed, transparent and invulnerable. I stood there with my hardened skin cooling, ticking, in the dawn light. I wasn't going home anymore.

"It only seems right I should get superpowers; if the zeta beam had hit me, maybe I would have had CoreFire's—did you ever think of that?

"I knew I had a decision to make, the same one you did, and Jason. I didn't have to be Erica the klutzy girlfriend anymore. So I decided to be Lily, savior of the thirty-fifth century, the future girl without a past."

She looks over the wreckage, making sure there's really no way for me to repair it. There isn't.

"One last thing. I really did go to the future once, you know, and saw the Blight. It was real. And you know where it came from? Costa Rica. It was that stupid hammer that started it all when it broke."

"But . . . there isn't any Blight. I moved the hammer. I shut it down."

"I know. I guess you saved the world after all. Take care of yourself, Doctor Impossible."

She kisses me on the cheek, then looks into my eyes for a moment, almost smiling. She stands in the entrance for a moment, rainwater sheeting off her back, then vanishes into the night.

CoreFire looks after her, too, with a funny expression on his face that I've never seen before. He looks almost thoughtful. I can't think of anything to say, and apparently he can't either, so we just sit there tied to our pillars. And that's how the New Champions find us when they finally escape from my dungeon.

CHAPTER TWENTY

GIRL MOST LIKELY
TO SUCCEED

For a while, there's fighting overhead—tremendous blows and counterblows that seem to shake the whole fortress. Then an eerie silence except for the hum of Doctor Impossible's machines. Then I hear footsteps coming closer and I think I'm finally going to meet CoreFire. But of course it isn't. It's the last new Champion.

"So this is where the popular kids hang out," Lily says.

"How did you get in here?" Blackwolf asks. "Were you . . ."

"I know how it looks, but no, I'm not with him." She looks us over, her eyes moving from one to another. "But I wasn't entirely frank with you guys, either. About CoreFire."

"I know he's alive," Blackwolf says. "The Pharaoh tried to kill him, so he faked his own death."

"He fucking what?" Damsel's head snaps around, for once taken off guard. Even Mister Mystic makes a noise behind his gag.

"Is that what he told you?" Lily asks. She sounds incredulous herself. "He lost up there, did you know that? The Doctor beat the hell out of him. Whipped him senseless."

"Wait, wasn't CoreFire your boyfriend? Or were you just pretending about that, too?" Blackwolf looks angry, but I wonder if it's only because he's been outsmarted for once. "Were you working for Doctor Impossible this whole time?"

"Jesus, no." Lily rolls her eyes. "Look, it was a stupid mistake. It's what I wanted to tell you; I just didn't think you'd listen. You want to know what really happened to CoreFire? Your hero friend?" She looks us all over, slowly. He wasn't my friend, I want to remind her. I never even got to meet him.

"We met at a warehouse party in London, you know, one of those fringe powers things. He was slumming, I guess, with some friends I didn't know. I already knew I wanted to switch sides, and we sort of talked. He wanted to go away for the weekend, to this place he knew in Costa Rica. He said he could just fly us there, that it would take a couple of hours. Anyway, I went. I was going to be a heroine now, right?

"We found a resort area he knew, abandoned, but a cool place to take girls to, I guess. But when we got there, it was obvious someone else had found it. When we found out it was the Pharaoh, I thought he was going to die laughing. You know, that villain from the seventies, with the makeup? So this was a hero fight ready to happen, and my first collar for your side. We all used to make fun of him, like the time he couldn't find his own sarcophagus at the Met. We'd just bring him in and slap him in jail for a while, and I'd be in from the cold."

"But wait a minute. Jason said it was Doctor Imp—" Blackwolf looks caught completely off guard for once. "God damn it."

"Yeah. I thought so." Lily doesn't look smug at least. But she's been waiting to tell this.

"We split up—CoreFire set me down on a hill nearby, told me to just watch the show, see how a pro does it. I only got in close at the end. Pharaoh was tired by then. He hadn't had time to put on his gold makeup. He'd been swinging that hammer for hours; his scraggly graying hair was matted; sweat ran down from his beard and under his armor. He gave me a look, like he knew why I was there. We'd met a couple of times.

"Whatever else you can say about him, the Pharaoh could take a punch. CoreFire's strength was irresistible, but the Pharaoh's hammer made him absolutely impervious to harm.

"It's like we always used to talk about, who could beat whom when it came to just power on power. Blockade versus the Living Diamond. Nick Napalm or Aquamarine. Grab Bag against the Bricoleur. A matchup like CoreFire and the Pharaoh was anyone's guess. How do you calculate it? Zeta energy against magical relic. Pharaoh had always been tougher than anyone bothered to measure, and if he had put his mind to it, he could have been a real threat, instead of a standing joke. Each one had a force inside him, fueling him, and now we were going to see what it was worth. When they met . . . something gave.

"The fight covered about a mile, back and forth; then it went down to the beach. The hammer was glowing; the rubies on it were incandescent. It was obviously the only thing keeping him standing. There were gouges in the landscape where CoreFire had swung and missed. The paint was coming off of it, and underneath I could see symbols carved there. CoreFire wasn't worried, more like baffled. Frustrated. You could see the confusion spreading across his face—why wouldn't this guy go down? His hands hurt from punching him. And he was sick of the Hammer of Ra coming back and catching him in the face in front of this girl.

"Then the Pharaoh . . . Nelson . . . hit him straight in the chest, knocked him back a few steps and he went to one knee. I saw CoreFire's face then. I thought, Oh God, he's going to kill him.

"I started to run in. CoreFire went a few feet off the ground, taking his time to deliver his old Sunday punch, a massive roundhouse, harder than he'd usually dare to hit a living power. More the kind of thing when he'd smash an asteroid or sink a ship. The Pharaoh blocked two-handed, and the hammer . . . broke. It cracked down its face. I heard a sizzling crackle that seemed to come from everywhere at once. I smelled an otherworldly whiff of alien or god.

"The hammer was at the center of a slow explosion, a cold blossom of negative energy, like a fluid. It had splintered; one of the pieces went through CoreFire's biceps, and he was bleeding. Whatever technology or madness made the Pharaoh invincible, it was coming out. The effect was spreading; it dragged at me. Light and color smeared toward it. In another moment, we might all have been sucked in. I had a sudden thought that it would consume the world, or our whole dimension. Maybe Mister Mystic knows.

"The Pharaoh shouted at me to run. He was muttering his power word, but I don't think it was working. I didn't look back.

"You know I can't fly, but I run pretty fast. I honestly don't know what happened then. The whole valley had iced over by then. It was creeping into the sea. I honestly thought we had started the end of the world.

"There was another explosion. CoreFire got blasted miles into the air, and it must have hurt him, thrown him into that coma. I thought he was dead. I guess that's where he got the brilliant idea of stringing it out like that. Unless it was you, Marc. It's got your stamp on it."

Blackwolf shrugs. Oops.

"I wanted to say something before, but . . . if anyone knew I'd been there, no one would have believed it wasn't me who killed him. I guess I wanted a chance to be the good guy for a while. You would have worked it out eventually. Fatale would have, I know."

"So what happens now?" I ask. Did we lose? Or win?

"I'm going upstairs after this, to stop that idiot from taking over the world. I'll be gone by the time you get out of this. I just want to say . . . thanks for giving me a chance to be someone else for a while."

"Lily . . ." I want to tell her not to go. That we need her here.

"Wait." She walks over to where Elphin's spear leans against the wall, hefts it once, then tosses it to Elphin through the bars. "If you're thinking of hunting me down when this is over, forget it." She turns to go.

I call "Good luck" after her, because someone should. She was one of us. She half-turns, nods, and walks off down the passageway.

Elphin picks up her spear and looks at it uncertainly. I stand up and spread my arms.

"Go on," I tell her. "I'm ready this time." The plan has formed in my head; I can see already it will work. If she hits right, like she did the last time, she can pull me out through the field that's been trapping me. Our cells aren't that far apart.

She frowns and takes aim. It goes through, just like before, and the barbs catch, but it doesn't even hurt. She's good. I let her pull me into the field. For a moment, all my systems shut down. I black out for a second, but when I come to, I'm out of my cell, and they're all looking at me. For a moment, I'm the only superpower in the room, and they're waiting for me to rescue them. I bend the bars of Elphin's cage, shoot out the lamps shining into Damsel's cell, and tear off Blackwolf's and Rainbow's restraints. For a second, I'm a towering figure helping the needy, forgotten, and helpless in a faraway place.

When we get to the surface, everything's already over. Lily is gone, and smashed machinery and fragments of mirror lie everywhere. The Hammer of Ra rests on the floor, cracked and useless. It must have been some fight.

And there, tied back-to-back at the central pillar, are CoreFire and Doctor Impossible, the greatest hero and greatest villain of the age. For once, neither one has anything to say.

Lily vanished into the rain after the battle. She must have some other way of getting around, because she's nowhere on the island—Damsel and I check the whole place. After a team vote, we decide not to look for her. Everyone is feeling pretty giddy anyway.

CoreFire himself is maybe a little disappointing. When I heard the thunder, I could hardly believe it. And now, meeting him, he's actually kind of cute, even bigger than I expected—untied, he towers over me. But for a guy who came back from the dead, he doesn't feel like talking much.

One thing CoreFire does do is show me one of the Doctor's secret archives. I don't know how he knew, but it turns out to hold the thing I've needed all along—the original file that Protheon kept on me. They photographed my passport and everything. They kept a record—not much, but name and medical history at least. Even a psychiatric profile. One last origin story.

There isn't much time to sort through it before we have to leave.

There's some technical stuff I never knew before, a few hints about abilities I haven't even tried. Biometric data explaining why I was a good candidate in the first place.

There are pictures of me, scanned from someone's holiday Polaroids. I only barely recognize the girl in the photograph. We look like half sisters at best—I could have passed her in the street. She stands in a fuzzy sweater, smiling at whoever is taking her picture, looking lost but hopeful. And the memories are gone, 1980s Christmases and high school French and the rest. But I don't think she was very happy. I spend a while at the databanks, downloading.

When I come out, I almost walk right into Blackwolf and Damsel, who are making out in the rain like high school kids. I feel my face go blank and slack; it's a familiar feeling that, amnesia or not, I can tell I've felt before. And there's this extra twist inside of me because it shows how much I was kidding myself all along. And although it's just about the most romantic thing I've ever seen, I don't much enjoy looking at it. I could tell them more than they know, about who Lily is or what they should do with Doctor Impossible, but they don't seem much interested in talking.

They don't even notice me, and I try to be casual about it, like it never mattered in the first place. Everybody pretends not to see me seeing them. Elphin's performing some Celtic victory ritual, so Mystic and I watch for a while. He even offers me his opera cloak to keep the rain off, but I decline. There's something gallant and a little sad about him.

Then they march Doctor Impossible out, Rainbow holding him by the collar. No one's ready to leave yet, so he's left standing there for a while, sagging in the chains, looking around at what remains of his lair. The rain is running into his eyes and there's a quirky kind of smile on his face, but it's the same guy. He's not looking his most evil with his helmet off and his hair all over the place and one black eye.

I stand there and let him get a good look at me, and he looks back. I want to grab him, shake him, make him talk to me, but what does one say on these occasions? A real hero would have all kinds of clever observations. I did at one point, but I can't remember my stupid speech at all. He's my nemesis, I guess, if I want one. Creator, savior, enabler, whatever he was. All these enhancements, everything that happened to me, was just fallout from his stupid, offhandedly brilliant plan, which I never even got to hear about. I'm looking at my whole life standing there, and what do you say to that?

My combat computer comes up with the answer. It starts as a growl that turns into a shriek and ends with a ferocious right cross, whose impact rattles my whole frame. He feels it—I doubt CoreFire could have done much better. It spins him almost around. His head goes back and his lanky hair follows, rainwater spraying everywhere. Even Rainbow Triumph's mouth hangs open with surprise, and I hear applause—Blackwolf, maybe, or CoreFire.

I'm finished. I think he mutters, "Sorry," but I'm already walking away.

I don't know what happens next, because at this point I just wander off to another part of the island, and I'm not really paying attention. I end up down by the water, at what looks like a little harbor area, a couple loading cranes and concrete piles in the water. He must have built it early on, but it never got much use. It's still pouring with rain.

Yes, sure, we won. Things overall are going to be okay. I don't know it yet, but we're all going to be famous again—some of us for the first time. Blackwolf's corporation will get rich off of patents gleaned from Doctor Impossible's island. Damsel's powers are coming back stronger than ever, reborn in the light of her mother's sun soaked into her. New senses, even a new power that will bring the ocean up over my ramparts to sweep away the remnants of the Doctor's robot army. Her skin looks greener than before. Gills more prominent, and they work properly now. Maybe she can even breathe on her mother's home world.

She's mounting an expedition there next year, and she's even talking about running for an open Senate seat when she gets back. Apparently the Constitution doesn't have anything prohibiting alien princesses, at least in the legislature.

CoreFire decides to disappear again for a while. The bruises healed in a couple of days, but this has been a PR disaster for him, a fake death and then getting beaten to a pulp by Doctor Impossible. He said he was taking off into space to be by himself for a while. Maybe the Moon, or maybe Titan. I was surprised—he actually seemed a little shy.

And we take Doctor Impossible into custody. He isn't talking much on the ride home, either. Not even when we hand him over to a pair of agents from the Department of Metahuman Affairs, who assure us they have some new ideas about containment, and that they "can totally handle him this time."

But I don't know any of that yet, sitting on the docks and wondering if maybe I will just rust away like the rest of Impossible's island. That's when Elphin arrives. She's carrying the Hammer of Ra, or halfway dragging it behind her. It must weigh a couple of hundred pounds. The gold paint is flaking off, revealing the stone underneath.

The rain starts to slack off when she arrives, which is a nice trick. She climbs up on a half-shattered slab of concrete, careful not to touch the bits of iron rebar poking out.

"I know you wish to leave us."

"Elphin, I . . ." I guess I'm surprised. She never seemed all that perceptive. "I was going to announce it later. I'll get a mercenary job somewhere."

"Why? Because you are not like CoreFire? Invincible?"

"I'm just not one of you."

The clouds are drifting away, and a full moon rises huge and orange behind her. Under the light, she's a silvery May Queen, perched on a neo-Gothic ruin. Moonlight strikes the water, showing every ripple. There's no wind.

"Come here. I want you to see this." She points back up to the cliffs, where Doctor Impossible's ramparts are still black against the sky.

"It's almost gone, but this was once a vast continent. Only this isle remains. This was where our castle stood, the fortress of the Western Sidhe. Once, they left offerings for us, the earliest people. That was long before the covenant, before we came to England."

"Before . . . How old are you, Elphin?" She turns away, ignoring it. I guess it was a rude question. But something about her is starting to make sense. For the first time, I can see past the teenage waif look and see how old she really is. And what she is now—a being partly sylvan goddess and partly animal, a fairy. She'd been left behind by everyone she ever knew, but she became something else, new and strong and strange. That's what Damsel did for her.

I can smell grass and forest loam. It's an uncannily warm night, and the sky is awash with stars—under 20× light amplification, you really start to appreciate it. Elphin has a point to make, but, as usual, she doesn't bother to explain for a while.

"I need you to help me."

"What are we doing here?" I ask.

"It is my mission, the geas Titania laid upon me before she departed to the other land. It has been so long, I thought it would never come.

"There," she announces, and hops down. She takes my hand, and I let her walk us down to the waterline together, feeling as if in a dream or a fairy tale. Next to me, she looks like a child.

She drags the Pharaoh's hammer a little way out onto the docks. Scrubbed of some of its tacky gold spray paint, the broken weapon still has a primitive beauty. I can't read the runes—the hammer keeps fuzzing out my video chip—but I can tell they aren't hieroglyphics.

"She said I would know my purpose when it came. And there were times when I thought it all a falsehood, or Titania's grim joke," she says.

"I know what you mean."

"I want you to tell me when it's midnight exactly." The clock inside me counts slowly down while we watch the moon rise. Neither of us says anything, but for once it doesn't feel awkward. It turns out to be a good place to think things over for a bit.

I suppose I ought to vow to oppose him forever; make a nemesis issue out of it. But it's a little beside the point. It's not like I'd get to hunt him down—we're about to send him to prison. And with CoreFire back, he's already got a nemesis. I'd have to be co-nemesis. And since he saved my life and gave me superpowers, I'm not 100 percent sure what I'm supposed to be angry about, if we come down to it. Although I do wonder what scheme or inspiration I was part of at the beginning. One day, I'll have to ask him.

It's almost twelve. I nudge Elphin and whisper, "It's coming. Now."

"Here," she says. She hands me the hammer. "I want you to finish this. Throw it out there. Far as you can." She points out over the water.

The hammer is surprisingly heavy, but once I get it off the ground I find I can handle it. No regular human could have lifted it at all. I set myself, grip the hammer's shaft, and wheel around once, then again. The forces are enormous, but my skeleton adjusts to the stress and pivots smoothly, as if it were designed for this.

The hammer hums in the air, massive, and there's an energy building in it that feels a little dangerous, and I wonder for the first time if I should be doing this.

I spin a third time, feel my muscles and metal skeleton straining to put more spin on it, and then with a grunt that unexpectedly becomes a scream, I let it go, hurling it farther than I would have thought possible out over the ocean. It disappears into the dark and I listen a long time for the splash, but unbelievably, there's no sound at all, then a distant crack of thunder. For a while, we stand quietly together on the shore, feeling something end. Elphin's free now, and I'm crying again.

When I think of the photograph of the girl I used to be, a stranger now, I think how much I miss her, and how she was never really happy in the first place. I still don't know why she went to Brazil, or if she meant to stand in front of a dump truck or not.

But she probably couldn't see in the dark, or walk on the bottom of the ocean, or take a punch worth a damn, or throw one. Maybe not everything changes for the worse. Maybe I just became what I needed to in order to survive. I miss the girl I was, and I wish I could tell her that.

But she got hurt really bad and I've been waiting such a long time for her to be okay again.

I bet she never dreamed she would live so long, or do the things she can do now. I wish I could tell her what she'd grow up to be, how strange and beautiful and unexpected she'd be. She'd probably feel a lot better if she knew. The sky and the stars are brilliant, and I think of how much she would have loved this.

CHAPTER TWENTY-ONE

NO PRISON CAN HOLD ME

If you had one single chance to get everything you ever wanted, to succeed, to win, what would happen? Would you make it, or would you go down in flames? Which kind of person are you? I used to ask myself that question. Now I don't have to.

It happened two weeks ago, but there hasn't been much else to do except think about it.

They chained me up outside, rain running into my eyes. Blackwolf and Damsel were kissing, like idiots. Blackwolf's mask came off, showing the shock of white hair he usually keeps hidden. They pretty much forgot about me for a while.

It didn't take much to finish me. Once the Champions were loose again, everything started to crumble. Elphin used her storm powers, and Damsel did something to the ocean so that it surged over the walls, washing everything in warm salt spray. The great dome of my laboratory cracked and broke. The sky opened up, and my much-ballyhooed Ice Age fizzled into a warm tropical rain. The water ran down through the laboratory, the armory, all my experiments, trickling down even into the lowest levels this time, through the subbasements and into the atomic furnaces far below, the secret fires.

It's a great moment for them. The New Champions are splashing around in the courtyard like giddy ten-year-olds, while I watch, helplessly trying to reach the padlock on my ankle. Why shouldn't they be happy? After all, it's their finest hour.

Elphin is aloft, chanting unintelligibly, weapon raised to the storm. And Mister Mystic's cloak flaps in the wind as he gazes dramatically off, stage left. He even winks at me. His ridiculous top hat finally seems to have found a purpose in keeping the rain out of his eyes. The cyborg hits me in the face, to the amusement of all.

Lily's gone, or Erica I guess, disappeared into the rain to find her own way home. She didn't seem any more eager to hang out with the New Champions than I was, and they didn't go looking for her. I still don't understand her role in this, whether she's a hero or a villain, or exactly what. I make a note to ask her.

But that was two weeks ago. Sitting here chained up in a DMA transport I have other things to think about. In about ten minutes, the smoke bombs will go off. I'll slip the handcuffs and get out the other side of the helicopter and into the uniform I cached there. After that, all I'll have to do is keep walking across the tarmac. With the briefcase, I might look a little odd, but it could just be somebody's baggage. That dummy I made out of seat cushions and parachute silk should fool them for just long enough. If not, I'll have to improvise.

In a few minutes, I'm going to be free again. But that's just the beginning of my problems. I still have my work to do. There's still the whole world to deal with.

What does it mean to conquer the world? Is there really a way to do it? Do you have to be the richest one, or the smartest one, or to beat everyone in a fight? Or just know you could? Is it to be invincible?

Does it just mean you get the girl you really wanted? Did CoreFire already conquer the world a long time ago? Did I? Or maybe there is no way to do it. No one could have tried harder than I have. Haven't I already fought a hundred battles, and lost every one?

Three minutes now. And yes, this could be a bigger problem than I thought. Nontrivial. I see that now. But that's no reason to stop. No more mistakes this time.

I can see a helicopter parked in front of its hangar, maybe six hundred feet off. That's what I'll make for, just slip into the pilot seat and start revving the engines for the dash across the border. It's even odds I'll make it. Who built Antitron? Who harnessed the limitless energy of Dimension Zeta? No hero did that; that was groundbreaking. I can beat these people, no question about it. Who moved the Moon? I did.

In a week, I'll be in Antigua, or Hong Kong, or Des Moines. And from there, I'll find a way. Something new, nanotech or superstrings or voodoo. I'm still the smartest man in the world. Soon, yes, soon I will be invincible.

When your laboratory explodes, lacing your body with a super-charged elixir, what do you do? You don't just lie there. You crawl out of the rubble, hideously scarred, and swear vengeance on the world. You keep going. You keep trying to take over the world.

APPENDIX

SELECTIONS FROM *THE INTERNATIONAL METAHUMAN DATABASE,* THIRD EDITION

HEROES

The Champions

Blackwolf—"the Ultimate Crime Fighter"
  Bio: When an autistic child loses his brother and sister, he transforms his life through discipline and training into an endless quest for justice.
  Powers: superlative martial artist, gymnast, tactical instincts
  Source of Powers: natural ability, intensive training
  Notes: no true superhuman ability; formerly married to Damsel

CoreFire—"World's Mightiest Hero"
  Bio: A scientific accident turns an Ivy League quarterback into the world's greatest superhero.
  Powers: flight, strength, invincibility
  Source of Powers: scientific accident
  Notes: missing; whereabouts unknown

Damsel—"First Lady of Power"
  Bio: Born to superpowers, she struggled to lead the life of a normal girl.
  Powers: flight, strength, force field, hand-to-hand weapon
  Source of Powers: inheritance—Stormcloud and unidentified alien princess
  Notes: nominal leader of the Champions; formerly married to Blackwolf

Elphin—"Warrior Princess"
  Bio: The last fairy, she was charged by her queen to live among humankind.
  Powers: flight, hand-to-hand weapon (spear), weather control
  Source of Powers: fairy
  Notes: origin story not verified

Fatale—"the Next Generation of Warfare"
> *Bio:* After a freak accident, a young woman is healed and transformed by new technology into a cyborg agent.
> *Powers:* enhanced strength, speed, intrinsic weaponry
> *Source of Powers:* cyborg enhancements
> *Notes:* possible psychological instability

Feral—"Savage Street Fighter"
> *Bio:* Half beast, half man, he roams the urban jungle in search of crime.
> *Powers:* strength, speed, toughness
> *Source of Powers:* unknown
> *Notes:* under investigation for brutal methods; volunteer in inner-city super-hero "incubator" program

Galatea—"Heart of Gold"
> *Bio:* An extraordinary machine devotes herself to humankind, and becomes more human herself.
> *Powers:* flight, energy projection, machine empathy
> *Source of Powers:* robot
> *Notes:* deceased; identity of Galatea's builder unknown

Lily—"Relentless"
> *Bio:* Born in the far future and stranded in the present, a superpowered outcast seeks her lost home.
> *Powers:* strength, toughness
> *Source of Powers:* far-future technology
> *Notes:* dual-listed as villain; unusual appearance

Mister Mystic—"Man of Mystery"
> *Bio:* A two-bit magician and con artist stumbles on the secrets of true magic and his life is changed forever.
> *Powers:* including but not limited to teleportation, telepathy, and energy manipulation
> *Source of Powers:* magic
> *Notes:* subject's powers remain largely unknown

Rainbow Triumph—"Teen Idol with an Attitude"
> *Bio:* When young Briony is diagnosed with a fatal disease, she chooses to undergo an operation that gives her new powers and a fabulous new career.
> *Powers:* enhanced speed, martial arts, enhanced strength, undisclosed gadgetry
> *Source of Powers:* prosthetic cyborg augmentation
> *Notes:* degenerative nerve disease

The Super Squadron

Go-Man—"Faster Than the Speed of Crime"
    Bio: An awkward navy engineer stumbles onto a secret government project
    and becomes the fastest man alive.
    Powers: superspeed
    Source of Powers: fusion reactor accident
    Notes: retired; whereabouts unknown

Lightwave—"In Darkest Night"
    Bio: A midwestern farmer investigates a mysterious light in the hills, only to
    gain astonishing new powers.
    Powers: flight, energy projection, dematerialization
    Source of Powers: overexposure to meteorite radiation
    Notes: emigrated to outer space

Paragon—"the Living Flame"
    Bio: A U.S. Army lieutenant captures a Nazi stronghold deep in the Black
    Forest and discovers a strange artifact in their looted treasure horde.
    Powers: flight, strength, telekinesis
    Source of Powers: artifact, possibly of prehuman origin
    Notes: deceased

The Pharaoh (1)—"Might of the Ancients"
    Bio: An archaeologist is granted power and insight by the ancient pharaohs.
    Powers: strength, truth ray
    Source of Powers: early Egyptian relic
    Notes: whereabouts unknown, following failed archaeological expedition

Regina—"Queen of Elfland"
    Bio: A childhood adventure reveals a young girl's destiny as a superheroine.
    Powers: strength, hypnotic ray, hand-to-hand weapon (Scepter of Elfland)
    Source of Powers: magic
    Notes: scepter a class-A magical object

Stormcloud—"Squadron Leader"
    Bio: An air force test pilot disappears over the Bermuda Triangle, only to
    return weeks later with amnesia . . . and the mighty power of a tropical
    hurricane.
    Powers: weather control, flight, invulnerability, strength
    Source of Powers: Bermuda Triangle incident
    Notes: former leader of the Super Squadron; retired

The Chaos Pact

Bluetooth—"Wireless Warrior"
> *Bio:* When nerdy UFO abductee awakens with startling abilities, he and his high school friend fulfill a childhood ambition to fight crime together.
> *Powers:* invasive telepathy
> *Source of Powers:* probable surgical modification
> *Notes:* subject's medical records sealed per FBI order

Phenom—"Most Valuable Player"
> *Bio:* A gifted athlete undergoes surgery to fulfill a childhood pact with his best friend; together, they seek to become crime fighting's greatest duo.
> *Powers:* enhanced speed, strength
> *Source of Powers:* surgical modification, pharmaceutical stimulation
> *Notes:* cited for bravery during chthonic intrusion in Chicago

VILLAINS

Baron Ether—"the First Name in Evil"
> *Aliases:* Lianne Stekleferd, Lester Lankenfried; real name unknown
> *Bio:* A diabolical genius stalks the twentieth century, battling its greatest heroes and committing its greatest crimes.
> *Powers:* evil genius (Malign Hypercognition Disorder); partial transmutation; various scientific enhancements
> *Source of Powers:* unknown
> *Notes:* accent indicates Eastern European nationality; currently under house arrest, New Haven, Connecticut; subject apparently close to one hundred years old, subject to distortion via time travel effects; extremely dangerous

Bloodstryke—"Deadly Inheritance"
> *Bio:* When his father dies, a mild-mannered accountant learns uncomfortable secrets about his family history, and its curse.
> *Powers:* vampiric drain, flight, energy blast (hemoglobin-powered armor)
> *Source of Powers:* cursed family artifact
> *Notes:* not a genuine vampire, possibly subject to mental domination by ancient cursed armor

Doctor Impossible—"the Smartest Man in the World"
  Aliases: Baron Benzene, Count Smackula, Doctor Fiasco, Smartacus; real name unknown
  Bio: An evil genius swears to take over the world.
  Powers: evil genius (MHD), enhanced speed, strength
  Source of Powers: unknown
  Notes: currently held in federal detention; treat as extremely dangerous; wants to take over the world; nemesis of CoreFire, and suspect in his disappearance

Doctor Mind—"Mind over Matter"
  Bio: An Oxford philosopher has a curious insight, with startling results.
  Powers: supergenius; telekinetic
  Source of Powers: unknown
  Notes: former hero turned villain; currently missing following ascension event (files classified)

Dollface—"Crime Is Child's Play"
  Bio: A neglected child develops her own playmates, and unleashes them on the world.
  Powers: mechanical assistants allow for varied capabilities—viz, gravity control, flight, heat ray, X-ray vision
  Source of Powers: inventor/constructor of mechanical toys
  Notes: no longer active

Kosmic Klaw—"Inhuman Power"
  Bio: A failed mercenary uncovers a crashed UFO and finds his luck has changed.
  Powers: strength, flight, armor
  Source of Powers: armor of extraterrestrial origin
  Notes: former mercenary; possible psychological deterioration

Laserator—"Professor of Peril"
  Bio: Thwarted in his bid for tenure, a bitter astronomy lecturer turns his talents to evil.
  Powers: energy manipulation, gravity beam
  Source of Powers: focusing/reflecting device
  Notes: subsequently reformed as legitimate scientist

Nick Napalm—"The Human Flamethrower"
  Bio: A disturbed lawyer manifests a mutant ability to project flame, and finds a new purpose in life.

Powers: pyrokinetic flame projection, flame shield
Source of Powers: mutation
Notes: exhibits delusions of a religious nature; tentative diagnosis of schizophrenia

The Pharaoh (2)—"Ramses Returned"
> *Bio:* When a young boy discovers a secret in the woods behind his housing development, he learns his life is connected to that of an ancient sovereign.
> *Powers:* hand-to-hand weapon (Hammer of Ra), invincibility
> *Source of Powers:* artifact (provenance unknown)
> *Notes:* missing, presumed inactive; not to be confused with Pharaoh (1), former Super Squadron member

Phathom 5—"Secrets of the Deep"
> *Bio:* A computer designed by a mad genius to further his schemes, develops a mind of its own.
> *Powers:* weather and tidal prediction, molecular manipulation, limited prescience
> *Source of Powers:* cybernetic construction
> *Notes:* supercomputer developed by Doctor Impossible

Psychic Prime—"Man of the Future"
> *Bio:* A man of unique talents is drafted by a far-future academy for psychics, only to flunk out and be returned to the present.
> *Powers:* range of telepathic abilities
> *Source of Powers:* psychic training academy
> *Notes:* incipient alcoholic

Terrapin—"Connection Man"
> *Bio:* A small-town stoner is gifted with strange abilities.
> *Powers:* psychoactive projection, pharmacological arsenal
> *Source of Powers:* unknown
> *Notes:* exhibits kleptomania; possible supplier of ordnance to larger-scale operators

A SELECTIVE TIME LINE OF SUPERHUMAN HISTORY

140,000,000 B.C. Baron Ether spends six years in the Cretaceous due to time-traveling accident.

147 B.C. The Champions and Doctor Impossible intervene in Third Punic War.

A.D. 1674 Elphin is excluded from mass fairy emigration.

1907 First recorded appearance of Baron Ether.

1937 U.S. military begins secret super-soldier testing program.

1945 U.S. government founds the Department of Metahuman Affairs.

1946 Super Squadron founded—world's first superteam.

1948 The Delinquent Five appear, world's first supervillain team-up.

1968 Mentiac is constructed, escapes into sewer system.

1979 Super Squadron announce their retirement.

1979 Baron Ether retires, following arrest in the Senate building.

1984 Doctor Impossible creates his first Doomsday Device Mark I, the Termination Machine.

1984 The Champions are founded by Blackwolf, Damsel, and CoreFire.

1985 Galatea, Mister Mystic, Elphin, and Feral join the Champions.

1986 Doctor Impossible unleashes Antitron (Doomsday Device Mark II).

1989 Blackwolf and Damsel marry.

1990 Doctor Impossible concocts the Fungal Menace (Doomsday Device Mark III).

1992 Doctor Impossible decants the Gray Goo (Doomsday Device Mark IV).

1996 Champions defend Earth in the Titan incident; death of Galatea.

1997 The Champions disband.

1998 Blackwolf and Damsel file for divorce.

2004 Doctor Impossible releases the insidious Meta-Metavirus (Doomsday Device Mark V).

2004 Doctor Impossible experiences his twelfth defeat and incarceration.

2006 CoreFire disappears.

ACKNOWLEDGMENTS

Thanks to Marty Asher, Zachary Wagman, and the team at Pantheon and Vintage.

I'm indebted to Julie Barer; Jami Bartlett, evil genius; Tina Bennett; Lev Grossman; Talissa Ford; Judith Grossman; Jennifer Jackson; Luke Janklow; Don Korycansky, who really did figure out how to move the Earth; Rowland White. Also thanks to Tom Farber, Bharati Mukherjee, and Jim Shepard for their wonderful fiction workshops. And to Marka Knight, for innumerable corrections and improvements—from nitpicking style points to basic premises of plot and character—and rescuing the entire project on at least two occasions.

And friends and family for support and encouragement throughout.

A NOTE ABOUT THE AUTHOR

Austin Grossman is a video-game design consultant and a doctoral candidate in English Literature at the University of California at Berkeley, where he specializes in Romantic and Victorian literature. He lives in Berkeley.

A NOTE ON THE TYPE

This book was set in Albertina, the best known of the typefaces designed by Chris Brand (b. 1921 in Utrecht, the Netherlands). Issued in 1965, Albertina was first used to catalog the work of Stanley Morison and was exhibited in Brussels at the Albertina Library in 1966.

Composed by North Market Street Graphics,
Lancaster, Pennsylvania

Printed and bound by Berryville Graphics,
Berryville, Virginia

Designed by M. Kristen Bearse and Chip Kidd